DEAD PULSE RISING

THE KYLE WALKER CHRONICLES VOLUME 1

K. MICHAEL GIBSON

SEVERED PRESS
HOBART TASMANIA

DEAD PULSE RISING

ISBN: 978-1-925342-21-5

PROLOGUE

Russia

"Бутырской тюрьмы 1980" (Butyrka Prison 1980)

Snow pelted the ashen gray grounds of Butyrka prison as Doctor Ivan Morozov ran, at sixty-three years old, ran for his life. He couldn't believe what he had done, couldn't believe he had actually gone through with it. He had let one of them free, one of those vile perversions of nature, one of those things that he had created. He tightly clutched the suitcase containing all of his notes in one leather-gloved hand. His hands shook so badly with adrenaline and fear that he nearly lost his grip. All he had to do was make it beyond the gate; get to the car the Americans had waiting for him. He was so naive to think that what he was doing was for the benefit of his people, now he knew better and he would not, could not, allow what he had created to be unleashed on any population. The gate came into view, and he slowed his pace knowing the guards would find it suspicious if he were running. It was bad enough that he was soaked in snow and sweat. A guard held out a gloved hand as he approached.

"Good evening sir, ID?" one of the sentries asked. Even though Ivan had worked at this facility for nearly twenty years, the guards still asked.

Doctor Morozov fumbled around his pocket and produced a plastic ID card with his credentials.

"Leaving kind of early today, aren't you Doc?" one of the guards asked. Ivan ran a hand along his sweat-covered forehead.

"Yes, well I've seemed to have come down with something, Mr. Vinokurov," Ivan responded sheepishly while reading the guards nametag.

The guard nodded and handed Doctor Morozov back his ID.

"Well, feel better sir," the guard said and began to raise the barrier that blocked Ivan's escape.

At that moment, the sirens went off. Ivan glanced nervously over at the guard, who instantly narrowed his eyes and began to raise the AK-47 that was slung across his back. A shot rang out from somewhere in the distance. Vinokurov fell to the side, half of his skull having disintegrated. Another shot rang out as a second guard emerged from the shack.

Ivan stared in shock as a hole erupted in the second man's chest, and he fell dead to the snow-covered streets. Headlights appeared in the distance as Ivan heard screams behind him. Ivan turned to face the prison knowing that his creation had found someone.

A voice with an American accent shouted from behind the Doctor. "Doctor Morozov I presume, this way sir."

Ivan turned to face his savior. Relief flooded Ivan's body as the American ran over and grabbed him by the sleeve of his coat and led him toward his new life.

CHAPTER 1

Where to begin I don't even know. It seems so long ago since anything was even remotely normal. I suppose, for record purposes, I should start at the beginning.

It was Monday morning, and my alarm came to life and scared the shit out of me at this early hour. I shot up to smack the long silver button to shut off the noise that I dreaded every waking day and damn near killed myself by tripping over one of my combat boots on the floor. My arm shot out, and I grabbed the closest sturdy object I could find. In this case, it was a large mahogany dresser that set next to the wall. The dresser's sharp corner dug into the palm of my hand. I winced involuntarily and shook the pain out.

"Shit," I whispered to myself in the darkness. My alarm clock set atop a monstrous-sized dresser surrounded by ceramic knickknacks and jewelry boxes. I had a thing about actual furniture, wooden furniture, not that prefab pressboard crap that breaks within a year after you snap it together. I was thankful for this fact, because if it had not been for the real wood, it more than likely would have come crashing to the floor with the impact of my 210 pound buck-naked frame. I had to concentrate this early in the morning to navigate around the items on the dresser and not send half of them crashing to the floor. I stared bleary-eyed at the black-and-silver contraption, my eyes blurring in and out of focus on the blindingly red illuminated numbers. My fingers hovered over the alarm clock button for a moment as I listened to a gravelly voiced female. I had come to hate that voice. The voice of Amelia on the early morning talk show that was supposed to be comical annoyed me to every fiber of my being, probably due in no small fact that every time I heard her, well, that meant it was time to get up and go to work.

She spouted off something going on in downtown Baltimore. Apparently, there was a shooting in front of a Starbucks on Eutaw Street. Amelia and her partner tried to put a comic spin on the serious situation.

"Maybe he was pissed that he couldn't get that half-caf skinny latte," I heard her partner Mickey say as they erupted in laughter. I often wondered what she and her partner looked like. I always assumed that to be on the radio basically meant that you weren't good enough to make it in television, perhaps, because you looked like a troll. I was never obsessed enough to research it, and what do I know anyway? They may just be the epitome of style and beauty. I dismissed my abstract thoughts, pushed the snooze button, and stumbled back into bed. I sat down and rubbed my tired face, feeling the gritty stubble that had seemed to sprout up overnight.

"Great, I'll have to take care of that, I guess." I turned over to my wife and kissed her gently on the forehead. She stirred for the slightest of moments and settled back into a deep slumber, snoring lightly. Her nostrils flared and mouth hung open as if to catch flies with each breath. I smiled at the thought of her by my side, snoring and all. She was beautiful, and if she ever read this, she would more than likely kick my ass for that description.

No matter, it took fifteen years, and a lot of hardship to finally make that happen. We had dated on and off, mostly on throughout high school, and a small stint in college. We ended up married to the wrong people. Neither one of us planned for things to end up in divorce; however, that's just the way things go sometimes. We each had children with said people who were, for all intents and purposes, my only reason for being for several years of my life. After a period of loneliness, we miraculously found each other anew, and with a much deeper sense of appreciation for each other. I don't know if I believe in fate or God or any of that other mumbo jumbo, but He, She, or It was there and on our side. I stared at her for a long moment, smiling as I watched her sleepy facial expressions form dimples in her slender cheeks. Her long brown hair nestled against her pale skin and fell into her creamy bosom. I gave her a slight squeeze and stood.

I walked over to the bathroom door, taking care not to have a repeat performance of earlier by kicking my boots out of the way, sending them clomping across the hardwood floor. I grabbed my uniform off a hook attached to the door and sniffed it. *Two days worn, it seemed fresh enough,* I thought as I slid the black polyester wool blend shirt on.

I worked on an armored car. The shirt's fabric was designed to wick away moisture in the summer and keep you warm in the winter. It sucked at both functions. Personally, I mused that it could have been made out of burlap; fact of the matter was that the contract for the garment went out to the lowest bidder. I slid into my pants and reached for my gun belt and ballistic vest. The vest was the kind that went over the shirt and was designed to blend in with the uniform. It was nice and supposedly worked, although thankfully, I had never put it to the test. I strapped the Velcro fastenings into place and secured my gun belt.

I strolled out of the bedroom, headed for the kitchen, and stepped on a Lego. Now, if you have children, then you've probably had this experience at least once in your lifetime; but if you do not, stepping on a Lego in bare feet is akin to having a railroad spike shoved into the tender under flesh of your foot. I hopped for several seconds on one foot, cursing the powers that be, and braced myself against the couch in the living room. I positioned my foot over my knee and plucked out the offending object that was embedded in my heel. I rubbed the now-sore appendage and shook my head. I scanned the floor, taking into account any danger areas of the Lego minefield, and then made my way into the kitchen. I paused in front of the refrigerator, reached up top, and grabbed my cooler.

The large red Coleman cooler was still full of melt water from the day before. I slid it off the top of the refrigerator and managed to brush up against a set of papers that were adhered to the front of it, sending them fluttering to the linoleum floor along with a barrage of magnets that clattered and skittered across its smooth surface.

"I don't have time for this crap," I said to myself and scowled at the mess. I emptied the Coleman cooler into the sink; the scent of the day was old tuna sandwiches. The odor wafted up and assaulted my nasal passages, threatening to overwhelm my olfactory senses. *It smelled much better the day before*, I thought as I tried not to gag (unsuccessfully, I might add). I opened the fridge, squinting at the light as it pierced the darkness. *Sandwiches again*, I thought as I grabbed for the salami and mustard on wheat and shoved it into my cooler. I liked good crusty French or Italian bread, but my wife insisted that whole wheat bread was better for me. A commercial for Fiber One Cereal shot through my head: A man standing with a shit-eating grin eyeing another man eating a bowl of cereal, with his wife standing over top of him, pouring a glass of juice. "She gave you fiber," he said, implying that she must love the shit out of him for caring about his bowel habits, and the man with the cereal chewed as contently as a cow with his cud. Stupid, I know, but that's what went through my head. Dumbass commercials make me lose brain cells every time I see one.

The stereo suddenly came to life again, the alarm only set into sleep mode. I heard Amelia say something about a disturbance at the train station as I rushed as quietly as possible into the bedroom, even though the point of that was lost at the fact the alarm was screaming like a banshee. I cursed quietly as I jammed my pinky toe on the bed frame; a shock of pain from the blow traveled all the way up to my knee.

"What in the hell does the universe have against my feet this morning?" I said in an irritated whisper. I smacked the alarm, and then smacked it again for good measure just to be sure it was indeed off.

I sat on the edge of the bed, cracked my toes, and rubbed away the pain, deciding that it would be a good time to pull my boots on. However, in order to do that, I needed that precious commodity of socks. In a house full of children, trying to find a matching pair of socks is like trying to actually locate your soul mate on eHarmony. They might be out there, but good luck finding them. Just for giggles, I stood facing my dresser and opened my sock drawer. Surprise etched across my face when there was actually a pristine pair of socks staring back at me. I grabbed the soft items and hastily slid them over my feet, fearing they may be some sort of a sleep-deprived mirage. The softness of the socks felt good against my battered feet. I slipped on my black Bates tactical combat boots and zipped them up the side.

I checked the clock and it was 6:27, only a few minutes left before I had to be on the road. I stood, made my way into the bathroom, and stepped into our walk-in closet. I reached up onto the top shelf and withdrew a small locked case from behind a stack of old file boxes. I swiftly unlocked it with a code, grabbed my weapon from the gun safe, and slid a speed loader full of FTX rounds into the cylinder and twisted the knob. The bullets slid home and, in one swift motion, snapped the cylinder shut and holstered the weapon. Yeah, make fun of me if you want; the police I work with often do. They would always poke fun at the fact I still carried an old-fashioned revolver, a Smith & Wesson .357 magnum, model 10 to be exact. My employer preferred to issue .38 caliber slugs, mainly because the less robust rounds were cheaper. I personally liked the stopping power of a .357 FTX round; unlike the slug, the FTX was a hollow point filled with an expanding polymer which allowed the bullet to flange out to its full potential effectively giving the target a really bad freaking day. The police I worked with would always praise the higher capacity semi-automatic Glock's they carried. I would in turn give them a joyful ribbing that it was easy to hit a target when you could empty a magazine in around 2.5 seconds. I was a firm believer in one-shot-one-kill shooting, whereas our standard training dealt more with instinct shooting. This is what you would do at high noon on the dusty streets of the old West. My skills were a little more honed by my previous years spent working for Air Force intelligence.

Acquire sight picture, breathe, squeeze the trigger were my instincts. In fact, it took quite a lot of practice to get used to drawing from the hip, whereas I was acclimated to a tactical leg holster. This was a little known fact for most, as I had to sign a nondisclosure form the size of a phonebook when I retired from active duty; my friends, my current job, and even my wife had no idea of the things that I had done in the past or that I had even been an enlisted man. I was recruited young due to strong test scores on a not-so-standardized test. I had recruiters calling me at the tender age of twelve. When I graduated high school, I enlisted and was supposedly rejected. In actuality, I spent a year at a facility in Nitro, West Virginia, training.

To the rest of the world, I was simply there living with my cousin, which I was; however, when he and our other roommates were out working at taco-hell, I was training on how to create improvised plastic explosives by scraping the sulfur off match heads. Needless to say, it took a lot of scraping. After my training was complete, I was reintegrated back home, and sent on *business trips*, and none were the wiser.

My alarm started screaming again, telling me that I still hadn't figured out which of the damn buttons shut it off for good. It told me I had but five minutes to get my ass out of the house. Quickly, I finished putting on my gear, grabbed my cooler and backpack, and headed for the door.

I opened the door and stepped out into the hazy summer gloom of an August morning. Sweat instantly began to bead on my forehead. I turned back toward the door, staring longingly into its air-conditioned interior, wishing I could just go curl back up next to my wife's soft form, but money had to be made, bills paid, and bread bought. I sighed and closed the door, having to slam it hard for the lock to catch, the humidity swelling the wood of the door frame. The whole frame of my manufactured home shook with the impact. I cringed, hoping against hope I hadn't awakened my wife. Not that it mattered much; she would be up soon welcoming her children that she cared for every day.

For the better part of ten years, my wife had taken care of the neighborhood children; and after a while, she decided to turn it into a business. She catered mostly to the low-income families in the area, which in this economy were plentiful; and since we lived close to a military base, the enlisted men and women transferring to Aberdeen proving-grounds were steady clients as well. In this day and age of conflict and war, business boomed.

I walked through the dew-covered grass, its wetness coating the black leather of my Bates tactical boots, and stepped onto the street to my car. I fumbled with my keys for a moment. I blindly located my ignition key and opened the door to my little white four-banger of a car. I drove a Hyundai Accent, not the most fashionable car on the planet; but hey, I got what I could afford, well, just barely, anyway. I opened the door, sat down, and plopped my cooler on top of about four weeks' worth of empty drink bottles that crunched with the added weight; several cans spilled off the seat and fell to the floor. The scene reminded me of a *Simpsons'* episode where Homer had been pulled over by the police, drunk as a skunk. When the cop asked him if he had been drinking, he said, *No*. When he shifted in the car, the tinny sound of cans rattled from the cartoon car's interior. I sighed and started the engine. "I really need to clean out this damn thing," I said to the air. The engine purred to life—oh, who am I kidding?—it more or less coughed, then spit, and then sputtered to life. I backed out of my driveway, taking great care to not hit the dumbass's car that was parked directly behind me on the opposite side of the street. For some reason, my neighbor, Ned, who I believe was an ex-Marine with severe—and I mean severe—PTSD, could not seem to bring himself to park his ugly ass red El Camino in his driveway. Several times I had actually kissed the piece of shit with my rear bumper. The first time it had happened, I was half asleep and rushing to get to work, and wham-o, I backed right into it. I pulled my car over to the side of the street, stepped out, and went up to his house and rang the doorbell. Now keep in mind it was like six thirty in the morning. He opened the curtain and peeked out at me. I waved at him, seeing that he was staring at me through what I thought were curtains. As I peered closer at the windows, I discovered the curtains were actually camouflage netting hung over the windows.

I smirked when he came to the door, fully decked out in camouflage BDUs. I grinned ear to ear at the sight and had to stifle a chuckle that would have totally screwed up any kind of apology I had in mind for my transgression. I started to explain what had happened.

The older man didn't seem interested in hearing a damn word I said. His eyes darted around from place to place as if he were looking for the ever-present man to pop out and read his mind, or perhaps abduct him, and whisk him away to some super-secret lab to perform highly classified LSD experiments on him. I was surprised as hell that he wasn't wearing a tin foil hat. After a moment, he looked at me and nodded as if just noticing my presence, and simply shut the door in my face.

I stared at the door for a terse moment, wondering what the hell had just happened. So ever since that little experience, so long as I didn't do any damage to GI Psycho's car, truck, or whatever the hell it was supposed to be, I didn't bother taking the time to inform him of my blunder. Besides, if he even gave a shit, he could always park in his empty driveway. Ceasing my reverie, I backed out, narrowly missing Ned's truck, and I started on the long trek to base.

CHAPTER 2

My job at Specter Armored was roughly about forty-five minutes away, give or take with traffic. Somehow, it always seemed on days I was running slightly late, there was traffic. Some jerk behind me leaned on the horn just as the light turned green, not even giving it a three count. I resisted the urge to flip him/her the bird and pressed on the accelerator.

The sun was just peering overhead with red and gold jet streams of color, forcing their way through massing storm clouds.

"It's gonna get nasty today," I said to myself. "Red sky at morning—sailor takes warning, red sky at night—sailor's delight." The old seaman's adage flitted through my wayward thoughts.

I took the entrance ramp to I-95 South toward Baltimore and merged into traffic at breakneck speed. The speed limit on this particular corridor was only fifty-five miles-per-hour; however, if you were to enter the highway at anything less than sixty-five, your ass was probably toast. As if to punctuate this point, a beat-up red SUV idled on the shoulder, with a green cavalier whose back end had been smashed in. A scrawny black woman with nappy hair exchanged, what I could only imagine were colorful words, heatedly with a large middle-aged balding white man in a stained wife-beater. I cruised by them doing seventy-five. The distinct sound of sirens reached my ears from the distance. Looking back at the fender-bender, I half wondered if the nappy-haired woman was going to pull out a neck brace.

I reached my exit and veered off, cursing as a MTA bus damn near took my front end off by merging clearly into my lane.

"I hate this town," I said to myself with a sigh and meant it. I sometimes wished I were back in the rolling hills and mountains of West Virginia. Here in Maryland, at least in Baltimore, everyone was always impatient, and with no good reason. Didn't matter if they were on their way to the emergency room or out to pick up antianxiety meds at Wal-Mart. The mentality seemed to be: *Get the fuck out of my way, bitch*. Like, *How dare you for being on the road at the same time as the rest of them*.

Before I had entered into the Air Force, I was required for clearance reasons to provide my address and at least one reference to testify that I did indeed live there and was not some kind of crazy dick. I had lived in an apartment building in Middle River somewhere around three years. When I had gotten my packet, I realized I knew absolutely no one in the building. I went door-to-door in my small apartment building, two apartments per floor. Of course, there were only three floors, so that meant I had only six chances at finding some help. I figured someone has bound to have seen me in passing. I had received two main reactions. Either they answered and promptly slammed the door in my face or looked through the peephole and pretended not to be home. It wasn't until I had reached the final apartment on the bottom floor that an elderly ex-Baltimore police officer, named Ed, opened the door, invited me in for coffee, and agreed to sign my affidavit. We sat around a small round table in his cozy apartment and talked about the job while his wife poured us steaming hot cups of brew. He told me a few of his old war stories. One I remembered in particular had to do with the introduction of crack cocaine on to Baltimore's streets.

He explained how the city seemed to take a complete downward spiral after that. Cases of homicide and robbery spiked into infinite levels previously unknown. He looked me in the eye and seemed to read me in a microsecond, and nodded in approval. He then told me he was happy to be retired and that the torch had been passed to the likes of me. He reached out, shook my hand, and then wished me luck. I appreciated his candor.

Baltimore was extremely different from the town I grew up in. In my little town in West Virginia, everyone knows everyone. You can let your kids romp around outside and know that your neighbors have got an eye on them as well as you do. In Baltimore, I was afraid to let my children out of the yard.

I pulled my attention back to the road and made a right into the industrial park that housed my employer. Specter Armored looked like any other nondescript business in the park. The only difference being the rows of concertina wire that surrounded the complex affixed to the top of chain-link fencing. I maneuvered my Hyundai into the parking lot and swung into a spot. Drawing my keys from the ignition, I clipped them to my already-heavy belt. The keys seemed to add another ten pounds as I stepped out of the vehicle and stared at the darkening sky. Wind had begun to blow in from the east, kicking up dust and grit in the parking lot. I shielded my eyes from the assault of dirt flying into my tired face. Surprisingly, the lot was relatively empty for this time of morning.

Great, I thought sarcastically. Missing officers meant more work for me and my coworkers. I looked around the lot briefly and noted that my partner's beat-up red-and-rust-colored pickup truck was there and smiled. *At least my crew showed*, I thought as I approached the gate.

From the front, Specter Armored looked like your average warehouse-type building with offices in the front. To the random passerby, it was a simple nondescript brick and mirrored glass building; however, that was where the similarities ended.

Gaining access to the structure was a multitier security system that required at least two people. You and a guard positioned within the complex. The first entrance was through the electrified chain-link fence. This housed a keypad and card scanner, as well as a speaker and microphone setup. Aside from swiping your card and entering a code, the guard on the other end of the speaker would have to verify your identity for you to gain access into the yard. The idea being if an officer happened to be compromised, someone with just a stolen key card and a code wouldn't be able to just stroll on in and steal an armored car.

I swiped my ID and keyed in my badge identification number; a few moments passed, and a tired, grumpy-sounding woman chimed in.

"May I help you?" she said as if to say, *What the hell do you want?*

"Yes, I'll have a large fries, pie, and a coffee," I said and smirked. Silence greeted me, and I could imagine Patty, the woman in the guard booth, simply staring at the monitor, frowning and tapping her fingers on the desk. "Fine, Walker, Kyle," I said, rolling my eyes. The door to the gate buzzed and allowed me entrance.

The yard was a sprawling area, rows upon rows of monstrous glossy black international armored cars lined parking spots. I scanned the area and noticed one particular car idling with the door open, waiting to be loaded.

My vehicle was one of the older trucks in the fleet. The paint job was rusting in patches around the bumper and the back doors. The air-conditioning sucked ass, but it had an awesome turning radius and a reliable engine. The company, over the years, had added some of the more modern systems that were being built in to the newer vehicles; however, the engine and body remained the same old American-made truck I had come to love. Some of the newer foreign jobs seemed to break down every other day. One thing I didn't care for with the new trucks was that they were longer with a lower profile; this made it easier on an officer's knees as we traveled up and down the small stairs, in and out of the trucks all day long. Problem with this particular design was you couldn't bust out a quick U-turn in the middle of the road if your life depended on it, and most of the time, it did.

I made my way to the heavy steel door of the complex and pushed the door buzzer, activating a camera positioned in my face, and gave the assholes inside a big cheese-eating grin. The door clicked, and I entered the building. The smell of diesel and bad hygiene assaulted my olfactory senses, and I had to strain to keep myself from gagging.

Smells, especially in the early morning, were my sworn enemy and always made my stomach do flip-flops for a few moments. I breathed out slowly, drew in a deep breath through my mouth, and blew it out. Composed and out of danger of retching, I made my way to the guard booth, skirting behind an armored vehicle waiting to be loaded. In stark contrast to the quiet outside, the inside of the complex was a whirlwind of activity. People raced back and forth through the large truck bay with bins full of numerous bags and boxes of jewels, currency, and whatever the hell else people thought was valuable for one reason or another. Personally, I couldn't care less what we were transporting so long as I got a paycheck at the end of the week.

I reached the guard booth and tapped on the thick bullet-resistant glass. Visibility through the glass was less than clear, and the image of those behind it was marred and obscured. The window was smudged with oil and pockmarks left over years of constant abuse. I eyed the time clock impatiently. In less than a minute, I would be late again, and I had to wait on a mean-spirited bitch named Patty to give me my timecard. She was currently stuffing her round face with what looked like an exploded pig from this vantage. She peered up at me with irritation and popped open a small slot in the window and passed my timecard through. I turned and reached for the time clock and . . .

"Fuck!" I said as I noticed the clock was now two minutes past my objective time. Scowling, I swiped the card and handed it back to a now-closed window. I crammed the card into a tiny crease between the window and the flap, and watched in disgust. Patty had gone back to cramming her meal into her face. Sighing, I tapped on the window again. Patty frowned and stared blankly at me through thick glasses. She reopened the window and snatched the timecard out of my hand, slapping the window shut again without so much as a *Good morning, sunshine*.

The phone inside the room rang, muffled by the bullet-resistant glass, and Patty answered it sourly. I chose to take that particular moment to beat a hasty retreat from the evil she-bitch before she could infect me with her disdain. I never could quite understand why, if you hated your job so much, that not only would you sit there and wallow in self-pity, but force everyone else around you to suffer. Why don't you just quit the damn job? There were plenty of them for those who were looking and not complete idiots. After doing this job for the last ten years, most of the time, I pretty much found it tolerable; other times I thought I may be better off working for a urinal cake factory. *At least it would smell better*, I mused.

After looking around for a terse moment, I found my partner leaning up against a plain concrete wall at the far side of the truck bay, arms crossed and eyes closed. *Probably asleep*, I thought. I couldn't count on two hands how many times throughout the course of a day I would have to pound on the door of the truck to wake him up so he would open the door. He would then swear up and down that he was just resting his eyes. I approached the old ex-Marine whose once muscular form had since turned to flab from lack of use. Not completely his fault, he was in his seventies and had his leg amputated from the knee down after a wound in Vietnam. He told me the story once. He had stepped into a pit and bamboo skewers had shredded up through his foot and into his calf muscle. The wounds were not serious, at least not at first. The Vietcong had apparently coated the bamboo skewers in piss and animal feces, and infection was ultimately what took his leg. His handlebar mustache twitched as I approached him. One eye popped open.

"I thought I smelled you coming," he said gruffly, and adding a smirk.

I slapped him on the shoulder. "Watch it, old man. I might have to break your hip," I jabbed.

"Bring it, whippersnapper," Marvin Winters laughed.

"So what's the sitrep?" I said, eyeing my partner.

"Same ol' bullshit. We're stuck here waiting for these piss-ants while they figure out what to do with their dicks." Marvin frowned.

"Call outs," I ventured assumingly.

"Yeah, what else. More than usual, though. Seems like half this joint is at home in bed."

"That sucks," I said, knowing that not only were we going to be delayed at hitting the street, but now we also were going to have an even larger workload. Banks still need money whether people showed up or not; if there weren't enough officers to cover the routes, then the rest would have to be divided between the ones that showed. *Got to love it, maximum work for minimum pay*, I mused. Marvin glanced over at me with an ear-to-ear grin.

"Got a surprise for ya," he said.

"Oh, you mean better than all this." I gave a wide sweeping motion with my right hand.

"Definitely better," Marvin chuckled with a snort. "Follow me," he said as he started walking toward the guardroom. He opened the door and beckoned me in.

We stepped through the door, and noise immediately assaulted my ears as our coworkers talked and joked noisily around the break-room table.

Marvin headed past them toward the armory and waved me along excitedly. "Yer gonna wanna see this," Marvin said as he opened a locker. "Here, try this on fer size," he said as he pulled out a brand-spanking-new Mossberg model 500 tactical shotgun and handed it over to me.

I cocked and eyebrow and hefted it into my arms, holding it up across my shoulders. "Damn!" I exclaimed. "I've got this same model at home. Mine is a bit older, but this is nice," I added, observing the weapon.

"Yeah," Marvin said in agreement. "Just got 'em in."

We had only recently been granted the ability to carry shotguns on the trucks, used to be common practice until some dumbass rookie had been playing with one, and it discharged. It sent scattershot, ricocheting all around the interior of the truck, striking him in the legs and arms. Lucky for him he was wearing body armor, and he survived. After that, they were banned on the trucks and were only used in the vaults. Recently, we had acquired a new chief of operations who had authorized their use with extensive training. Up until now, we had used a standard generic pump-action shotgun. Nothing like this, though. The Mossberg, I knew, was a serious weapon.

Marvin reached into the locker and produced a box of ammo, and cocked an eyebrow. "Breach rounds," he said, holding up the box as if it were an idol to be worshiped. Teflon-coated steel core slugs were a force to be reckoned with, not to mention extremely hard to come by. Marvin pulled out a box of scattershot rounds as well. "Brought these from home," he said and smirked.

"Christ, Marvin! You expecting an army?" I said.

"Dunno. Personally, I'd rather deal with twelve peers in a room than six carrying my casket," he said, spouting off the standard law enforcement motto for better safe than sorry.

The radio clipped to Marvin's shoulder squelched to life, and Patty's gravelly voice chimed in.

"Beta team, you're up in one," she snarled.

"Your wife's calling you," Marvin said and chuckled.

"Fuck you," I replied and flipped him the bird as I headed out of the door to the vault.

We wandered past the bay full of armored cars, avoiding an oil spill in the middle of the floor. We stepped over it and approached the heavy gray steel vault doors located on the opposite side of the room. I reached the door handle as Marvin made his way out toward the yard to grab our vehicle. I pulled on the door, and it held fast. I cocked my head in the direction of the guard booth, and shouted, "Pop it!"

A moment passed, and an audible clank sounded as the magnetic lock allowed the heavy door to spring forward from its mount. I entered into a small gray brick room with another heavy steel door directly in front of me. A set of fluorescent lights buzzed and flickered above, casting an almost eerie bright and unkind light around me; it seemed to sap the energy from my being and caused me to struggle momentarily to keep from yawning. The top of the steel door clanked as a guard on the other side disengaged the locking mechanism and swung the top half of the door open, revealing the interior of the vault.

Behind the door, a scowling figure, Josh, I believe was the man's name. In all honesty, it might very well have been John or Jake or Bob for all I knew. I never had much use for our vault personnel other than to check my shit out and get us the hell out of there. Josh was a skinny kid with close-cropped hair, a hook nose, and thick glasses. He wore a baby-blue lab coat with only one pocket large enough to accommodate a small pad of paper and a pen or two. The idea being the less pockets, the less of a chance they had shoving wads of hundred dollar bills in them.

"Trust no one, Mr. Mulder," rolled through my brain, thinking of the old *X-Files* shows.

Josh yanked a large rolling cart over to the window with a grunt.

"Damn things will never just . . ." Josh gave a hard pull, causing the cart to scrape across the concrete floor. "Roll!" Josh shouted the last part as he slammed the cart against the lower half of the steel door. "Sup, man," Josh hissed in his high-pitched voice, causing me to wonder if this boy had even hit puberty yet, although I knew you had to be at least twenty-one to work for

Specter. Josh must have just turned the qualifying age, and turned it very recently. I personally was only thirty-five, but looking at the young man made me feel slightly old. I nodded at Josh, and Josh handed me a small dark gray PDA.

I tapped the power button on the PDA and awoke it from sleep mode, and then keyed in my personal identification number to log into the system. The PDA was basically our entire business on the street. It held all pertinent information about the day's job. From addresses, maps, GPS location as well as all delivery information, we could operate without it, on the off chance the system went down, with a packet of paperwork that was handed to us in the morning.

Josh then handed me a large ring of keys, spare batteries for the PDA, a clipboard full of paperwork, and extra ammunition for the shotgun and my .357 revolver. I took a moment and used the PDA to scan everything into my truck's inventory. When I returned from our route in the afternoon, a guard would then scan everything back into the vault. If anything was missing, there were mounds upon mounds of paperwork to be done, and you avoided that situation like the plague.

After all of my tools were scanned into the system, Josh began handing over bags of currency slated for today's delivery. I frowned inwardly when I noticed the amount of packages that were listed in my PDA.

"Definitely gonna be a long day," I groaned to Josh, and Josh smirked.

"Better you than me, dude," Josh said wearing an oily grin on his face that made me want to punch him in the forehead. I continued scanning the items and sorting them into small mail bins that I would later load onto my truck, keeping out only what was slated for whatever section of the route we were in, while the rest was locked into a steel cage. I clipped a key to a lanyard around my neck and tucked it beneath my ballistic vest that would be used to retrieve said packages once we entered a new area. Josh handed me the last package and said, "Done. Now get the fuck outta here." I eyed him for a moment, and then looked down at my PDA and shook my head.

"Uh, you missed one." I held up the PDA, the screen facing in Josh's direction.

Josh frowned and mumbled something unintelligible and began scanning the inside of the vault with his eyes. Josh seemed to recognize something, and he strolled out of sight for a moment. He reappeared a few seconds later, carrying a large black metal case struggling slightly against the weight of it.

Josh heaved the case onto the counter. It was huge, only slightly smaller than a suitcase, but definitely larger than your standard briefcase. Next to the handle, embedded into the metal, was an electronic keypad and what appeared to be a biometric scanner designed to accommodate a single thumbprint. A red LED flashed next to white lettering that stated "Armed."

I cocked an eyebrow and whistled. "That's some fancy shmancy security. What the hell is it?"

Josh shrugged. "No freaking clue, man. All I know is that it's supposed to go to Brantley and Reese," he said, flicking a small card that was tied to the case's handle with a black zip tie.

"Great," I muttered sarcastically. Brantley and Reese was one reason why I had been assigned to this particular route. Although my company knew nothing of my military past, my clearance level was still one of the highest in the armored car industry, which made me a vital player when it came to picking up various government and high-security facilities. Brantley and Reese was one of those facilities. The company itself, from the public standpoint, was nothing more than your simple run-of-the-mill electronics outfit that made everything from alarm clocks to smart phones. Their business, however, expanded way beyond that. Contracted by the government, they also built such things such as aircraft, submarines, and missile defense systems, as well as a whole menagerie of experimental weaponry that even my high-clearance level was not made privy to.

I grabbed the handle of the case and tossed it into my own cart, barely even registering its weight. I had done this job for years, and the case couldn't have weighed more than fifty pounds. My slightly toned, but muscular arms, took the weight with ease. I eyed Josh and smirked. *Girly, man*, is what rolled through my mind, but I decided to keep the rude comment to myself and remained professional.

"That it?" I spat out.

"Yeah," Josh replied.

"You sure—nothing else hiding in the shadows back there? I really don't want a call later telling me to bring my ass back here to get something extra that you forgot about."

Josh suddenly grabbed a log book off to the side, just to double check. "Nope, that's it, man," he said.

I nodded, watching as Josh closed the upper section of the vault door, leaving me once again to the stuffy claustrophobic room. I stowed all of my mail tubs into the rolling cart, stacking them directly on top of the black metal case. My curiosity was piqued just a bit. Normally, I couldn't care less about what I was carrying; however, the case was somewhat intriguing. I delivered currency to their location on the regular; however, that usually consisted of a handcart full of coins and a bag of money, which was always packaged in clear plastic. This was something different. For all I knew it may very well be a nuclear bomb; I shivered slightly at the thought but quickly disregarded it. Shrugging, I pushed a green button located on the wall next to the door marked exit, pushed the cart through the heavy steel door, and into the truck bay.

I waited by the door for several minutes until the large, rolling truck bay door slid up the track, allowing our vehicle to enter the complex. The large black armored car rumbled through the garage to the opposite end near an exit door. I pushed my cart to the back of the truck and suddenly jumped backward as the armored car's rear doors flung open, almost catching me in the shoulder.

"What the hell took you so damn long?" Marvin growled.

"Sorry, there was a slight SNAFU in the vault," I stated simply.

The ex-Marine nodded, understanding SNAFU for the military slang that it was, situation normal all fucked up, in other words, a typical day. "Well, let's get this shit loaded so we can get our asses on the road," said Marvin sourly. "It's bingo night." He cocked a sheepish grin in my direction.

I raised an eyebrow. "Is that before or after the five whiskey sours you pound down nightly?"

"After," Marvin stated truthfully. "My wife makes me go hang with those old fogies. Personally, I'd rather eat my gun," he chuckled.

I loaded the mail tubs full of packages into the rear of the truck and handed Marvin the key that was tucked into my vest.

Marvin opened the cage in the rear of the truck and picked up a tub and braced himself with his prosthetic leg, and then heaved the heavy tubs into the cage. Marvin may have been in his seventies and was operating with only one leg, but he didn't let any weakness show.

This task completed, we set about loading a skid of coin boxes that a forklift had dropped at our rear. The boxes were heavy as hell; however, I tossed them one handed into the back of the vehicle with ease.

Marvin crouched and stacked them neatly in rows, separating them by denomination for easy access.

The humidity from the approaching storm made this a difficult task, having infused the cardboard boxes with ambient moisture, which made them harder to slide across the metal floor of the truck. I drew my sleeve across my forehead, wiping away beads of sweat that had formed and began to soak the inside of my shirt collar.

"It's too damn early to be sweating," I said sourly. "There should be a law in place. No sweating until after noon."

Marvin nodded in agreement. "I'll send a stern letter to our congressman," Marvin said in a sarcastic tone.

Sighing, I slammed the rear doors of the truck closed.

A few moments passed. Marvin had exited the building and pulled the armored car around to the large chain-link fence. I walked beside the truck and moved to stand by the exit gate. An alarm beeped as the gate slid along its track and opened. I walked to the other side of the gate and waited for my truck to pull through the opening. I keyed the radio clipped to my shoulder.

"Clear," I said into the microphone, and the gate almost immediately began to slide shut. When the entrance to the complex was secure, the side door to the armored car popped open, and I boarded the truck sitting in the rear.

Marvin sat in front of me to my left, and spoke, "Ready to rock, son," he said, glancing over his shoulder.

"No, but were gonna go anyway," I replied with a hint of disdain.

Marvin grinned and nodded.

"Buckle up, Bucky," and with that, the truck lurched forward, and we were on the road.

CHAPTER 3

Fat droplets of rain began to fall from the graying sky and splatter across the windshield, leaving spidery tendrils of water sheeting across the thick bullet-resistant glass. Marvin squinted and mumbled something about Mother Nature being a bitch and flicked a switch activating the sorry excuse for wiper blades. The tiny blades screeched across the flat surface of the windows and barely cut a path through the streams of water falling onto the hood of the truck, making visibility difficult.

I stared listlessly out a side window watching trees whip by, wondering if my wife had awakened yet. I pulled my cell phone out of a case attached to my gun belt and flipped it open. No messages. Either she hadn't awakened or she hadn't picked up her phone yet. I typed a quick message that stated simply: *On the road again, love. I'll be home as soon as possible*. I hit send, closed the phone, and returned it to its leather pouch.

Looking down at my clipboard, I planned the logistics of my day, in a nanosecond, figuring out where to start and where to finish, as well as the approximant time of day we would be getting home. I sighed with the knowledge that it would more than likely be well after dark before we got home. I tossed the clipboard into a mail tub.

"Bank of Amara," I said, letting Marvin know where our starting point would be. We always tried to move things differently along the route, never showing up at the same place at the same time from day to day. It tended to piss off our clients, but as I explained, *If you don't know when we're coming, neither do the crooks*. It was sound logic mainly because after running and gunning for the past ten years, I hadn't had my ass shot off yet. *Knock on wood*, I thought.

Marvin took an exit ramp that was meant to be traversed at fifteen miles-per-hour at around sixty-five. I grabbed hold of the *oh-shit* handle next to my seat and braced myself in between it and a large air-conditioning unit that was bolted to the floor on my left side. Marvin slammed on the brakes as we hit traffic at the end of the ramp. I jerked forward in my seat belt and heard a loud metallic scraping sound as a handcart in the rear of the truck slid forward, and then caught me square in my left calf. Fiery pain exploded in my leg, and I kicked the handcart and sent it skittering to the rear of the truck.

"Son-of-a-bitch, Marvin, what the hell!" I shouted. Marvin looked over his shoulder and glanced back at me.

"Sorry, man," was all he said.

I had to seriously resist the urge to pull my weapon and shoot him in the face. I rubbed my calf and hiked up my pant leg to observe the damage. My calf was an angry red, but the skin was not broken. It was, however, going to leave one hell of a bruise, though.

"What the hell is this?" I motioned irritably to the traffic ahead of us.

Marvin rose up slightly and looked down the road a bit.

"Dunno, ton of cop cars, though."

I looked at my watch. "Fantastic," I said sarcastically. "We're already an hour behind."

"Hence, why I was speeding," Marvin interjected. "Sorry 'bout the leg, though. You okay, boss?" Marvin frowned slightly.

"I'll live. Can we get around this crap?" I said and made a sweeping motion with my hand.

"Not unless the cops let us through or we take a short cut through the median, but I don't feel like getting arrested today." Marvin shrugged.

"Okay, I'll see if I can get us through, or at least see how long this is gonna take." I unbuckled my seat belt and pulled my windbreaker on; the jacket didn't do much against the rain. God forbid that the powers that be pay a little extra for water proofing. It would help keep the chill from the driving rain down a bit. I stood, and Marvin popped the door open with the bus bar, and I exited the vehicle.

I stepped out into the elements. The rain seemed to have picked up a bit. I pulled a baseball cap out of my back pocket and seated it on my head. The rain pelted the brim of my hat and still managed to run into my eyes. I frowned, shook my head, and looked down the road. Cars, vans, and trucks stretched for what seemed like a half mile and obscured my view of the commotion ahead. The only indication I had that something was amiss was a series of bright red and blue light flashes in the distance. I zipped up my windbreaker and flashed my driver a *thumbs-up* and began walking.

I followed the shoulder of the road absently taking notice of annoyed and impatient drivers and passengers as I walked by. A mother yelled at her kids loud enough that I could hear her quite clearly with her windows up and the sound of the rain enveloping me. I cringed and wondered if those kids still had any hearing left after that ear assault. Apparently, they did not or more than likely just didn't give a damn, because they kept on acting stupid in the back of the car. I thought back to my own kids probably up and romping around at this point at my grandparents' home in West Virginia, where they were spending the remainder of their summer vacation.

Gravel scraped across the wet asphalt as I walked. The clouds were all encompassing with no break in sight. Ambient light seemed to cast a gray-blue hue over everything. As I rounded a curve, three police cars came into view. The gray and yellow cars instantly identified the department as the Maryland transportation authority.

"Good," I said to myself. I had worked with these guys before. As always, there were a few pricks, but most of them seemed to be decent people. Several officers stood around a dark-green minivan, in black vinyl rain gear. One of the officers shined a flashlight into a window while another spoke into his lapel mic. As I approached, an officer standing slightly away from the scene took notice of me. I waved as I walked forward.

"How ya doing, Officer?" I said as I put on my best fake smile. The transportation cop looked over his shoulder nervously and hurried toward me. "So what's—"

"Sir, you need to get back in your vehicle!" he ordered and pointed back in the direction I had come from. He came to stand nose to nose with me. "Sir, I gave you an order."

I stood there and looked stupefied at him. *One of the pricks*, I thought. "Sorry, man. We're in an armored car down the road, and we're just wondering if we could possibly get through. Got a lot of liability on board, and we're sitting ducks back there." I thrust a thumb in the direction of my vehicle.

That line of logic usually got them thinking about them possibly being held responsible. I snuck a quick peek over his shoulder and noticed flashlight guy trying the door handle.

"Look, I don't give a shit if your wife is about to have the first alien baby." He thrust his arm up and pointed toward the accident scene. "We have a serious situation and you need—" A scream from behind him stopped him midsentence.

Both of us instinctively went for our sidearms. Officer Dickhead whirled around and froze in horror. I looked past him and noticed it too. We both stood there, mouths gaping for a moment. Flashlight guy was clutching his face as blood poured through his fingertips.

What got out of the van took us completely by surprise. I was half expecting some belligerent and drunken bruiser with a shank in his hand, and what emerged was a blond-haired kid who reminded me of Dennis the Menace. The boy stumbled out of the front door and fell down on all fours. The kid was covered head to toe in gore. His blond hair was matted to his head with blood. Flashlight guy backed away from the kid as he crawled toward him.

"Fuck, man, help! Little shit just bit me!" Flashlight guy spat blood on the ground. Radio Cop just stared at the boy stupidly, apparently not sure what to do. When it's an adult and you don't have a half mile's worth of angry people in cars with camera phones, you can pretty much thump the shit out of anyone who has attacked a police officer, but this was just a kid. If they handled the situation even the least bit wrong, their asses would be plastered across Facebook and Twitter in a matter of seconds, YouTube video's taken with random cell phones would make it on the six o'clock news. I glanced over my shoulder and noticed several nosy Nancies dangling cell-phone-laden arms out of windows trying to get a good shot of any carnage taking place. Probably hoping someone would get shot so they could end up on *Dr. Phil* talking about how horrible it was, and how it had scared them to witness such brutality, however, internally loving every second of national attention. Next thing you know they have a reality show and a fucking Chihuahua in a purse.

Another yelp from flashlight guy snapped me back to reality. He was backed up against his cruiser, holding his torn face, blood still pooled over his fingers, and soaked into his gray woolen shirt. Dennis the Menace still crawled on all fours toward him.

"Will somebody grab this kid? Something isn't right with him!" Radio cop started to walk around the car toward the boy. He stopped in front of the open car door and looked down at the boy as if deciding how to best restrain him. Should he cuff him, or simply just pick him up in a bear hug and restrain his arms? They were taught how to deal with punk ass teens and drunken adults, but seven-year-old kids, not so much. He decided his course of action, reaching behind his back for the handcuffs attached to his duty rig.

At that precise moment, a growl seemed to emanate into the air, and a hand shot out of the passenger-side door and grabbed the officer by the arm. Thrown off balance, he pitched backward into the open car, his head disappearing into the SUV's interior. A split second later, he screamed, red liquid sprayed across the windshield and out of the open passenger door. The officer's legs kicked and spasmed. He jerked and writhed as if trying to throw something off. A wet gurgling sound was all I heard. Hearing another scream, I looked to my right. The young boy grabbed onto flashlight guy's leg and sank his baby teeth into his muscular calf. The cop kicked out and reached for his sidearm. Officer Dick-head seemed to pull himself out of shock and drew his own weapon.

"Stop right there!" he shouted at the boy. The boy took his attention from flashlight guy, mouth open in a snarl covered in fresh blood, and focused on us. Slowly, the kid got to his feet and snarled.

Normally, the growl of a pissed off seven-year-old would not strike fear into my heart. I did, after all, have five children of my own. This boy, however, made my skin crawl. Aside from the blood and gore that seemed to cake every inch of the kid's body, his eyes, even from this distance, bloodshot and cataract laden, stared at us with such intense hatred they made me want to turn tail and run back to the safe confines of my black and gray three-quarter-inch steel-plated armored truck.

"Be smart, son. Don't move!" Officer Dick-head said as he pointed his weapon in the general direction of the boy. His hands shaking as he stared down the barrel of his .44 Mag. At this point, I noticed flashlight guy crumple to the ground like a discarded piece of paper; he started to shake and convulse violently.

"Hardy! Winters!" Dick-head shouted, still gripping his pistol, with white knuckles. At this point, I realized that happened to be the other officers' names.

Odd, I thought. My partner's last name is Winters also, wonder if there was any relation. I know he has a kid in the prison system, guard that is not inmate. Not sure if he has any relations in the police department; I'll have to remember to ask.

I noticed off to my left, Officer Winters' legs begin to twitch inside of the car. A hand slowly seemed to grasp for the door, trying to gain purchase, shaky and unsteady. Not Winters' hand, mind you. Unless Officer Winters wore a bright-pink watch and a marquise diamond ring that would make the average man say, *Holy shit, how did you afford that?*, and had the kind of hands that you would find in a jewelry catalogue out of JCPenny.

The boy stumbled forward, looking slightly confused, like when you pretend to throw a scrap of bacon to a dog. The dog then spins around the room for a moment and then looks at you as if to say, *What the hell, man?*

Officer Dick-head took a step back and, in effect, left me closer to the boy. The boy eyed me with the look of someone who had a serious case of the munchies. I inadvertently took a step back as well. Dick-head looked at me, and I nodded and drew my sidearm slowly. The boy crept closer.

Officer Dick-head shouted, "Stop right there, kid!" I noticed his finger slip off the trigger guard and into firing position.

Holy shit, I thought, *he is actually going to shoot this kid.* I glanced over my shoulder and noticed people starting to slunk out of their cars, trying to get a better angle of the action. "Fuck!" I said out loud without realizing it.

There was a commotion at the SUV. The door suddenly shook on its hinges, and a woman's body slumped out of the car, sliding over top of the still form of Radio Cop um . . . Winters, I suppose was his name, at least that's what Dick-head had called him. The woman hit the ground with a wet thud. Blood pooled from her mouth, seeping down to the pavement. Slowly she raised her face, and Dick-head and I gasped. Her cheek had been torn completely off, exposing bloody teeth and muscle tissue. Jagged pieces of cheekbone protruded at awkward angles on her otherwise attractive face. My first instinct had been to run over to the woman and see if I could help her. However, her expression seemed to drain my body of blood, starting at my head and ending at my toes. Every single hair on my body stood on end, and a chill settled in my chest and spread out to my fingertips in waves. Anxiety, I realized, and I had to force myself to calm down, to breathe. I held my gun in my hands and sighted down the barrel. Although at first glance, she was a meek slender wisp of a woman, something in the inner recesses of my mind, in the areas ingrained in all of us, the areas built in for survival, perceived this woman as an immediate threat, and I turned the business end of my weapon in her direction.

Her sightless eyes locked on mine, and she let out a terrible hiss. Fighting the instinct to turn tail and haul ass to anywhere but here, I took a chance, and glanced over at the police officer standing next to me. He was frozen in place, his eyes never leaving the child and his fallen comrades behind him.

"Hey, hey!" I shouted to Officer Dick-head. He jumped at the sound of my voice and glanced at me over his shoulder. "What do you wanna do? Shouldn't you call this in or something? You know, call for backup, Dann-o," I said with a slight edge of sarcasm. Don't judge me; it's a defense mechanism. The officer nodded his head, reached for the microphone clipped to his shoulder, and keyed the receiver.

"Dispatch, this is unit fifty-three requesting backup multiple ten fifty-threes, two suspects ten dash twenty-nine H," Dick-head said, sounding like he was programmed, which in a way he was.

My police lingo was not the best. In the military, we had an entirely different code structure, which I had to deprogram and adapt when I became an armored officer. In that code, what he said didn't make any sense; basically in our lingo, he just said he had multiple bathroom breaks and was stopping to grab a sandwich. I shook the thought of the man sitting in a bathroom with his tighty-whiteys around his ankles eating a sub from my mind. Although I mused, that would be an extremely efficient way to gain nourishment while ridding the body of toxins. I searched my memory and figured out he said something along the lines that there were multiple men down, and the suspects were extremely hazardous.

Yeah, no shit, I thought. The radio chirped, but before we had a chance to register something that was being said, the woman and the child both seemed to spring at once. The boy, being closer, ran straight for Dick-head, looking like some savage cross between Dennis the Menace and a fucked up Eddie Munster.

The boy barreled into Dick-head's legs, causing him to lose his footing. His firearm discharged, sending a .44 caliber hollow point into the rear windshield of a police cruiser. The windshield popped and spider-webbed into thousands of tiny cracks, screams from the observers in the idling cars sounded with deafening alarm. The cop fell on his ass and tried to scramble away from the snarling boy. His sidearm skittered across the pavement and came to a halt under the rear tire of his police cruiser.

"Shit, shit," Dick-head whimpered, trying desperately to put some distance between him and the crazed child. The child fell on him and sank his teeth into the heel of the officer's boot. "What the hell is wrong with him?" the cop shouted desperately and kicked with his free leg, trying to dislodge the boy.

The woman took me by surprise as I was momentarily distracted by the child. I instinctively opened fire as my training took over. I fired two shots. One went wide and missed her completely; the other struck her in the shoulder and sent her spinning around. She fell to her knees stunned momentarily. Time, seemed to slow down as adrenaline flooded my body. Noises were muffled, and the world seemed to take an almost dreamlike quality. Everything moved in slow motion.

I noticed the first officer who was attacked begin to convulse once more. Suddenly, he shot up, his eyes flaring wide. His pupils looked impossibly large, like black disks. He let out a scream that sounded so shrill it was practically inhuman.

Officer Dick-head continued to struggle unsuccessfully, the child still gnawing on his boot.

"Help!" he shouted over to me. I looked at him dazed for a moment, holding my gun downrange, watching the woman struggle to get back to her feet. It registered what the cop was yelling to me, and I snapped out of it.

"Hang on!" I shouted and ran around to the cop. I frantically glanced between the woman and now the flashlight guy, who were both struggling to get to their feet. I grabbed the boy by the back of his shirt and yanked him off the cop. The boy kicked and flailed in my hands, and I was forced to toss him aside like a sack of potatoes. His mouth snapped and snarled in midair as he fell to the ground and landed with a thud.

Quickly, I helped Dick-head up to his feet. I scanned the area and noticed that another figure was standing to my left.

Radio Cop had appeared on his feet again, which, by the looks of him, was impossible. He stood there, a ragged, bloody mass of skin, bone, and cartilage hanging around the area of where his throat should be. Blood still seeped from the wound and stained his gray wool shirt and tie.

Someone off to my left, a woman I think, let out a shrill scream upon seeing the officer's mangled form. His gaze left Officer Dick-head's and my direction and seemed to focus on the source of the noise. His arms outstretched and his mouth agape, he let out what I could only imagine was a moan; however, all that emanated from him was a gurgling seepage of air escaping through the ragged hole in his throat. Blood bubbled out of the opening, and I had to steel myself against a wave of nausea. I looked over at Dick-head, and both of us stared at each other in disbelief.

A shrill scream sounded to our left as Radio Cop latched on to a woman in a Volkswagen Bug. She had been recording the entire endeavor with her smartphone. He grabbed her arm and was pulling it to his gaping mouth when I was suddenly knocked backward.

My head struck asphalt, and white bursts of light clouded my vision. I felt something heavy on top of me, clawing at my chest.

As my vision cleared, I realized it was the woman whom I had shot only moments before. I felt her mouth ripping at my chest, and I struggled to raise my gun. At this range, it would most likely be suicide to open fire. I don't care what you see in the movies; shooting someone that is right up against you is never a good idea. Bullets react funny when they strike bone; they can go all sorts of ways, including into me. I chose to bash her in the skull with the barrel of my gun. I cocked my arm back and struck her as hard as I could manage. The blow I administered would have taken down a 260 pound meth head; this meek woman with a gunshot wound and a mangled face hadn't even flinched. I think all I managed to do was piss her off. I looked frantically around for Officer Dickhead, seeking help, and noticed the boy and flashlight guy stumbling my way.

Shit, I thought, struggling underneath the weight of this crazy-ass woman. "Where in the hell did that son-of-a-bitch run off to?" I said, trying my best to look around the area. It was at that point I came to a decision. I have a wife and five kids, and I am not planning on checking out today. Not here, not in the middle of a goddamn traffic jam. I raised my gun up, put the barrel to the back of the woman's head, and said a small prayer. Hoping that the bullet would be deflected by my vest and not bounce off into my forehead. I put my finger on the trigger. At that moment, there was a large crash behind me. I craned my head backward to see what this new threat was. Cars were being strewn out of the way as something large, something powerful barreled through them. A sound of metal scraping on metal flooded my ears and then was followed by the blaring of a horn.

Oh shit, I thought as the upside-down image of an armored car plowed its way toward me. "Oh shit, oh shit, oh shit," I said as it registered in my mind what my partner was planning. We had an unspoken rule on the trucks. In the case of a robbery, our drivers were instructed to leave the area, thus taking away the temptation from the perp. This was good in theory but wound up leaving officers like me pretty much screwed, and at the mercy of some pissed-off crook that just had his cookie jar taken away.

"I might be ordered to leave, but nothing says I can't hit the bastard on the way out," was what my partner had always said. He spotted me and gunned the engine. Black smoke poured from the exhaust pipe as he revved the engine. He brought the truck's rpm's up to speed and surged forward. Wet gravel slung from under the truck's enormous wheels and sprayed the surrounding traffic as the tires sought purchase on the soggy asphalt.

Quickly, I grabbed hold of the snarling woman, with both hands grasping onto her shoulders. I thrust my knee into her gut and dislodged her mouth from my shirt. Brackish thick blood, drool, and mucus clung to my shirt, stretching into long, thin tendrils as I thrust her upward—just as the fifty-five thousand pound armored beast roared over top of me.

The bumper connected with the top of her head and snapped her neck backward with an audible crack. Her face scraped along the oil and dirt-encrusted surface and began to tear away flesh in chunks. I watched as her noggin bounced up and down as the undercarriage passed over and peeled her face off in beef-jerky-sized strips. I could almost hear the wet slurping sound as the flesh tore, even though thinking about it later, I knew that was impossible due to the intense rumbling noise the truck made. Flecks of blood and bone showered my face. I squeezed my eyes and mouth shut and held onto her as hard as I could. The reverberation of the impacts sent shockwaves down my arm, grinding my elbow into the pavement, and I almost lost my grip. Then the muffler connected with the side of her ruined face and ripped her head completely off. Her body went slack in my now-bruised hands. A thick viscous blood seeped from the wound and pooled around my neck, running underneath my ballistic vest. I was almost amazed at how slow the blood seemed to trickle out. Arterial blood always shot out hard and heavy like turning on a fire hose.

The truck came to a halt just before it had completely passed me over. My arms struggled against the dead weight and finally gave out trembling. I dropped the corpse, and she landed hard onto my chest, knocking the wind out of me. I saw fading at the edge of my vision, and I fought to take in ragged breaths to prevent myself from passing out. My ears rang, and I could hear the blood rushing through them. There was an audible pop and muffled footsteps, then something grabbed me. Panic shot through me as I thought it was one of those things out there coming back for seconds. Officer Dick-head pulled with all his might, managing to slide me out from underneath of the dead woman's corpse and the truck. He helped me to my feet, and I staggered, almost losing my footing.

"Come on!" he shouted, half carrying, half dragging me to the side door of the truck. One arm positioned under my armpits while the other, I noticed, carried my brand new Mossberg. The door to the truck popped open, and a familiar voice shouted.

"Get your candy asses in here!" said Marvin and the cop shoved me inside. I hit the reinforced metal floor and crawled my way in. Pain was starting to register in my arms from the repeated impacts with the roadway. I gritted my teeth against the pain and moved myself forward to make room for Officer Dick-head. "Look out!" Marvin shouted out to the policeman.

The cop whirled around and fired a shot, knocking one of his former partners in the chest, sending him sprawling to the ground. The crazed officer was unfazed and was getting back to his feet to have another go.

Dick-head hastily climbed into the cab, and Marvin shut the door and slammed down on a red button located on the dash. Loud clicks sounded around the interior of the truck as the automatic throw bolts slid into place and sealed the truck up tight. The truck rocked with impacts as several people plowed into the sides of it.

I managed to get to my feet and peer out the window. At first, all I saw was the two cops and the little boy. They pounded fruitlessly onto the sides of the armored vehicle, and then there were more, a lot more—passengers of the trapped cars. I realized some of them still clutching their cell phones in their bloodied hands.

"What the fuck," I breathed out in disbelief.

Marvin twisted around in his seat and looked at me and then to the heavily breathing cop and then back. "Will someone please tell me what the hell is going on?"

INTERLUDE 1

Director Don Hammond sat behind a heavy oak desk in the office of Homeland Security located on the outskirts of BWI airport. He thumbed through a stack of reports that had cluttered his desk for the past week and sighed.

All dead ends, he thought. They had been tracking a suspected group of homegrown terrorists with the aid of the FBI and the NSA, so far with absolutely nothing to show for it except some vague money trails. Some suggesting ties to Al-Qaeda, others to North Korea, however, nothing definitive, and perhaps as far as the intel was concerned, not even related. Don dropped the stack of reports on to his desk, cupped his face in his hands, and rubbed his eyes. The familiar pain of heartburn began creeping up to his throat, and he swallowed hard in an effort to force the acid back down. He reached across his desk and grabbed a cup of coffee sitting on a plate warmer and took a sip. He scowled and set the cup down on the edge of his desk, reaching into a drawer by his side. He rummaged around and produced a bottle of Irish whiskey. He unscrewed the cap and poured a bolt into his steaming cup. A knock at the door startled him, and he fumbled with the bottle, hurriedly trying to replace the cap. He stashed the bottle back into the recesses of his dark cherry wood-finished desk, and said, "Yes. Come in."

A slender man in his mid-forties entered the scantly adorned office of Director Hammond. In the office sat two burgundy leather office chairs facing the director's large wooden desk. Stacks of unread file folders brimming with reports lay somewhat strewn about the office. The director's waste basket was overflowing with crumpled-up papers that now spilled over and onto the gray-brown carpeted floor. Light illuminated the office from a single bay window off to the agent's left, casting an almost-cold and sterile hue in the small room. The agent wore a navy-blue business suit that had appeared to be ironed and had a tight, crisp look to it. The man ran his fingers through his neatly trimmed graying hair. He wrinkled his nose in disgust, detecting the faint alcoholic scent of whiskey that hung in the air.

This early in the morning, he thought to himself and eyed the director dubiously. He held a manila file folder in his hands containing the first action reports of the day. Only 9:00 a.m. and the folder was already a half an inch thick. The director eyed the folder and raised an eyebrow.

"Already, Bishop? I haven't even had my coffee yet," Director Hammond said with a sigh.

Alex Bishop glanced at the coffee mug on the director's desk and smirked. "My thoughts exactly, sir," he said coldly.

Hammond frowned and snatched the folder from Agent Bishop's outstretched hand, and then pretended to skim over the action reports. Alex Bishop was an ambitious weasel and after Hammond's job, and he knew it. Standing there, showing off in his pressed suit and silk tie, the director could almost swear the man had eyeliner on as he stared intently at Bishop's dark piercing blue eyes. If Hammond could find anything to fault the man on, he would gladly send him over to the TSA giving strip searches to fat men with herpes at the airport; unfortunately for Hammond, Bishop's record was flawless.

"Anything actually worth my attention here, Bishop, or is this just more fodder for the paper shredder?" Hammond said slightly annoyed at the fact Bishop was still standing there.

"Mostly the usual, sir. Guns, drugs, money and a bomb threat or two. There was one report that stuck out from the rest, though. The call came in just a few moments ago via cell phone from one of our agents stuck in a traffic jam. Called to tell us he was running late when seemingly all hell broke loose. Police involved shooting apparently—"

Hammond cut him off with a wave of his hand. "What the hell does a police shooting on the road have to do with Homeland, Bishop?" Hammond shot Bishop an irritated glance.

"Because it involved an armored car, sir," Alex said to Hammond expectantly.

"So? Armored cars are the Fed's problem."

"Sir, if you look through your reports from the past few days, you will find that we have some um . . . materials being shipped to an NIH research facility at Brantley and Reese. We believe this was one of the vehicles bound for that destination. We lost contact with our agent before we could confirm it."

Hammond looked down at the files on the desk and sighed. "What kind of materials, Bishop, and why in the hell wouldn't we use our own people?" Hammond growled.

Bishop paced the length of the room and stopped in front of the bay window, and then gazed out over the graying city. Dark clouds swirled ahead and tiny raindrops splashed upon the glass. "Biological research," Agent Bishop said, pausing. "It's all in the report, sir."

Hammond cast a longing glance at the drawer that contained his liquor bottle. He already knew that the reason behind their choice in transport, if the public had gotten wind that Homeland Security was messing with biotech, it would cause an uproar that would undoubtedly have lasting repercussions to the current administration. People had already begun to speculate that Homeland had all sorts of nefarious agendas, for instance, buying up caches of weapons and ammo. They were correct in that assumption, but they didn't need to know that. The reason they had just recently started looking into and studying biological entities was due in no small part to the alarming amount of weapons being offered on the black market.

Hammond reached in his drawer and withdrew the bottle and two glasses; he poured the amber liquid into the glasses and held one out to Agent Bishop.

Bishop cocked an eyebrow at the director.

"Trust me, Bishop, you're gonna want this. Your day is about to get a hell of a lot more complicated," Hammond said and knocked the shot back. Slamming the glass down on top of his file folders, he reached for the phone on his desk. "Tracy, put me in touch with the secretary of defense."

CHAPTER 4

Karen sat around the kitchen table staring at a tiny laptop screen. Pale blue light cast across Karen's smooth feminine features as she tried unsuccessfully to input information for the day's attendees. She rubbed her temples and massaged her face, trying to stave off the headache that was brewing in her brain. Children ran about the small trailer crazily as Karen rubbed her temples.

"Chill out!" she screamed, and the children, as usual, completely ignored her. Karen stood from the wooden kitchen chair and stormed into the living room. The eight young boys and girls immediately stopped what they were doing and stared at her. Karen held her breath; quietly, she exhaled.

"Okay, who wants to play a game?" she said calmly. Karen looked at her charges and quickly thought of the game on the fly. She arranged all the children in a circle around the living room. Karen stood in the center and clapped her hands together in front of her face. "Okay, now who knows how to play Duck, Duck, Goose?"

Tiny hands shot up in the air.

The first boy to be *it* was a chubby blond-haired, seven-year-old named Rich. Richie, to everyone who knew him, walked around the circle, patting the other children on the head as he went.

"Duck, duck, duck, goose!" the boy shouted and slapped a wisp of a girl named Sophie on the top of her head, causing her to involuntarily wince. She jumped up and frantically began to run around the circle while being pursued by the chubby boy. Richie ran as fast has he could, hands outstretched almost touching her long auburn hair that fluttered behind her. Just as he was about to tag her and relive himself from being *it*, he tripped over his own two feet and stumbled head first into one of the front bay windows, smacking his head against the double panes of glass. Sophie sat back down in her spot and smiled smugly in satisfaction. Richie, who was now tangled in the forest-green flower-patterned curtains, shook and spun around frantically, trying to dislodge himself as if caught in a giant spider-web. He caught a glimpse outside of the window in the graying landscape and froze. He gasped suddenly.

Richie stumbled backward and shook his little head back and forth, trying to clear the invisible cobwebs that suddenly clouded his rattled brain. He opened his eyes and shuddered. Richie backed away from the window slowly, his mouth dropping open and lip quivering. He raised his right hand and pointed toward the window.

Karen had been watching the little boy and asked, "Richie, you okay?" she said, furrowing her eyebrows with concern.

"Mmm . . . Mrs. Karen, there's a man outside and he's, he's . . ." Richie stammered, unable to finish the sentence.

Karen quizzically eyed the boy. She stood and walked over to the window. She pulled the curtain open and peered outside.

"What the . . ." she whispered to herself. A man was crouched down not two feet from the window. He appeared to be holding something in his hands and chewing on it. His head seemed to bite down on something and frantically jostle back and forth and tear away at the object he was holding. Karen stared intently at the man, noticing a stream of blood running down the disheveled-looking man's fingers. "Holy shit!" she said a bit louder than she meant to.

"Aw! Mrs. Karen, you said a wordy dirty!" the kids exclaimed.

The man stopped his feast and lifted his head in the direction of the home. He cocked his nose in the air and sniffed. He snarled, baring his bloody teeth, and dropped what appeared to be the corpse of a neighborhood cat.

Karen backed away from the window in a panic. The man suddenly shot up and ran for the window, slamming face first into it. Blood and saliva oozed down the surface of the glass and smeared as he began to pound on the window. The first pane of glass began to crack under the onslaught. Karen looked around wildly; quickly, she moved to the children's cubbies and grabbed a red backpack that contained essential supplies for the kids. She shouldered the bag and looked at the children, trying to remain calm as the crazy man assaulted her window. She risked a glance over her shoulder and noticed the man still slamming into the pane of glass. It seemed others had joined him; panic momentarily moved across her face. *What the hell is going on?* she thought.

"Okay, boys and girls, I want everyone to line up and follow me." She appeared to be calm and in control; however, her insides were doing summersaults.

Quickly, she led the children into her bedroom, shutting and locking the door; she then proceeded to lead them into the bathroom and into a large closet. Her husband—thank God—had insisted that the closet be well-stocked with food and water, as well as weapons hidden behind a false wall. She hated the thought of having guns in the house; however, they were unknown and inaccessible to the children, and she had tolerated the idea. At this moment, she was grateful she had relented to his paranoia. She piled the children inside of the small space and closed and locked the reinforced door just as there was a loud crash inside of the living room. The closet plunged in darkness, and the kids screamed.

"Shhh, shhh, shhh!" Karen exclaimed. "It's okay," she whispered and felt around the shelving units for a windup lantern. She found what she was looking for and turned it on. The small lantern flooded the closet with a dim fluorescent light.

Karen shrugged off the red backpack and began rooting through it, pulling out some crayons and a few coloring books.

"Okay, who wants to color a picture?" she said, trying to remain calm.

A little girl with blonde pig tails and a flower-patterned dress looked up at her and asked, "What's going on, Mrs. Karen? What was wrong with that man?"

"I don't know, sweetie," she replied. "But we're safe here," she assured them all. Karen silently prayed that she was correct. She handed each one of the children a coloring book and a small pack of crayons, and then listened to the sounds of her home being ransacked by strangers. She eyed the far wall of the closet and contemplated if she would be willing to open it and retrieve the firearms that lie beneath the drywall. If it came down to it, she would do whatever it took to keep the children in her care safe, which included facing her fears, and going against her beliefs. In the dim light of the lantern, her mind drifted back to the past.

Karen stood in her friend Jenna's home; she was thirteen. Her parents were at work, and Jenna and Karen roamed around the neighborhood until there was absolutely nothing left to do. They ultimately wound up at Jenna's house planning on watching some MTV and eating chips and dip, conversing about boys and hot rock stars. As they entered the house, Jenna's brother, Seth, was lying in a pool of blood at the bottom of the stairs. A neat hole bore through the boys left leg. He lay there unconscious, blood spreading out and seeping into the carpeted stairs and landing beneath. A hunting rifle that had belonged to their father lay next to him on the stair landing. The girls screamed and were paralyzed and rooted to the floor, staring at the young man.

Jenna moved and ran to her brother, crouching down beside him. She frantically called his name and shook his shoulders, trying desperately to wake him. Karen looked around, found the phone, and proceeded to call the police. The police and ambulance showed up a little while later and took the boy to the hospital.

Ultimately, Seth had lost the leg. The bullet from his father's hunting rifle had shattered the bone and caused so much nerve damage that the leg caused more pain than it was worth. After years of therapy, treatments, and pain management, Seth decided just to have the damn leg removed in favor of a prosthetic.

Karen remembered the pain that one bullet, one mistake, had caused and had loathed the use of firearms ever since. She stared at the false wall warily. If it were absolutely necessary, she would do what she had to do. She just hoped it wouldn't come to that.

CHAPTER 5

Marvin darted his eyes back and forth, tapping on the armored car's steering wheel, searching for an exit.

I gazed out of the windows and watched in abject horror as more and more people seemed to be devoured and, only moments later, get back up and add to the onslaught of bodies now assaulting the perimeter of the armored vehicle. The black behemoth visibly swayed back and forth under the immense pressure being exerted by the assailants. Those unfortunate enough to be pressed against the solid steel armored car were split open and crushed into a bloody pulp under the combined weight of so many gathering in. I watched in revulsion as the head of a gangly man burst like a melon in a microwave. Blood and brain matter shot out and oozed down the heavy ballistic glass and armored plating. Quickly, I turned my head and fought the urge to vomit. I tried in vain to unsee the carnage, but that in itself was about as effective as trying to unsee a half-naked fat chick in a Go-Go skirt going down on my hairy-as-an-ape neighbor, behind the privacy fence in the backyard, when my brothers and I were hiding in the trees behind our house as children, playing army men with the other neighborhood kids. As I recall, I puked then too.

"Marvin, buddy, are you planning on getting us the hell out of here anytime soon?" I tried to come across sardonic, but it more than likely sounded like a whimper of panic. I really didn't have time to care, if I'm honest. I was visibly shaking at this point. I hadn't been this scared since the time my ex-girlfriend cheated on me, and I had to go through a battery of tests to make certain I didn't have any kind of VD. It had taken weeks upon weeks of anxiety and flat-out fear before those tests results came back and let me know she hadn't infected me with anything except a major case of the heebie-jeebies. As it was, I was somewhat of a freak when it came to germs.

When I was a kid, I developed a habit of washing my hands at every single possible opportunity that I could get, trying my damnedest to keep any of the invisible horrors away. Finally, my mother got fed up with my neurosis and decided to do something about it. She crammed my hands in the dirt and forced me to sit there for about an hour and would not, for the life of me, let me get up and wash my hands. I panicked, I cried, pretty sure but not entirely certain that I went into convulsions, and then finally I relented. After she was satisfied that I was not going to end up like Adrian Monk and suffer a nervous breakdown and never leave my house, she let me get up and wash my hands, and be done with it.

Marvin began to speak and snapped me out of my revelry.

"I'm looking. I'm looking. Quit pestering me. I can't just drive off and plow over a bunch of people," Marvin insisted.

"Dude, seriously, they are trying to kill us," I pleaded.

It was at this point the cop that was with us piped up, "He's right. You know, if you wait much longer, we're not going to be able to drive out of here. There's just too many of them. I say just roll over the bastards and let God sort it out later."

Marvin cocked an eyebrow at the officer. "You know that's your own men out there, right?" he said incredulously.

"God damn it, don't you think I'm aware of that?" the officer growled letting his emotions slip. He then softened. "Look, those men out there are like brothers to me. However, right now, they seem to be more like the enemy, so get this bucket moving before we all end up like them." The officer pointed out the window halfheartedly at the massing brood.

Marvin shook his head back and forth and let out a sigh. "You may want to buckle up then. It's gonna be a bumpy ride." Marvin cocked his head to the side in thought. "Hell, it's a bumpy ride even without all of this shit going on." Marvin threw the vehicle in first gear, depressed the clutch, and pressed down hard on the accelerator. The engine roared to life. Marvin revved the machine several times, halfheartedly hoping the noise rumbling forth would give pause to the people standing in front of the truck. Sadly, it did not. If anything, it seemed to aggravate them even more, and they redoubled their efforts assaulting the side of the vehicle.

Marvin released the clutch and began moving the vehicle forward, slowly knocking bodies askew. As the truck's speed increased, the bodies seemed to almost fly out of the way, reminding me of a man with a leaf blower cutting a path through fallen leaves. Figures fell away and began to give chase, some of them simply hung onto the bumper and mirror assembly. Just as we started to break free of the crowd, we heard sirens begin to amass in the distance.

The officer's ears perked up. "Finally, the fucking cavalry has decided to grace us with their presence," Officer Dick-head said, gazing out the truck's tiny window trying to spot the telltale signs of emergency vehicles.

Sirens grew louder and seemed to come from all directions, converging on our location. They, however, were not the usual local PD that we had expected. White SUVs embossed with the Homeland Security seal surrounded the area of the highway that we were currently attempting to drive on.

"Why the hell is Homeland here?" I asked no one in particular. Everyone just simply stared out of the windows, wondering the same exact thing. I gazed out of the portal at the oncoming vehicles and noticed a large jet fly overhead. Military, from the looks of it, but I was uncertain if it was even related to what was going on. Being so close to the airport as well as an Air National Guard station, it could have been in the air for any number of reasons. I dismissed it and watched as the Homeland vehicles approached.

The Homeland Security vehicles amassed ahead of us, positioning them in a semi-circle around the front of our vehicle. They parked a mere two hundred or so yards away. Marvin had to slam on the brakes to avoid skidding across the wet road and ripping through the Government SUVs like pieces of tin foil.

A graying-haired man dressed in black and gray BDUs with a gold badge attached to his belt, and a lanyard around his neck, stepped out of the passenger side of the SUV, holding what looked like a megaphone. Our efforts to get away from the approaching horde appeared to be in vain as the Department of Homeland Security usurped our actions. White SUVs appeared behind us in the distance, effectively surrounding our location, and blocking any means of escape. Men in black BDUs and balaclavas seemed to materialize out of every nook and cranny, each armed with what looked like MP5s. With the heavy armor of our vehicle, the 9 mm rounds would do nothing more than scratch the paint. The man with a megaphone sidled up beside the lead SUV and began to speak as the horde of sickened people once again gathered around our vehicle.

"Fellow officers." The commander, at least that's what I assumed he was, tried to play to our egos. "We need you to please remain calm, turn off your vehicle, and allow us to deal with this situation. We will then escort you out safely."

I shook my head in confusion and looked at my companions.

"We were getting out of this situation just fucking fine till these D-bags showed up," Marvin said with trepidation.

"Yeah," I replied, feeling my anxiety spike even higher, if that were somehow possible. "What should we do?" I said with a ragged voice, swallowing hard. At that moment, the police officer chimed in.

"I've been working with these guys for a while now. We should probably comply. Besides, it doesn't seem like we have much of a choice," the cop said, and pointed to the group of federal officers.

Suddenly, there was a high-pitched scream from somewhere outside of our vehicle. The fact that we even heard it inside of the armored truck behind three-inch thick ballistic glass told me that the shriek had to have been extremely loud. We scanned the area in front of the windshield and saw the attention of the Homeland Security officers looking beyond us.

I jumped out of my seat and ran to the rear of the truck and peered out of the almost nonexistent rear windows. The windows themselves were actually a small piece of ballistic glass covered with a sort of reinforcing steel mesh. Through the dirt and grime that covered the small portal, I strained my eyes to see what was going on. A black-clad officer was kicking ferociously at what I assumed was a man lying face down in the street, dressed in what appeared to be mechanic's overalls. The officer was shouting something at the man and waving an MP5 in his direction. The figure slowly crawled back to his hands and knees.

The agent continued shouting, and although I couldn't make out anything he was saying, I could imagine he was telling the once-man-thing to stay the hell down. *Dumbass*, I thought.

All at once, the mechanic seemed to spring into a standing position and lunge at the officer. The Homeland agent recoiled back and raised his weapon. He let out a savage three-round burst that struck the mechanic square in the chest. A red mist exploded from the attacking man's back and shower the ground behind in gore. I watched in horror as the mechanic continued his assault, not having been slowed by the barrage of lead. He reached his victim and grabbed the offending weapon in one hand and latched onto the agent's shoulder with the other.

Other agents who were standing in close proximity finally seemed to react. Stunned at first, I imagine they had never seen any real violence since the initial terrorist attacks in 2011 that had formed their agency. They ran to aid their fellow officer, but they were too late. I watched helplessly from the confines of my truck, powerless as the mechanic bit deep into the agent's neck region, tearing through the soft material of his balaclava, sending jets of blood spurting high into the air. The agent, seemingly in a last ditch effort, squeezed the trigger of his weapon, sending a barrage of 9 mm rounds harmlessly into the air.

"Kyle!" Marvin shouted and brought my attention away from the window.

Turning toward him, I noticed he was staring at something out of the side window. I followed his gaze. The horde of people that had been relentlessly pounding on our truck had suddenly galvanized and began to move away. Moving toward new and easier prey, like sharks drawn to a drop of blood scattered in the sea, they headed in the direction of the fallen agent and his fellow officers to our rear. Gunshots erupted from all over the area. I dove for cover instinctively, inwardly slapping myself as I came to the realization that I was standing in an armored truck. Poorly aimed shots bounced off the hull of our vehicle, sending shots skittering across the glossy black paint job on the Specter Armored car. I made my way once again to the rear of the truck and took position at the window to watch the carnage.

Through the dirty, greasy window, I watched the horde descend on the unsuspecting fools who had positioned themselves around the area.

"Shit, shit, shit!" I exclaimed as I watched the horror unfold, feeling completely helpless. I wanted to jump out and do something. I saw the crowd plow into the group of unsuspecting officers, but what the hell could I do? All I had was this stupid six-shooter and a shotgun . . . Wait.

"The shotgun!" I shouted and scanned the interior of the truck, trying to locate the newly acquired tactical shotgun. "Marvin, where the hell is the shotty?" I said, looking at a confused driver.

He looked at me and then behind his seat. Quickly and without question, he reached behind the seat and withdrew the black steel weapon and handed it to me.

Its large black frame felt heavy in my hands; I motioned to him to hand me the carton of buckshot that he had hidden in his bag. The cop that was with us regarded me and nodded, sensing what I was about to do and made himself ready. The sounds of gunfire and screams of pain intensified, and from what I had seen previously, it wouldn't take long for those men who had been bitten to turn and join the assault against their own comrades. I frantically loaded the Mossberg and watched the cop eject and check his magazine.

Marvin's mouth hung open, looking to me, and then to the officer. "What the hell do you think you're doing?" he said with a twinge of fear entering his voice.

"We need to help these guys, Marvin," I stated flatly, my mind already made up.

Marvin furrowed his brow. "The hell you do! I say we aim this truck and that line of SUVs and bash our way through, and then get the hell out of here," Marvin said, shooting me an angered look.

"Marvin, think it through. How many cars do you think we can knock out of the way before the engine either burns out or is simply crushed?" I said.

Marvin shook his head, and then realization hit him like a ton of bricks. He knew as well as I did the hull of our truck was armored; however, the engine compartment was not. There may be three-fourth-inch steel wrapped around the entirety of the cabin cargo area as well as three-inch ballistic glass; however, only a thin layer of fiberglass covered the entirety of the engine compartment. The sturdy bumper would probably knock a few vehicles out of the way; however, as soon as one smacked into the hood, it was game over, and we would be trapped like rats in a barrel at sea.

When Marvin had come to my aid earlier, he had managed to ram several vehicles out of the way, but part of me figured that had a lot to do with a bit of luck being on our side. I wasn't quite sure at how much further our luck would hold out. No, we stood a better chance of getting out of here if we thinned out the herd a bit; perhaps the favor wouldn't go unnoticed with Homeland. As the old saying goes, "You scratch our backs, and we'll scratch yours."

"Well, fuck it then! If that's the way you're gonna be, I'm coming with you," Marvin spat, reaching for his sidearm. He carried a silver Glock .45 caliber pistol with a faux wooden grip. I looked at my friend and partner of ten years, and shook my head no.

"Marvin . . ." I paused considering my words. "I need you, hell, we need you here." I smacked the hard steel door of the truck with the palm of my hand for emphasis. "We're gonna need someone to let us back in here if things get too hairy. Besides, even if you left the doors open and came with us, what's to stop these bastards from climbing right inside and cutting us off from our only means of escape?" I said in all seriousness.

Marvin scowled but acquiesced to my orders, which was a good thing. Fact of the matter was, if Marvin had put his foot down, I didn't know what I was going to do; there was no real way I could have stopped him from coming with us if he was dead set on it. Thankfully, he let common sense reign.

"Fine, but don't go getting your asses killed." He pointed a stubby finger in my direction. "If I have to explain to your wife that I let you die out here, she'll cut my balls off, and hang them from her rearview mirror." Marvin seemed to squirm uncomfortably in his seat. I nodded in compliance, knowing for a fact that my little fiery Italian woman was perfectly capable of raining fury down on those she deemed deserving.

"Yes, Mom," I said, cutting a crooked smile. I sat there for a moment transfixed on the gray metal of the truck interior. I took in a deep breath, trying to clear my mind. I cocked the Mossberg to chamber a round, then I reached down to my holster and unsnapped my .357. It was always a good idea to be ready to rock 'n' roll rather than get your ass chewed off fucking around with a stupid snap.

I glanced over at the police officer who was riding with us; it was at that moment I realized I still had no idea what the hell his name was. *I couldn't very well go around calling him Officer Dick-head, although the name fit quite well*, I thought. I looked over at the man sitting across from me. His gray police uniform was covered in dirt and grime, and torn in several places; he had close-cropped blond hair and a scar on his right cheek. His hardened brown eyes spoke volumes of a tough life. I noticed he only had one stripe on his arm, indicating that he was a patrolman. He looked to be in his mid-forties, more than likely a career cop still stuck at the low level of patrolman. I regarded him for a moment, wondering why that was, but quickly dismissed the thought.

"I'm Kyle by the way." I reached out my hand in a vain attempt at a long overdue introduction.

"Richard," he stated simply and looked at my hand.

I had to forcefully bite back the urge to laugh my ass off. Richard, Dick, was his actual name. If he told me his last name was head, I was going to lose it.

"So are you cocksuckers going to get off my rig, or are you going to start reading each other poetry?" Marvin snapped gruffly, calling me back from my internal ministrations. I shook my head, stepped over to the door, peered out of the window, and scanned the immediate area. The expanse around the truck seemed to be clear, the strange people having taken more of an interest in the influx of free-roaming Homeland Security agents that now strolled around the road. I looked over my shoulder.

"You ready, Dick?" I said, holding the Mossberg across my chest.

"It's Richard," the officer chided through gritted teeth.

The heavy rain outside pelted the windows, making visibility difficult beyond the rear of the truck. I glanced over at Marvin, and he nodded uncertainly. I gripped the shotgun, with white knuckles, and Marvin pushed the bus bar, opening the door with an audible pop. Rain assaulted my face and salty sweat on my forehead ran down my skin and stung my eyes. Rubbing the liquid away, I allowed my eyes to adjust to the din.

I stepped onto the small stairs and descended to the ground. My eyes darted back and forth, frantically scanning the area for threats. I took a second to process all that I had seen in that short moment; our area, at least for a hundred yards or so that could be seen, appeared to be clear. Beyond that, Homeland agents were locked in what sounded like a full-fledged battle. Officer Richard stepped out behind me. I cast a quick glance over the guardrail of the highway, down a grassy embankment, looking for any other potential avenues for escape should we not be able to make it back to our armored sanctuary. A very steep incline down to the street below took that option off the table, lest we end up as roadkill. I shuddered slightly at that thought.

We walked swiftly and quietly to the rear of my truck, our footsteps splashing on the wet asphalt. We pressed up to the side and cautiously peered out into the falling rain. Cars set scattered all over the roadway beyond, rain pouring in sheets off their painted surfaces. Steam arose from overheated hoods as engines on some of the derelict vehicles still ran, emptied of their previous inhabitance. Acrid smoke filled the air and stung my nostrils; I've heard guys on the gun range often refer to this particular scent as *the smell of cordite*, in actuality it was most likely the scent of nitrocellulose, one of the common components in modern day gunpowder; in any case, the amount that hung in the air added with the biting aroma of burning metal made my nose want to retreat to the inside of my face.

To my left, I heard sounds of a struggle. Fifty yards from my position, I could just barely make out the shape of two men. A Homeland agent, I realized, was pinned to the ground by what looked like a giant. A large gelatinous man sat atop him struggling to bite the man in the face.

The agent held the monsters girth at bay, but just barely. The fat man, I noticed as we approached, wore a tattered gray buttoned-up shirt, and a red ball cap. *A truck driver*, I realized. The fat man easily topped four hundred pounds.

The Homeland Security agent's arms twitched like dried kindling ready to snap. His arms shook violently trying to hold the man-beast's gnashing teeth away from him. He didn't have much time.

Quickly, I ran toward them, not wanting to use my shotgun for fear of hitting the officer. I sprinted, reared my leg back, and landed a savage kick to the truck driver's kidney. Any normal man would have crumpled into a ball clutching his side and more than likely would have been pissing blood for weeks. The fat beast, however, didn't even register the pain that should have followed. I drew my boot back and struck again and again, each blow just barely jiggling the man's fat girth.

A hot wisp of air whizzed past my ear, and the top of the man's head cracked open like a walnut. Blood shot from the newly formed wound as the report of the cop's .44 Mag reached my eardrums.

The fat trucker ceased moving and landed squarely on top of the Homeland agent, its dead weight pinning the man to the damp ground. The man pushed with all his might, trying desperately to dislodge himself from under the dead trucker's bulk. Richard and I ran swiftly over to assist the Homeland agent, feet slapping against the wet pavement. I grabbed the fat man by the collar of his soaked gray shirt and pulled. I felt the muscles in my back strain, and my spine start to pop. The fabric of the man's shirt started to slip from my grasp. A little known fact, rain-slick fabric and blood do not make good gripping material. Richard quickly grabbed the fat man's belt, and with our combined effort, we managed to move the beastly figure off to one side, rolling him onto his back. Blood oozed out of the trucker's head wound and mixed with the falling water. It spread out in a pool surrounding the body, seeping into the gravel and dirt. The blood was strange and didn't look normal, almost too red I thought, more of a burnt orange.

The Homeland agent rolled to his side, gasping for air and coughing all the while. I stepped over to try and help him to his feet, but he waved me off.

"Thanks," he said, his voice sounding raw and strained. He propped himself up and took some deep shuddering breaths, and after a moment, he got to his feet and composed himself. He cast us a glance and nodded. He swung the MP5 that still hung from a strap wrapped around his shoulder into his arms. He checked the magazine and looked squarely at us. "I didn't even have time to get a shot off," he said visibly shaken. He popped the magazine back into the weapon.

We heard more screams in the distance.

"Come on. We need to see if we can help the others," the agent said and sprinted off in the direction of the screams, swiftly disappearing into the rain and gunpowder-laden haze. I looked at Richard and shrugged. Hoisting my shotgun into the ready position, we began to jog in the direction the Homeland agent had taken off in.

I glanced back once more at the dead man lying on the ground, blood continuing to stream out in bright red-orange tendrils as if it had a mind of its own, like it possessed some kind of sinister purpose. His red ball cap still clung to his head, a ragged hole blown in the top. His bloodshot eyes remained open, collecting droplets of rain water that pooled into his sunken orbital sockets. Shuddering, I turned my attention forward and continued moving in the direction of screams and gunfire.

Richard ran beside me silently. A blank look etched across his face. I wondered if the man was in shock. I would have to keep a close eye on the officer, not wanting him to do something stupid that might get us both killed. We continued forward, expecting the worst.

INTERLUDE 2

Director Hammond paced the length of his office, frequently glancing at the clock hanging above the door, then at the black and gold old-fashioned telephone that set atop his desk.

"Damn it," he cursed to himself. Almost an hour had passed by since he had dispatched a team led by Agent Bishop to retrieve vital records being transported via armored car to their medical research facility in Bethesda Maryland. The records by themselves were not damning in the least; however, if combined with the other five reports, they could definitely do some damage. Several months ago, they had received intel of a biological weapon that had been obtained by a known terrorist organization operating within the U.S. borders. True, they received such threats almost on a daily basis, whether it be dirty bombs, suitcase nukes, cyber-terrorism, you name it, they saw it. This particular tip was not so much any more threatening than any of the others, except that their teams had managed to procure a sample of this particular bug. They had intersected a cell just outside of Washington, D.C. The assailants apparently meant to release the pathogen during one of the President's press conferences.

They had disguised themselves as reporters for the *Washington Herald*. Acting on a tip from an informant, they managed to catch the would-be assassins, more or less, out of luck. With the blanket of national security, they had been able to setup checkpoints along the back roads and interstates that led into the Washington, D.C. area. Armed with the knowledge their informant had provided, they managed to stumble upon three individuals matching the assailant's descriptions.

The first search of the vehicle and its inhabitants turned out to be a bust; however, under orders, the men were detained. After they were taken into custody, their clothing was removed, and more thoroughly searched using the latest scanning technology. The scan revealed a series of small syringes no bigger than a strand of human hair located in normal pat-down areas that most police and security forces were trained to utilize. Their plan, apparently, had been simple but brilliant. Knowing security would have found any kind of explosive devices, aerosols or large syringes, weapons or even small vials, they had implanted hair-like needles within the groin and armpit areas of their suits, designed to be brushed over on the way up and catch the tender flesh of the hand on the way down. The infected needles would then break off in the hand of the security personnel, like an invisible splinter. The thin nitrile gloves that the security officers would have worn would not have protected them in the least. The security forces would have then proceeded into the building and somehow manage to infect everyone they had come into contact with. Not much at this time was known about the pathogen, other than it was designed to take out everyone at the press conference, including the President.

In the weeks following, their scientists had discovered it was some kind of prion disease, something similar to—Hammond searched his memory for the name—kuru, yes that was it. The disease also exhibited similarities of hemorrhagic fever, a horrible disease in which the carrier would crash and bleed, infecting anyone who came into contact with contaminated blood. However, this viral component was merely speculation at this point. Hammond had absolutely no idea what the two diseases had in common with each other or even what they did. According to Homeland's medical science division, the prion disease would have taken years to do any real damage, although hemorrhagic infection pretty much guaranteed a quick and gruesome death. *But then what was the purpose of the prion? What would be the point of releasing a disease that would take years to kill you?* Hammond thought to himself. It was above his scope of knowledge; however, politics were more his area of expertise. So the preliminary findings and the pathogen itself were being shipped to one of their bioweapons research labs.

Their field office in Arbutus was not equipped with the materials or the equipment needed to detect any other anomalies in the disease cocktail. So they had shipped it to their biolab in the most discreet way possible. The biolab, otherwise known as the ARC (American Research Centers), housed some of the world's most notorious diseases: Ebola, Anthrax, weaponized small pox, plague. To the public's knowledge, there were only two-level five biolabs in the entire country: the CDC in Atlanta and the United States Army Medical Research Institute of Infectious Disease, otherwise known as USAMRIID. In truth, there were somewhere in the neighborhood of thirty-five of these labs spread nationwide. Most of which were privately owned by powerful pharmaceutical companies who had enough clout to buy the cooperation of the U.S. Government.

However, under the newly imposed Patriot Act, Homeland Security was able to acquire several of these labs for their own use. In order to provide secure transport of these items to the ARC, Homeland had separated the files and shipped them via six separate armored car companies. There were two main reasons for this: one, without knowing exactly how much of the pathogen these terrorist cells had procured, there was a slim chance that what they had intercepted was the group's only viable sample, and they couldn't risk those materials falling back into the wrong hands. Hammond had his doubts about this scenario, but he felt compelled to agree that it was indeed a possibility.

The second reason simply had to do with secrecy. The last thing the public needed to know was just how close they had come to losing their newly acquired president. This was something Hammond, the President, and his constituents agreed should be kept under wraps until they had more information—not wanting to cause any unnecessary panic. Using the armored cars for this task seemed like a good way to handle both issues; it also had the added benefit of not being tied directly to his department. The fact of the matter was the United States had received information about this particular bug some time ago. Homeland was unaware of that fact until just recently; however, when the threat had become an actuality, and they had made some inquires. Problem was, if the public knew they had been sitting on this info . . . Hammond furrowed his brow in thought. Well, that meant heads were going to roll, and being this information now resided with his department, that meant his head. Hammond had no illusions that the current President would let this stick on him, no; the President would undoubtedly throw him under the bus.

Hammond frowned and scratched at his balding noggin, feeling nervous tension building within his temples. Earlier this morning, when he and Bishop had discussed the traffic problem on the highway, Agent Bishop and the director both agreed that the accident could have possibly been a decoy. A way for the terrorist cells that were still active to hijack one of the armored cars and their materials; as it stood, the five other transport vehicles had not made their scheduled deliveries to the research facility either. Hammond shook his head. They needed to get those materials to that lab. If another terrorist cell contained more of this pseudo-virus and hit a populated area, there was going to be a hell of a lot of blame flying around. The director wanted to come out smelling like roses or at least have some sort of preliminary action plan in play, instead of saying, *Oh yes, we had the virus sample, however, we fucked up and lost it*. Old Joe public would crucify them. No, Bishop would obtain the samples and documentation. Hammond had been abundantly clear of the outcome if he and his teams failed in their mission. Hammond sat down in his burgundy leather office chair, with a thud. Staring at the phone once more, he picked up the receiver. He was tired of waiting; he had to know what was going on.

"Tracy, get Agent Bishop on the line . . . I don't care that he is in the middle of an OP, just get him on the phone." Hammond slammed the phone down and impatiently drummed his fingers on the desk, waiting.

CHAPTER 6

Agent Bishop watched the carnage unfold in his wet, black and gray BDUs; he had changed out of his normal day-to-day attire and dressed in his standard-issue field gear in order to join his men. He stood next to his white government SUV, a pair of thermal binoculars pressed to his face. Black-clad operatives stood less than twenty yards from him, firing incisively at anything that moved. The scene he observed was chaotic. The screams and moans added together with the reports of gunfire were almost deafening in his ears. It reminded him of his days overseas. Days spent entrenched in the sand, pumped with adrenaline and fear, days he honestly wanted to forget. Agent Bishop could see the infected's fevered bodies clearly through the binocs. Their bodies seemed to glow a brilliant red in the Flir's optics, a sign that their temperature was far higher than that of any normal man on the field.

Bishop watched in horror as his men were systematically brutalized and devoured right in front of him. At this point he didn't know what to do. His first instinct was to call his men in, but those cases they were ordered to retrieve contained information, information they could use to possibly combat this disease. He wasn't sure how the outbreak had occurred, but here it was, there was no mistaking that now. His only guess was that another terrorist cell had been dispatched when he and his operatives had foiled their last attempt to release the germ. *How could this happen right under our noses?* Bishop thought, and scowled. He had read a bit about this disease and knew it was dangerous; however, had not expected this. This was just pure madness.

A flash at the corner of his eyesight caught his attention; and without so much as a blink, the agent released the binocs and drew the pistol holstered against his thigh. He brought the muzzle to bear and squarely pointed it at the forehead of one of his men. The man skittered to a stop and threw his hands in the air.

"D-d-don't shoot," the man stammered, holding something in his upturned hands.

Agent Bishop held his position for a moment then gingerly holstered his Glock. "What is it, Private?" Bishop uttered in his gruff, slightly annoyed, monotone voice. Private Simmons, a young man in his twenties dressed in the same black uniform as his compatriots, exhaled slowly. The private held out his hand.

"Call for you, sir. It's the director. He wants a status update." Simmons handed Agent Bishop the comms device and stepped back.

Bishop eyed the bulky olive-drab SAT phone dubiously. "Are you fucking kidding me?" he whispered under his breath and watched droplets of water fall and splash off its flat surface. Bishop rolled his eyes and held the phone to his ear. "Sir?" Bishop questioned, trying his best to disguise his annoyance.

"Agent, report," Director Hammond spat out impatiently.

"Sir, frankly, we're in the middle of a shit-storm, and this is hardly the time to—"

"What do you mean hardly the time? Is the armored crew offering resistance? I find that hard to believe," Hammond questioned sardonically, wondering just what kind of a shit-storm they were in. Two or three people, even people armed with an armored car, couldn't possibly be causing that much trouble. There seemed to be a long pause on the phone before there was any kind of response. Static and noise hung there for agonizing moments.

"No, sir, they're the least of our worries." Bishop gazed around the area from behind the cover of his SUV. "The contagion has been released, sir. We're in the process of trying to contain the situation now," Bishop stated flatly.

"Released? What do you mean released?" Hammond said with alarm rising in his voice.

"The disease has been released sir—on the public. It's spreading much quicker than we had anticipated." Hammond began to cut in, but Bishop silenced his words. "Sir, there is more. From what we're seeing on the ground, those whom have been infected are the ones attacking us. I don't know what those fuckers in the science division told you, but it's much worse than what was in the report." Bishop paused for a moment composing himself. "Sir, at the moment, I'm not totally certain that my men are being effective. We keep firing on them, and they simply just keep coming. They're feeding on my men, sir," Bishop added trying to stifle his anger.

"That's unfortunate, Agent. I understand how you feel, however, the mission, remains the same, except now it's of even more importance. Now we're dealing with and actual outbreak and not just a threat of one. Retrieve the case at all costs, Bishop. Once you have it, evacuate your men, and we'll pacify the area," Hammond said coldly.

"What about the armored truck's guards, sir? Bishop asked.

"I don't care, Agent. Take 'em out if you need to. Just get that damn case." —There was a pause on the line— "On second thought, it would probably be best if there were no survivors, if you catch my drift. After all, they could be infected, and we just can't take that chance." The director finished, and before Bishop could protest, the Director abruptly hung up the phone.

Bishop scowled inwardly at the order. *Fucking asshole*, he thought. Sure, he had killed before, but that was usually some homegrown nutcase with a bomb packed inside of a van parked outside of an elementary school. These guys were lawful citizens, just grunts doing their jobs. Sighing, Bishop acquiesced. An order was an order, and who knows, perhaps it wouldn't come to that. More gunfire erupted close by causing Bishop to jump slightly. Wet thuds resounded as the infected dropped to the ground off to his left.

The infected were advancing, and he needed to act quickly. Hammond's use of the word *pacify* meant that more than likely, a flight crew had been given the green light to drop a small yield, fuel air bomb. Basically, incinerating anything that lived within this small corridor of I-95, knowing that one of the cars contained the case that housed a small sample of the pathogen they had dubbed K-5 Variant, they had prepared for the slim chance that the virus could be released unintentionally. At present time, Bishop did not believe the infection had stemmed from the armored car, for the simple fact that the guards were still operational. Agent

Bishop looked over at the expecting private, who was obviously waiting for the agent to return the SAT phone.

"Simmons, was it?" Agent Bishop stated more than asking.

The private nodded.

"I need you to relay an order. Director Hammond has authorized us to take that armored car and its contents by force if necessary. Understood? Tell the men to bring them in for questioning if possible," Bishop gave the man a look that practically dared him to question his orders.

Private Simmons simply nodded, feeling the tension that radiated off of the man, pressed a button on the side of his headgear, and began to relay the order.

CHAPTER 7

I caught up to the black-clad agent who stood still in the middle of the smoke and rain-soaked field. His black gloved hand was pressed against his ear as if trying to hear something. I skidded to a stop just behind the man to avoid slamming into him. The agent glanced at me from the corner of his eyes, his brow furrowing, barely visible underneath his balaclava. I scanned the area for threats and noticed a trio of crazed people stumbling around to our far left. They saw us standing stock still and began heading in our general direction.

"Um," I started, and the agent held up a finger in front of my face as if to say shush. I waited mouth agape and glanced over at Richard. He cocked a crooked smile and shrugged. The insane ones were moving in. "I think we should get moving," I said in a loud whisper.

The agent turned around, annoyed, and shouldered his MP5. "Stop right there!" he shouted.

The three figures paused for a brief moment, as if studying the agent. One of them, a man dressed in a rumpled business suit, let out a deep moan. Another, a woman in a torn muddy red dress, with long flowing tangled brown hair, screamed a shrill and piercing wail, and then took off running straight for us. Her compatriots followed suit.

The agent took a step back and repeated his order, his voice beginning to quiver ever so slightly.

"Shit," I said. I nudged him aside and pulled out my revolver, taking aim, and letting the Mossberg drop to my side where it dangled from a nylon strap. They were less than thirty feet away when I took my first shot. The .357 round struck home boring a vicious wound through the once-beautiful woman's face.

Her head snapped backward with a *crack*, obliterating the attractiveness that had once been. The back of her head exploded into the face of a guy who looked as if he just stepped out of the gym. He then tripped over her crumpling form and sprawled to the ground, with a grotesque slap.

Joe Blow Forbes in the business suit growled and ran past the duo, closing in on our position fast. Next to me, the MP5 roared to life, unleashing a three-round burst that struck the man in the chest, the rounds seeming to have no effect as he moved forward.

"What the fuck?" the agent exclaimed as the snarling figure headed toward us. I kicked out with my right leg and struck the man in his ruined chest, feeling it give way under the pressure of my attack. Ribs cracked and blood pooled out from around my boots. I could feel the soft tissue of organs underneath, and I had a fleeting thought that my heel just touched his still heart.

"Shit!" I yelled as I realized my foot was lodged in this man-thing's chest. He clawed at my leg and craned his neck down, trying unsuccessfully to bite me. I tried desperately to pull my leg away. I brought my gun hand up and tried in vain to get a shot, but no joy. The violent motion of the man's movements kept throwing my aim off, and I was more likely to shoot myself in the leg. "Help!" I screamed as thoughts of my wife and children came rushing into my mind.

We toppled to the ground hard. My shotgun tore away from the nylon strap that had secured it and it bounced off out of sight, landing somewhere in the mud. At that moment, the businessman's head violently jerked sideways, a neat hole appearing in his temple.

The man slumped to the ground, his head striking the wet asphalt. Blood and brain matter oozed out of the wound, mixed with rain water, and washed away into the smoke.

I gasped for breath and positioned my other foot over the man's stomach. I kicked hard and pulled my right leg with a jerk. It came free of the man's rib cage prison. My boot was covered in gore. Red and orange goo dripped from the soles to the wet ground below. "Fuck me," I gasped as I started to get myself to my feet. Richard stood facing me, arm still held out clutching his Glock.

"You okay, brother?" he said, holding his hand out to help me up.

My eyes went wide. I slapped his hand out of my way and aimed my weapon at his legs. Richard looked at me with fear and shock.

"Move, dumbass!" I shouted. Richard dove to his left, and I fired. The barrel of my Smith & Wesson exploded, sending fiery hot lead into the brain of the muscle-bound freak that had tripped only moments ago. "Christ!" I exclaimed as I scanned the area for more dangers. It was then I noticed the Homeland Security agent standing several feet away. His weapon trained on us. I raised my brow in shock and rose slowly to my feet. I holstered my sidearm and raised my hands up in a placating fashion.

Richard stood there, still aiming his weapon.

"Lower your weapon, sir. I don't want to kill you," the Homeland agent said smoothly.

"What the hell is going on here? Did we not just save your ass?" Richard yelled.

"Sir, I have full body armor, and your little pea shooters are not going to do anything more than piss me off, so I suggest you stow it," the agent said through gritted teeth.

"I think he's serious, champ." I shot a look over at the cop.

"Fine!" he snarled, and in one swift and fluid motion, he slid his weapon into his hip holster. "Now what's this about? If it's about those people we just took out, there was no—"

"No," the agent said, cutting him off. "Thank you for your assistance, Officer. You are free to go. This man, however"—he pointed the muzzle of his weapon at me—"is wanted by the department of Homeland for questioning," he finished.

"Questioning? What the hell for?" I said, furrowing my brow.

"My orders are to bring you in, sir. You and your partner, it's a matter of national security," he said flatly.

"What? I . . . No . . . wait a minute, my truck. You assholes want the truck. Why?" I asked.

"Sir, I don't know anything about that. Now let's get moving," the agent said.

"Don't sweat it, Kyle. I'm not going anywhere. I'll stick around until we clear up this misunderstanding," the cop said, surprising me a little.

As we walked down the road, the sounds of gunfire and screams reverberated out in the distance. We remained quiet as we walked, doing our best not to draw any unwanted attention to ourselves. My brain tried its best to understand what the hell the Department of Homeland frigging Security wanted with me. *Or was it me? Was this a robbery?* I thought, and shook that notion from my mind. I was fairly certain with all their appropriations and black budgets that they weren't hurting for money, so that couldn't be the reason, unless of course this particular bunch had grown tired of playing the lottery pool in the office. With everything that was going on I seriously doubted that there was any kind of sideways agenda, but what was it then?

I searched the day's and week's happenings to try and recall some sort of link to this unexpected turn of events and was coming up empty. The morning had started out pretty much like clockwork. I went to the shop, picked up our shit, and hit the road. Next thing I know we're stuck in traffic and all hell broke loose. No, it had to be something in the truck, I just didn't know what. All I knew based upon what I had read about was, once Homeland got their claws in you, you were pretty much screwed. No trial and indefinite imprisonment based on nothing more other than being labeled a person of interest. I had to figure out what the hell was going on.

My thoughts went to my driver, Marvin. He was currently sealed up tight in one of the most formidable vehicles cruising around the roads of the United States. He was under orders to keep it sealed up tight in case of an emergency and to relocate to a safe location if it came under attack. Pretty much he was not allowed to open the vehicle for anyone other than me. If anything, it would seem that gave me a little leverage.

I suddenly remembered the radio mounted to my shoulder. I could try to warn my driver, but that could end up with my ass being shot off. I nervously glanced over my shoulder and noticed the Homeland agent looking around the area for threats. I slid my hand as inconspicuously as I could manage and depressed the send button on my radio three times, resounding with three quick clicks on the receiving end, a code for danger if I had become compromised. Hopefully, my partner would remember that part of our training. The more I thought about it, the more worried I became. My partner could barely remember what he had for lunch that same day, let alone an hour's worth of training in a brain-sucking fluorescent-lit concrete room with a trainer that had the personality of wet cardboard.

"Shit," I whispered to myself.

"Keep walking," said the agent. I sighed inwardly, trying to figure out what the hell I was going to do. What was this all about? Why was I being escorted to answer questions about something I knew absolutely nothing of? Then it dawned on me. The only strange thing that I could possibly think of on our rig was that odd case. Could that possibly have something to do with all this? At that moment, the microphone on my shoulder squelched loud in my ear.

"Kyle! Where in the hell are you, and what the fuck is going on?" my partner shouted damn near, making me deaf. I could feel the Homeland agent's eyes on me.

"Well, what are you waiting for? Answer him."

I stopped and stared at the Agent, in confusion.

The Agent scowled and said, "Tell your man to rendezvous with us half a klick to the north at the roadblock, then the agent in charge can sort this shit out."

I hesitated for a moment, narrowing my eyes, and nodded. I clasped the microphone in my hand and positioned it to my mouth. "Marvin, I don't know what the fuck is going on, but get your ass off this highway. These guys want something on our truck. I think it might be that damn case! Go, run . . ." I said in a frantic and hushed tone. Suddenly, something struck me in the back of the head—I saw flashes of bright light and fell sprawling to the damp earth. I heard the sound of an engine roar in the distance, tires squealed, and the horn blared. I raised my throbbing head up and glanced over my shoulder, seeing the large armored vehicle come barreling down the highway, knocking derelict cars askew. "Go Marv, go," I said grinning weakly, face plastered in mud, everything faded to black as I was struck from behind once more.

CHAPTER 8

Marvin Winters sat in his Specter Armored car at the edge of the highway obscured by the rain and the haze of smoke. The warning from his partner's microphone sounded clear within the truck's confines and reverberated off the steel walls echoing in his ears. Marvin glanced behind him, looking directly at the cage that contained the strange case they had been given to safeguard. A dull red glow emanated from within the shadows of the compartment. Marvin realized there was nothing that he could do to retrieve the case, his partner having the only key. Marvin thought about his partner's words; he knew that in the event of trouble, his orders were to leave the scene. However, he had misgivings about leaving his partner within this mess, but what could he do? Marvin wasn't even certain where his partner had gone.

Marvin glanced in his rearview mirror; and even among the specs of rain that obscured his vision, he could see armed agents closing in on his position.

"What the fuck?" he grunted to himself. Marvin decided to heed his partner's warning. Normally, he would not consider running from the authorities, but something about this was just all wrong. The agents, six of them as far as he could tell, approached the armored car, with weapons raised. Marvin chuckled to himself; they were shouting something unintelligible at him. They may as well of been speaking Chinese. The armored car, aside from being bulletproof, was also, for the most part, soundproof.

The agents motioned to him to open the door.

Marvin glanced at them, gave them the middle finger, mouthed the words *fuck you*, and smiled.

One of the agents began pounding on the door. Shouting at him, he held up a federal ID.

Marvin smiled and in turn pointed to his own federal ID that was pinned to his chest, and then shrugged. The agent seemed to get fairly pissed off at this.

Marvin noticed movement off to his left-hand side; stumbling figures emerged from behind cars and seemed to materialize out of the smoke and gloom, from the looks of it, dozens of them. The figures made a beeline straight for the agents.

The man who was pounding on the door saw Marvin's expression.

Marvin frantically raised his arms and pointed in the general direction of the advancing horde.

The agent turned abruptly, shouted something, and opened fire. The bullets tore into the crowd. Red and orange blood began to fly in all directions. Some of the advancing figures took rounds in the legs and fell to the ground; however, it only managed to slow them down a little. The ones that fell kept coming, pulling themselves along the ground with their fingertips; most of the oncoming figures had taken bullets directly center mass. The onslaught of lead that was sent their way, unfortunately, was about as effective as giving them a vitamin shot. They surrounded the truck and slammed into the agents. Their ragged fingertips tearing and clawing at body armor.

Marvin saw one of the ghouls sink his teeth into an agent's neck, sending arterial spray toward the truck, and coating the windows. "Fuck me!" Marvin exclaimed and he threw the truck in gear and floored it. The engine roared, and the truck barreled forward, smashing derelict cars in its path. He watched as blood oozed down the windows and mingled with rain water. He flipped on the windshield wipers, trying to clear his view, but the little dime-store wiper blades didn't do jack-shit for the size of the heavy window. He tried to maneuver the hulking vehicle in and out of cars, and other people. At least he thought they were people. At this point, he wasn't sure who was a friend or who was foe.

Marvin's mind drifted back to his days stationed in Vietnam, reminded of the bloody conflict amid all the carnage. He was a demolitions expert during the war. The enemy built a bridge; he took it down. He recalled one particular engagement where he and his squad had been given orders to clear out a system of tunnels that had been discovered days previous by a recon team dispatched into the jungle. They stumbled upon an entrance and sent a lone tunnel rat inside; upon his return, he reported back that a massive underground command post occupied just a half mile or so in. Rather than risk the lives of his men trying to clear out a bug hole underground, with rifles in blind close combat, Sergeant Michaels of force recon called in the boom squad.

Marvin's unit responded to the call. They were to place demo charges in and around the tunnels, and blow the piss out of them. Shit went wrong. One of Marvin's squad members, upon placing his charge, fell into a trap while working his way back to the rendezvous point. He crashed through a well-hidden hole in the ground right into a cluster of sharpened bamboo. As the shafts pierced through his chest cavity, the soldier depressed the trigger of his detonator, causing it to blow before the rest of his squad's charges were in place. As a result, Charlie swarmed out of the tunnels with the knowledge that they were under attack. In the end, the tunnels and the command center housed within were destroyed, but at a price. When the smoke cleared, seven Americans lay dead or bleeding out on the jungle floor. Marvin survived that conflict, and by God, he was going to survive this.

Marvin sped across the rain-soaked asphalt, crashing through cars and bodies alike, trying his best not to enter full on panic mode. His eyes focused on the ongoing carnage in his rearview. Too late, he noticed, the roadblock of white SUVs that lay directly in his path. Marvin had a choice to make: slam on the brakes and risk skidding into the roadblock and more than likely flipping the metal beast over due to the trucks top heavy nature, or put the pedal to the metal, and ram the bitch. Marvin had a split second to make his choice.

"Ramming speed!" Marvin shouted to himself, following with a smirk. He flipped on the siren and blared the truck's horn, trying his best to warn the Homeland agents of his intentions, hoping to cause as little collateral damage as possible.

The agents took the hint and ran scattering in all directions, diving for cover as the armored car slammed into the roadblock, sending metal and fiberglass debris flying about. Some of the Homeland agents opened fire on the truck as it roared past in a futile attempt to slow him down. Sparks rained off the hull of the armored car as he sped by. Marvin felt the truck jolt as bullets slammed into the run-flat tires; no matter, the truck was designed to take that kind of abuse and could operate at speeds of up to fifty miles-per-hour even if all six tires had been shot out.

Marvin throttled the armored car toward the open expanse of highway in an attempt to put as much distance between himself, his cargo, and his would-be pursuers. At that moment, Marvin heard the loud whirr of an engine overhead. A Black Hawk helicopter emerged out of the rain and smoke, and positioned itself directly in front of the armored car.

"Fuck!" Marvin shouted, not sure of what he should do. He could outrun SUVs and cars all damn day but not a freaking gunship; there was just no way in hell. Marvin suddenly remembered an overpass on a side street that was just up the road. It was narrow enough to accommodate only one vehicle at a time. Marvin just hoped that the truck would not become lodged underneath the small train bridge.

No time to think about it. Marvin shifted gears and gunned the engine. Steam rose off the engine hood from droplets of water that evaporated almost instantly as they pelted its black exterior. The gunship fired a volley of warning shots at the ground in front of the vehicle, sending broken shards of concrete and asphalt raining down on the windshield. Marvin flinched and reflexively swerved to avoid the gunshots. The damaged tires caused the truck to slide and fishtail for a moment, nearly causing Marvin to lose control and go spinning off the road and into nearby trees. Marvin turned into the skid and regained traction; he then took a sharp right onto an exit ramp and headed for the side street that would take him to the train bridge.

The loudspeaker of the helicopter shouted at him to stop, audible even within the nearly soundproof confines of the armored car.

"I hope this works," Marvin prayed to himself and any god that would listen as he began to bear off to the left. Marvin turned the wheel, and suddenly, the truck shook with such violence it caused him to slam face first into the ballistic glass. An explosion rocked the truck, causing it to flip end over end. Fire encapsulated the entire vehicle, metal began to creak and groan. Marvin hung upside down from his seat belt, his head throbbing with pain. He noticed blood dripped from his eyebrow and sizzled as it landed on the truck's ceiling.

"Fuck me," Marvin gasped, coughing and choking on smoke that arose in feathery tendrils from the currency that lay strewn around the interior of the truck being systematically burned into charcoal.

"What the hell just happened?" Marvin groaned. It was then he noticed the smoke drifting up from underneath him. "Ah crap, I think it's time to go," Marvin said to no one in particular, realizing that if he sat in the oven-like vehicle for too long, he was going to be cooked alive. Not wanting to become the first human pot roast, Marvin fumbled around with the seat belt clasp and depressed the button. It held fast. *Shit*, Marvin thought and frantically looked around for something he could use to cut his way out of the restraint. The truck was starting to heat up, sweat beaded on his face and mingled with his blood and stung his eyes.

Marvin remembered that he carried a pocket knife on his duty rig. He stretched his shaking hand toward his waist and found the pouch that contained it. He undid the clasp, and the knife slid out and went clattering to the inverted ceiling. "Shit!" Marvin shouted and stretched his arm out, trying desperately to grab the knife that he was only able to just touch with his fingertips. Marvin pushed up with his good leg, straining against his restraint. *Just a bit farther*, he thought. His fingers burned as he touched the ceiling area around the knife. He ignored the pain and grasped hold of it, with a grunt. Marvin raised his arm in midair and flipped the blade open, light from the flames outside bounced off the blade and flickered in the interior of the truck, casting an array of dancing shadows. Marvin began to steadily saw at the orange nylon belt. It frayed with each passing stroke until it gave way under the old man's weight. Marvin fell to the floor, or ceiling rather, in a heap.

He hurried and scrambled to his feet, trying to avoid being pan fried. Marvin stood, feeling his bones creak and pop as he did so. *I hate getting old,* he mused. Marvin tried to listen to hear if the helicopter was still in the area, but it was useless between the

71

foggy ringing in his ears and the distortion sounds the truck's metal hull made as it was heated.

Marvin glanced around the truck, looking for anything useful. He noticed the strange metal case lying on the floor, the truck's cage door hanging open, the framework distorted from the impact of the truck flipping over. Marvin reached down and picked up the case and looked it over. It was scratched, dented, and warm to the touch, but otherwise, it was no worse for the wear.

Marvin set the case on the floor and bent over to peer through the truck's back door windows. It was hard to see anything through the dirt-encrusted glass, but from what Marvin could tell, the coast looked clear. Marvin reached for the door's latch and tapped at it to check for heat; it was warm but not burning like the area in which Marvin stood. He could tell there was something burning underneath the truck due to the fact that the soles of his boots were starting to melt. *Guess the shoes they make us buy for work aren't fire resistant*, he mused, chuckling slightly.

He needed to make a hasty retreat, and he needed to do it now. Marvin grasped hold of the door's latch and pulled up, releasing the thick metal bolt that held the doors secure. He pushed and felt a little give; however, the door would not open. "God damn it," Marvin cursed as he figured at the angle the truck laid; the doors must be lodged into the earth. Marvin pushed with all his strength and managed to open a gap, with just enough space to squeeze through.

Marvin turned around and headed back to the front of the truck and retrieved his backpack, remembering that his wife had packed him some sandwiches and cans of Ensure. He would need food if this shit lasted longer than just a few days, in these types of situations you never knew. He also kept some other bare essentials within the bag for just-in-case purposes, a habit left over from his old military days. It contained things such as a lighter, map, compass, extra ammunition, as well as some water purification tablets.

Marvin slung the backpack over his shoulders when he heard a noise coming from outside. The sound reminded him of a juicy steak sizzling on his old charcoal grill at home. Curious, he made his way over to the back door and peered out.

Marvin jumped back, nearly slamming into the upended passenger seat as a snapping, snarling face appeared in the door's opening. The beast was disgusting. Marvin realized the sizzling noise he had heard was the sound of the flesh on this man roasting in the fire that still surrounded the armored car. The creature reached toward him and let out a groan. Marvin frantically fumbled for his sidearm and unsnapped it just as the figure started to force itself through the opening. Pieces of putrid burnt human flesh tore free from bone in sheets and fell to the vehicle's floor with a wet slap. Marvin had to force back the bile and vomit that threatened to overtake him as he brought his weapon to bear. His hands shook with fear and revulsion as he took aim. Marvin squeezed the trigger of his Glock .45, sending a round straight through the figure's eye socket.

The thing's head snapped back and slammed against the open door. The round exited the skull and struck the armored door, causing it to ricochet and reenter the man-thing's head. Its forehead burst outward, sending blackish orange blood spewing Marvin's way.

Marvin involuntarily ducked as he felt the bullet whiz past his head only millimeters from his ear. Marvin reached up and touched the side of his head and felt around to make certain the bullet hadn't struck him. Satisfied that it did not, he slowly approached the rear of the truck, dizzied a bit from the loud reverberation of the gunshot. He nudged at the still form on the floor, with his still-melting boots. It did not seem to be moving any longer. Relaxing slightly, Marvin pushed the corpse back out into the burnt grass.

Carefully, he stuck his head outside and scanned around the area. "Holy fucking shit!" he let escape as he noticed about a dozen or so figures heading his way. Quickly, Marvin reached down and grabbed the metal case that still lay on the floor. He glanced at it for a moment, wondering what the hell was in it to make the Department of Homeland Security damn near blow up his truck for it. Well, whatever it was, he was going to make certain they answered some questions about it before they got their grubby little hands on it.

Marvin sucked in his seventy-three-year-old beer gut and squeezed through the rear door's opening, feeling the heat from the fire that still raged on around the truck. Marvin crouched, trying his best not to be seen by the approaching forms in the distance. Through the smoke, rain, and steaming haze, he could not tell if the figures heading his way were normal or the infected. Marvin searched around the area for a path of escape. He remembered the train tracks and, more importantly, the forest surrounding them. Marvin stepped carefully over the remains of the ruined man at his feet and made his way toward the side of the road, doing his best to conceal his movements.

Hurriedly, Marvin jogged toward the train bridge that he was trying to make it to before his truck had been struck with what he could only imagine was some kind of missile. Judging by the small crater that was left in the road where Marvin had been driving, he could only assume that they had missed, or perhaps they were only trying to stop his truck rather than destroy it. He wasn't quite sure, and there was really no point in dwelling on it at the moment.

Marvin made his way over to the embankment at the bottom of the stone, train bridge and started to climb his way up to the top. He had to work slower than he would have liked, but the fact of it was he was an old man. He was in relatively good shape for his age but still old nonetheless. Taking his time to avoid slipping in the wet grass that covered the hill, Marvin ascended to the top of the bridge. He went into a crouch, feeling his bad knees groan in protest, and headed toward the forest, taking care to gingerly step over the train tracks and rocks surrounding them. He eyed the heavy case held in his left hand, a small LED light blinked silently in the shadows of the forest entryway. *This thing is like a God damn beacon*, he thought. Reaching down, he snatched up a clump of wet earth and smeared it across the LED's surface, effectively obscuring the light. *That ought to do*, he mused. He took a moment and peered out at the flaming wreckage, surprised at the fact he actually made it out of there alive. He ducked down low as Homeland agents descended on the broken truck. He angrily spied on them for a moment, and then silently slipped away into the trees.

CHAPTER 9

Karen sat Indian style with her charges on the hard wooden floor of the closet, doing her best to keep her "big girl panties" on and not panic at the sounds of the invaders banging around and most likely destroying her home; well, more so than the children had done already. She cringed as she heard the crash of glass breaking on the kitchen or quite possibly the living room floor; it was hard to tell in the small space with the drone of sobbing children.

"Shhh, shhh, shhh, shhh," Karen tried her best to soothe the children packed into the confines of the dark closet like sardines in a can. She had wished that she had told Kyle to put a new light bulb in the ceiling fixture, this one having blown out several weeks ago. Chances are she probably had and it just slipped his mind. She frowned at the fact that the replacement bulbs were all the way on the other side of the house, inside of the laundry room cabinet, not that it would do her much good even if she had one. With her short stature and no ladder, there was no way in hell she could even attempt to replace the bulb, unless she climbed up a shelving unit and risked falling on top of the kids.

She reached up and grabbed the windup lantern that she had been using earlier, off a nearby shelf. The shelf contained nonperishable food, water, candles and other useful items that had been put there specifically for this type of emergency. *Thank you, emergency preparedness workshop*, she thought to herself, remembering the state-mandated training courses she had to take in order to keep her business running. Funny, she never actually thought they would come into any practical real-world use. Normally, she absolutely despised taking the time to even go to such things; it was usually eight or so hours stuck in some smelly school gymnasium with an instructor that was just as excited to be there as she was.

Karen located the recessed crank on the lantern just as the light started to dim and blink out. She snapped it open, and began to spin the charging handle, it made a whirring sound as it spun up. She cringed at the noise the machine made as she cranked it, hoping that it wasn't nearly as loud as it seemed to be inside of the closet's confines. She cranked the handle for what seemed like an eternity, cranking so much that her wrists began to ache from the effort. She flipped the switch, and six bright LED lights flooded the room, illuminating the tear-streaked faces of her surrogate children. "It's going to be okay, guys. Don't worry, you're safe in here." She hoped. At that moment, a loud crash shook the wall with such violence it caused tiny cracks to appear within the drywall behind racks of clothing.

Sophie, a seven-year-old girl with pigtails, let out an ear-piercing scream as drywall rained down from above and pelted her in her small head. The other children started crying with renewed vigor.

"I wanna go home," cried one.

"I want my momma," cried another.

"I know, I know. Quiet now, quiet please," Karen said with futility, panic beginning to enter her voice. It had already been too late, Karen knew. Whoever it was on the other side of that wall definitely heard the commotion. The sound of footsteps pounded through the home, causing the floors to shudder under their urgent pace. Karen heard the weak hollow outer door to the bathroom creak and splinter as it exploded open, then something slammed into the closet door hard, causing the entire room to shake. Fists pounded frantically on the reinforced closet door, even above the children's cries and screams.

Karen could hear the figure outside snarling like some kind of rabid animal. She backed up away from the door instinctively moving the children behind her. She watched in fear as the frame surrounding the heavy reinforced door buckled and began to crack under their would-be attacker's abuse.

Quickly, Karen rushed over to the far wall of the closet and began throwing boxes of books and old video tapes and other assorted junk in front of the door, trying to build some kind of barricade. She reached up and slid aside a row of her husband's clothing. Reaching behind his detritus, she located a length of rope that was drilled into the wall and pulled. A false drywall panel dropped away with a thud, revealing a large safe located behind it. Karen tapped the panel located next to the safe's handle, and a digital screen powered to life, basking the room in a dull blue glow. Karen typed in her personal ID that her husband had set up for her. He used a number he knew she would not forget—their anniversary date. She keyed the number in and pressed her thumb to the glass panel. A LED light flashed green, indicating that her thumbprint and code key matched in the system, and the door popped open.

Karen grabbed the closest weapon she could find; in this case, it was a Mossberg 500 tactical special purpose twenty-gauge shotgun. She opened the breach and reached for a box of rounds. She had no idea what rounds did what; she just reached for the closest shotgun ammunition she could find. She fumbled with the cartridges, trying to control the shaking of her hands, loaded in six shells, and pumped the weapon feeding in a round. She hadn't had much experience with any of the weapons, but her husband had shown her that much, even against her protests. At the moment, she was glad he had.

The door continued to shudder and crack, raining bits of dried paint and wood to the floor. The kids shifted terrified, wide-eyed glances back and forth between the door and the newly acquired shotgun that she now held in her quaking hands.

Bang, bang, bang! sounded around the closet, the noise all encompassing. Karen's heart pounded, threatening to rip out of her chest. Her vision narrowed and blurred around the edges, her pulse roared in her ears. She had to fight back her anxiety to prevent herself from passing out.

"Breathe," she told herself. "You have to protect these children." The word *protect* became the new mantra in her mind.

BANG, BANG, BANG! The door was beginning to come loose. *BANG, BANG, BANG!* The door came crashing in, the hinges finally succumbing to the onslaught, the metal shearing clean off the door frame. The door fell in and landed propped against the far wall of the closet. For Karen, time seemed to stand completely still; she could hear the sounds of the children breathing heavy and sobbing. She stared at the door, expecting something to emerge through the portal; nothing happened. One of the children tugged on Karen's pant legs.

"Mrs. Karen," he whispered softly.

She glanced momentarily down Richie's reddened tear-soaked face.

He gazed up at her with bloodshot blue eyes and freckled cheeks and was about to tell her he had to pee, of all things.

Suddenly, a growl escaped from beyond the door; and like a feral dog, a figure came bursting through the opening, slamming straight into her before she could even react. The shotgun clattered to the floor as she was knocked back into the children. The kids were scattered back into each other and the shelving units that lined the wall, sending canned food and other assorted odds and ends raining down, pelting everyone like falling meteors.

A can struck Karen in the shoulder, but she had no time for the pain to register as the snarling man's fingers dug into her sides and the back of her neck. Pinned down to the floor, she kept his snapping jaws at bay with her right hand while she groped blindly around the floor with her left, searching for the shotgun or anything, for that matter, in which to defend herself and the children.

Thick saliva dripped from the sweaty feral man's yellowed teeth and landed on her cheek as she let out a scream. His jaws moved closer, her strength beginning to ebb away. At that moment, something struck the man in the forehead, a can of tomato soup bounced off the man, seeming to stun him for a moment, his attention briefly shifted away from Karen, and he looked directly at the children. Karen glanced upward behind her and noticed Richie, little Richie, holding the shotgun—pointing it right in the face of the attacker.

"G-g-g-get off her," he stammered weakly, his chubby little form shaking from head to toe.

The man growled at him and shifted his attention back to Karen, not caring or even knowing what the weapon was that was pointed in his direction.

Karen pushed up at the monster with all her might using what seemed to be the last of her strength. "Richie!" she shouted over at the boy. "Use the gun, Richie!"

The little boy backed away, shaking his head frantically. "I-I-can't," he stuttered.

"Yes, you can! Just point and shoot just like you do with your toys," she pleaded with the boy, in desperation, grunting with exertion, wanting anything to get this asshole off her.

The boy pointed the Mossberg and held it away from him; he squeezed his eyes shut and looked away. He pulled the trigger; the recoil of the powerful weapon sent the boy sprawling to the floor, knocking the other children over like bowling pins.

In the same instant, a large high-velocity Remington slugger round struck the beast directly in the forehead, obliterating and shearing most of his head completely from his shoulders, spraying the far wall of the closet in dark viscous blood and brain matter.

Karen pushed the dead man off her and slid out from underneath. Completely stunned by everything that had just transpired, she barely noticed her arms covered in bright red and orange gore.

She approached Richie lying on his back, still clutching the shotgun in his tiny hands. Karen reached out for the boy and he shrank away from her in wide-eyed horror. She looked down at her blood-slick hands and tank top that was anything but white anymore and decided to just liberate the firearm from the boy's trembling hands.

"Richie," she said soothingly, "I know that was hard for you to do, but I need you to be a big boy and understand that it had to be done…if not…" Karen let the comment hang in the air, not knowing exactly what to say. I mean, how does one explain to a child that killing a man was necessary?

Richie nodded in silent understanding and wiped snot and tears away from his childish face.

"I-I-didn't want him to hurt you, Mrs. Karen," the boy sobbed.

"I know, honey," she replied. "Thank you, Richie, you saved my life." She smiled weakly, tears welling up in her eyes.

Karen took in a deep breath and stood. She motioned to the other children to help Richie to his feet, not wanting to touch him with her grotesque hands. "Okay guys, we have to see about getting out of here." She didn't wait for them to reply. She scanned the area of the closet and found some quilted bed comforters tucked into a shelf that lay just within her reach. She chose an old one that she used as her *time-of-the-month* blanket and draped it over the now-dead man's body lying half in the closet entryway.

She carefully peered around the edge of the shattered door frame, listening intently for sounds of any other intruders; all was silent, save for the whimpering of her daycare charges. She carefully and gingerly stepped over the still form of the dead man on the floor. Blood from the horrific wound beginning to seep through the thick pale green flower-patterned comforter. Gore coated the walls and door frame and hung in wet chunks of matted hair and skin; Karen forced down her revulsion.

She managed to step out of the breach into the bathroom proper and nervously looked around, searching for any other possible threats.

The children peeked with their small faces out of the opening and watched her move silently around the bathroom.

Karen quietly motioned for them to stay where they were, and then held her finger to her lips. "Shhh." She walked over to the edge of the bathroom and gazed out into the bedroom beyond. Upon seeing no immediate danger, she pulled off her gore-covered shirt; thankfully, her bra and blue jeans had seemingly been spared. She stepped over to the sink and turned on the faucet, and positioned it to nuclear hot. She proceeded to scrub her hands and arms, with thick viscous layers of soap and bubbles until her skin was red and raw. She watched as the strange-looking blackish red and orange blood went swirling around the drain in spidery tendrils. She wasn't a doctor, not by a long shot, but she knew something had been very wrong with that man, and the first thing she needed to do was disinfect. She finished with her extremities and started working on her hair and face, squeezing her eyes shut like a vice trying to prevent any of the possibly infectious bodily fluids from entering her bloodstream. She had no clue as to what it was that ailed the man, but it was bad.

Karen stepped quickly and lightly into the bedroom. Standing in front of her large mahogany dresser, she slid the drawer out, grunting as she did so. These old dressers tended to last forever but sucked in functionality; she would have Kyle grease the wheels later when he got home.

Her thoughts drifted to her husband for a moment, wondering what he was going to think about all that had transpired this day in the Walker homestead. She would call him once she had the children safe and contacted the police. She shook her head at the thought of how traumatic this was going to be to these children and how much time this was going to consume over the course of the next few days. She wondered exactly how this was going to affect her business. She wracked a quiet sob that hitched in her throat and stifled a tear. Her thoughts went back to the children still cowering in the back of the closet. She selected a gray and white camouflage tank top, slid her arms and then her head into it, and pulled it down to her waist. She grabbed a hair tie out of a small ornate treasure box on top of the stained mahogany dresser, and pulled her still-wet reddish-brown hair back and let it tumble to the nape of her neck, feeling the moisture from her hair run down her spine, causing her to shudder involuntarily with a slight chill.

She took a moment to compose herself, taking a long deep breath and blowing it out slowly. It did nothing to calm the nerves that were seemingly on fire throughout every continuous cell in her meek body. It was then in the stillness of that moment she could hear the faint sounds of rushing cars; a siren blared in the distance muffled by the thin walls of the double-wide trailer she and her husband resided in. She could swear she heard the sounds of screams. Acid rose in the pit of her stomach, a strange sensation brewing within her core; tingling began in her extremities as waves of panic started to overtake her.

She turned around from the dresser and faced the window. Curtains allowed only a meager amount of illumination to enter into the dim room. Slowly, she crossed the room, stepping around the bed. Leaning over a potted elephant ear plant, she drew the curtains across and stared out into the street.

She watched in confusion as people of all ages seemed to be running every which way. Cars raced back and forth in front of her home. She watched in horror as a red sedan barreled into an elderly woman and spun off the road, striking a fire hydrant, sending water cascading into the streets. A group of people went sprinting toward the scene; Karen thought for a moment that they were bystanders coming to the aid of the crash victims, until she noticed a group of them fall onto the ruined old woman, who now lay in the center of the road.

Another group snatched a bleary-eyed wisp of a man who clung bleeding to his steering wheel in defiance, as the horde of men and women drug him from the window, kicking and screaming. Karen's stomach lurched as she saw the figures begin to tear into the poor man's flesh. Ripping off bacon-sized strips of meat and opening a floodgate of blood. Several of the cannibals reared their heads back in unison and let out triumphant roars.

Karen let the curtain fall, her hand covering her mouth, in shock. "My God," she gasped. Karen slowly backed away from the window and the offending scene of carnage that lay beyond. *What the hell was going on?* she thought. Was this just happening here, everywhere? Was Kyle okay? "What the hell is going on?" she repeated to herself aloud this time. She heard the kids in the other room getting restless, picking up on her sense of panic, she assumed. "What am I going to do?" she whispered.

Quickly, she stepped into the bathroom, and walked around to the closet. They needed supplies, something to help them sustain and ride, whatever the hell this was, out. Second, they need a plan of escape, and last but not least, they needed a place to escape to. Some place much, much stronger than a double-wide Fleetwood.

She peered at the legs of the man that lay in her closet. *He had gotten in easily enough,* she thought. She walked over to the entryway, gritted her teeth, grasped the corpse by the legs, and dragged him out into the bathroom. The kids shrieked as she did so, probably thinking the mean man was getting ready to stand back up and come and get them. She deposited the body next to a large whirlpool bathtub that resided in the corner of the bathroom.

She put on her best fake smile and stepped into the closet to address her charges. "Okay, boys and girls"—she clasped her hands together—"remember the fire drills that we've had to do sometimes?" wishing now that she'd actually practiced them like she was supposed to.

Some of the children nodded fearfully.

"Okay, good." She smiled wanly again. "I'm going to round us up some things to take with us, and then we're going to run to the van and go somewhere safer," she explained, wondering just exactly where safer would be. There was the drugstore on the corner of her development, which was their designated storm shelter in the event of a hurricane or tornado, those were extremely rare in their area, but with today's funky weather patterns, you just never knew.

There was the middle school, but she assumed that to be out of the question, due to the fact that it would most likely be filled to capacity with people. People, at the moment from what she'd just witnessed, she would rather avoid. Then it hit her, her mother-in-law's place. Terry was constantly calling her husband whenever there was a particularly bad storm heading their way, fearful that her little boy would be swept away in their meager little trailer. Karen would tease her husband about it all the time, telling him she could see where he got his paranoia from. It made perfect sense, though. Her mother-in-law's home was located within a small forested area. There were several homes surrounding the property, but they were still somewhat isolated. Their home was built into the side of a small hill, the lower two levels being the ground floor and the basement, which were constructed of poured concrete and red brick, while the upper levels of the house, where the sleeping and storage areas were, were constructed of wood.

Firmly decided on her course of action, Karen grabbed Kyle's hiking pack and began to fill it with nonperishable food items, water purification tablets, diapers, and several liter-sized bottles of water. She then began looking through the armaments that adorned Kyle's gun safe. She reached up and withdrew a tactical ballistic vest, one of Kyle's spares. She slipped the garment on and secured the Velcro straps in place, adjusting them as tight as they could go. The vest was fucking huge, well, on her at least. By comparison, Kyle stood about two feet taller and had a solid hundred pounds on her.

She secured the shotgun to her back with a strap and slid an extra ten shells in the cartridge holders that adorned the shoulder straps. She then grabbed a duty rig and wrapped it around her waist, snapping it in place with a clasp.

The kids stared at her wide-eyed when she withdrew a Glock 9 mm pistol and slid it into the duty rig's holster.

She then pulled out five full magazines, each holding fifteen rounds. She secured two of them to the gun belt's magazine holders and tossed the extra three in to the side pocket of the backpack. She then grabbed a few extra boxes of ammo. She limited the amount due to the weight of the ammo. As small as she was, the backpack was already almost more than she could handle.

She shouldered the heavy pack, letting out a grunt as she heaved it onto her back. *Goddamn thing had to weigh at least sixty pounds*, she thought as she wrestled it into place. She turned toward the children, almost laughing at the looks on their small faces as they eyed her with what looked like a sense of awe and astonishment.

Karen steeled her expression and addressed the children. "Okay, guys, I want you all to line up behind me and hold hands. I want you to focus on getting into the van. Do not worry about anything else that is going on, just get in the van. Can everyone do that?" she asked.

The children nodded frantically in unison.

They were scared, Karen could tell; and from what she'd just seen outside, they had every right to be. "First thing we are going to do is walk into the living room, and then I'm going to look outside and make sure it's safe for us to go to the van. I need you to be brave and very quiet, and when I say go, I need everyone to hurry over and get in the van. Don't worry about who gets what chair, or even buckling up, just get in and sit down. Am I clear?" The children nodded again, most of them tightly holding their lips closed to help them against making even the slightest peep.

Karen led them through the bathroom, instructing them to take care avoiding the patches of sticky coagulated blood that coated the floor and walls of the closet. Slowly and quietly, they made it to the living room. Karen held out a hand, motioning for them to stop while she crept forward. She reached up next to the open door frame and retrieved her car keys that were hanging on a wooden hook, trying her best to keep out of sight as she did so. She grasped the van's electronic lock transmitter in one hand and slowly pulled the Glock out of her holster with the other. She debated hitting the button for the remote starter her husband had installed for her last Christmas, but decided against it, not wanting to draw attention to her and the children until they were in the vehicle. She drove a dark-blue Honda Odyssey van, and she was thankful that it sat eight and came equipped with automatic sliding doors that could be controlled with the transmitter she held in her hand. This would save them some time and allow them to jump right in as they ran; not having to stop and open the doors could possibly save their lives. Now the only thing she was concerned with was getting them shut fast enough once they were inside.

Karen slowly craned her head around the open storm door; the outer screen door was completely demolished. The screen itself was torn to shreds, and the aluminum frame was bent all to hell. She looked around the immediate area of her home and the driveway, and it appeared that the coast was clear. There were people running or milling around just a few houses down, so they would have to make this quick, or they were going to be in a world of trouble. She motioned to the children to come and stand behind her. "Are you ready, guys?" she whispered.

The kids nodded fearfully.

Karen took a deep breath and held it as she stepped around the door. Crouching low, she began to push the ruined screen door open. She gritted her teeth as the warped bottom of the aluminum door caught on her wooden front porch. The door scraped along, and she hoped to hell that the sound was louder in her head than it was outside. Quickly she looked up, hoping they hadn't been spotted. She realized that the thought had come too late, as a figure standing only two houses down heard the noise and stopped what he was doing and turned in their direction, cocking his head to one side like a dog. Like a very mean, feral, rabid dog. "Shit," Karen hissed to herself as she prepared to make a run for it. She hit the button that controlled the van's sliding passenger door. The door shuddered for a moment and began its cycle.

At that moment, the confused man realized there was something there worth his attention. Several others in the area also turned at the noise.

"Run!" Karen shouted to the children as she slammed the screen door open and held it for the kids—ushering them through. She pushed the button to the remote starter, figuring stealth was no longer a concern, and the engine sputtered and started up.

The rabid-looking men and women seemed to come alive at that moment. They howled and began running straight for her and the children.

"Get to the van!" she shouted as the kids piled through the porch gate and down the rickety wooden stairs, several of them nearly tripping as they headed for the open door to the Honda Odyssey. She had to give them credit as she watched them hop into the van, not a one of them argued about who was going to sit where or complained that such-in-such was touching them. *So this is what it takes to get them to behave in a car*, she mused.

A ghoul was getting dangerously close as she throttled off the steps. Karen lifted the 9 mm and opened fire on a man. Three rounds punched him center mass, and it seemed to do nothing but piss him off. "Holy shit!" Karen screamed as she ran to the van. Quickly, she grabbed the sliding door's handle, and gave it a yank. Slowly, painfully slow she thought, the door began to close. Karen stood there, guarding the entrance as the man with the three holes in his chest ran straight for her. Karen kicked out with her foot and planted the sole of her tennis shoe right into his ruined chest, knocking him back and to the ground. The impact caused her knee to buckle slightly, and pain shot up to her thigh.

Quickly, she limped over to the driver-side door and flung it open; she climbed into the driver's seat as the man she had just kicked scrambled to his feet. The elderly woman she had seen get bitten from the window surprised her and slammed right into her open door, pinning her leg halfway in and halfway out. Karen pushed the door open hard, knocking the old bat back a step, and yanked her foot in.

She barely registered the gash in her ankle as she thrust the key in the ignition and hit the gas. The car shot forward in the driveway, slamming her into a basketball hoop in front of the house, knocking it over, it smacked against the side of the home, and Karen cursed at her own stupidity. She threw the car into reverse as five other infected people came hurtling into the sides of the van. They began beating on the doors and windows with such ferocity Karen was afraid they would break through the windows.

The kids were screaming in the backseats, huddling together to get away from the snarling faces of their attackers.

Karen hit the gas again and spun the wheel as they rocketed out of the driveway, crashing over three people in the process. The van rocked back and forth as she threw it into drive and thrust forward, feeling the distinct crunch under the tires as bones were ground into paste on the asphalt. She sped toward the intersection at the end of her street, barely slowing as she veered right and swerved to avoid a derelict jeep parked in the middle of the roadway.

As she looked around, she noticed people running at her from all directions. Bodies were strewn across manicured lawns; homes were set ablaze with black smoke, making it hard to see much of anything in front of her.

Karen slid to a stop as another car sped her direction, struck a pedestrian, and slammed into a concrete guardrail, almost flipping up and over into the creek bed below. It fell back and landed on its roof and teetered back to the roadway. Karen pulled the van around, trying her best to avoid the shattered glass and debris. A flat tire at this point in time would more or less spell doom for her and her precious cargo. Karen made it through the chaos of the streets in her neighborhood and turned quickly onto Route 40. She hoped against hope that she would be able to make the fifteen-mile drive to her mother-in-law's place in all of this madness.

She dug around in her pocket for her cell phone. She pulled out her Nokia, pushed number one, and hit send. The phone speed dialed her husband's cell phone, and she held it to her ear. Before it could even connect, the phone clicked, and then made a horrible screeching sound. Karen pulled the phone away from her ear and stared at it wide eyed for a second before returning her attention to the road. "What the hell was that?" she asked of no one in particular.

She tried the call again and again; she got the same strange noise. "Damn," she stated, annoyed. She hoped that when Kyle made it home—*if he made it home*. The thought entered her prefrontal cortex before she could stop it, and she shuddered involuntarily. He would figure out where she had gone. It was a logical choice being that she was from out of state when they got married, and she had only had a handful of friends in the area. Yes, there was no doubt in her mind, he would figure out where she'd gone. She hoped at least because she had no idea how in the hell she was going to get through all of this without him. She had always teased him about his paranoia, but on the other side, she had always said she felt pretty sure of herself that if the shit hit the fan, she would be fine because he knew what to do. Now she was alone with a car full of kids, and the shit was in fact hitting the fan. She rocketed forward and prayed. She was an atheist, but what the hell. *It couldn't hurt*, she thought as she sped down the roadway.

CHAPTER 10

I slowly pushed myself up off the asphalt; tiny pebbles clung to my face and bit in to my cheeks and bottom lip, causing pinpricks of pain that, at that moment, barely registered in my brain's pain sensors. I made my way shakily back to my feet and watched wide eyed as my partner smashed through the barricade. I silently prayed that he would make it when I saw the attack helicopter. My heart sank, and the expression on my face went sallow. I started to run in the direction of the barricade when a voice from behind, and a resounding click of a gun's safety being disengaged, grabbed my attention.

"Stop! Don't make me shoot you!" I heard the Homeland agent state dryly.

"You can't do this," I said coming to a halt, worry evident in my voice. I watched in horror as a stinger missile launched from the Apache's weapons bank. The rocket struck the roadway directly in front of the Specter Armored truck. Its flat black surface illuminated in flame as it flipped end over end and slammed into the newly formed crater, with a deafening crunch. "Fuck!" I screamed in frustration, feeling completely helpless as my partner of ten years was undoubtedly cooked alive inside of the wreckage. *No one could have survived that*, I thought as my head dropped down in defeat.

A second explosion rocked the area as the armored car's fuel stores caught fire due to the intense heat. This momentary distraction took the Homeland agent off-guard for a moment, and Richard took that instant to act.

I heard a commotion behind me, sounds of a struggle. I spun around to see Richard locked in contest with the Homeland agent, his hands gripping the soldier's MP5, forcing it upward, taking me out of the line of fire. I ran forward, balling my hand into a fist and lashed out with all my remaining strength, striking the agent in his face, knocking his head back, stunning him, allowing Richard to wrench the weapon from his hands. I changed tact and thrust an open palm upward striking the agent below his chin, causing him to bite down hard on his tongue, sending flecks of blood skyward.

He stumbled backward and tripped over his own two feet. He fell to the ground hard with a resounding thud.

I pulled my pistol and aimed for his forehead. "Tell me why the fuck I shouldn't blow your fucking head off!" I spat as he shook his head groggily.

Richard shouldered the MP5 and took up position scanning the area, doing his best to cover our six.

"Make this quick, boss," Richard said to me over his shoulder.

"Answer me, motherfucker!" I said, taking my finger off the trigger guard.

The Homeland agent held his hand up in a stalling fashion and spat; blood dribbled from over his split lips and ran down his bruised chin. "Thuck," he said with his newly formed lisp while running his dirt-encrusted arm across his face.

"I'm waiting," I said, applying about three of the seven necessary pounds of pressure to activate the gun's trigger. That got the agent's attention and he sighed.

"I downt know thwat your asthking of me. I wasth justh following orders," he said, struggling to form his words with what I could imagine was a split tongue and a broken jaw.

"Then who the hell would know? I need answers. I need to know why my partner had to die for your fucking national security." I spat the last part as if it were a curse.

The agent leaned up on his elbows and cocked his chin toward the roadblock. I could see the agents that were left in the area scrambling around their SUVs. I heard someone begin to speak over the Homeland agent's shoulder mic.

"This is Agent Bishop. Target has been eliminated. Evac to rally point for containment measures conformation code echo echo seven five seven nine six," said the tinny voice of their commander. Then the line went silent, following a slight static burst.

"We were your target? With all this madness going on, we were your fucking target? What for, and what the hell do they mean by containment measures?" I asked with confusion, crossing my hardened features.

"To answer your firsth question, all we were told was your truck may have contained a possible bioweapon, and we were under orders to apprehend you and, if necessary, neutralize you," he said with some difficulty, but his speech seemed to get marginally better now that the cobwebs of his assault were starting to clear.

"We gotta go, Kyle. We're starting to draw a crowd," Richard said nervously, noticing a group of Homeland agents heading in our direction.

"Containment, how, what the hell are they going to do?" Richard grabbed me by the sleeve and pulled.

"We need to go now!" Richard said, trying to pull me along.

"Wait!" I shouted and shouldered him off. Richard screamed in my ear:

"There's no time," he said, pointing as agents and crazies alike were starting to swarm in our general direction.

"Fuck!" I shouted. "Fine," I said. I spat on the downed agent, and we took off at a run in the opposite direction of the incoming hostiles.

I frantically searched the area, looking for a place to escape. I had a dreadful feeling starting in the pit of my stomach, the word *containment* repeating itself over and over in the forefront of my mind. My thoughts went back to the plane I had seen fly overhead earlier. It had meant nothing at the time, but now it seemed altogether sinister in its appearance. In my experience in the private sector, before I had been cast out to live a normal life, I had seen some of what the government deemed as containment. It typically involved the complete destruction of an area. Usually, biological outbreaks of a critical magnitude burned themselves out due to the speed and virulence they possessed without any human involvement; they simply let nature run its course. Being the government had called for containment measures meant that they had no fucking clue what this was and were freaked out enough to level the area. In this case, I suspected a fuel air bomb judging by the size of the aircraft I had seen do a flyover previously. The bomb would be dropped from the aircraft where it would then bust open, saturating the area in a highly combustible compound that would then ignite at temperatures so hot it would literally suck the oxygen out of the area, creating a vacuum, obliterating everything within its calculated radius. I had no idea how far this thing had spread, but I knew we had to get the hell out of Dodge—and get the hell out fast. I shot a look over my shoulder as we ran to see that the Homeland agents were helping their fallen comrade to his feet. Oddly, they seemed to ignore us completely as they pointed toward the oncoming crazies that approached them.

Agents toward the roadblock boarded their SUVs and started to speed off into the distance. My gaze landed upon the ruins of my armored transport, and I felt a pang of regret enter my mind, knowing that my partner had most likely been killed as a result of my actions. *What am I going to tell his wife?* I thought. Richard smacked me in the shoulder, tearing my attention away from the wreckage.

"No time to dwell on it right now. Come on, this way." He pointed at a police cruiser not too far from our position.

We ran past crumpled cars and still forms of ruined bodies that lined the roadway. Some of them still twitched as we ran past.

As I jogged past a small red Mini Cooper that was set ablaze, the paint beginning to bubble and peel, a hand shot out from underneath and sent me sprawling to the ground. I kicked out with my boot as I noticed a charred figure trying to pull himself forward and out from underneath of the burning wreckage, and take a chunk out of me with his teeth. I kicked him in the head. My foot slid off, taking bits of burned flesh, revealing his bone-white skull underneath. I gasped at the fact that this individual was still even moving. I raised my leg up and stomped down hard, splitting the skull open, sending bits of congealed brain matter splattering across the ground like a squashed bug.

Richard thrust a hand out and helped me to my feet, and we continued on, picking up the pace as I heard the roar of a plane's engine in the distance.

"Shit," I said, and Richard shot a side glance over to me, a questioning look on his face. "We need to hurry," was all I said in response.

"Thanks, Captain Obvious," the officer replied.

We reached the gray and yellow police cruiser, nearly out of breath.

Richard thrust his hand down to his duty rig and located a set of keys that were attached with a metal ring. He unclasped the key ring and fumbled around with them for a moment until he located the key he was looking for, thankful that the department had keyed all of their standard cruisers with the same locks. Richard inserted the key and gave it two quick turns to the right, disengaging the car's locks, and climbed in.

I hurriedly followed suit. I slapped on my seat belt and looked in the rearview mirror just in time to see an F-18 Hornet throttle out of the horizon.

"Get this bitch moving, Dick!" I said with an edge of fear in my voice.

Richard followed my gaze to the rearview to see what I was staring at. "What the hell is that for?" he said, observing the scene.

"That's winged death," I said in response. "They're planning on torching this place."

"How in the hell do you know that?" he questioned.

"Just trust me and get this bucket moving," I said in reply.

Richard cocked an eyebrow and started the engine. The police cruiser purred to life; he threw it in gear and hit the gas pedal. The police car accelerated smoothly.

I cocked a short-lived grin when I thought of how cushy the vehicle felt in comparison to the monster car I cruised around in all day. The police car took the roads bumps and curves with ease, and among all the tension, I had to stifle a laugh.

Richard glanced over at me. "What?" he questioned, looking confused.

"Nothing." I smiled and shook my head. "I was just thinking how smooth this thing runs. If I were in my truck hitting some of these bumps, my head would be smacking the ceiling." I involuntarily touched the top of my head.

"No shocks." It was a statement more than a question.

I nodded my head in agreement.

"Well, our vehicles are the best the taxpayers have to offer," he said and followed with a grin. At that moment, there was a huge concussive blast that shattered the cruiser's rear safety glass and hit with enough force to cause the car's back wheels to rise up off the roadway. Richard fought with the steering wheel, doing his best to control the vehicle that had briefly hopped up onto its two front wheels. He had just regained control when our eyes went wide in unison as we saw a massive fireball headed our way.

"Ahhhh, shit! Step on it, Dick!" I shouted, glancing behind us nervously.

"I'm stepping on it! I'm stepping on it, and by the way, the-name-is-Richard!" he shouted back. The cop reached down and tapped the turbo button on his cruiser's console. There was a momentary burst of energy, and the car rocketed forward. Richard's face was perspiring, his brow furrowed in intense concentration as he whipped the car around almost unintelligible obstacles. He maneuvered the cruiser with the precision of a surgeon as he avoided stranded cars and debris.

The fireball struck, moving way too fast for us to outrun. I just hoped we were far enough away to not be vaporized immediately. An intense heat struck our backs and flooded superheated air into our nose and mouths, making our lungs feel as if they were on fire. The car shot forward, no longer under the power of its own engine, but being forcibly projected by the intense pressure of the blast. Control of the vehicle was futile as we were propelled forward; the cruiser rocked on its antiroll suspension and was forced sideways, and then flipped over like a newspaper blowing in the wind. Feeling the inertia as the car began to flip, I wrapped my hands behind my neck and bent down, tucking my head into my knees like they tell you to do in a plane crash.

"Duck and cover, people!" The line from some movie I cannot remember obscurely flitted through my thoughts. The car rolled several times before landing squarely on its roof, spinning like a top, showering the area with sparks that were barely visible with the surrounding fireball that engulfed us. The car slid about fifty or so feet along the highway before being slammed into a guardrail, and finally coming to a rest.

I watched bleary eyed and dazed as the flames blazed around the car, reminding me of a blast furnace. I felt my skin begin to burn under the intense heat. *This is it*, I thought as I squeezed my eyes shut, feeling the sting of tears that attempted to fall but were being immediately evaporated into the air. I opened my eyes and gazed over to Richard through heat-distorted waves. He groaned in pain, a large welt beginning to form on his forehead. I watched the fire as it roared by, and I let my thoughts drift off to my wife and children. If I was going to die here, I wasn't going to let my last thoughts and feelings be full of fear and remorse. I thought of my daughter and the four sons that we shared. I thought about Boy Scout meetings and trick or treating on Halloween, our last Christmas, where my wife and kids had all pitched in to get my car detailed.

I wished I was there now. Instead, I was stuck here in this hell. I stared out of the window, wondering just how much time we had left; and as if by some miracle, the flames ceased just as fast as they appeared. I heard a whoosh of air flood around the car. Smoke poured from the roadway and surrounded us. I had to wonder if we had just survived the explosion only to die from smoke inhalation. However, it seemed that the police cruiser, even as banged up and shattered as it was, helped to keep most of the offending toxins outside of the cab.

I closed my eyes, feeling incredibly dizzy, a sense of nausea overtook me and I vomited. Acidic bile ran out of my mouth and up my nose as I hung upside down still strapped into my seat belt. I aspirated on the putrid liquid and began to gag and cough uncontrollably. My lungs spasmed trying to remove the vile fluid from within them. I took in a ragged breath of hot air and began coughing anew; white spots started entering my vision like mini explosions going off in my optic nerves. I fought for consciousness but lost as everything started to fade to black.

CHAPTER 11

Marvin Winters crouched low on the forest floor atop of a hill overlooking the roadway where he had just narrowly escaped. He kept quiet and out of site while he tried to catch his breath; he rubbed his throbbing knee, the artificial metal joints adhering his prosthetic leg gave him hell in the best of times, and that was when he was sitting on his ass all day pushing down on a gas pedal. Now that he was up and moving, running for his life, he was living through pure torment. He felt the grinding of the metal joint against his muscle tissue with every slight movement.

"I'm getting too old for this shit," he grumbled as he watched a group of Homeland agents approach his rapidly burning vehicle.

Marvin watched somewhat amused when he noticed the gas tank on his ruined rig catch fire. "Get ready for a big surprise you fuckers," he said to himself, cocking a sly grin. Marvin, however, knew better than to stand there, gawking like some civi. As a former Marine and a demolitions expert to boot, he knew one of the first rules pertaining to explosives: if you were close enough to see it, you were close enough for it to kill you. So Marvin backed farther into the forest's shadowy interior. As quietly as he could, he navigated his way through the thicket of trees and underbrush. As far as stealth goes, he could have sworn that he sounded more like a bull in a china shop rather than the cunning fox that he was trying to be.

"Fuck aging," Marvin said to a squirrel that happened to be in his path. The squirrel apparently heard him coming from a mile away and subsequently scurried up a nearby pine tree in response. His thoughts drifted back to his glory days in the Marine Corps, moving as quietly as a tiger in the grass ready to pounce on its prey as he and his crew planted explosive charges behind enemy lines to halt or even cripple their operations.

The sound of an engine in the distance snapped him out of his reverie, and he gazed upward at the gray sky. It had been a while since he had heard the sounds of military aircraft, but he could pick out the urgency in which it seemed to travel. The unmistakable drone of a jet engine hurtling toward his position, he knew that when there was that particular sound, a shit-storm was sure to follow. He just hoped Kyle had enough sense to get out of its way, if the kid was still alive, he thought.

He stood there sullen for a moment. Kyle was a smart kid, little bit full of himself at times but a smart kid nonetheless, not to mention that he loved his family more than anyone he had ever seen. That became keenly apparent if you happened to work with the man aside from his constant rambling about his wife and kids; he would quite literally run his ass off just to get home to spend a little more time with them. Marvin took in a deep breath and continued forward through the trees, wanting to put as much distance between him and this place as he could. If only for his family, Marvin knew Kyle would make it. Besides, the boy was just too damn stubborn to die.

Marvin looked down at the mud-encrusted metal case that he gripped in his left hand. He had to periodically swap the case in between his hand's, alternating arms due to the strain the heavy case put on his weathered shoulders. He winced and spat as he walked directly into a large spider-web. "Shit," he spat again as he wiped the offending strands of spider silk from his face with his free hand. Their rough calloused surface brushed along day-old gray stubble. "Should have shaved this morning," Marvin mumbled.

He debated taking a moment and trying to force the case open, figuring it to be rigged with a GPS locator, not to mention finding out exactly what it contained that our illustrious government was willing to kill for. However, still mindful of the jet heading his way, he decided he should probably keep moving; he had a very bad feeling about that sound. He would, however, have to ditch said case probably sooner rather than later, lest they use it to track his position. If they did, he doubted very seriously that he would survive a second go-round with Homeland's goons.

Marvin cut a path through the vegetation, knowing that soon he would run into the side street that bisected the main road from which he had just departed. He hoped that among the smoke and confusion, no one had noticed him slip away from the wreckage; he knew they would figure it out sooner or later, but he hoped he'd be long gone before then.

Marvin approached a drop off in the landscape. Peering down below the smoke and gloom, he could just make out the roadway below. It was a narrow stretch, probably a service road to the main highway, he mused. Using his free hand, he gripped onto the base of a spindly sapling and started his way down the steep incline, taking care to avoid slipping on the now-damp and slick leaves that coated the earth. The rain had all but ceased to fall; the only droplets cascading down upon him were the result of water collected atop the leaves of the trees he disturbed while making his descent. After several minutes of slipping, sliding, and cursing his way down the slope, Marvin reached the edge of the forest and crept silently toward the roadway, doing his best to stay out of sight.

He gazed skyward to see the military jet go screaming by. "Shit," Marvin hissed and ducked down low, not knowing exactly what to expect next. A moment later, the earth surrounding Marvin's feet shuddered and quaked beneath his boots. Trees atop the hill flattened with the concussive blast that resounded throughout the expanse. Old growth oaks and pines tumbled down the hill in waves like something you would see in old turn-of-the-century logging camp films.

Marvin jumped out from his hiding place and dove to the drainage ditch aside the roadway, moving quickly as adrenaline fueled his tired body. Immediately going prone and using the metal case as a shield to protect his head, dirt and debris rained down upon him for what seemed like an eternity. Bits of earth and rock pelted the metal case. To Marvin, the sounds of the debris striking the case sounded a bit like popcorn popping in his eight-hundred-year-old thermonuclear microwave oven. The ancient contraption looked akin to something they would have produced out of Three Mile Island instead of something he and the Misses picked up at Macy's sometime in the early eighties.

The sounds of material striking the case grew steadily slower until it came to a stop. Marvin slowly removed his head from underneath his makeshift shield and brought his gaze upward. He stared in shock and awe at the miniature mushroom cloud that plumed beyond the hill, and he then noticed a giant timber that teetered above him merely yards away, hanging directly above his position.

Marvin quickly scrambled to his feet lest a squirrel farted in the wrong direction causing the massive oak tree to come tumbling down into his hidey-hole. He climbed his way out of the drainage ditch and stepped onto the roadway. He glanced in both directions, still having the presence of mind to check for any threats that may be lurking about. Thus far, he had been protected from the insanity that had befallen the area, enclosed within his nearly impermeable armored shell. Now much to his chagrin, he was right in the thick of it. Marvin set the heavy metal case on the gravel road beneath his feet.

First order of business was his personal safety. With what he had witnessed thus far, the world, at least in this general vicinity, had gone insane. People were attacking without justification, government agents were dropping bombs on American soil, and this was all too much for him. Something had gone terribly wrong, and he suspected whatever was in that case— he eyed the suitcase with disdain—had something to do with it. Marvin reached to his side and checked to make certain his .45 Glock was still firmly attached to his hip. It was; at least there were still some small miracles. Next thing he needed to do was get as far away from here as possible. With his bad knees, Marvin knew he wasn't going to get very far before something caught up to him. At the moment, the gravel roadway that he stood on appeared empty; however, he knew he would have to find some sort of transportation if he were going to make it anywhere. He wondered briefly if he could catch a bus, then dismissed the thought. That would be a sight, an armored guard with a large case standing on a bus. Might as well just paint the target on his back. Not to mention all the other shit going on at the present time.

Marvin looked up and down the roadway trying to decide in which direction he wanted to travel. He guessed his best option was to make it back to HQ; now if only he knew which direction that was. Marvin looked down at a button compass embedded in his watch strap. He changed his position until the red needled directed him roughly to the north, knowing that he and his partner had traveled about twenty miles south of their home base, might as well have been a hundred in his condition. He would need to find a ride, or at least a phone; he wanted to check on his wife of the past forty years. With Homeland's boys on his tail, he wasn't certain if that was the best course of action, however.

Marvin kicked the case onto its side and pondered the locking mechanism. It was from all outward appearances a biometric lock, nearly impossible to open without the proper thumbprint or at least a good set of tools, neither of which he had. The case, however, had sustained a good deal of damage when his truck flipped over. Marvin glanced around the roadway until his gaze came to rest on a rather large hunk of rock.

"Ah, what the fuck," Marvin said while plucking up the mini boulder. Marvin knelt beside the case; he held onto the side of its now-dented surface and raised his hand up in the air. He brought the bludgeon down with as much force as he could muster. A loud pang reverberated through the air, sending shock waves up his arm. Marvin winced and struck the lock again. To anyone who may have been within earshot, it would have sounded akin to someone working metal on an anvil. Seven or so attempts later and nothing to show for it other than a slightly cracked LED screen. Marvin gave up and decided to move on lest someone get curious as to what the hell that banging was. Marvin had to laugh at the thought. Here, there, was just a massive explosion, and he was thinking someone would give a shit about his hammering. He shrugged.

He glanced over his shoulder and then did a double take; his neck cracked in response to the unexpected movement. Marvin squinted at what appeared to be two figures stumbling out of the brush, one of them lost their footing and plunged face first into the drainage ditch. Marvin cocked an eyebrow in amazement at the fact that the man or woman—he couldn't quite tell at this distance—did a straight up face plant into a concrete drain pipe, not even bothering to put out its hands to protect itself. Its companion then tripped over the now-still form of its partner, successfully tumbling in the ditch after it.

"What the fuck," Marvin snickered. "They must be stoned out of their gourds." It was then he noticed the two tangled figures begin to slowly emerge from the shallowly depths of the embankment; both figures were covered in what looked like a mix of blood and mud caked over with bits of gravel. Both of them reached out in Marvin's direction and let out a ghastly snarl. Marvin's stomach began to sour like curdled milk; it was at that moment he decided it was time to go. If anyone could take a fall like that and still keep coming, it's time to bug out.

Marvin reached down and grasped the handle of the case once more. He toyed with the idea of leaving it behind and retrieving it later, but he could barely remember what he had for breakfast that day, let alone trying to remember where he stashed some flipping case in the middle of the woods. Glancing behind him and taking note of the position of his new fan club, Marvin set off down the road.

He moved at a brisk pace, well, at least as brisk as a seventy-three-year-old ex-Marine with an artificial leg could manage. Even at his current stride, he still managed to lose sight of his pursuers. He had traveled about two miles along the service road before he reached the entrance to the main thoroughfare through town. An odd feeling came over Marvin as he entered the town proper; the usual noise and hustle and bustle of commuters and tourists flying in from BWI airport were strangely absent. Even the locals who normally traversed the neighborhood were missing. It was as if he strolled into a ghost town.

Marvin looked skyward. The rain had stopped, and from the looks of things, the clouds were starting to disperse. It even appeared that the sun was trying to make an appearance. Marvin gazed up and down the roadway. He scratched his balding gray head and continued walking.

There was a gas station that sat on the corner of the next street over, the type that housed a decent-sized convenience store as well as a garage. As Marvin approached the store, he noticed a red and white sign that hung in the garage window that read mechanic on duty.

"Wonder if he's good enough to fix an armored car that was hit with a fucking missile," Marvin said dejectedly with a hint of sarcasm. He made it to the parking lot of the gas station, cautiously approached the glass double doors, and peered inside. The store was in complete disarray. Snacks of all shapes and sizes lay strewn about the floor; Slurpee-type machines set with the valves still open, draining the frozen treat onto the floor. Magazines clung to the tile drenched in the sugary swill, causing the ink to leech and run off in a rainbow of unnatural colors. Marvin shook his head; it looked as if everyone had just picked up and left.

"What in God's green Earth is going on here?" Marvin questioned himself. Slowly, he opened the door; he wanted to find a phone and call home. With everything that was going on today, Homeland Security will be damned. He wanted to know if his wife was okay and, more importantly, if this shit was going on there as well.

Marvin stepped inside; a bell chimed as he entered. He paused and looked around expectantly, waiting to see if a merchant would step out of a backroom somewhere. When none appeared, he called out. "Hello, anyone home?" he said in his normal gruff tone. His gaze flitted around the store. "I need to use your phone." He stepped farther into the store, cheese puffs crunching underfoot as he approached the counter. Marvin leaned over the countertop to see if their phone was hidden within; he stepped back in shock, almost knocking over a rack of comic books as he saw the disemboweled corpse of an Indian man lying in a puddle of blood on the floor.

"Holy fuck!" Marvin hissed as he grabbed the side of a display rack to keep from falling over. "Shit, shit, shit," he spit out in rapid succession, his feeble heart raced in his chest; and for a moment, he eyed a bottle of aspirin that lie on the floor, wondering if he should take one now just in case. "It's just a body," he said to himself. "Nothing I hadn't seen before," he said trying to calm his quaking nerves. He took in a deep breath, walked back toward the counter, and peered over once more.

The man on the floor was in horrific shape. His face looked as if it had been peeled back with a vegetable peeler then nibbled on by carnivorous raccoons, half-moon shapes dotted up and down his caramel-colored flesh in between the torn rags of clothing. Marvin wasn't even sure if he could identify the sex of the victim. Marvin held his breath and scanned the contents of the shelves that were in his vantage point. A black old-fashioned rotary phone set opposite his position, underneath a lotto machine on the other counter.

"Damn it," Marvin muttered, knowing that he would have to walk behind the counter and over the mutilated corpse if he wanted to use the ancient device. "Didn't even know those damn things still existed."

Marvin walked around to a small swing door attached to the rear of the counter behind a row of coffee machines and carefully pushed it open. The door swung open easily on well-oiled hinges and clanged as it struck the door jamb behind it. Marvin winced involuntarily at the noise that resounded. He quickly glanced around the empty store to make certain nothing was creeping around to attack him. He stepped in through the door frame, carefully avoiding a puddle of sticky congealed blood that matted the gray-and-black-speckled linoleum floor. Marvin skirted the edge of the counter, standing on his tiptoes, trying his best not to step on the dead man's form that lay in the space's center. It was at that point Marvin noticed what looked like the pistol grip of a pump action shotgun poking out from underneath a shelving unit, only inches from the bloodied man's hands; well, what was left of his hands that is. Marvin noticed three fingers had been torn from their respective moorings, bloodied bits of torn skin, and sinew occupied the space where the fingers should have been. He looked around the area half expecting to find them lying close to the body, but they were nowhere to be found. That gave him pause. The more he looked, the more he noticed other things missing as well. In Vietnam, he had seen his share of eviscerated corpses, and this man seemed to be missing a hell of a lot of his internal organs. Marvin shivered at the thought.

He tore his gaze away from the man and turned it instead to his objective. Marvin reached down and retrieved the phone from its perch on the shelving unit and set it atop the counter. Picking up the receiver, he placed it to his ear. "Well that figures," Marvin said, realizing that there, of course, was no dial tone. He rapidly depressed the disconnect button several times, trying to get a response from the stupid machine. "Fuck!" Marvin shouted, and then tossed the phone aside in frustration, sending it clattering across the countertop.

Marvin turned around and froze as he noticed the corpse that was on the floor just a moment ago was currently standing directly in front of him. The man's dead eyes focused seemingly on nothing as it steadily swayed from side to side like a crackhead standing on the corner of Fayette Street, its entrails squirmed out of his body cavity spilling waste and other fluids onto his pants and down to the floor.

Marvin began to reach for his sidearm when the man's gaze abruptly seemed to polarize on him.

Out of nowhere, he lunged, closing the slight distance between them in an instant. The man clutched onto Marvin's arms as he brought his snarling face into Marvin's shoulders and bit deep. Subsequently, Marvin's body armor saved his life as the man wrenched his head back, chewing on a mouthful of polyester fabric.

Marvin, placing his foot in between the shelving unit's baseboard and the floor, pushed forward, bringing his left hand up, striking the ruined man in what was left of his chest. The man lost his grip and stumbled backward, tripping over his own intestine, sending him sprawling once again to the floor. Marvin ripped his pistol from its holster and opened fire; the .45 caliber rounds punched neat holes through the man's snarling skull. The back of his head exploded outward adding to the gore-strewn linoleum.

Marvin breathed heavily, not taking his eyes off the beast that lay at his feet. A loud banging noise from his rear caught Marvin's attention. He spun around bringing his pistol up in the direction of the noise. To Marvin's amazement, his two pals from the roadway stood, pounding on the gas stations front door. "What the hell?" Marvin said in astonishment.

Upon closer examination, he could tell these two were in just as good of shape as the man on the floor. Bits of flesh were torn away from sections of their arms and faces. Marvin saw now that one of them was a female, a young woman, and an attractive one at that, at least she had been. The other was a middle-aged man in trucker's overalls, both left smears of blood on the thick glass of the entryway. Marvin decided it would be a good time to get out of sight, not wanting to wait around until the duo either shattered the glass or figured out how to pull open the door. He had to wonder, *how in the hell had they found him; he'd lost sight of them on the roadway about two miles back.* He shrugged off the thought; it didn't matter. All that mattered was that they were here now.

Marvin turned back around, glancing down at the body on the floor. He kicked at the still form with the tip of his boot to make certain the son-of-a-bitch decided to stay dead this time. At this, Marvin remembered the shotgun. He grinned as he pulled it out from the recesses of the shelf. Upon further examination, he also found a small box of birdshot cartridges hidden behind a money order printer.

"Got to love the ol' U.S. of freaking A," he said as he pocketed the shells. Marvin slid his sidearm back into his holster and held the shotgun in one hand. He picked the metal case up off the countertop where he had left it and searched the walls until he spotted a door at the far end of the store that he assumed led into the garage area. He hoped there would be a drill or a hammer and chisel, something he could pop this fucker open with. Stealing another glance over his shoulder to see his newly formed entourage was still there, which they were, Marvin began to make his way toward the door.

CHAPTER 12

Alex Bishop stood observing the explosion from a mile or so away from the target zone, tucked inside the relative safety of a local middle school parking lot. Their white SUVs stood in stark contrast to the school's bland red brick facade. Rows of dogwood trees swayed with the gentle wind and dripped with resonate moisture from the stalled rainfall. Clouds still hung low in the sky casting wan shadows across the dim landscape; grays and whites now illuminated in a red and orange glow above the blast site. Bishop and his men could feel the heat resonate from the eruption even at this distance.

Alex checked his watch. About twenty minutes had passed since he had relayed the information about the armored vehicle and subsequent outbreak of the kuru variant pathogen. Director Hammond, along with other suits in Washington, had ordered him to launch Prometheus protocol. Prometheus was the code name for a small localized fuel air bomb designed to be launched in the event of a biological attack on the United States, to aid in the prevention of the spread of whatever contagion may have been released. It was, of course, an extreme measure; however, the threat of a wildfire disease being released in a major U.S. city or, in this case, an international hub with flights not only traveling to every major U.S. city, but also every country on the planet, was an extreme situation. The collateral damage would most likely be minimal by comparison to the entire country's population; however, the casualties would most definitely haunt their lives and dreams for years to come, but what could they do? Orders were orders, and in this case, he believed those orders to be justified. From the initial report that Bishop had read, this shit was beyond nasty. He, however, had not expected the disease to infect and spread via cannibalism though; that after all was just crazy, but here it was and if it were allowed to spread even further than it had been, well, he didn't want to even think of that possibility.

He watched as the small mushroom cloud engulfed the portion of I-95, where they had just been. Cars that weren't immediately vaporized under the intense heat were blown off the overpass like autumn leaves scattering in the wind. Concrete and asphalt jutted skyward in a plume of dust and debris, reminding him of the aftermath of the World Trade Center attacks. Refrigerator-sized chunks of asphalt rained down for about a quarter mile of the blast site smashing cars and careening into buildings.

Bishop saw more than one structure collapse under the manmade storm. A man from Bishop's squad came running over to his position. He came to a halt in front of his commanding officer and stood expectantly waiting for Bishop to acknowledge that he was there. Bishop ignored him for a moment, still observing the aftermath of the bridge bombing. He wondered just how the brass was going to spin this one. *Terrorists, fuel tanker explosion, solar flare*, he laughed at that last thought, knowing how the pinheads in Washington worked, he wouldn't put it passed them.

"Ahem," the agent by his side cleared his throat in an obvious attempt to wrangle his attention.

Bishop removed his face from the binoculars that he was peering through and brought his gaze upon the man that stood beside him. "What is it, Corporal?" Bishop asked with a hint of impatience entering into his voice.

"Sir," the corporal snapped off a salute. "I was given orders to monitor the GPS readings you provided on our target."

Bishop raised an eyebrow. "And what do you have to report?" Alex had quelled most of his worries about the damn case when the armored car was struck with a stinger missile, and then blown to shit when they enacted Prometheus; unfortunately, they hadn't had time to search the vehicle before the jet was radioed to be inbound.

The corporal shifted uneasily under his captain's scrutiny. "Well, sir, it's moving," the subordinate replied.

Bishop stepped toward the man, his head cocking to one side in irritation. "Moving? How in the hell is it moving?" The question was rhetorical, and Bishop really didn't expect an answer from the man. He was just the messenger, and Bishop did, in fact, want to shoot him.

"Damn it," he spat in frustration, abruptly pacing a few feet in thought fairly certain he already knew the answer to his query. The driver must have escaped. How that was remotely possible with everything they had hit it with he didn't know, other than he must have drastically underestimated the capabilities of that damn car; more importantly, he must have underestimated the resolve of that car's crew. He made a mental note to find out who exactly was operating the armored transport. *No matter*, he thought, they could track that case to the ends of the Earth so long as there was a satellite still in orbit to do so. "Did you get a location?" Bishop said calmly, steeling himself a bit.

"Yes, sir. It appeared to be about two klicks west of our current position."

Gunshots erupted sporadically to Bishop's left on the opposite side of the middle school. He keyed his lapel mic, and shouted, "Who in the hell is firing?" Bishop waited for a response and got nothing. "Who's firing?" he called again; the hiss of broken static was his only reply.

"Damn it," he hissed and grabbed his MP5 and motioned to the corporal along with several other agents that loitered around the area. "On me," he ordered and began to run toward the opposite end of the parking lot. He stopped dead in his tracks upon seeing several figures burst out from the tree line directly ahead. He could tell by their jerky movements and feral faces that they were infected with K5, the kuru variant strain, which meant Prometheus had failed to contain the outbreak, or perhaps there had been more than one release site. At the moment, it didn't matter. Bishop opened fire at the advancing men and women.

Under normal circumstances, his men would have questioned their superior officer as to why he had engaged a group of unarmed civilians, not being privy to the information that he was provided with. After what they had just faced on the bridge, they didn't query, and quickly followed suit.

Bullets tore into the tree line, striking into the advancing figures punching neat holes into chests and torsos, spraying the leaves and trees with pink and red mist. The first volley hit the group mostly center mass and had barely even slowed their pace. One man in a rock and roll T-shirt and blue jeans took a round just above his left eye socket and fell in a heap to the grass-covered ground. Bishop took note of this and quickly adjusted his aim.

"Aim for the head!" he shouted, barely audible above the sounds of gunfire and roars of battle. The tactic seemed to be working as the infected people's progress seemed to stall.

Then from behind the carnage, there were more, a lot more. Bishop stared wide-eyed in horror and amazement at the onslaught of people that began to materialize from out of the shadows of the forest. There were dozens, possibly even hundreds of them; it was hard to tell with the way the trees broke up their sight pattern. Bishop checked his rifle and then checked his spare ammunition. There was no way in hell they were going to be able to hold this position. Making a head shot was difficult enough even when firing at full auto, but to take the time to aim and fire one round at a time, which was the only way they could possibly even stand a chance at thinning this horde, they would be overrun in a matter of minutes. Alex glanced around, gauging his options. They could go for the vehicles, but then what? They would be on them before they could even get the engines started, and with this many bodies heading their way, there was no way they'd ever be able to push through them. The middle school was their best and really only option at this point. Thankfully, this morning's excursion was prior to the school's opening; and with the firefight and the threat level raised, the school was automatically closed, which is why he and his men had chosen it as a rendezvous point. Bishop shouted out, barking the order to his men. "To the school! Everyone get inside!" he admonished, sounding a general retreat.

The men quickly ceased firing at the advancing infected and turned tail. They ran through the rows of dogwoods and on to concrete sidewalks and through the brick columns that formed the entryway to the school. The men reached the door and pulled—locked—as if they expected anything else. One man panicked and kicked at the door violently with no effect.

Before Bishop could stop him, the man pulled up his weapon and fired at the locking mechanism. The bullet struck the heavy metal door, causing its brown paint to chip away and dent. The bullet ricocheted off its surface and struck the agent just above his knee. Flecks of blood sprayed outward and stained the door's silver handle. He fell to the ground, dropping his weapon, sending it clattering across the concrete sidewalk and coming to rest in the grass that lined the entryway. He clutched his wound and shouted obscenities through gritted teeth as blood seeped through his fingers.

"You dumbass, didn't you notice this door is made of metal?" Bishop shouted at his subordinate.

"Goddamn it, sir. I wasn't thinking," the agent hissed as he rocked back and forth on the ground, trying to dull the fiery pain that now resonated through his entire lower half.

Meanwhile, the infected were surrounding their position.

"Guys, set a perimeter." Bishop motioned to his remaining men, ordering them to get into a defensive position. "Jones!" Bishop shouted, looking for his second in command. A large black man jogged over to his position.

"Yeah, Cap?" the former special forces soldier said with a slight Mississippian drawl.

"Get us in that door," Bishop stated, needlessly pointing past the injured agent laying abreast the door frame.

"You got it, sir," Jones answered almost casually.

Jones walked across the forecourt and inspected the door and its lock, looking for the weakest entry point. He could possibly pick the lock, but judging the distance of the advancing horde of drooling attackers, he didn't think that they'd have that kind of time. With the threat of children being abducted or just plain massacred by crazed armed gunmen entering the premises, the school had really upped the ante on security. The red brick building held rows upon rows of tempered security glass, the kind with the waffled wire pattern running through its center. Jones had often wondered what would happen if he pushed a man's face through that glass. *Would it cube him?* He thought and chuckled in spite of himself. He wondered if he could test the theory with one of the advancing infected, but then decided against it, not really wanting to get that close. Those people looked really fucked up.

"Gonna have to blow it, Cap," Jones said flatly, a slight grin crossing over his features.

"Do what you gotta do. Just get us the fuck out of here!" Bishop shouted to be heard above the gunfight that raged on as his men engaged the enemy.

"You, uh, might wanna move Albert Einstein here unless you want that leg amputated explosively. How 'bout it, Simmons?" Jones quipped.

"Go to hell," Simmons hissed while Bishop grabbed the man under his arms and began to drag him away from the door.

Jones snickered as he lifted a Velcro strap on his body armor and retrieved a small foil packet from within the recesses of his vest. He peeled off a thin layer of film and began to manipulate the small amount of plastic explosive within.

"Gonna need a few minutes here, boss," Jones said calmly while studying the lock intently.

"Make it quick, Jones, or we're all dead," Bishop said as he propped the injured Simmons up against a concrete and wooden bench that lined the forecourt's entryway. "Can you still shoot, Simmons?" Bishop asked.

"I think so, sir," the injured man replied. Bishop retrieved his weapon from the grass in which it had landed and handed it to him.

Simmons reluctantly took it and propped himself up giving off a grunt, an expression of pain moving across his pale face as he took aim downrange at their attackers.

Bishop did a quick head count on his men. There were eight of them, eight out of twenty, he realized, not knowing exactly what had befallen the rest of his squad whom he had ordered to set up perimeter around the school. The fact no one had answered his call, and the gunfire from that side of the school had since ceased, led him to assume the worst. Bishop took up position next to Simmons, kneeling and setting his elbows atop the bench to help steady his aim. He opened fire.

His first target appeared to be a half-naked homeless man. Torn pants drooped around his dirty ankles; his penis, flopping around with each stumbling step. He looked as if he had bought it while trying to take a piss. A large neck wound shown beneath his long graying beard.

"Ouch," Bishop muttered and shot the man in his scraggly face. He acquired another sight picture and fired, bringing another infected down, and then another. Bodies began to pile up in front of the forecourt, creating an almost symmetrical half circle, and yet they still gained ground. "Anytime now, Jones!" Bishop shouted.

"Another sec, Cap," Jones replied as he spooled out wire away from the door. "Cover your ears, bitches!" Jones shouted almost gleefully and depressed the trigger, activating the small detonator.

A loud bang sounded as a piece of the locking mechanism broke away and whizzed through the air, buzzing by Bishop's neatly trimmed hair. Bishop recoiled instinctively, thrusting his hand up to his head.

"Holy fuck, Jones! Check your shit!" he shouted, momentarily losing his usually cool demeanor.

"I said cover your ears, Cap. No worries, though. It didn't mess up your hair." Jones gave Bishop a sideways grin. The door hung open on undamaged hinges. The door's lock was all but obliterated by the small Semtex breach charge Jones had used to open it.

Bishop glanced over at the approaching infected, now merely yards from their position. "Everyone, get inside!" he ordered.

The men started to pullback from their cover positions, operating in tandem; one group would retreat while the other covered. They operated smoothly and with precision.

Bishop motioned over to Jones to get his attention. "Grab his legs," he said, motioning to Simmons who still sat beside the bench, firing in a futile effort to stem the tide that threatened to wash over them. Bishop shouted down to Simmons, "Cease-fire! We're getting out of here!" Simmons either didn't hear him, or he simply ignored the order altogether. "I said, *cease-fire*, damn it!" Simmons risked him a glance.

"I can't, sir. They're right on top of us," his voice quivered.

"You have to. Don't worry, troop, we've got ya," Bishop said with confidence.

Simmons ceased-fire and braced himself as Bishop and Jones gathered the man up in their arms and hoisted him up into the air.

Bishop's squad formed a protective barrier around the trio as they retreated toward the open door. Men fired volley after volley of shots, doing their best to hold off the infected that were now merely feet from their targets.

Jones and Bishop struggled to carry Simmons in through the doorway just as a member of their squad was caught from behind. A scream of panic and pain cried out as an infected grabbed him by the back of his head and sank his teeth into his tender flesh. Arterial spray jutted out from the man's neck as the thin layer of flesh surrounding his windpipe and arteries were torn away; his compatriots turned and fired on the attacker. The infected went down in a heap, taking their squad member with him. There wasn't time to check on their compatriot. The man was finished, and his squad knew it. The infected were on them, so close they could almost feel their hot, fevered breath on their faces. They began stumbling into their ranks threatening to overrun them.

The remainder of the men ran for all they were worth, bursting through the school's entrance, managing to shake its sturdy frame and pulled the door quickly shut just as the throng slammed into the door. The men held the door tightly as the infected pounded on it in frustration, nearly knocking the three men who fought against the tide to the flat tiled floor. Bishop and Jones set Simmons down next to a potted rubber tree, off to the side of a small display case that appeared to house assorted science fair projects, no doubt the best the school had to offer.

Simmons eyed the detritus as the hammering of the infected became more belligerent; he ignored the noise and the commotion and tried his best to fight back the pain radiating in his leg. "I'm such a fool," Simmons whispered to himself, shaking his head listlessly, finding it almost hard to believe he'd done something that stupid. His squad was never going to let him live this down.

Bishop looked around frantically, trying to find something, anything—to bar the entryway. "Hurry, we've got to find something to keep this damn door shut!" Bishop shouted to Jones.

"Already on it, Cap!" Jones shot back, trying his best to be heard above the din. At that, Jones took off down the dimly lit corridor and darted into an open doorway, Bishop following him with his gaze.

A few seconds passed, and Jones poked his head out and waved Bishop over. Jones cupped his hand to his mouth and yelled, "Over here! Give me a hand!"

Alex complied and ran over to the man. They stood in front of what appeared to be the principal's office.

"In here, boss." Jones pointed over to a heavy-looking receptionist's desk that set facing the doorway.

The two men jogged over to the desk, each of them taking up position on opposite ends.

"Ready?" Jones asked.

They both grasped the ends of the desk. "One, two, lift!" The men grunted with exertion and hefted the monstrosity a few inches off the floor. With as much expedience as they could muster, they began to carry it toward the office door.

Bishop, who had his back to the doorway, turned slightly, glancing over his shoulder. "Is this fucking thing going to fit?" he said, eyeing the opening.

"That's funny, Cap. My last girl friend said the same exact thing about me," he joked with a grunt.

Bishop shook his head, his breathing growing heavy with the strain. "Tilt it to the side, or we're gonna crush my damn hands."

Jones smiled and did as instructed.

They managed to squeeze the large desk through the opening and, with effort, carried it down the length of the hallway.

They positioned the desk in front of the main entryway, pushing it up as close to the door as they could get without pinning the men who were holding it in place. Bishop and Jones stood behind the desk, ready to heft it into place.

"On my order, get ready to move. Got it?" the captain said to his men.

The men nodded in understanding, flashing each other nervous glances.

"Now!" Bishop screamed and slid the desk forward.

The men dove out of the way as the desk slammed into the front door. An infected hand managed to penetrate through the momentary crack and became lodged in between the double doors. The hand wriggled frantically in place, trying its damnedest to gain purchase on something.

Bishop and Jones didn't give it a chance as they threw all of their combined weight behind the desk. The sounds of snapping and grinding bones reverberated through the small expanse, causing the two men to grimace in disgust. After one final shove, the hand sheered away from its owner and fell atop of the desk, twitching and writhing on its surface like a headless viper, its final nerve impulses firing and evaporating away without stimuli to control the movement. The twitching receded after a moment, finally bringing it to rest across the desk's polished surface.

Bishop stared at the dead hand in disbelief, bloated veins and arteries hung limply, giving way to waxy pale skin. Deep crimson blood stained with spidery tendrils of orange seeped from the severed hand and soaked into the porous wood. He leaned hard against the desk and slowly exhaled; he pushed himself off and turned his gaze to focus on his men, the beasts outside still relentlessly wailing on the door.

"This isn't gonna hold 'em long, guys. We need to find whatever we can and put it in front of this door." He paused. "Jones, I need you to round up and inventory the remaining ammunition. Redistribute it accordingly. We have no idea of knowing if this building is in fact completely empty or not, so watch your asses."

The men nodded in understanding, and Jones stepped over to them.

"Yo! You heard the man, people. Ante up!" the big man said loudly, holding out an open black backpack in front of the men, waiting impatiently as each of the five agents emptied their weapons and spare magazines into the open pack.

Jones carried the less-than-heavy pack over to a row of cushioned chairs that lined the wall and set it down; the magazines and loose rounds jingled as they shifted position in the pack. He eyed Bishop dubiously and emptied his own ammunition in to the pot.

"You too, Cap. Let's have it." He grinned with pearly white teeth that stood out in complete contrast to the dark-skinned man's features.

Bishop stepped over and dropped his own share into the bag.

Nodding, Jones knelt down beside the chair and began removing the rounds and placing them one by one on the floor. After all sixty-three rounds were placed along the tile in neat rows, Jones stared at them incredulously.

"You gotta be fucking kidding me," the big man said, looking to each man within their group. "All right, who's holding out?" The men glanced at each other, uneasily shaking their heads. "Really, well, goddamn," he exasperated, shaking his large head. Each of his squad had left Homeland's base of operations at BWI this morning carrying at least one hundred rounds of 9 mm ammunition a piece, normally way more than they would ever need. Unfortunately, he mused, most had probably been stored within the group's SUVs.

Jones split the cache of ammo six ways and divvied it out to the men. "Don't use 'em unless you have to. We need to make this shit count," he said as he passed out the rounds. Each man nodded in turn and began refilling their magazines. That task being fulfilled, Bishop split the men in to three groups of two.

"First things first, we need to put some weight on this door." He pointed needlessly at the shuddering door frame for emphasis. "Check the surrounding rooms and look for anything we can use— filing cabinets, chairs, copiers. Hell, I don't care if it's the damned soda machine out of the teachers' lounge. We need to buy some time till I can radio the cavalry and get us the hell out of here." Being that his corporal had informed him that their target was still at large, he wasn't quite certain if the cavalry would indeed be coming; unfortunately, the man he had tasked with the job of tracking the case was one of the men that were killed during the fight with the infected only moments ago. So, the only information that he had to go on was that the case they were seeking was roughly two miles to the west of their location, and given their current situation, getting there to complete their mission was going to be easier said than done.

Bishop needed to get some answers. He had read the report on the K5 virus and knew it to be a bioweapon of sorts, developed in some other country he believed, but that was about as far down the rabbit hole he could go. Everything else was mere speculation on his part. On the other hand, Hammond, if he could get off his lazy drunken ass and be bothered enough, had the clearance level to get the entire story, which could be why he was so gung ho about retrieving the files in that case.

The men separated into their respective pairings and set off into the dimly lit recesses of the school.

Bishop and Jones walked down the corridor to their left, passing by the principal's office from where they had retrieved the receptionist desk. The desk at the moment seemed to be holding, but Alex didn't want to count on it against the pressure being exerted by all the bodies on the other side of the doorway. As they walked, Bishop and Jones flitted glances into open classroom doorways, first checking for danger, second looking for objects they could add to their makeshift barricade.

Jets of pale light filtered in through semi-closed vertical blinds, illuminating bits of dust particulate that hung in the air, giving the classrooms an ominous appearance. The pounding on the main entryway became slightly muffled as the duo stepped into one of the adjoining rooms.

Bishop studied the student's desks, taking notice that most were covered in childish scrawls in ink, with such phrases as "Justin was here 98," and "Keith rocks." Bishop scanned around the cluttered room, taking in everything in an instant, bulletin boards covered in brightly colored construction paper shapes hung on egg-yolk-stained cinderblock walls that oddly reminded him of egg salad. Standing there, the room brought back memories of his misbegotten childhood, sitting at his desk as a preteen child as a hook-nosed, crater-faced Ms. Rice droned on about something he couldn't remember at this point in his life. As he recollected his youth, he thought the one thing he missed about school was the extra sleep.

Bishop dismissed the thoughts and got back to the task at hand. Stepping around the meager children's desks, he located a heavy-looking HON file cabinet that set in the corner of the room. Its black-painted surface dented and scratched from years and years of constant abuse. A white-crocheted doily set atop the cabinet and held a potted fern. Bishop motioned over to Jones, who was curiously rifling through the teacher's belongings.

"Jones!" Bishop snapped, bringing the big man out of his stupor; he brought his attention to Alex. "This ought to do." Bishop smacked the side of the heavy cabinet. "Here help me clear this junk off, and we can drag it out of here." Bishop heard a slight noise behind him, an almost imperceptible, shuffling sound.

He turned, half expecting to see one of his men, when suddenly a figure lunged. The infected was too quick for him to react, and something that felt like a broom handle connected with his forehead caused his neck to snap backward. He fell into the filing cabinet, sending the potted fern sailing down onto the man-thing that pounced on top of him like a feral cat. Bishop thrust his hands outward, trying to block the man's snarling mouth before it gained purchase on the exposed flesh of his face.

Jones reacted without thought and savagely kicked the man in his face, striking Bishop's outstretched hand in the process in the heat of the moment.

Bishop didn't even notice as three of his finger bones fractured under the assault.

The figure dressed in dark-blue custodian's overalls lost his grip on Alex and fell backward onto his ass. Blood seeped from an open gash on the custodian's face and absorbed into his uniform's fabric. Greasy, sweat-covered dark hair hung limply over insane bloodshot eyes. The man snarled, exposing tar-stained teeth as he lunged for Bishop once more.

Bishop kicked his foot out and sideswiped the man in the temple, bringing his head to the floor trapped between his two legs. Alex contracted his leg muscles and applied pressure on the thing's neck and twisted his hips, causing the custodian's neck to snap.

Its flailing arms and floundering legs fell to the floor and ceased to move all the while his mouth continued to open and shut as if still trying to bite; his eye's stared angrily, flitting back and forth between Alex and Jones, seemingly trying to figure out a way to get to them.

"Holy Mary, Mother of Christ," Bishop said as he released the snapping head from his legs' grasp and pushed its still body away. He forced himself to his feet and stared at the thing, in wonder. He had broken the thing's neck, completely severing the spinal cord. He felt it pop like a chicken leg being separated from the thigh.

"How the hell is that thing still moving?" Jones said incredulously, cocking an eyebrow.

"I don't know," Bishop replied as he walked over to the figure and raised his boot in the air, bringing it down hard on the flailing thing's writhing head.

Its skull ground into the tile floor and split under the pressure of Alex's heel; pink brain matter seeped out of the opening and spilled onto the floor followed by what looked like a mixture of blood and pus.

"What the hell is this shit?" Bishop breathed and gazed down at the infected. The beast's head spread out across the tiled floor like a cracked egg.

As far as Bishop knew, the bioweapon that he was informed of was nothing more than some kind of weaponized hemorrhagic illness that terrorists had somehow managed to get a hold of, but this? This he couldn't even comprehend; these assholes didn't just get sick and die like one would expect. As a matter of fact, it seemed almost as if the disease actually increased their strength while decreasing their vulnerability.

Footsteps came pounding down the hall way in unison; both Jones and Bishop raised up their MP5s ready to gun down whatever fiends came rushing through the classroom door. Two men appeared through the portal, guns raised at the ready as well. Bishop and Jones sighed, a measure of relief flooding over their adrenaline-flooded bodies.

"Son-of-a-bitch!" Bishop exclaimed, lowering his weapon slightly. "We thought you were more of those things." Bishop exhaled not realizing he had been holding his breath and pointed over to the massacred body of the janitor lying on the floor.

"Where in the hell did he come from?" one of the men asked as he glanced nervously around the room as if waiting for the boogeyman to jump out, which, in this case, wasn't too farfetched. Bishop shrugged.

"Must have been in here cleaning before the alert went out. Hopefully he's the only one," he said but doubted his own statement.

Jones stepped over to the captain. "You all right, Cap? Son-of-a-bitch clocked you pretty good. Oh, and I think your hand is broken," Jones said with a cringe, noticing the odd way several of the finger bones on his left hand were angled.

Bishop lifted his own hand up to his face and studied it. "So it would seem," he said coolly, eyeing the big man, remembering that it was his boot that had struck his appendage. As if on cue, pain began to radiate up his disjointed fingers and consume his whole left arm. Bishop, however, did nothing to show any discomfort; he was just glad that he was right handed.

"We should probably set that, Cap," Jones said, nodding to his injured hand.

"Yeah, yeah, after we get this stuff in front of that door. I don't want any more surprises. Then we can worry about my hand." The big man nodded in agreement and set about with the other two men to drag the filing cabinet out into the hallway.

After making several more trips to various classrooms surrounding the one-story middle school without incident, the men had discovered just about every classroom housed a similar filing cabinet. After a lot of dragging, grunting, and swearing, the men had built quite an impressive-looking barricade in front of the school's lobby doors that looked similar to the first real world game of Tetris.

Bishop was impressed. The infected outside who were still attempting to break the door from its moorings were nearly imperceptible under the stack of cabinets and desks that lined the entryway.

Bishop looked to the men. "You, um, Jackson?" he pointed to a rather short, scrawny light-skinned black man who seemed to hold a grimace permanently etched on his face, tattoos lined his muscled arms and neck.

"Yeah, Captain?" he replied in the typical laid-back Baltimorean accent.

"I need someone to establish comms with command. You think you can handle that?" Bishop raised an eyebrow, knowing full well that he could.

"Yeah, man, I can do that. Might have to get up to the roof, though. I don't know about you all, but I ain't gettin' a signal for shit," he said, looking down at the signal indicator on his radio gear.

"Do what you gotta do, and consider yourself promoted to comms officer. Take Scotty here with you." Bishop pointed over to a burly red-haired bruiser of a man named Ian McBride; he had gotten the nickname Scotty when his unit had found out that his family had immigrated to the United States from Scotland some seventy years ago. He was as full red-blooded American as they came, though, down to his deep Southern draw and the beat-up four-by-four Ford trucks that he drove. "That goes for everyone. No one goes anywhere alone from this point on, got it? Everyone needs to stay on point and watch each other's asses. Am I clear?" Bishop instructed.

Everyone who remained in the small detachment acknowledged his order with a simple "Hooah," being most of his men were former military, primarily Army special forces or ex-Navy Seals. Bishop had become accustomed to the reply.

"While Scotty and Jackson set up communications, the rest of us are going to search this school top to bottom, make sure we're not in for any more surprises. If you get into trouble, don't play hero. Shout. This school's not that big. I'm sure we'll be able to hear each other."

The men nodded in turn and broke up into their respective teams, and began to head out into the school to perform the tasks they were assigned.

CHAPTER 13

Consciousness flirted with me like a lost lover. Blurry shapes began to emerge only to seem to evaporate in to the void once more. My eyes watered and blinked rapidly as they fought to stave off the assault of noxious smoke and gasses that flitted around the cab of the police cruiser and entered my shallow breathing form. Muffled sounds entered into my nightmarish world barely audible over the roar of the blood coursing through my ears. All at once, reality seemed to crash in. I awoke with a start and gasped, sucking in deep breaths of lung-burning fumes. I coughed harshly to the point of near vomiting. It was at this point I realized I hung upside down, still adhered to the passenger seat by the thin strip of nylon seat belt. Its thin edge dug into my side, restricting my breathing.

I felt myself begin to panic and reached my hands up to the harness and fumbled around in the gloom, trying to locate the release mechanism. My hands trembled as I grasped onto the latch and depressed the button. I fell, hard, landing awkwardly onto of the cruiser's broken windshield. Bits of shattered safety glass crumpled as I maneuvered myself to my hands and knees. I looked around the car, thanking God or any other deity that was listening for the fact that these cars were equipped with roll cages. I coughed hard again, raising my hand in front of my face almost instinctually as I tried to stifle the burst. The smoke was making it near impossible to see, but I was still close enough to make out the form of the police officer. Richard hung aloft in a similar position to myself. He, however, remained unconscious; at least I hoped he was just unconscious. I outstretched a bloodied hand and placed two fingers to the side of his neck to check for a pulse. I didn't really know exactly what I was doing, but it was something I had seen done in just about every single crime drama ever produced on television, so I figured there had to be something to it. I was somewhat surprised when immediately I felt the steady thrum of the man's heartbeat in his neck.

"Thank God for late night episodes of *Criminal Minds* and *ER*," I whispered to the unconscious man.

After several moments of examining the man, I did not see any obvious signs of injury aside from some cuts and bruises. I quickly glanced myself over and discovered much of the same; a wound on my forehead bled like a stuck pig, dribbling salty blood into my eyes, nose, and mouth. If I had to make a wager, I figured if anyone had seen me at the moment, they would probably figure me for one of those crazy assholes running around outside.

Those crazy assholes, I repeated slowly in my thoughts. I had all but forgotten about those people, those things outside. The thought spurred me into action. I knew if we sat around in this burning wreck of a car for too long, the cop and I would be done for. I crawled up close to the upside-down man looking at him almost nose to nose and began slapping him gently in the face.

"Rich, hey, Rich, wake up, dumb fuck. Rich, Richard. Hey, pig!" I shouted the last part, sending droplets of blood and spittle into the man's face as he shot awake and immediately threw his arm up to his waist, reaching for his gun. I ducked back and threw my hands up in a placating gesture. "Hey, man, relax. It's just me, just ol' Kyle." I did my best to smile; the whites of my teeth were covered in blood along with most of my face, making the act look more menacing than cheerful.

"Aw, fuck," Richard groaned and touched his hand to his now-throbbing head.

"Yeah, I pretty much had the same reaction. Here, let me help you get out of that thing." I reached up to unlatch his seat belt, and Richard batted my hand away.

"Get the fuck off," he spat. "I'll get it," he said, wincing in pain.

"Not a morning person either, I take?" I said lightheartedly.

He ignored me and undid his seat belt, falling to the windshield in similar fashion as I had previously. He clutched his ribs as he landed, screwing up his face, and letting out a litany of swear words that would make my grandmother blush from her grave.

"You okay, tough guy?" I said as he did his best to roll over onto his side, wincing in pain as he did.

"Yeah, think I cracked some ribs is all." He took in a deep shuddering breath.

"Damn, I broke a nail," I quipped, trying to inject some levity into the situation.

Richard grunted in way of reply and looked around the cab. "We need to get out of here," he stated flatly. I wholeheartedly agreed. I reached down and checked to make certain my sidearm was still attached to my hip, and then checked to make certain my speed loaders were still in place. All was accounted for, and I did my best to take a gander outside of the window to gauge what we might be up against.

"Can't see shit," I said, wiping at a small section of unshattered glass with my hand. I cocked my head to the side like a dog in an attempt to hear anything that might be lurking outside. All I could hear was a series of creaks and pops as heat from the blast ebbed away from the vehicle's surface.

Although I could not see outside, I sensed a foreboding of what we would perceive once we exited the police cruiser. The fact that there were people still trapped in their cars as crazies and Homeland agents alike battled out in the street, I knew that the outside of this wagon would be the scene of widespread carnage like one would see only in times of war, or at least in the movies. I wondered briefly if exiting the charred remains of the vehicle at this point was our best course of action. *Perhaps we should take a moment to formulate a plan.* That thought quickly receded as memories of my wife and children entered my mind. They were, by far, my only priority. I had to wonder once again if this, this affliction, had struck home as well.

A crack and crunching sound wrenched me from my revelry as Officer Richard struck the windshield with both boots, trying to knock it free from its resting place. He coughed violently, clutching his side as he completed the motion; a small trickle of blood escaped his lips and dribbled onto his chin.

"Damn, dude," I exasperated. "I think you better take it easy. I'm pretty sure your injuries are worse than you think," I said as I eyed the bit of crimson spittle on his lips, a look of concern crossing my features.

"I bit my fucking tongue. I'm fine. Let's . . . let's just get this damn window off so we can get the hell out of this death trap."

I nodded, even though I seriously doubted that it was even perceived in the smoke-infested car.

I pivoted myself into position, lying on my back, and raised both legs, bringing my knees up toward my chest.

"On three, one, two, and three!" Both of us launched our assault on the windshield at the same time, the combined force of the attack sending the fragmented glass hurling out into the dead space in front of the car. It landed with a grinding *thunk* as it struck the scorched asphalt, skittering to a stop at the base of a melted median. I scrambled my way around until I was facing the open portal and carefully, slowly inched my head out of the opening, doing my best to listen for any signs of trouble. I heard nothing.

"I'm going to check it out. You stay here. I'll let you know if it's safe." Richard started to protest, as I have come to learn in the short time I had known him was his usual way, but I held a finger to my lips, essentially shutting him up. "Shhh." I dragged the rest of myself out of the open window, gingerly avoiding bits of glass and rubble. I spotted a rusted nail along the roadway and thought what a screwed-up thing it would be to cut myself on it and die of tetanus after living through all of this. I avoided it, getting to my feet, crouching low to keep from braining myself on the crumpled hood of the car as I duck-walked out into the open air.

My imagination could not have prepared me for what lie outside of the wreckage. The police cruiser sat astride the edge of what could only be described as a small crater. From the looks of it, it had to be at least a half a mile wide. Smoke flitted up from charred rock and sizzled as the storm's last remaining droplets of rain pelted its nearly molten surface. The pit itself, however, was not that deep, perhaps only twelve or fifteen feet, high enough, however, that I would not want to take a fall down its jagged sides.

The bridge on the interstate where we had resided was all but destroyed; all that remained of it was a small slip road that winded uphill toward a series of train tracks in the distance. I heard a noise and spun around, hand on my sidearm ready to draw, only to see

Richard clambering out from underneath the wreckage. I relaxed a bit and held my hand out, grasping a hold of his wrist, helping him to his feet. He grudgingly accepted it, although I had a sense he was not used to receiving aid from anyone lest it be a lowly security guard. *If he only knew*, I mused.

"What on God's green Earth happened?" he said in utter amazement as he gazed upon the destruction.

"Fuel air bomb," I stated matter-of-factly.

He eyed me quizzically. "You know this how?" He cocked an injured eyebrow.

I smirked. "I know a little bit about a little bit," was all I would reply.

Thankfully letting the matter drop, we turned to observe our only escape route, unless we had the intention of walking across semi-molten asphalt, which we did not. We began to walk; well, okay, it was more like a spirited limp down what was left of the open roadway. What was left of the remaining cars on the roadway looked more like some kind of crap modern art you would see located outside of a random skyscraper in downtown Baltimore than the remnants of a Honda Accord or a Nissan Pathfinder. I wondered how many commuters or mothers taking their kids to school were on the interstate this morning when those assholes decided to bomb the shit out of it. I sighed, shaking the thought out of my head, and reached my hands up to rub my temples. I winced as my fingertips grazed the abrasions on my forehead. I looked over at the exhausted-looking police officer.

"So what now?" I asked.

"We need to get down to the station," he said, looking around from side to side, still clutching his rib cage.

"Dumb question, why the police station?" I asked.

"The best thing we can do right now is get help. Besides, I need to get these ribs wrapped, and if anything else, there are a hell of a lot more guns and ammo there than what you and I are carrying."

I nodded my head, all the while thinking that I wanted, no, *needed* to get home. Alas, I was a good thirty miles from there. If what I had seen earlier this morning was any indication of how things were going down all over, I was going to need some type of ride; well, mainly being the fact that mine was blown to shit by our illustrious government, but I digress. It was what it was.

"Okay, about how far are we from your station?" I asked, having a sneaking suspicion I knew exactly where it was.

"BWI, a few miles that way," he said and pointed in the vague direction of the airport.

"Are you flipping insane?" I chastised. "If you hadn't noticed, the Department of Homeland Security has a hard-on for us."

"Correction," Richard interjected, raising an eyebrow, "they have a hard-on for you."

I sighed.

"It's no matter. I want to head to our substation located on Fuel Farm Road. There we have more cars, weapons, ammo, and perhaps we can get a read on just what the fuck is going on. You know where I'm talking about?"

I nodded, and in fact, I knew it well, being that I passed the damn road every single waking day. The road itself got its name for obvious reasons. The area where it was located housed several massive fuel tanks that held, of course, you guessed it, jet fuel. I wondered for a moment if that's where the powers that be procured the fuel for the bomb they had just dropped on hundreds of innocent people.

There was only one major flaw in his plan: the bridge leading toward that particular area of the airport was just blown to smithereens, which meant, of course, we were going to have to backtrack to the side roads and make our way around, which was going to add more time than I wanted to give. Personally, I just wanted to start hoofing it home; but I knew on foot the thirty mile-or-so trek might as well have been a hundred, especially if whatever this was affecting the townsfolk here had spread beyond the roadway we currently occupied. As much as I hated to admit it, I understood why Homeland had launched the attack. In my previous experience with the military, I had seen such atrocities take place in the jungles of the Congo while squaring off against militant warlords who threatened to overthrow and destabilize the region. My unit was sent in to gather covert intelligence on their troop movements and assist the local government in quelling such uprisings.

There were, quite frankly, several times my team and I could have taken down several of the power players who ran these militant groups; however, our hands were completely tied with bureaucratic red tape. I hated that shit, but alas, we were on strict orders to remain eyes only lest we inadvertently cause some kind of international incident, even though we resided there for the simple reason that their own government had requested it, but I guessed that the African government feared looking weak among their own people when Americans were doing their dirty work.

During one of our reconnaissance missions into the jungle, we witnessed a small village become afflicted with one of Africa's infamous strains of Ebola. As men and women fell ill, surrounding tribes did their best to quarantine and isolate themselves from it; but as the disease spread and killed with quick and cold precision, the remaining unafflicted peoples took action, burning homes and even entire villages in an effort to contain the deadly infection. We wanted desperately to intervene; however, all we could do was sit idly by and watch as the chaos unraveled.

The area that Richard and I walked was eerily silent; come to think of it, I don't even think we heard so much as a lonely cricket chirping in the distance. That thought made me once again think of my wife. Why, you ask? Well, I'll tell ya. My wife, the little four-foot-nine powerhouse that she is, was deathly afraid of crickets, not grass hoppers, not spiders or snakes. Her biggest fear in this entire Earth, aside from being abducted by aliens and shot face-first into the red planet, was crickets. I know it's irrational, but it's true. She grew up in an area around Georgia where to hear her speak of the insect, they were the size of Mac Trucks, sported fangs, and carried 9 mm handguns. Anytime we were outside tending the lawn or weeding the garden during the summer months, I would give it almost exactly ten minutes before I would have to go and rescue her from the evil little buggers.

The sounds of gunfire erupted in the distance, bringing me back to the here and now, snapping my mind to the present like a taut rubber band. I exchanged knowing glances with Richard. If there was gunfire then almost certainly, Homeland's attempt to quell this disease had most likely failed. Unless we were lucky, and it was just your good old-fashioned, run-of-the-mill, Baltimore-style violence.

As if we had been choreographed by Paula Abdul herself, Richard and I simultaneously checked our sidearms. We continued to walk the remainder of the devastated roadway, navigating our way around charred hubcaps and fenders, and headed for the adjoining town surrounding the airport and directly toward the sounds of battle. I wasn't sure what would be worse, infected crazed people, or another run-in with Homeland. At least as far as I could tell, the infected didn't shoot rockets at you. I shrugged; whatever was going on lay directly in our path, and we would have to deal with it one way or another.

CHAPTER 14

Marvin stepped through a door leading into the gas station's adjoining garage. The smell of old oil and gasoline flooded Marvin's olfactory senses, bringing back memories of sitting in his father's garage as a kid. The room was small, only set up to handle at most four vehicles at a time from the looks of things. Dim light permeated the area through windows situated in heavy garage doors, illuminating an old dusty blue Dodge Charger. The car set atop a hydraulic lift in the garage's center. It appeared as if some bodywork was being done to the old car as patches of primer were visible among the remnants of blue paint.

Marvin swept the area with the shotgun, making certain that nothing was going to come barreling out at him from behind one of the large, red and silver tool boxes that lined the gray cement block walls. When all seemed normal—well, as normal as things were going to get in this situation—Marvin turned and shut the entryway to the storefront. Securing the door, Marvin searched the area until he found a workbench residing in the far corner of the shop.

He approached the bench and set the strange case atop its surface, knocking over coffee cans full of loose nuts and bolts, sending the fragments of metal scattering to the cement floor. Ignoring the noise, he leaned his shotgun against the workbench's side and studied the dented case's exterior, trying to figure the best way to gain access to it. Looking it over, he noticed the hinges that held the lid in place were recessed and impossible to jimmy open by simply popping out the pins that held them together. *That would be too easy*, he thought, scowling. However, the small cracked LCD screen had just enough space along the panel's edge to perhaps fit a small tool into and pry it away from the case's bent edge. At least the rocket that struck his truck had been good for something; Marvin doubted seriously that if it wasn't for the humongous dent on the top of the case, the panel would have absolutely no flaws in its security, period.

Marvin stepped off to the side and began to rummage through one of the toolboxes until he found a small flathead screwdriver and a pair of needle-nosed pliers. Smiling, he stepped back over to the workbench. Leaning down, he inserted the edge of the screwdriver between the infinitesimal gaps surrounding the LCD screen and gently worked it up and down, and side to side, until he felt the satisfying pop of the panel's retaining pins. Using the pliers to grasp the LCD's edge, he gingerly pulled it away from its housing, taking care not to sever any of the leads that connected it to the circuit board that lie beneath.

Marvin wiped sweat away from his forehead that threatened to run into his eyes. He smiled, reminded of the days he used to disarm bombs in very much the same way he was working this lock. Of course, the technology had changed, a lot, but the premise was still pretty much the same. From what he figured, if he could locate the panel's main power supply, the one that powered the LCD and the biometric scanner, and somehow manage to overload it even if for the slightest of moments, it may just complete the circuit in similar fashion as if someone had actually placed the correct appendage to it. It was only a theory, of course, but it was all he had lest he wanted to try drilling into it for several hours, which, by the sounds of things in the store, he didn't figure he'd have that long. The sounds of the infected's assault on the door seemed to intensify as if more were drawn to the noise that their brethren were making.

Marvin followed the lead wires until he located what he perceived to be the main power conduit. *Red was always the obvious choice on these types of things*, he thought, drawing on his demolitions experience. Using the needle-nosed pliers he had obtained, he snipped the red wire in twain. He looked around the workshop until he found a small length of generic speaker wire; this he would use to connect to some sort of power source. He would need to find a way to regulate the incoming power, or he could risk completely frying the circuit, which would then render the mechanism useless. He would also, in turn, have to connect the thumbprint scanner into the circuit, crossing the leads to complete the connection. He wasn't quite certain if this would work, but he figured, *what the hell*? If anything else, he could always resort to plan B and simply nail the thing with a hammer until he could pry the fucking thing open.

Marvin used the pliers to strip away the plastic sheath on the speaker wire, exposing the copper beneath. He found what looked like a charging cord for an electric drill and snipped the head of the cable off, figuring the adapter at least would regulate the power to a low nine volts, a bit less than if he were to plug this thing up to a car battery. Marvin snipped the lead connecting the biometric scanner, spliced the cabling into the speaker wire, and subsequently infused that wire with the power relay and the adapter cord.

Marvin stood poised to plug the adapter in when a loud crash reverberated from within the store. *The bastards managed to get in*, he thought. The sounds of shelving units and product hitting the floor as the mass of crazed people stumbling about could be heard in the relative quiet of the garage bay. Marvin looked down and made certain his shotgun was still within easy reach; he'd been moving around the workshop so much he had all but forgotten where he'd set it exactly. It rested right where he had left it, propped against the workbench that he now used.

Marvin jumped as the first of the infected slammed into the door, as if they could sense him somehow inside of the room. *That's not possible*, Marvin thought. Had they seen him come in here? No, they couldn't have between all the crap in front of the door. There was absolutely no way they could have known where he'd disappeared to. The pounding on the garage door's entryway grew more and more insistent as if more of the infected were following suit. Figuring he didn't have much time, Marvin thrust the power adapter into the wall. Sparks showered the concrete floor, and the smell of burning metal fumed into the air with slight wisps of white smoke. To Marvin's surprise, the locking mechanism actually disengaged, and the case popped open. "Holy shit, it actually worked," Marvin said with amazement. He quickly yanked the power cord from the wall plate as the silicon circuit board began to sizzle, as if about to catch fire.

The door to the garage began to shudder with each resounding impact as the infected waged war upon it. The frame began to splinter under their assault.

Marvin jerked open the case. These assholes would be through the door any minute now, and he wanted to get this shit done and bug out before they made it inside. He cast a quick glance over at the garage's bay doors and hoped against hope these things had not managed to figure out that it led in here. Marvin peered into the case, a simple manila folder set in its center, stamped with the seal of Homeland Security and marked "Classified" in large red print across its surface. A small flash drive set off to one corner of the case secured in by what looked like a Velcro strap. Marvin threw off his backpack, let it rest atop the workbench, and fumbled with the zipper. He opened the bag, then snatched up the flash drive and the contents of the folder, and tossed them unceremoniously inside and resecured the zipper. He didn't have the time to look at the folder's contents here; he wondered briefly if he even should, then shook off the thought, knowing that he damn well should look at it being they just blew up half a city block trying to get at it.

Marvin shouldered the pack, grabbed his shotgun, and moved his way across the garage to the bay doors. He cringed as he pushed the up button located on the wall next to the door. The bay doors slowly began to rise; the sound of the garage door opener and chain seemed to scream in his ears as the infected on the other side of the door worked themselves into a frenzy, like piranha's sensing prey as it entered the water. As soon as the door was at an acceptable level, Marvin quickly clambered underneath just as the doorway adjoining the storefront burst outward. About six infected stumbled over one another into the garage at first, looking lost and confused, until one spotted Marvin making his getaway, and then the six men and women seemed to polarize onto his position.

"Shit," Marvin spat and racked a round into the chamber of his newly acquired, albeit antique-looking, Winchester shotgun. He pumped his aching legs as fast as they could take him and turned, opening fire on the first of the infected to stumble through the doorway. The scattershot caught the man dressed in a ball cap and torn Orioles baseball shirt center mass, virtually blowing apart his ribcage—sending bits of bone and deep viscous red blood spraying into the mass of infected beyond. Amazingly, the son-of-a-bitch kept coming. Marvin racked the slide again, ejecting the plastic shell and sent it clattering to the gray asphalt while simultaneously loading another round.

He adjusted his aim slightly and pulled the trigger once more. This round went a little high, blowing the top of the Oriole fan's ball cap laden head off. The man fell to the ground in a heap, tripping up the remaining infected behind him. Marvin retrieved another round from his pocket and slammed it into the weapon as he ejected the spent cartridge. He knew looking at the old nineteenth-century shotgun there was not a snowball's chance in hell that he could hold off the remaining five having to load each individual round into the weapon. Man, he wished he had his Mossberg, but he had sent that out with Kyle, thinking that he was safe and sound in his nice armored fortress. "Yeah, that lasted long," he muttered to himself.

Turning around, Marvin limped his way on bad knees to a derelict Chevy Nova parked at the gas pump, hose still situated in the tank. He walked around the car as the infected began making their way back to their feet, seemingly unsure of how to do the action. He glanced inside the window, hoping that there were keys or something still within the confines of the old car that he could use to get as far away from this place as he possibly could. After a brief search, he came up empty.

"Fuck, fuck, fuck!" he hissed as he aimed the shotgun once more and opened fire on another infected that had managed to get too close. This one, a young teenage boy, fell to the space in between the store and the gas pumps; the others sidestepped the corpse and kept coming. Marvin ejected the spent casing and loaded another round. He couldn't keep this up for long, he thought as he glanced at his surroundings and noticed another ten or so infected-looking people cresting over a hilltop to his rear.

"Holy shit!" he shouted, knowing if he didn't do something, he was completely and utterly screwed. *Where in the hell were they all coming from?* he thought. Only a few short hours had passed since this all began on the highway; he wondered briefly if all of these people had managed to escape the blast, fleeing from it like cockroaches from light. He wasn't quite sure how many souls were on the highway that he had previously occupied, but with the amount of gridlocked cars, he had to assume it was upward of a thousand or so people. Marvin looked around frantically for another avenue of escape; he knew he wouldn't be able to run for long or even far for that matter. Damn artificial leg.

Funny, he thought, when he had received the implant, he imagined he would be like the Six Million Dollar Man. He had even joked with his wife while he was in physical therapy, making the *"ch-ch-ch-ch-ch-ch"* sound effect from the show as he moved his legs as he learned how to use the implant; but unfortunately for him, nothing could be further from the truth. In all honesty, he was fairly certain that his knees ached more now than they ever had before.

"Gotta love tech . . ." his voice trailed off as he noticed a nearby cell phone tower hidden on the opposite side of the gas station, in a small copse of trees. He would have to make it somehow past the remaining four infected that were still approaching him, but he figured even on his weak old bones he could manage a short sprint and outrun them, at least he hoped. Marvin fired another round into the advancing group, not particularly aiming but using the scattershot to knock them back a step or two and slow them down a bit to buy himself a small measure of time.

Marvin slammed in another round and took off like a bat out of hell, or at least he thought it was like a bat out of hell. In all actuality, though, it was more like a turtle out of purgatory, but he still miraculously managed to slip past the remaining infected. He made a beeline for the dumpster corral positioned aside the gas station, slipping through a chain-link fence that had green strips of plastic running through its links, and scrambled to the top of the dumpster. The cell tower lay just beyond, up and over a small wooden fence.

The infected had turned toward his direction and found him within the enclosure; one of the bastards caught the heel of his boot and tried to grab him. Marvin kicked out and watched as skin literally peeled away from the older woman's scalp; her hair and skin fell away to the pavement with a wet slap. Marvin recoiled, clambering back away from the woman as she continued to claw at him, not even noticing that her grizzled skull was now exposed to the elements. Marvin backed into the wooden fence that the dumpster had been sitting against. He turned his body and latched onto the top of the fence with the palms of his hands and hefted himself up. The cell tower lay just five or so feet away. He glanced over his shoulder, taking notice that the other infected, who had joined their little party, had managed to slip in rather quickly.

Marvin's pulse quickened as one of the infected attempted to climb the dumpster. It failed, and then tried again. It was only a matter of time until it actually made it to the top and came within biting distance. Marvin took a deep breath and jumped over the fence, landing hard at the base of the cell tower. He pulled himself to his feet as another two infected made their way around an opening in the fencing.

"How did I not see that?" Marvin cursed. "I'm getting too old for this shit," he stated as he reached for the utility ladder and began his long ascent. By the time Marvin had reached the first maintenance platform, he had drawn quite the crowd; his arms and legs ached from the constant assertion. He pulled himself up and over the landing's railing and found that there was just enough room for him to sit if he dangled his legs over the edge. He sat down hard, panting like a dog, while sweat seeped from every pore of his body. Marvin pulled off his backpack and rested it on his legs. He retrieved a Lexan water bottle from the pack, popped the top, and took a long pull on the lukewarm liquid. He wiped the sweat from his eyes and looked down on the massing horde of infected that gathered at the base of the cell tower, roughly a hundred or so feet below. Marvin cleared his throat and spat a massive ball of phlegm onto one of the onlookers' upturned faces. It didn't seem to mind as the grotesque ball of yellowed snot dripped down its face and mingled with its own nasal secretions. He heard them making strange keening noises below, formless mutterings and guttural growls almost like animals.

"What the fucking hell is wrong with you people?" The old man spat again, this time unable to work up a good projectile from his lungs. He took another sip of water, the tepid liquid sliding down his throat doing little to quell the adrenalin-fueled thirst that brewed within.

Exhaustion began to set in as his body's defense mechanisms relaxed and his chemically induced stamina ebbed and faded away. The remembrance of battle fatigue from his glory days in Nam flooded his memories. He knew it well, and they were old friends you could say. He also remembered the warnings of succumbing to such afflictions while on your post could often be met with dire consequences.

His thoughts drifted back to a time when he had first enlisted into the Marines before the training that would essentially determine his war career in demolitions. He was young, the age of seventeen, having lied to gain entry into the military. It was a way for him to get away from his bastard of a father who took capital punishment to a whole new level. He was young, stupid, and barely even a man.

He recalled one night in the jungles of Vietnam working sentry duty on the edge of his platoon's encampment. He had been exhausted after a full day's forced march through the thick, inhospitable and unbelievably humid jungle, and being the newest member of the platoon, he drew the short straw for guard duty. He took up his post and kept watch, a Lucky Strike lit and dangling from his lips. The next thing he knew, he was being struck in the face by a large meaty fist. His eyes shot open as he landed in a heap on the moist jungle floor and he reached for his sidearm. A large jungle boot landed square on his throat, nearly choking the life out of him. He tried to gasp and immediately brought his hands up to try and wrestle away the boot and clear his airway. As spots began to form in his vision, the pressure behind the boot relaxed slightly, and a man stood above him, pointing a finger in his direction. He recognized the man but couldn't remember his name, but from the insignia on his uniform, Marvin knew he was a major.

"If you ever, ever, fall asleep on this post again, soldier, I will personally put a bullet in your ass! Now get the fuck up!" the major screamed, reached down, and plucked him up by the collar. The major leaned in closely to Marvin's ear. "If Charlie would have attacked while you were taking your little fucking snooze and one of my men had died, they wouldn't have needed to court-martial your worthless ass, because I would have seen you strung up here in the jungle. Do you get me, soldier?" the major spat angrily in Marvin's face in a harsh whisper.

Marvin nodded his dazed head frantically in acquiescence.

The major brushed out Marvin's uniform and handed him a cigarette. "Now take yourself over to the mess and get a cup of coffee. Hell, make it two. I'll hold your post until you get back." The major didn't have to add the words and *see this never happens again*, because that had become abundantly clear to Marvin. Ever since that day, even with the onset of old age, Marvin had conditioned himself to function even with total lack of sleep, albeit it had gotten progressively harder with age.

Marvin glanced down at the backpack resting on his legs, remembering the manila folder he had taken from the briefcase only moments ago; it felt like a lifetime, however. *Yet another effect of adrenaline*, he mused. He reached into the backpack and withdrew the classified document. There was a small red string wrapped around a round tab that held the folder closed. Marvin slowly unwound it, almost afraid to see what the folder contained. He placed his thumb inside the folder, pinning down any documents to prevent them from blowing away in the slight breeze that made its way to the top of the tower as he opened the folder.

INTERLUDE 3

Director Hammond still sat at his desk rubbing his temples as reports had started to flood in from his agents in the field. The airstrike on the only known infection point had failed. Prometheus had failed, their only defense against this type of crisis. Somehow the contagion had still managed to spread, and as reports came in from around the country, it had appeared that Maryland had not been the only target affected. In the matter of only a few hours, every major airport, train station, hell, it seemed even bus depots around the United States had been silently attacked. K5 was being deployed on American soil.

"K5," Hammond hissed, running his hand nervously over his balding head.

He pulled up the media player on his computer and located a file marked Kuru Variant Nanoid. A prompt displayed on the screen requesting a user ID and password; Hammond entered his credentials and pushed play.

The file that played was badly distorted being that it originally had been on an old reel-to-reel thirty-five-millimeter tape that had been digitized once the technology had become available. On the bottom of the screen read "Бутырской тюрьмы августа 1975" (Butyrka Prison August 1975). A man dressed in plain tattered prison garb sat strapped to a metal chair in the center of a small brightly lit room. He struggled with his bonds in a futile attempt to recoil from a man or woman dressed in what appeared to be an old version of a hazmat suit. The figure held what looked like a petri dish in one gloved hand and a scalpel in the other. The hazmat-clad figure then ran the blade along the surface of the dish just barely scraping the culture within.

He or she then walked over to the prisoner, turned and held the knife up in view of the camera, and said something in Russian that Hammond could not understand. He decided he would read the translations later, although he wasn't quite sure what that would do other than fuel his acid reflux, if anything. The doctor then turned toward the sobbing prisoner, tears streaked down his grizzled face as the doctor gripped his chin hard with a gloved hand, jerking his tear swollen face toward the camera, making it clearly visible to the camera that the young man looked to be in good health. Without hesitation, the doctor ran the scalpel across the surface of the prisoner's cheek; a small thin line of blood appeared from the minute scratch. The doctor backed slowly away from the prisoner, scalpel still raised in the figure's hand, never taking his or her eyes off the subject.

After a tense moment, the prisoner's eyes rolled back into their sockets, exposing nothing but the whites of his eyes. His head listed off to one side and hung still and limp, a small trickle of blood and saliva oozing from his mouth. There was silence for what seemed like an eternity.

The doctor stepped over to the man and placed two gloved fingers against his carotid artery. The figures remained still for a few seconds more, and then without warning, the prisoner began to violently convulse; the doctor quickly jumped back, losing his or her grip on the scalpel. The small metal object clattered to the floor and skittered out of site. The man in the chair convulsed so violently the leather straps that confined him to the piece of metal furniture tore free from the bolts that held them, as if someone had flipped a switch; the prisoner's gaze snapped in the direction of the doctor. The infected prisoner lunged, grabbing the doctor and immediately tore into her suit. Hammond could tell it was a woman now that the suit lay splayed open, exposing a naked breast underneath.

The female doctor screamed in agony as the prisoner sank his teeth into the soft, tender flesh of her breast. He jerked his head back, removing her once pink and supple nipple and swallowed it, ingesting flesh and blood. He lunged again, missing her, as this time she ran off frame, presumably pounding on the door as she pleaded for her life.

The infected prisoner regained its bearings and charged after the woman. Another scream erupted, and then the entire screen flooded white as the observing scientists purged the room with fire, effectively destroying anything living within the smallish space. Director Hammond leaned back in his chair, removed his bifocals, and rubbed his eyes with his thumb and forefinger. If this was the disease that had been released, then plausible deniability was the least of their worries; and if the reports from his field agents were valid, and he had no reason to doubt that they weren't, containment was really their only viable option. Problem was, *how exactly does one combat a foe you can't see?* The President, however, disagreed per his words:

"This virus will be contained. Neither I nor my administration will be held accountable for your incompetence, Hammond. Your people need to fix this, or I will see you hanged in the middle of the Whitehouse lawn before you bring me down."

The President had practically screamed at him through the phone. Hammond, who is well-schooled in the art of self-preservation, knew that what the President had said was, in all seriousness, the truth. He would do his job. His men would track down and retrieve the cases that tied them to this whole ugly business, and as far as containment—well, as far as he was concerned—medical containment was the job of the eggheads at the RID. Homeland could set blockades and lock down Townes all in the name of national security, but beyond that, they were helpless.

All things considered, in reality, they knew very little about this disease. It had been brought to the attention of the United States sometime during the 1980s at the height of the Cold War, when a scientist by the name of Ivan Morozov defected after his conscience finally caught up to him, seeing firsthand at some of the biological cocktails that his government was having them cook up on a daily basis. Weaponized anthrax, Ebola containing strands of RNA that would normally only be found within rhinovirus, otherwise known as the common cold, allowing the disease to be spread via sneezing or coughing rather than the crash-and-bleed response the virus normally triggered. That in itself was scary beyond belief, but K5 took the cake.

Doctor Morozov explained that with the increasing tensions between Western-led NATO and the Eastern Warsaw Pact, Russia had toyed with an idea of a first strike offense that did not involve a nuclear response. The biological cocktail itself was designed to infect a nation's population and alter their brain chemistry, causing extreme violence and social unrest, and ultimately have them destroy themselves from the inside out. The pathogen K5 was the Russian attempt at mind alteration, similar to the United States' own MK-Ultra experiments from the early 1960s. The U.S. had used drugs such as LSD or some other designer, more potent substances that had never made it onto the streets. The Soviets took a different approach, using a designer virus merged with a prion disease that would normally take years to affect the brain of the host organism. The viral component that was still yet unknown broke down the body's defenses, allowing the prion disease to multiply and infect the brain at a much, much faster rate. Unfortunately for the Soviets, they had never succeeded to develop a working vaccine to inoculate their own population, so the project was scraped.

It would be thirty years later before even a hint of the pathogen would surface. After the fall of the once-great Soviet Union and its subsequent demilitarization, a vast black market surplus of weapons and equipment opened up to the rest of the underdeveloped world. With dual wars being fought in Iraq and Afghanistan, and tensions toward the United States and its allies surging to its inevitable critical mass, it was Homeland's firm belief that one of the many terrorist organizations of the region had procured this nasty bug, and from Internet and cell phone chatter Homeland and the NSA had intercepted, they planned on using it to purge the infidels from the planet.

Hammond rubbed his sweat-coated temples and reached for his lukewarm cup of whiskey-spiked coffee. He took a long pull and slammed the cup on the desk just as the video respooled and began playing again. He snatched up the mouse and clicked the stop button, leaving an image of the bound prisoner staring toward the camera's eye, his face contorted and full of fear. Hammond stared at the screen for a brief moment; the whiskey that he had been pounding all morning was beginning to catch up to him. He wasn't sure if it was panic or the booze, but his head began to swim. There was a pounding outside his door, not on the door itself, but somewhere off down the hallway from the sounds of it.

Hammond swooned and steadied himself on his desk as he reached for the phone. He picked up the receiver, expecting his perky intern to answer. After four or five rings, he hung the phone up, figuring perhaps she had gone to use the facilities. Strange, as far as he could tell, the woman never seemed to even leave her desk throughout the day. Well, not unless she was popping outside to grab a smoke, which she actually only did on a rare occasion; and even when she did, she'd always informed him that she was doing so. He waited a few moments, picked up the phone, and tried again; still he got no response. He arose from his desk, wobbling as he did so, and stumbled slightly over to the door, pressing his ear against its cool wooden surface, listening for any sounds of movement.

Hammond jumped a bit as another bang resounded on the other side of the door, closer this time. It was then Hammond noticed the smoke lingering outside of his window. Curiously, he left the door and approached the large bay window that overlooked the street from eight floors up. His vision blurred slightly as he peered out into the gray-cast sky; vertigo started to set in as he looked down into the direction of the street. At first appearances, everything seemed to be normal, everything except for the car that was smoking from underneath its hood. *It had more than likely just overheated*, he thought.

"Sucks to be you," he said with a slightly drunken laugh. People walked back and forth along the street, or so it seemed. The more he gazed down at the figures on the sidewalks and streets, the more he noticed something was off about them. Everyone was walking, but no one seemed to be going anywhere. They just kind of lumbered around as if they all had a touch of the spirits this morning. Hammond blinked his eyes rapidly, trying to clear away the fog of the booze so that he could interpret the situation.

A figure came tearing ass out of a building across the street, a woman, as far as he could tell. Several others pursued her arms outstretched as if trying to snatch her right off her feet. Hammond leaned close as the others that had only moments ago been milling around, seemingly without purpose, galvanized and joined the chase.

"What the fuck?" Hammond said as the group of people chased down the screaming lady. He watched as she tripped on a curb and landed face down on the sidewalk, trying desperately to get to her feet as the others piled in on top of her. Hammond's face drained, the effects of the liquor all but vanishing.

"I-it's here," he whispered to himself and began to back away from the window, not wanting to watch any longer, not wanting any of this shit to be happening. A heavy weight slammed into the door, causing Hammond to nearly jump out of his pallid skin. He spun around, facing the door as it jolted again, this time sending wood splintering from its frame. Don ran quickly to his desk and flung open the bottom drawer; the door cracked again as it took another hit, this time the hinge at the top of the door buckled and rattled in its place. Hiding underneath a pile of discarded paperwork was Don's old .45. It set among the detritus in the desk unused for, Christ, years, he thought. He found the magazine still loaded and squeezed into the edge of the drawer propped up alongside a small basket of colored paperclips. The door shuddered again as Don frantically tried to place the magazine into its socket. As he thrust the magazine upward, it caught on something and fell to the floor, skittering underneath the desk. Don held up the weapon and inspected it. A fucking Post-it note had lodged itself within the cavity of the gun, crumpled up in a little ball. Don drove his index finger into the slot, trying desperately to dislodge the foreign object, having difficulty maneuvering his digit with its fatty exterior. All of a sudden, the door gave way.

CHAPTER 15

Fear and shock passed across Karen's features as she sped down the roadway toward her in-laws' homestead. Figures ran freely along the streets and sidewalks, some screaming, fleeing in panic, scattering to and fro like seagulls amassed on the roadway, some giving chase. She had to swerve on many occasions to avoid colliding with any of them. One pregnant woman stood outside of a doughnut shop, waving her arms frantically in the air, screaming for help.

Karen was about the pull the van over to her position and pick up the frightened woman, taking her out of the chaos erupting all around them, just as a man ran straight at the lady from inside of the doughnut shop, crashing through the large plate glass windows that encompassed the front of the store, seeming unaffected by the shards of glass that penetrated his neck and face.

He grabbed the pregnant lady and sank his teeth into her exposed neck, causing her to fall to the sidewalk in front of the store. Several others seemed to take notice of the fallen woman as she screamed in pain and horror. They came running over, falling on her as well. Several of them fought with one another like rabid dogs fighting over a piece of meat.

The last thing Karen had seen of the young woman was her bloodied, outstretched hand protruding from underneath the teeming mass of the infected. She shuddered at the scene and sped off. Karen passed through sections of derelict cars, cars that had seemed to be abandoned on the sides of roads, and sometimes directly in the center. She could tell that most, if not all, were still running, by the exhaust that fumed out of their tailpipes.

Karen exited off Route 40 and took side roads until she reached the outskirts of a town called Colora. It was a small spit of a town, the kind of town that you could spit from one border to the next. If you were driving and you blinked, you would quite literally pass straight through it without even knowing it was there. Her in-laws lived near the town's eastern edge, away from the town proper, and somewhat off the beaten path. Things were still and quiet as she maneuvered the van through winding forested-lined roads. Normally, whenever she and her husband had taken this drive, there were signs of life everywhere you looked—a deer running across the roadway, carrion birds feasting on the carcass of a not-so-fresh piece of roadkill. As of yet, however, there seemed to be nothing but silence. As much as she wanted to avoid the more populated town center, she had no choice but to travel through it in order to reach her destination. She had to wonder if this affliction, or whatever the hell it was, had made it this far into the countryside. After leaving the main road, most of the chaotic activity had seemed to drop off all but completely. The fact that she hadn't seen so much as another car along the roadway gave her pause.

As Karen pulled to a stop at an intersection several hundred yards away from the town proper, she let her hand rest on the shotgun that rested on the passenger seat. She eyed the seemingly quite streets and buildings with dismay; she had hoped to see the usual bustle of activity that the summer months seemed to turn out, but none had presented itself thus far. The sun started to show through the gray expanse of cloud cover, casting brilliant reflections off pools of water that flowed toward the town's storm drains.

"Miss Karen," one of the boys in her care broke the silence.

She turned around to meet his gaze and saw him pointing down the road. Karen followed the boy's outstretched hand to a man stumbling in the roadway about a hundred yards away.

"Shit," Karen whispered under her breath. She hoped that it was just some old man out for a walk after the morning rain, but something gnawed at her gut telling her otherwise. It was the way he walked, she supposed, his strange jerky movements—almost as if he were being controlled by some unseen puppeteer. She squeezed her eyes shut trying to will the image away. Sadly, when she opened her eyes, the man remained, only he had shuffled a few feet closer. Another man came around the side of an old brick building across the road over by the next intersection. The man stepped off the curb into the street, tripped, and fell face first into the asphalt. "I want everyone to hang on," Karen said as she revved the engine.

The kids squirmed nervously in the back of the van, clutching on to one another. The children whimpered as the van thrust forward into the intersection.

She moved the vehicle forward, cautiously at first, looking back and forth around the streets and buildings, scrutinizing possible escape routes should things go south. At the moment, the two infected that had stumbled into view were still far enough away that they didn't pose much of a threat. The man in the middle of the street was slowly pulling himself onto his feet, focusing on the moving van. She gazed at him as she pulled past. His eyes—oh, Christ, his eyes—they were completely and utterly vacant. They were the eyes of the dead.

Karen unconsciously sped up, keeping her eyes on the lanky grizzled man who reached out from the roadway, grasping at the air trying in vain to get her in his clutches. The van jolted, and the children screamed as she struck something in the roadway. She ground the van to a halt as she slammed on the brake pedal. Blood coated the windshield; spidery cracks formed on the glass where something had impacted.

"Oh my God," she breathed, not knowing if what she had hit had been normal or infected. With all the noise, figures inside of row homes and shops began to stream out into the streets, hundreds of them—as if they had been waiting for her to hit the center of town. Karen threw the van in reverse, but the infected were pouring out in droves from in front and behind. "Shit, Shit, Shit," she hissed.

Something slammed into the side of the van; one of the figures began pounding on the side window hard enough to cause it to shudder under his assault.

The kids screamed in fear and panic.

"Keep your heads down!" Karen shouted over the increasing noise as the men and women outside shrieked with rage and fury.

The kids ducked down low, some of them even coming out of their seats and lying on the carpeted floor.

Karen stepped on the gas pedal, moving slowly, trying her best to push the men and women aside as she plowed through them. Figures fell to the ground and sent the van bouncing up and down as if riding over speed humps. Karen gritted her teeth and held back tears as she moved. She had to get to safety; she had to get these kids out of here. Her mind at that moment drifted to her husband and her own children. Christ, among all the chaos she hadn't even had time to think about her own kids. What kind of mother did that make her? She hoped that they were safe, that this disease, or whatever it was, had not spread that far and wide.

She was always happy with the onset of summer, which was the time when she and her husband would drive the kids out to a small town in West Virginia to spend several weeks with Kyle's grandparents and cousins. The kids loved it there; there wasn't much in the way of entertainment out there in the holler; however, the kids were free to make their own fun. One problem with living this close to a city like Baltimore was the incessant crime made a parent fearful to even let their children play out in one's own yard, let alone run the neighborhood.

In Tornado, however, everyone knew everyone else; and if your kid was doing something stupid, you could count on one of the neighbors to round them up and march them straight home, by the ear if necessary, as if they were one of their own. Karen herself loved the freedom it provided her as well. She spent so much time with children working with them during the day and dealing with them all night long. Sometimes it seemed as if she never got a break, never had a day off, so she relished in the time they spent away. She missed them, of course, but as she would tell them, "The farther away you are, the more I miss you." She would grin and smack them on the behind.

The passenger-side window shattered as several hands thrust inside of the van's cab. Karen tried to jerk the steering wheel to the left, but the bodies surrounding the van prevented the vehicle from maneuvering. One of the infected managed to get a grip on her arm as she tried to reach for her shotgun in the passenger seat. Karen gripped the steering wheel firm and hit the accelerator. The van lurched forward at what seemed like a snail's pace as she rammed into the bodies of the infected that lay beyond. The man's grip on her arm loosened and then wrenched free as she moved forward; the infected, however, managed to remain clinging to the inside of the window.

She grabbed hold of the shotgun one handed, raised the weapon up, and placed the muzzle up against the man's open mouth. He bit down on the cold metal as she screamed and pulled the trigger, sending blood and brain matter flying out into the crowd. The recoil of the weapon damn near knocked her arm out of its socket; her hand stung as she dropped the gun back into the seat. The man's body slumped over the broken window. She gripped the steering wheel with both hands and floored it.

The large Honda slammed into the teeming infected, throwing them askew like cordwood. She plowed up and over the fallen and finally broke free of the crowd and onto the open road. Several clung to the bumper in an attempt to reach them but failed as the rough asphalt tore away their clothing and flesh. She watched them roll away from the van, in the rearview as she rocketed forward, leaving the small town behind.

She veered off onto a side road that would take her toward her mother-in-law's home; light faded and flitted by as she crossed under trees that hung over the roadway. Her eyes scanned the tree line for threats as she moved forward. She glanced into the rearview mirror to observe the children.

"Everyone okay?" she asked, trying to hide the tremble in her voice, but failed as the words caught in her throat.

The kids cried and whimpered but were otherwise unscathed.

She focused her attention back toward the front of the vehicle and studied her forearm for a moment. Finger-sized bruises formed on her wrist and ached slightly. Thankfully, it appeared that she had suffered no other damage. Finally after what seemed like an eternity, she pulled into the driveway of Mr. and Mrs. Walker. She sat in the car for a long moment and studied their home, searching for any sign of life. Trees swayed and leaves rustled in the breeze, droplets of rain just beginning to evaporate under the emerging sun. For all intents and purposes other than the craziness that they had all just endured, it would otherwise be a beautiful day. She shut off the engine and turned in her seat to face the children.

"I'm going to check things out. I need you all to stay here and stay quiet. Can you do that for me?" Karen asked, faking her best smile. The children reciprocated by nodding and slinking down into their seats.

Gathering up the shotgun, its grip reminding her of the stinging that still resounded through her wrist, she cringed as she noticed the blood-caked barrel. Coagulated gore clung to the end near the large bore at the front of the weapon, a fragment of tooth sticking in the drying viscera. Taking care not to touch the contaminated barrel, she gripped the stock, and opened the door.

She stepped out into the humid air and quietly closed the door behind her. The smell of earth hung deep in the air as the breeze wafted scents of the surrounding forest. It was almost peaceful. She cautiously walked around the front of the home and peered along its side, studying the expanse of trees for movement. Carefully, she walked down a hill, around to the rear of the home, and onto the patio. She approached the sliding glass door and cupped her face, placing it against the glass, and peered inside. The basement area was dark and empty. She tried the handle, but the sliding door held firm.

"Damn," she stated. She continued around to the other side of the property as one of the children let out an ear-piercing scream. Karen hauled ass around the side of the building and collided with an infected that just seemed to be standing there. A woman, a neighbor Karen realized, stumbled backward and fell to the ground snarling. She quickly began to scramble to her feet as Karen brought the shotgun up high in the air and screamed. She struck the woman in the temple with the business end of the shotgun, snapping her head back with a resounding crack. Blood oozed from an open head wound as she brought the shotgun up and struck again, sending the older woman to the ground.

Karen stifled a cry as she heard the kids scream once more. She ran around to the front of the house just as a large black man in nothing but boxer shorts and socks reached into the van through the broken window on the passenger side. She could just make out the scene of the children cowering in the far corner of the van, all of them piled on top of one another. She ran up behind the man and smashed the shotgun into his wide, exposed back.

He halted his assault, extracting his head from the open window, and turned slowly to face her. He was massive, his face contorted in a mix of agony and rage.

Karen stepped back a few steps, gripping the stock of her weapon like a shield. The man let out a low rumbling growl and took a step forward; Karen raised the shotgun and hesitated. If she fired this close to the van, she would almost certainly hit one of the children. Karen made what her husband called a command decision; she took another step back as the humongous man took another lurching step forward, raising his large meaty hand out toward her. Karen spun on her heels and ran for all she was worth, hoping to draw the beast away from her charges. Her plan worked as the large man gave chase, lunging and sprinting in her direction.

Karen ran for her life, the man's large stride easily catching up to her. She could feel his fevered breath on her neck as she broke right and plowed straight into the forest, hoping to slow him down. Branches struck her in the face and thorns tore into the tender flesh of her legs as she ran. She could hear the man come crashing through the underbrush as he pursued her. She wanted desperately to turn around and shoot this asshole, but she knew if she stopped for even a second, she was done for.

She saw her opportunity as she ran directly for a fallen tree; quickly she hopped up and over, hoping that the infected man lacked the coordination to mimic her maneuver. She was correct as the beast slammed headlong into the exposed roots of an old rotted oak. He scrabbled at the tree in an attempt to somehow get over the top. Karen darted to the left, effectively running in a circle, doing her best to work her way back around to the children. The infected noticed and reacted as she darted past through the underbrush. Karen burst back out into the yard and charged toward the van, fumbling with her keys as she ran. She had put a little distance between herself and the infected man, but he was still too close for comfort. She depressed the button to open the van's automatic sliding doors and called out.

"Everyone, out of the van! Get to the house!" Nothing moved, however. No children frantically scrabbled out into the driveway desperately running for the house. Karen reached the car door and thrust her head inside. The van was empty. She gasped and stepped back, looking frantically from side to side, searching the area for her wayward children. The large half-naked black man burst out of the woods and ran straight toward her, snarling and howling like some bloody devil. A noise to Karen's right caught her attention as her mother-in-law's front door burst open; a smallish graying-haired woman frantically beckoned her over.

"Karen, get your ass in here!" the woman shouted.

"Terry? The kids," Karen replied, motioning toward the van.

"They're inside. Come on, hurry. He's getting closer!"

Karen looked back at the charging figure that was only about twenty feet away from her position. She spun on her heel and took off running, still grasping the shotgun.

Terry grabbed hold of her by the arm and ushered her inside, slamming the door behind them just as the large man crashed into the sealed ingress.

Karen panted on the other side of the door, sweat running down her forehead; her heart hammered in her chest as the man on the other side of the portal slammed heavy fists on the door in frustration. Karen eyed her mother-in-law, who stood before her, holding out her hand.

"Don't worry. I don't think he can get in. Come on. The others are upstairs." Terry took Karen by the hand and helped her to her feet. Shaking and exhausted, they ascended the stairway.

CHAPTER 16

Richard and I continued our march along the ruined streets surrounding BWI airport. Although the rain had stopped and the sun was trying its dandiest to make an appearance, ash from the blast flitted slowly down out of the sky like snow, giving the area an almost surreal visage.

We traveled slowly and deliberately, watching every step we made, taking care to observe the areas around abandoned cars. Between the two of us, we were able to guard each other's flank. I kept watch over our right, while Richard guarded our left. Every so often, one of us would turn and walk backward for a few feet just to make certain we weren't being pursued by the infected, or anyone else, for that matter.

"This shit sucks," I said, breaking the silence. "I mean, how the fuck does this even happen?" I said more as a statement then a question.

Richard looked over at me for a moment and shook his head. "Does it really matter? It is what it is, and we're stuck in it, so do us a favor and get a grip and just deal, or we're both gonna die." He turned his gaze forward once more.

Another gunshot resounded out in the distance, this time closer that it had been previously, which meant whoever was doing the shooting was remaining stationary. *Last stand*, I thought to myself and hoped that if it were some wayward survivor, that Rich and I would make it in time to do some good. I was fairly confident at this point that it was not Homeland's goons, however. If it had been Homeland's boys, I believed there would be a hell of a lot more gunfire going on. If one thing was certain about those assholes, they traveled in packs. *Pussies*, I mused, giving myself a small grin.

I was snapped out of my revelry as I tripped over a hubcap that lay rusting in the middle of the road. It skittered noisily across the road's surface and into the surrounding grass. There it was again, the universe trying its hardest to fuck up my feet. I felt an ache in my pinky toe, and I was reminded painfully of the knock I took this morning as I banged into the dresser at home.

Home, I sighed. All I wanted to do was get there, see my wife, make certain she was okay, and then get in touch with the kids. As much as a pain in the ass the little buggers were, I missed them now more than ever. I just hoped like hell this disease, or whatever it was, hadn't made it out there to West Virginia. If it did, I hoped my grandparents were keeping my little miscreants safe. As we walked, Richard looked over at me wide-eyed.

"Are you trying to get us killed?" he said eyeing the wobbling hubcap. I shrugged, and we continued walking.

We reached the end of the highway and walked down an exit ramp that led into the surrounding town. It was funny; I had driven by this same expanse hundreds of times over the past ten or so years and never really gave it too much thought. Every so often I would wonder about a lonely shoe that rested on the shoulder, curious to what had become of the shoe's occupant. I was always reminded of the old cartoons, you know, the ones where some cartoon character is standing on the side of the road as a car zooms by and tears all of its clothes off. I shook the image from my thoughts and concentrated on the task at hand.

We walked toward several rows of small buildings, most appeared to be office buildings of some sort. There was even a 7-Eleven off to one corner. I wondered if I could get a cup of coffee. That was until I noticed it was on fire. It was difficult to see from our vantage point, but gray, black smoke squeezed itself through what I assumed were the doors on the other side of the store and ventilation ducts on the roof. I could take a good guess at what had started the blaze, being that there must have been a ton of flaming debris raining down all over town after the bomb had been dropped on the highway. I wouldn't be at all surprised if we encountered more infernos along our route. Which kind of sucked being that it would seriously limit our options if we ran into any trouble and needed to beat a hasty retreat, and hold up somewhere.

As we approached the end of the off-ramp, we noticed what looked like the remnants of about five cars smashed into one another effectively creating a barrier of twisted metal at the end of the exit ramp. The cars were piled up in such a way that it looked as if one or two on the end had just abruptly stopped, causing the others to plow into them. You could see the evidence of this judging by the skid marks that lined the roadway up to that point. Richard and I exchanged furtive glances with each other, both of us undoubtedly wondering the same thing. What caused them to stop? From the looks of things beyond the pileup, at least from our perspective, the roadway seemed to be perfectly clear. Sure, there were several cars parked along the sides of the road, and a few scattered in parking lots, but the road itself looked completely empty. As we neared the sight of the collision, I noticed what had caused it. At the end of the off-ramp set two concrete barriers, the same type you would find separating most roadways. I looked at my companion and raised an eyebrow.

"They trapped these poor bastards."

Richard nodded in agreement. "I think it's safe to say that the feds had no intention of letting anyone off this road alive," he said, never taking his eyes off the wreckage.

As we moved forward, I scanned the area surrounding the vehicles for signs of escape. Sadly, there were none. Doors still remained closed; airbags that had been deployed were deflated, hanging limply from steering columns—many of them with a body slouched over top of them.

I started in the direction of the closest car, readying myself to peer in the windows, when I heard something scrape along the ground under my feet. My first thought was that I had gotten a lone pebble stuck in my shoe, but the object felt oddly cylindrical. I raised my boot off the material and inspected it. It was a shell casing, 9 mm to be exact. As I gazed along the ground, I noticed several more casings littering the area. I reached the first of the cars and looked in at the driver. His still form sat leaning up against his seat. He wore a typical Walmart business suit and looked as if he had been on his way into work, probably an accountant or something. A cup of coffee lay on its side in his lap, leaking sticky brown liquid across his previously pressed trousers and dripped to the gray-carpeted floor. The brown liquid mixed with a coppery-colored substance that pooled at the man's feet. I gasped when I noticed a single gunshot wound to the side of his head. Blood and brain matter coated the window and passenger seat. Closer inspection showed a small hole chiseled through the door frame where the bullet must have exited the vehicle. I shook my head.

"This guy was executed," I said, standing up straight and looking at Richard.

"Was he infected?" he asked.

I shook my head. Honestly, I had no way of really telling. I mean, I was no doctor, but the man seemed to look perfectly normal, at least compared to what I had seen earlier that day.

We walked around the other cars and found the same story in all of them. It hadn't really fazed me much until I found the van. A mother lay across her dashboard, her head looking as if it had been caved in with a blunt object, perhaps even the butt stock of a rifle. Three children in the backseat, each of them with looks of terror forever etched across their little faces, a single gunshot wound to the forehead is what had ended their short existence. I nearly wept as I stumbled back away from the vehicle.

"Why would they do this?" I croaked out.

Richard walked up behind me and laid a hand on my shoulder. "Come on, friend. We should probably get going. Really not much we can do to help them."

I fell to my knees and gripped the handle of my .357. "They killed them. For no fucking reason!" I shouted pointing toward the cars. "They blocked them in here and then they killed them!" My anger rose as I gritted my teeth.

"I hate to say this, but perhaps they felt they had no choice," Richard offered in a detached tone.

I was on my feet in a second. "You're defending this?" I motioned toward the vehicles and the barrier as I rapidly approached him. My anger over took me, and I lunged at Richard, pushing him hard, slamming him into the side of one of the wrecked cars. Metal and glass crunched as his body struck.

Richard put his hands up in a placating gesture. "Hey, I'm not saying what they did was right. I'm just trying to play Devil's advocate here. Figure out what their thought process was. Kinda what we cops do."

I released the man, my anger flowing out of me like air from a balloon. I shook my head, trying to wrap my brain around all of this. The fact that Homeland had set up this roadblock and done it rapidly had told me one thing. They had anticipated this, which meant they knew something like this could happen. It was like 9/11 all over again. The feds knew that shit was coming and did absolutely nothing to stop it, just simply mopped up the mess afterward

Richard broke my thought as I heard him shout.

"Shit!" I looked over at the man and saw him bring up his weapon. I followed his gaze. Several lumbering figures came sprinting in our direction, a dozen of them at least, my outburst most likely having drawn their attention. I looked at them in disgust as one of the figures appeared to be badly burned; his flesh flaked off as he headed in our direction.

"Christ, that one is still smoking." I pointed out and drew my pistol. I flipped open the cylinder and checked to make certain that all six rounds were present and accounted for. I slapped it back home and made certain to twist it until it locked into place. It would suck to pull the trigger only to have the weapon misfire and blow off part of my hand. Richard and I quickly took up position behind the concrete barrier.

We knelt, supporting our weapons on the Jersey wall's edge and took aim. Richard fired first, letting a three-round burst strike the closest infected in the chest. The 9 mm rounds tore through fabric and flesh and lodged into at least one other infected who walked closely behind. It stumbled backward for the moment but barely seemed to notice the three new holes that bore through his chest. Richard cursed and raised his aim, this time striking the bastard in the head. The top of his head disintegrated under the assault, and he stumbled forward once more and then fell to the ground in a heap.

I watched in amazement as the one behind him actually sidestepped his fallen comrade. I raised my weapon and peered down the barrel. The creatures—I didn't feel comfortable calling them human any longer—were still a good distance away, and accuracy at this distance with a .357 was sketchy at best. I didn't want to wait for the son-of-a-bitch to be right on top of me before I opened up. I aimed for his head and then adjusted slightly higher to compensate for the bullet's natural drop-down effect as gravity did its job and pulled the projectile toward the Earth.

I fired, and almost to my and Richard's amazement, the bullet struck home, entering the short bald man's skull just above his right eyebrow. The back of his head exploded outward in a show of gore as the large bore round exited; his body pitched backward with the impact and landed on the burn victim, who was nearly knocked off his feet.

I almost lost my breakfast again when the bald man struck the creature behind him. Strips of incinerated flesh peeled off in large ribbons as the man slid down its midsection. The burned victim was probably the most disgusting thing I think I had ever seen in my entire life, and that was a lot. He or she, for that matter, being all traces of sex had been melted away. As it crept forward, it reminded me of a marshmallow that had been held in a campfire for a little bit too long. A black crust engulfed its entire body; it cracked and bled as it moved forward, sending rivers of dark blood flowing from each wound with every step it took. The only thought in my head was to try to put the poor bastard out of its misery. It saw me as I took aim in its direction. It reached out a charred hand and opened its mouth, revealing blackened teeth and a swollen tongue. It released a gurgling, ragged wail that sent shockwaves of fear down my spine. The others that moved along with him seemed to follow suit, crying out in what could only be described as sounds of intolerable pain.

A twinge of guilt struck me in the chest as I wondered if these things, these people, were still able to feel pain; perhaps they could, and perhaps they were just unable to control their actions. I gritted my teeth and squeezed the trigger, ending the poor thing's existence. Its skull shattered like glass as the flames that had burned the figure had most likely left the bones dry and brittle. I gagged at the sight.

Richard glanced over at me. "Steady, friend. This is the best we can do for them," he said, almost reading my thoughts.

I nodded and did the best to steel myself.

We managed to take down the rest of the infected in short succession and decided it was best if we double-timed it away from the area, figuring that if these things were attracted to noise, it wouldn't be long before more showed up. *How many more could there be?* I wondered. I hoped against hope we had seen the brunt of them; however, I had my doubts.

CHAPTER 17

Alex Bishop stood atop the roof of the middle school and stared out at the teeming mass of infected below. There must have been two hundred of them at this point. He was shocked at just how fast this bug infected. He knew a bit about the disease from the reports that he had recently received before they were sent out on this mission. He narrowly had time to read any of it on his laptop aboard the SUV as they headed to the outbreak site this morning, but from what he knew, the pathogen infected its host and screwed with their brain chemistry, somehow causing them to behave violently and irrationally. He also knew that those infected with K5 couldn't be reasoned with. They would basically stay in permanent attack mode until they were destroyed or succumbed to the virus, but he never anticipated this. Most of the victims seemed to have suffered severe trauma of some sort, some of them with whole limbs missing, either torn off by another infected, or just close enough to the blast site from their attack on the highway to have parts of their bodies blown away.

Bishop had to wonder how in the hell any of them were still up and walking around. Any normal human would have most likely gone into shock and succumbed to injuries; he just couldn't wrap his head around it. There had to be more to this disease than what the higher-ups had told him about. That, however, was a question for another day. As of now, as far as he was concerned, they were still under orders to procure the cases that held vital information about the disease, information that they could possibly use to stop this shit in its tracks; and at this point, the longer it took, the faster this shit would spread.

Alex glanced over at his new communications officer, Jackson; he believed that was his name anyway. He was on the opposite side of the roof, setting up what looked like a small satellite dish. "Any luck, troop?" Bishop asked.

"Not yet, sir. Still trying to locate a viable signal. I think the grid must be overloaded with cell phone traffic or something." The man cursed as his finger struck a hot lead.

Bishop watched him as he stuck his stinging finger in his mouth and sucked on it. "How about the case? Still in the same position?" Bishop asked, smirking slightly at the man.

The tattooed black man with chiseled features took notice of his captain's amusement and removed his finger from his mouth. He reached over to a supply case and removed a small PDA; he depressed a tiny button on its side and powered it up. A few seconds passed as the small machine went through its boot cycle. Jackson pulled a stylus out from its side and pressed the GPS locator application. It acquired the signal within a few moments, and Jackson had to wonder why they could pick up the GPS SAT and not the communication's satellite signal. He shrugged, figuring to be some technical garbage he would most likely not understand. He waited a moment for the information to display and looked over the readout on the small screen. "Yes, sir, it seems to be remaining stationary. Two klicks west of our position!" Jackson said, shouting across the rooftop.

Bishop nodded in understanding. It had been a little over an hour since their arrival at the school. The fact the case had ceased to move meant one of two things: either the man who possessed it was trapped as they were, or dead, which, in any case, it meant they still had a chance at completing their primary mission. Now if they could only manage to get the hell out of here.

Alex chewed his lip, mulling over several escape scenarios that he and his men could use to get out of this predicament. The best option being extraction via an HH-60 Pave Hawk helicopter, a resourceful aircraft that could pluck them off this very rooftop and shuttle them wherever they need to go along with whatever cargo and supplies they could carry. However, all of that hinged on whether or not they could establish comms with their headquarters. Judging by the look on his comms officer's face, he doubted that would be anytime soon.

Bishop cursed; they needed a plan. Unfortunately, during their sweep of the school, they had blown through several more rounds of precious ammunition as they discovered part of the school's cafeteria staff that must have come in early to prepare breakfast and prep for lunch. They had to put down three hearty women who damn near made lunch out of half of his remaining men. How the disease had managed to infected the staff at the school was somewhat of a mystery to him. The only thing that he could surmise was that one or more of them had to have come into contact with it some time before arriving at the school, which meant by the time they had responded to the outbreak on the highway, it had already been too late. Alex brushed the thought aside.

He turned his attention back toward the front of the building and gazed out over the parking lot and his government SUVs that remained practically surrounded by infected at this point in time. Getting to them, however, would be their best option at resuming their current mission. At last count, he and his men had roughly fifteen rounds of 9 mm ammunition between them. That wasn't going to get them far. Unless they could get these dumb fucks to stand in a straight line, they were going to have to get creative. If they could manage to distract the infected below, get them to gather on the opposite side of the building and make a run for their vehicles and the supplies that were held within, they might stand a chance.

Bishop rose up a gloved hand and keyed his shoulder mic; he tilted his head and spoke, "Jones, what's your twenty? Over." A few moments passed with nothing more than a slight hiss resounding from the speaker, then a voice broke through the static.

"Basement level. Shit, Cap, I'm surprised I even picked up your transmission down here, over."

"Everything down there clear, over?" Bishop asked.

"Yeah, nothing down here but plumbing and old books," Jones replied.

"Good, I need you to double-time it up to the roof. I have something I want to go over with you, over." Bishop waited a moment for a response.

"Copy that, Cap. I'm on my way. Out." The radio fell silent.

Bishop waited patiently as he figured it would take a few minutes for the hulking man to make it up to his position.

Jones burst through the heavy metal door that led onto the rooftop; he scanned the area and located his commander. He jogged over to where Bishop stood.

Alex was slightly impressed; the big man looked as if he had run flat-out up three floors of stairs and had barely broken a sweat.

"What's the sitrep, Cap?" Jones asked, looking out over the rooftop. "Damn, where in the hell did they all come from?" Jones asked raising an eyebrow.

Bishop glanced over at the big man.

"Your guess is as good as mine," Alex said, looking back over at the horde.

Several of them stared upward at the duo, with outstretched arms, keening like a pack of wild dogs.

"We're running out of ammo," Bishop stated matter-of-factly.

"No shit," Jones replied.

"We're going to need to get to our vehicles. Resupply and bug out," Bishop said as Jones nodded in agreement.

"No chopper?" Jones asked, glancing over at Jackson.

Jackson noticed the big man looking in his direction. The man put his hands up in the air, shrugging.

"I'm getting a signal now but . . ." Jackson shook his head.

Bishop strolled over toward the man. "You're getting a signal, but what?" Alex asked.

"I can pick up the satellite now—full signal in fact." Jackson motioned toward the LED readout on the communications array. "But no one is answering," Jackson said with a look of confusion crossing his features.

Bishop eyed him quizzically.

"What do you mean no one is answering?" Alex could understand the interference in the network, but once they had a working connection, getting an answer from dispatch shouldn't be an issue.

"I mean just that, sir. Full signal strength, no answer. The problem has to be on the other end." Jackson looked at his equipment as if it would provide all the answers the captain was looking for.

This turn of events sent acid roiling in Bishop's stomach. With the amount of money the oversight committee had spent on upgrading their communications equipment, there should be no way in hell they weren't being heard. So that meant only one of two things: either the equipment had been damaged somehow, or there was simply no one in place to receive their transmission. Bishop made a conscious effort not to reveal his concerns.

"Keep trying, Jackson. Try a few other frequencies just in case there is some sort of interference from the blast." Bishop knew better, the blast shouldn't have affected their equipment in the least, but he figured it would give the man something to do and, more importantly, not insight panic among his men.

Bishop stepped back over toward Jones, who still observed the infected milling around below. He watched in surprise as a few of them tried their best to claw their way up the side of the building to no avail. Bishop tapped his second-in-command on the shoulder, causing him to flinch.

"What the hell you trying to do, Cap, give me a heart attack?" Jones said, arching his eyebrows.

Bishop smirked. "Sorry. What do you think about all of this?" Alex motioned to the infected below.

"I think it's fucked, Cap," Jones stated simply.

"Hooah," the captain replied. "We need to come up with a plan to distract these bastards, get 'em away from our transports. We have a good lead on our target, and we need to get moving on it before it disappears."

"So I take that as a *no* on the chopper then?" Jones exasperated, shaking his head.

Bishop smiled. "Since when did we need a chopper to ferry our asses out of hostile territory?"

Jones looked over at the man. "Yeah, well, I don't know if you've noticed or not, Cap, but you're getting too old for this shit." Jones cast a glance at the captain's graying hair.

Bishop stifled a laugh. "Yeah, well, I'm not getting any younger, and neither are you. So any ideas on how we can get these assholes out of our way?" Bishop looked expectantly at his second-in-command.

Jones furrowed his brow in thought. "I think I might. Saw some cleaning supplies we might be able to use but . . . we're gonna need bait."

Both men turned to eye the wiry-looking communications officer at the other end of the roof.

Jackson's neck hair stood on end as if detecting their stare and looked up. "What?" he asked.

Both men grinned.

Bishop and his crew all met in the middle school's gymnasium. Bishop chose the location due to the fact that there were no windows in which the infected could spot them, although he was under no illusions that they were going anywhere, not on their own at least. The fuckers knew they were in there and wouldn't stop until they got hold of them.

Alex eyed the remainder of his men. A now-ragged-looking bunch that stood at ease in a line toward the center of the gym. Bishop paced in front of them, debating on how he wanted to lay this plan out to them.

"Okay, as you know, we're up shit-creek at the moment." The men nodded in response. "We have a mission to complete before any of us can go home. Hooah!"

"Hooah!" the team responded.

"In order for us to do that, we need to get back to our vehicles and get on the road. Now that being said, Major Jones and I have come up with a plan to do just that; however, as with anything in our jobs, it's gonna pose some risk." The commander stopped, gauging his men's response.

Each man looked back and forth to one another, wondering what in the hell was in store for them now, after all they had just gone through hell and back to make it to this point.

Bishop looked up and down the row of men. Not counting himself, only six men remained of his squad; Simmons was out due to the injuries he had sustained earlier. "I need two of you"— Bishop shot a glance at Jackson—"to create a diversion long enough for the rest of us to make it to the explorers. What I'm asking is that you draw the infected away from our position. As far as we can tell, these bastards are drawn to sound and movement. I've already selected Jackson to be our point man on this. He will need backup." Bishop looked up and down the line for volunteers. When none were exactly forthcoming, he sighed. "Look, I know this is some fucked up shit, but we cannot stay here indefinitely. If you want to get home to your families, we need to take care of business. Hooah!"

"Hooah!" the men replied.

A slender-built wisp of a man with a hawk nose and pockmarked skin stepped forward. The man's name was Salvador Vindetti. Although he was only in his mid-thirties, the pallor of his cratered skin made him appear aged way beyond his years; he was fit for his build with ropy muscles that stretched taut over his compact frame. Sal motioned toward the communications officer.

"I'll go with him, Cap," Vindetti said with a voice that sounded like gravel being rolled in a tin can.

Jackson tilted his head up to the man in a gesture of thanks.

Vindetti nodded in reply.

"Good. Now, this is not a suicide mission. As soon as we are clear of the building, you two will need to haul some major ass around to the SUVs. Don't worry, we'll be waiting. Scotty, I'll need you and Hoop to stay on the ground level and help Simmons out to the trucks. Jones and I will take sniping positions on the roof and pick off any stragglers that get in your way. We'll also provide cover for Jackson and Vindetti," Bishop said, laying it all out to the men.

"How will y'all get out, Captain?" Scotty asked.

"Jones and I will repel from the roof after everyone else is clear. First order of business is we'll need two of you to be ready to clear the door once we draw the infected away. Scotty, that job will fall to you and Hoop as well. Jones spotted some cleaning supplies that we can use to make incendiaries and hopefully take a bunch of these assholes out. We'll drop Vindetti and Jackson over the back wall where they'll grab those dumb fucks attention and run like hell."

"It will be like a big game of tag, except if you get caught, it means you get torn apart," Jackson quipped nervously.

Vindetti looked at the man and grinned savagely. "You afraid of a little dash and crash?"

"No, I'm afraid of getting my black ass chewed off," Jackson responded.

"Okay, enough of the bullshit. Let's get this party started," Bishop ordered.

The men broke off into their respective groups and set about their tasks.

Vindetti and Jackson headed toward the roof to set repelling lines.

Scotty and Hooper "Hoop" began moving some of the larger debris away from the main entrance, taking care not to remove too much until the time came to bug out. They didn't want to weaken the barrier while the entrance still teemed with the infected.

Bishop and Jones set about finding cleaning supplies; they headed toward the janitorial closet located at the end of the school over by the cafeteria.

The janitor's closet was not so much a closet, but a mini storage room, complete with an exit door for easy access to the school yard for mowing. A large riding lawn mower set in the end next to a rust-colored rolling door. The first thing Jones grabbed was a small two-gallon gasoline jug and a can of motor oil; he shook the jug of gasoline and gave a *thumb-up* to Alex. Bishop spotted a large bottle of industrial cleaner. He grabbed the plain white bottle and flipped it over to study the label. He grinned as he spotted the ingredients he was looking for.

"We're going to need to hit the cafeteria and probably the science room," Bishop stated, eyeing the bottle.

Jones nodded in understanding.

The chemicals were a great find, but they needed something to house the improvised explosives, glass being their best option, as well as a few other ingredients that they would doubtfully find here. Bishop also found a box of nails and screws and stuffed them into a small trash bag that he had found during their search.

The two men exited the room and headed for the cafeteria. The bodies of three fat women still lay there in the kitchen area in pools of their own coagulating blood, stinking as they strolled in.

Jones covered his nose with a gloved hand. "Holy fuck! Smells like they've been in here for a week." The bodies had already begun to bloat, releasing cadaveric gasses into the air.

"Yeah, they seem to be decaying much faster than normal." Bishop observed with raised eyebrows, wondering why exactly that was. He pushed the thought aside, knowing that particular information wouldn't help them in their current objective. Alex walked around the bodies, careful not to step in their contaminated blood, and opened a cabinet. After a short search, he found what he was looking for. He pulled out a large box of foil and set it on the countertop. He then handed Jones a box of dishwashing powder.

They stuffed the supplies into the bag and quickly took off down the hall in search of the science department. Glass and plastic bottles were what they were after, something to assemble the explosives in. After reaching the science room and gathering up bottles and rubber stoppers, they headed up to the roof. Jackson and Vindetti eyed them curiously as they saw the two men carrying a large black lawn bag through the door.

"What the fuck you gonna do with that, Cap?" Jackson asked.

"Oh, just a little science project, something to hopefully help buy us some time and maybe thin this herd out a bit." Bishop smiled at his cohorts and set the bag down carefully on the tarred black roof. The sun was at its zenith now and blazing down on the four men, making their jobs that much harder. The black uniforms and heavy body armor didn't help their situation either.

Bishop withdrew the glass bottles from the bag and set them up in a line. He handed Jones the gas can.

Jones started to fill the bottles with gasoline. He then added a bit of motor oil and then soap powder, effectively creating a homemade version of napalm. When lit, the explosive would burn like a lantern; then as it impacted their respective targets, the glass would shatter, allowing the viscous substance inside to cling to whatever it touched. You could stop, drop, and roll all you wanted, but it more than likely wouldn't do you any good. He tore strips of fabric he had found earlier in another one of the classrooms and began stuffing them in the jars to allow them to wick up the flammable liquid.

Bishop set to work on his own concoction. He removed the box of foil and pulled out a large sheet. He tore the foil into strips and began dropping them into plastic beakers. He then filled the remainder of the containers with nails; he glanced over his shoulder at the two men who were awaiting orders to go up and over and start the distraction. "When I seal these bottles, you've got about thirty seconds to get up and over that wall. It will take about three minutes for this thing to explode, but once it does, you don't want to be anywhere near it. I need you to get these dumb fucks moving toward you so these little bad boys can take some of them out. Hooah!"

"Hooah!" the two men replied in understanding. Bishop pulled out the bottle of cleaner; he popped off the spray cap and started emptying its contents into the plastic beakers. He swished the concoction around in the vessel and stuck a rubber stopper firmly in each one.

"Go!" Bishop shouted as he began to drop the plastic bottles over the side of the building. Several of them bounced and rolled off to the side. Bishop hoped they would be in the right position when the infected came stumbling around.

Jackson and Vindetti grabbed the repelling lines in tandem and began their descent over the rear of the building.

Vindetti's boots hit the ground first. He quickly unsnapped the rigging lines and brought his MP5 up to bare, and then scanned the area for any immediate threats.

Jackson landed just after and followed suit.

"Getting slow there, kid?" Vindetti asked in his gruff voice.

"Don't worry, old man. I'll make sure I run faster than you," Jackson replied, looking the slightly older man up and down.

Vindetti grinned.

"Let's get this done." Vindetti crept around the side of the building just to make certain none of the infected were right there, waiting to chomp down on them.

Jackson keyed his shoulder mic. "It's go time, everyone," he whispered, letting his fellow men know they were about to proceed with the distraction and to get their asses in gear. They only had one shot at this, and they needed to make it count.

Jackson and Vindetti stepped around the side of the building and began to shout.

"Hey! Hey dumb fucks, over here!" Jackson shouted at the top of his lungs, waving his arms around like a madman.

Vindetti stood behind him and covered their backs, being that with his twenty-plus years of smoking Camel Wides, he wasn't screaming at anyone.

Slowly one of the infected stumbled around the building to investigate. It paused for a moment as if confused, and then let out a horridly, sickening wail. This seemed to get the attention of the other dumb fucks at the front of the building.

"Yeah, hey you, asshole! Over here! Come see if you can get a bite off my black ass!" Jackson said, starting to have fun with this distraction.

Vindetti eyed him dubiously. "Why does everything have to be about your black ass?" he quipped.

"You wouldn't understand, whitey." He shot a look back at his partner, who just simply rolled his eyes.

After a moment, the group of infected began to stumble around the side of the building, being drawn by the noise and commotion. One of them took off in their direction, sprinting toward them.

"Oh shit!" Jackson shouted to Vindetti and started to back up hastily.

Vindetti raised his MP5 and smoothly dispatched the fast mover. He hit the ground hard and slid several feet before coming to a halt.

The others began to pick up speed, heading in their direction.

"Now?" Jackson asked.

"Now!" Vindetti concurred.

The two men turned and began to jog in the opposite direction. They had only gotten about thirty yards away when an explosion ripped through the moaning horde. Jackson and Vindetti hit the deck as nails shot out and whizzed past them, tearing limbs away from the group of infected. Another explosion fired off merely a second later. The two men watched in amazement as the shrapnel tore into infected flesh, tossing blood and body parts into the air. The men covered their heads as bits of flesh and gore rained down around them.

"Shit, I think some got in my hair!" Jackson shouted.

"Worry about it later, princess. They're still coming," Vindetti said, pointing at the remaining hundred or so infected that rounded the school.

"Holy shit!" Jackson exclaimed as he and his partner scrambled to their feet.

At that moment, the duo spotted a flaming bottle pitch over the side of the rooftop, landing squarely on the infected below. They watched as flames engulfed the advancing figures. Amazingly, the bastards didn't seem to mind that they were on fire. They just kept coming.

"Time to roll, hoss," Vindetti said, grabbing Jackson by the strap of his vest and hauling him forward.

The two men took off toward the woods. The remaining infected polarized on their position, some of them breaking into a drunken run. The men tore into the forest, branches whipping into their faces and legs. They hoped that they would be able to lose the sons-of-bitches in the thick overgrowth, and then double back to the SUVs without being noticed.

A moment later, they heard the sounds of footsteps come crashing into the woods behind them. "We got to put some distance between us and these assholes," Vindetti said with an exhale. He could almost feel the infected people gaining on them.

"What do you think I'm trying to do? Christ, I think I just got a thorn up my ass," Jackson said irritably.

"Quit your bitchin' and get moving, or would you rather they chew it off?" Vindetti said, pointing backward toward their rear.

Jackson thought about it briefly and picked up the pace.

The two men cut a wide swath through the woods moving in a half circle so they would emerge on the far left side of the school, where they could make their way around to the front and escape to the SUVs. At least, that had been the plan.

Jackson emerged from the forest first, looking behind himself as he did so. He could see Vindetti shouting something, but he couldn't quite make out what he was saying. All of a sudden, Jackson ran headlong into the body of an infected. Apparently, not all of them had been stupid enough to follow them into the woods; several of the creeping bastards stayed on the outskirts and followed the noise—basically triangulating their position.

Jackson went down tripping over top of the beast whose face had been ruptured and torn to pieces. Several nails protruded from his head, face, and extremities. Jackson screamed as the man snapped his head down and bit hard into his forearm. The infected tore a chunk of flesh away from his arm, exposing bone and sinew.

Blood poured from the wound as the beast chewed and swallowed and lunged for another helping. Jackson screamed in agony and raised his uninjured fist and slammed it into the forehead of his attacker. The infected's head snapped back with a crack, effectively shattering his spinal column.

"Fuck, fuck, fuck!" Jackson screamed as he realized five other infected converged on his position.

Vindetti burst out from the tree line and opened fire on the assholes that were attacking his friend. Bullets tore through them, but did virtually nothing, being that none of them found their mark in Vindetti's haste to get to his fallen comrade. Sal reached down and grabbed his friend and hauled him to his feet.

"Get up, soldier!" Vindetti said through gritted teeth.

"I've been bit," Jackson said, shock starting to overtake him.

"Never mind that now. We've gotta roll, hoss!"

Shots rang out above their heads as Jones and Bishop targeted the infected surrounding the men on the ground. Jackson and Vindetti took off running toward the front of the building.

Jackson clutched his bleeding arm and fought with everything he had to avoid collapsing from blood loss.

Vindetti spotted Jones and Bishop as they raced to the other side of the roof, presumably to repel to the street and into the cars.

As Vindetti and Jackson rounded the building, several infected held in tow.

Bishop and Jones had just made it to the asphalt.

Scotty and Hoop stood at the SUV, doors held open, and shouted at their compatriots to haul ass and get in. They opened fire on the infected that chased behind the distraction team and bought them enough time to dive into the vehicles.

Jones and Bishop hurriedly launched themselves at the cars, quickly jumped inside, and fired up the ignition. Scotty and Hoop were the last to get in. Bishop hit the gas, not waiting for anyone to get strapped in, and tore off out of the parking lot just as the remaining hundred or so infected started to show themselves from around the opposite side of the school building.

Jackson clutched his arm and cursed as they drove off. Vindetti studied the wound and flinched as he saw the distinct pattern of bone underneath the blood-soaked rags of his shirt.

Bishop looked in the rearview.

"What the fuck happened?" he stated with an edge of anger encroaching in his voice.

"Jackson, sir. He was bitten. Some of those bastards took him by surprise," Vindetti said somberly.

Bishop cursed under his breath. "Okay, what's done is done. Sal, apply a tourniquet to that arm, and then dress the wound as best as you can. There's a med kit under the backseat. Hopefully we can get it before the infection has time to set in."

Vindetti nodded and reached his hand down to locate the medical kit.

"Jones, get on that locator, and get us a position on that case. I want to get this shit done once and for all. Hoop, start reloading mags," Bishop barked out the orders to his men and took off down the street.

INTERLUDE 4

Director Hammond scrambled to reach his magazine as the door to his office exploded open. He finally managed to grasp hold of the slippery bastard, and slap the clip home, as a large man decked out in black BDUs and balaclava stormed into the room, brandishing what looked like an M16A2 fully equipped with laser sights and scope. Hammond's hands trembled as he pointed the gun in the direction of the man.

"Sir, put the weapon down. We're to take you out of here!"

Hammond relaxed, slightly lowering the weapon, realizing the man that had entered was one of his own. Several other black-clad men filed in and remained in the hallway, apparently keeping watch on their backs.

"What the hell is going on?" Hammond spat out in irritation.

"Sir, you need to come with us. This site has been compromised," the lead agent said as he walked over to Hammond and grasped him by the arm.

Hammond shook him off. "Now wait just a damn minute. What do you mean, *compromised*? Compromised how?" His mind swirled in alcohol-induced confusion. As if to punctuate his question, one of the agents in the hallway opened fire. He watched in horror as a female, one of the office workers, was gunned down upon entering the hallway. "What is the meaning of this?" Hammond growled as the woman, someone Hammond recognized as one of the mail room clerks, jumped back on her feet and charged one of the agents guarding the hallway.

The agent screamed and let off a sporadic succession of rapid fire as the woman's smallish form leaped on top of him and bit deep, sinking her snarling teeth into the agent's exposed neck. Blood shot out, coating the door and the walls. More carnage followed as the agent's stray rounds tore into his cohorts. Men clutched their arms and chests as bullets ripped through flesh and impacted body armor, sending screams of shock reverberating off the confined space of the hallway. The agent bled out in seconds and dropped to the floor under the little woman's weight.

The large man in the room with Hammond backed up against the director, taking aim with his assault rifle. He opened fire just as the woman arched her head back in a primal howl. The 5.56 mm round devastated the woman's forehead, causing it to explode outward.

Her corpse fell atop of the other agent, who lay twitching on the floor; red and orange blood pumped out of her grizzly head wound and mingled with the slain agent and pooled around the injured men. Orange tendrils seemed to seek out the fallen as they lay there on the drab gray tile.

Hammond and the soldier in front of him both recoiled as one of their fallen brethren began to convulse violently on the floor, underneath of the near-decapitated form of his female attacker. Shortly after, the other agents seemed to follow suit; some of them let out cries of agony and fear; others convulsed in silence. Several moments passed, and as if in tandem the men, all the men in the hallway, ceased to move.

"Sir, we need to get out of here, now!"

Hammond stared at the carnage in the hallway in silence and disbelief.

"Sir, we need to go. There's a chopper waiting on the roof to evacuate you," the big man said, grabbing Hammond by the arm once more.

"I-I—" A shriek resounded from out in the hallway, causing Hammond and his protector to jump.

One of the fallen agents had somehow regained his footing and was now standing there in the doorway, as if studying the two men. His face twisted in rage, and he took off straight for the two men in the office.

Hammond retreated behind his desk, pointing the pistol he still held in his hands toward the oncoming man.

The agent sent to lead Hammond to the extraction point on the roof was taken by surprise as one of his partners crashed headlong into him.

Hammond shrunk back, not knowing what to do as he clutched the .45 caliber handgun in his trembling hands.

The large agent lashed out at the infected, landing a glove-clad fist square in the man's gnashing jaw. The sounds of jawbones cracking went off like fireworks in the office. The agent kicked out with his boot and managed to flip the infected over onto his back. He rolled jumped to his feet, and brought his boot down hard—slamming the man's head into the plush carpeted floor. A sickening crunch followed as the agent repeated the maneuver, effectively grounding the infected man's skull into a bloody pulp.

Before Hammond could protest, the black-clad agent grabbed him one last time, pulling the balding director around the desk and shoving him toward the door.

"Move!" the agent ordered as they stepped quickly into the hallway.

Hammond noticed the other fallen agents beginning to writhe and twitch on the floor. "Christ almighty," Hammond gasped as his protector picked up the pace and pushed him down the hall.

The two men turned the corner just as a howl escaped from the corridor they had just occupied.

"Go, run, get to the stairs!" the agent shouted as black armor-clad infected rounded the corner.

The two men took off down the hallway.

Hammond gasped as he moved, his heart hammered in his chest as his alcohol-thinned blood flowed through his aging veins. He feared he may have a heart attack before they even reached the stairway door.

The two men ran through rows upon rows of cubicles, cubicles reserved for many of the agencies intelligence analysts whose job it is to decipher these threats.

Hammond shrieked as one wayward hand shot out from behind one of the work spaces.

"Help me," a young man rasped.

The agent simply nudged Hammond forward while at the same time batting the analyst's hand away. The young man lay there, clutching a ragged wound in his side.

"Keep moving, sir," he said as they made their way toward the emergency door.

"B-but he's . . ." Hammond stammered.

"We can't help him now, sir. Mission priority is to get you topside and out of here," the soldier replied.

Hammond reached the door to the stairwell and flung it open. A scream resounded from the cubicles as the infected agents found the wounded analyst cowering on the floor of his office space. Several of the more persistent infected continued forward toward their prey.

Hammond was shoved aside into the stairwell as his protector forced his way through, slamming the door shut, and then scanning the area for threats. Seeing none, he turned and flipped the door's underpinning. It wasn't going to do much, but it may just buy them some time.

The agent faced Hammond as the first of the infected slammed into the door. "Listen carefully. We don't have much time. That door is not going to hold for long. I need to clear these stairwells. You stay close. Don't lag behind. Got it?"

Hammond nodded his head nervously while salty sweat dripped into and stung his cobalt-blue eyes. He wiped the offending excretion away with the back of his hand.

The infected wailed on the door, causing it to shudder and quake under their onslaught.

The agent sent to guard Hammond glanced at the door. "Time to go, sir," he said and started off up the stairs.

Hammond glanced at the door, and then glanced at the four levels of stairs that he would have to ascend. He steeled himself and took off after the agent, not wanting to be left behind, although he was pretty certain the grunt would do no such thing. He was under orders to protect him with his very life. Hammond allowed himself a small measure of satisfaction with that thought. It was short lived, however, as he heard a loud bang from behind. The door, it was about to give. Hammond quickened the pace to catch up to the agent who now stood eyeing the next three levels.

The agent briefly inspected the small window in the door looking for threats; he knew that none of the other doors were secure, and infected, if there were any, could come pouring through those doors at any time. He quickly moved to the next landing, Hammond following close behind; he paused only to kick the door props down as they moved past.

"Clear," the agent said and advanced to the next level, following the same process.

Hammond kept close watch on their backs as they ascended. With one more floor to go, the door on the first level they had entered crashed open. Shrieks and howls filled the stairwell and echoed in their ears as footsteps pounded up the stairs below.

"Move!" the agent yelled as he pushed Hammond behind him and up the stairs toward the final level.

At the top lay a small ladder that led to the roof. Hammond moved as fast as he could manage. He nearly reached the top when the door adjoining the upper level quietly swung opened. Hammond gasped as a twitching shape emerged; the man standing in front of him drooled and growled in a low drone. Slowly, Hammond reached for his pistol, never taking his eyes off the snarling man in front of him.

Shots from one level below distracted the infected momentarily as Hammond brought his pistol to bear. He fired a round at the man, striking him in the temple. The man managed to turn his gaze toward Hammond as he pitched to the side and fell over the railing; he struck the bottom level with a thud.

The agent came running up the stairs, shouting, "Up the ladder! Up the ladder!" He turned and fired another burst, the rounds striking one of the advancing infected just above the knee, cutting the appendage in twain, sending him sprawling into the group behind him, it did little to stall their advance but bought them a few precious seconds.

Hammond climbed as quickly as his weathered body would allow and emerged from the hatch. The day's bright sun and heat blinding him as a group of awaiting soldiers grabbed him and pulled him up the rest of the way.

The men ran with him toward an awaiting helicopter; the rotor wash bore down on him causing his gray wrinkled suit to ruffle and flap as they quickly ushered him inside.

The agent that initially extracted Hammond from the building emerged through the portal. He quickly slammed the hatch shut as the other men stared at him in silence. He stood there breathing heavy, a look of grim shame etched across his blood-covered features. Another of the agents stepped forward to see if the large man needed any aid and he shot him a fierce look.

"Y-You okay, Sarge?" a younger man asked. "Where's your team?" he added reluctantly, already knowing the answer.

"Dead," the sergeant replied, "all for this sniveling little pinhead." He motioned toward the helicopter. "Come on. Let's get the fuck out of here."

The men boarded the flying machine and ascended out into the din.

CHAPTER 18

Marvin Winters sat atop the cell phone tower, thumbing through the contents of the case that he had managed to crack open. So far, none of it made any sense to him—charts, graphs, the occasional medical jargon that you would either have to be a medical doctor or fluent in Latin to even begin to comprehend.

The only part in the file that seemed to make any sense to the old war vet was a single photo. It was titled "Kuru Variant Stage 5." The image was a close-up of a man's face; the man himself really didn't seem to be anything special, other than the fact that he was strapped down to a table, and quite frankly, looked pissed as all hell.

Marvin stared at the image for a few moments and then looked down at the gathering figures at the bottom of the cell tower. He looked back at the photograph, and then as if out of thin air, the image seemed to click. It was the look on the man's face. Not just a look of anger, it was a look of primal rage. The same look that he got from the groaning figures below.

"Son of a bitch," Marvin breathed. "These bastards knew about this shit," he spat in disgust.

Marvin closed the file folder and wound the tie string back in place, keeping the documents secure in the folder. He gazed upward as the sun reached its peak in the sky. Its rays bore down on him like a heat lamp, causing his delicate paper-like skin to break out in small welts. He retrieved his backpack, which he had set off to one side of the landing and stuffed the file back inside.

He looked down at the mass of infected below and sighed. Up here he was fucked and he knew it. There had to be at least twenty of them amassed at the base of the tower, and from this height, there was not a snowball's chance in hell he could take them out with scattershot. He could probably pepper a few of them with the bird shot and maybe get lucky, but he didn't think he'd be able to take them all out. Even if he did, by the time he climbed down, the noise would most certainly draw more of them to his location.

Marvin unzipped the front pocket of his backpack and fished around until he found what he looked for. In his pack, along with essential survival gear, a habit left over from his days in the service. He withdrew a pack of good old Swisher Sweets cigars. He would have preferred a good Arturo Fuente, but at the moment, he would take what he could get. He slipped the slender box out of the unzipped pocket and withdrew one from its interior. After replacing it back into the pocket, he grasped the tab and unwrapped the cellophane that protected the sweet-flavored cigar. He scrounged around his backpack until he found the small waterproof container that housed his limited supply of matches. Normally, he would chastise rookie survivalists for doing such things, as fire in the wilderness could potentially mean the difference between life and death, but fuck it. He was a seventy-three-year-old man stuck on a cell tower above something like twenty crazy assholes. Not to mention he was far from the wilderness at this point.

Marvin popped the cigar into his mouth; the sweet aromatic tobacco wafted into his nostrils and flavored his lips as he struck a match and lit it. He took a long satisfying draw on the cigar, held it for a moment, and then exhaled with a slight cough. If his wife knew that he was smoking again, she would most likely whip his ass from here to Nantucket. For a small wrinkled old biddy, she could still throw him for a loop. He inhaled another drag and released it slowly. The smoke swirled around his head and drifted up into the heavens where it hung briefly and dissipated. He still loved his wife even after all these years that they had spent together. It never waned over time. Sure she could get on his damn nerves like no other, but he even learned to love her little ticks, her anal compulsions toward the cleanliness of the home that they had shared for the past forty years. He hoped she was all right; she had dealt with type-one diabetes for the latter part of her golden years. She was nearing an age where she would plum forget to check her blood sugar, and he would then have to remind her, not to mention help her with her insulin shots.

He looked up into the clouds as they drifted along toward the blazing sun. Feeling the warmth on his face, he was reminded of his younger days when he had first met his wife, Madelyn. *Maddie,* as he liked to call her, lived the next town over just across the river. He remembered in their early days; he was sixteen to her fourteen, and her father was a mean overprotective son of a bitch. When Marvin first came sniffing around, the lanky old man pretty much threatened to cut his balls off and feed them to him if he so much as laid a hand on his Madelyn. Marvin stifled a laugh; he was fairly certain it was her father's overprotective nature that had caused her to end up running into his arms in the first place. Marvin couldn't really blame the man upon reflection; the old man had lost his wife shortly after Madelyn was born due to complications from pneumonia.

Before he was finally accepted into the family household, Marvin could remember sneaking out for their little midnight rendezvous. Marvin would slip out of his home, which was easy enough as his father was an incessant drunk and normally passed out by ten; and his mother, well, she just didn't care. He would follow the game trails through the forest until he reached the edge of the river, where he would strip naked, and stuff his clothing into a small backpack. He would then tread across the river, doing his best to hold the pack up and out of the sluggish water. When he emerged on the other bank, he would dry off, redress, and go meet his girl at the train tracks that led away from the coal mines. A low series of moans from below broke him from his internal ministrations.

Marvin took another drag, inhaling deeply; he gazed down at the writhing mass of people, and well, *people* being a loose term as they seemed to act more like wild animals. He stared at them for a long moment, as if debating his options. As his cigar began to burn down to a nub in his fingertips, he eyed the glowing cherry and smiled. Leaning forward, he flicked the burning ember downward into the mass of infected. The hot projectile bounced off the forehead of a young woman in yoga pants and a brightly colored pink shirt, and caused her to pause slightly and look down at the cigar butt, seemingly studying it for a moment in confusion.

"Dumb fuckers, aren't ya?" Marvin smirked. He eyed the distance to the infected, and reached down to his waist, unsnapping his Glock .45. He slid it from its holster and racked the slide, making certain there was a round in the chamber. He stood and peered over the side, taking care not to lose his footing on the tall tower. *How much would that suck? To run your ass off, climb a tower only to tumble down right into the clutches of the enemy? It would be a perfect end to a perfect day*, he thought sarcastically.

"Pssst! Hey! Hey, shit heads!" He waited and watched as the infected below predictably tilted their heads upward. Marvin took aim at the woman he had marked with the cigar and squeezed the trigger. The .45 caliber round struck the woman just under her right eye, blowing the brain stem out of the rear of her skull. He watched as she collapsed, cursing at the fact that he'd been aiming for her forehead. No matter, at least the shot had found its mark and effectively did its job. He would have to take care; he had a total of fourteen rounds left in this magazine and another two full mags strapped to his belt. If he could manage to clear these assholes away from the tower, he may be able to manage with the shotgun on the ground. Bird shot was great for hunting; however, it's lethality on a human was limited to close range, hence why scattershot was the prime choice for close quarters combat. He also knew from this range it would most likely do nothing more than irritate them like a swarm of mosquitoes.

He took aim again, this time at a man dressed head to toe in what looked like tweed, like he'd just stepped out of a J.Crew store. He never did like those preppy naturalist types. He pulled the trigger, ending his miserable existence. He scanned along the next contestants and selected yet another target. He pulled the trigger, and nothing happened.

"Shit," Marvin spat as he realized the gun had jammed. He racked the slide and tapped the magazine to clear the jam as he heard the familiar sound of an engine heading in his direction. "I'm saved," he said to himself as a white SUV rounded the corner. Marvin's eyes widened as he realized whom the vehicle belonged to. A familiar logo that he had spied almost daily now for the better part of ten or so years was painted on the door of the SUV.

"Fuck, oh fuck, oh fuck," Marvin whispered, feeling his stomach acids roil in his gut and sting his esophagus. As quickly as he could manage, Marvin crouched as low as he could go, trying his best to remain still and unnoticed by the approaching Homeland Security vehicle. He glanced around nervously as if looking for some avenue of escape, but what could he do? He was trapped. At least he knew that perhaps they would take notice of him, kill the infected below, and then . . . what? They blew up the entire fucking road for Christ's sake. They would probably capture him and lock him away for the rest of his remaining years, perhaps after they tortured him for whatever information he possessed, which, of course, was absolutely nothing. Marvin quickly slung his backpack over his shoulders, wondering why they were here. Was it merely a coincidence or . . . The realization dawned on him as he noticed them pull into the gas station below. The case, they were tracking it. Marvin had hoped he had disabled the damn thing when he managed to fry the circuitry and force it open.

He watched as several black-clad agents exited the vehicle. The driver, a white man with graying hair, motioned to the rear of the SUV, and two men piled out half carrying a wounded black man.

Marvin gazed down at the group of infected, the fencing obscured their view of the agents in the gas station's parking lot, but slowly they began to take notice of the easier prey. Several of them began to shamble off in the direction of the noise.

Marvin looked back up at the agents just as a massive man stepped out from the passenger side of the Ford Explorer. The shambling mass caught his attention and he pointed toward the fence line. Marvin ducked down low, hoping they wouldn't take notice of him. With any luck, these agents would draw away the infected and he could climb down and escape before anyone was the wiser. He watched as the gray-haired agent and the large black man shouldered what looked to be MP5s; they took aim at the advancing horde and began systematically dispatching them. The remaining two men helped the injured agent toward the door of the gas station.

One of the men, a white guy with a burly red beard, disengaged himself from the trio, and quickly opened the door to the gas station and stepped inside. Marvin watched from his perch, imagining the man sweeping the interior of the gas station. The man emerged and Marvin saw him motioning toward his fellow officers, giving them the all clear and to get inside. The gray-haired man started barking orders, and Marvin had to assume that he was their commanding officer. The remainder of the agents scooped up the injured man and retreated into the interior of the gas station. Marvin exhaled with a sigh of relief not quite realizing he'd been holding his breath. He gazed down at the heap of bodies that lay in the parking lot; there were still a few figures shambling around, but the majority of them had taken a keen interest on the newly acquired meals under glass.

Marvin knew he needed to act quickly if he had any hope at all of getting out of this shit-creek he had paddled himself into, but goddamn, his knee was throbbing. He swung his body around and draped his legs over the ledge and attempted to step down. He got to the first wrung of the ladder that led to the ground below, and felt fiery pain shoot out from his kneecap and up his thigh as he put all his weight on it.

"Fuck," Marvin said with a harsh whisper, gritting his teeth against the pain. A voice from below drifted up and caught him by surprise.

"Hey, hey, you up there. What are you doing?" a deep voice floated upward toward him.

"Shit," Marvin cursed and closed his eyes, shaking his head. Marvin glanced over his shoulder down at the massive black man he spied getting out of the explorer just a few moments ago, apparently going back to the vehicle to retrieve supplies. *He should have known better*, Marvin thought.

"Come down here, man!" the large man shouted up to him.

Marvin rose up one hand in a placating gesture and nodded. "I'm working on that," the old man said sardonically.

The massive man leveled his weapon in Marvin's direction. "I said get the fuck down here, now!" the large man said irritably.

"I heard ya there, rib eye. I've got bad knees and an artificial leg. It's going to take me a minute, *prick*." Marvin did his best to work his way down the ladder. The man below him fired off a shot, killing another infected that managed to wander a bit too close. Marvin turned his gaze downward just as another man, an agent, ran outside. Marvin saw the big man turn in his direction.

"What the hell's going on?" the gray-haired officer said.

"Hey, Cap, look what I found." The big man pointed his weapon upward toward Marvin.

"Well, I'll be damned," the captain exasperated. "Get him down and bring him inside. We're seeing to Jackson's wounds and then we'll deal with him. You get the kit I asked for?" the captain said. The big man shook his head and pointed toward the SUV.

"Sorry, Cap, I got a bit distracted." The large man shrugged.

"No problem. I'll grab it," the captain said and opened the rear door of the Ford Explorer, pulling out a large medical kit, shutting the door, and motioned in Marvin's direction. "Hurry up with this one. I'm pretty sure he's one of the ones we're looking for," and with that, the captain shut the car door and headed back off into the gas station.

CHAPTER 19

Richard and I crouched low, going prone, hidden among a small grove of trees atop a hill, watching as a white SUV—the same type we had spied on the roadway earlier this morning—went roaring past our position. Richard and I looked at each other in wonder. The white SUV disappeared from sight just around a small bend in the road.

Shrugging, I stood and began tentatively brushing dirt and twigs off my uniform. Richard looked at me as I did so and I shot him a sideways glance. "What?" I asked as I felt his expectant stare upon me.

"Don't you want to see what they're up to?" Richard asked.

I cocked an eyebrow. "Do I want to go chasing after the assholes who just tried to vaporize us? Not particularly," I said, still trying to brush the remainder of gray dust away from my pants.

Richard sighed. "Well, regardless, the police station's that way. If your plan is to get home, you're going to need help and a vehicle, both of which are that way." He paused for a moment, pointing in the direction the SUV had traveled. "Unless you want to hoof it through zombie land," he said, finishing the outspoken thought. I grimaced and shot him a mournful stare.

"Don't call 'em that. That's just stupid."

Richard looked at me with a confused expression. "Don't call them what? Zombies? What the hell else would you call them?"

I looked off down the road in the direction we needed to travel, and then off into the woods in the direction of my home and my wife. Looking back at Richard, I said, "I don't know. Not zombies, though." I shivered a bit even in the summer's oppressive heat at the thought.

"Why not? What would you say they were? They sure as hell look like zombies to me," Richard said, his eyebrows raised.

I got angry. "Have you ever seen a zombie movie or ever read a zombie novel? What always happens in those, huh? Dead people walking. First thing, I haven't seen a corpse rise up out of the ground yet. You? Second, in every single one of those books or movies, the human race ends up completely fucked. I refuse to believe that, whatever this is, ends up meaning our extinction. Not if I can help it. So let's not give into tempting fate by calling them fucking *zombies*. Let's just say infected or something."

Richard sighed and smiled. "Okay, *infected land*. Are you done?" He shook his head.

I nodded satisfied.

"Come on, we need to get moving if you want to get home before dark," he said, eyeing the sun, which still set high in the sky.

It would be a good eight or so hours before night fell, and I hoped like hell that I would definitely make it home way before then.

Richard and I descended the grassy hill away from the woods and walked out onto the street, following the path Homeland's SUV had traveled. I wasn't too keen on the idea of catching up to them, which, being on foot, I doubted was even going to be possible anyway until I heard what sounded like a volley of gunshots just up and around the bend in the street.

Richard and I paused and looked at each other for a moment, and then as if on cue, we set forth in a jog to the side of the road and up an embankment, and once again made our way into the tree line. We followed the roadway from atop the forest-covered hill, doing our best not to trip on storm-blown branches. The ground was still wet from this morning's rain, and it was a struggle to keep upright as we occasionally slid on slippery leaves. We caught up to the source of the noise as we overlooked a small mom-and-pop gas station, complete with convenience store and garage. A group of infected bore down on Homeland's goons and we watched as they quickly dispatched the majority of them.

We saw two of them gather up a man whom appeared to be wounded and usher him inside. The remaining two men, a large black man and a white-haired guy decked out in full body armor, retreated inside of the convenience store moments after the other three.

Several of the infected still remained and began to wander around a small wooden fence that set to the rear of the gas station.

I looked over at Richard. "What do you think they're doing here?" I asked.

Rich gave me a puzzled look. "Hell, if I know, maybe they've got a hankering for Twinkies. Probably best if we stay out of their way, though."

I nodded in agreement. A rather large hairy tree spider decided to take that moment to crawl up and over my hand. "Shit," I exasperated as I shook the little devil off my exposed hand.

Richard cocked an eyebrow at me. "All this crazy shit going on and you're freaking out over a little spider?" He grinned ear to ear.

"Did you see that motherfucker?" I said in a harsh whisper.

"Yeah, I saw him," he said in a condescending tone. "If you thought that one was big, you should see the one on your back," he said and glanced up and cocked his head at my backside.

I spun my head around to try to see if he were telling the truth or just full of shit.

As I was inspecting my shoulder, a loud booming voice caught my attention from below. I turned my gaze back toward the gas station to see what was going on. The large black agent that we had spied only moments ago had returned to the parking lot. It seemed he was shouting at someone. He pointed his weapon, what I knew to be their standard-issue 9 mm machine gun, in the direction of a cell phone tower. I followed his line of sight and let out a resounding gasp.

"What?" Richard said, adjusting his position and narrowing his eyes to try to make out what I was seeing.

I took in a deep breath and exhaled slowly. "That's Marv," I said in disbelief. I'm not sure what shocked me more, the fact that he was still alive, or the fact that he had actually managed to climb a freaking cell phone tower. I guess the threat of being eaten alive can be in itself a powerful motivator. Seeing the asshole in the parking lot holding my elderly partner at gunpoint made me wish that I had some kind of sniper rifle instead of my little pea shooter.

"We've got to do something," I said aloud, sending a glance at Richard.

He returned my gaze and furrowed his brow in thought. "What do you suggest?" Richard said.

I studied the parking lot for a moment, eyeing the large soldier, then glancing between the gas station, and then to my partner. I rolled over onto my side and began patting myself down. Richard seemed to stare at me with some confusion. After several moments of fishing around my pockets, I located what I was searching for. Reaching into my top-left vest pocket, I extracted about three dozen rubber bands that I used daily to bind packages together. I removed them along with several cigarette butts, a few paper clips, and some scribbled notes. Underneath it all was my trusty black-and-silver Zippo lighter. I grinned over at Richard as I flipped it open and struck the wheel, igniting the expected flame.

"These assholes tried to blow us up. Let's return the favor," I said and flipped the lid closed, snuffing it out.

"And how do you propose we do that? Do you know how hard it is to set that shit on fire? It doesn't just take a simple little thing like a lighter to make it go *boom*. If that's all it took, it would happen all the time," Richard said, shaking his head. I took a moment to think it through, gazing once more down at the gas station. Marvin was still struggling to climb down the ladder's lengthy rungs, the soldier still holding a gun on him, ordering him to move faster. It's a wonder he didn't just come tumbling down.

"There." I pointed down to the edge of the parking lot just beyond the gas pumps. On the edge of the lot set a large tanker truck obscured behind several trees and hidden partially by the pumps. The tanker must have been in the middle of restocking the gas station when the shit hit the fan. The door to the truck still hung open as if the driver had beat a hasty retreat. I could see various hoses still attached to the ports that lay recessed in the concrete slabs imbedded in the parking lot.

"There what?" Richard said, not quite getting the gist of what I was saying.

I rolled my eyes. "Dude, the tanker. We blow up the tanker." I pointed down at the tractor trailer again, looking at my companion as if to say duh. "If we can manage to disconnect one of those hoses, or even cut the damn thing, fuel will leak. If the fuel leaks, it evaporates. When it evaporates, its explosive," I said and made a gesture with my hands mimicking an explosion while making a boom noise with my mouth.

Richard nodded, finally getting the idea. Richard seemed to perk up. "We could manage that, I think. What about the incredible Hulk down there?" Richard said, motioning to the large and intense-looking figure standing in the parking lot below. We saw another man exit the gas station briefly. It was the commander, I believe, but my attention was on Marv at the time, watching as he slowly descended the cell phone tower.

"We need a distraction," I said matter-of-factly.

Richard nodded in agreement.

CHAPTER 20

Bishop stepped through the doorway to the gas station, glancing over at Vindetti as he passed; Vindetti covered the parking lot from the interior of the store, watching the area around Jones intently lest something sneak up behind the big man. Bits of broken glass crunched underfoot as Bishop made his way toward the back of the store where two of his men tended to his wounded communications officer. One of the men looked up to greet him.

"Where's Jones?" Scotty asked as he reached a handout expectantly.

Bishop passed the medical kit over to him and looked back toward the front of the store.

"Jones managed to find one of our lost armored car guards. An elderly man stuck up in the cell tower out back, probably the driver, doesn't look like he could do much else." The captain shrugged. "He's getting him down, so we can question him." He plucked a bag of beef jerky off one of the fallen shelves and ripped it open. He savored the salty meat snack as his communications officer groaned in pain. "Jackson, hey, Jackson, stay with us, man," Bishop said, snapping his fingers and handed him a thick strip of beef. "You might want to bite down on something," he said, eyeing the crude tourniquet wrapped around Jackson's injured arm.

Jackson tried in vain to bite down on the tough piece of meat, but he cringed in pain, and it merely slipped out of his mouth and stuck with drool to his cheek.

Bishop looked down at the two men attending to him. "You know what needs to be done, right?" he said to the two men, looks of confusion crossing over their weary faces. Bishop sighed and knelt next to Jackson's squirming form. "Jackson," Bishop said softly, the man did not respond. "Desmond."

Jackson's eyes flickered open at the sound of his first name, something that the soldiers seemed to never use unless the situation had gone from bad to worse. Desmond's pained gaze fell on his commander. "Yeah, Cap?" he said through gritted teeth.

Bishop looked down to Jackson's arm, and then came to look into his officer's eyes. "We need to remove that arm," the captain said softly.

Jackson shut his eyes and nodded, trying his best to stifle a sob.

The other two men stared at Bishop with shock.

"We have to cut his fucking arm off?" Hoop asked with disbelief.

"Yes," Bishop answered coldly, "it's the only chance he has." Bishop reached over and grabbed the medical kit from off the floor where Scotty had laid it. He fished inside and removed the standard scalpel that came with the kit, along with a vial of morphine and a syringe. Bishop unwrapped the syringe and withdrew it from its cellophane packaging. He plunged the tip of the needle into the vial of morphine and drew back the plunger, filling the hypodermic to what he believed was the proper dosage for a man of Jackson's size. He thought about it for a moment and then added a bit more. He removed the needle from the container and tapped the end as he depressed the plunger to remove any trapped air that lay inside. Bishop rolled up the remainder of Jackson's sleeve and located his humeral artery; quickly, he plunged the tip of the needle into Jackson's arm and injected the liquid painkiller in one fluid motion. Looking toward his men, who currently were looking in the other direction, he snapped his fingers, and they quickly looked toward him.

"I'm going to need one of you to find me something I can use to break his arm," Bishop said as his men looked at him dubiously.

Unbeknownst to most, removing a limb was not as easy as one might think. It wasn't like in the movies where a quick flick of the wrist with a sharpened sword would lop the appendage off. Normally, under hospital supervision, in order to remove a limb, it took two things: one: a skilled surgeon, and two: a saw or, in some cases, a scalpel to disconnect the tendons that held the joint in place. In this case, however, Bishop intended to break the bone, allowing him to remove only the infected portion from his comrade's arm, thus hopefully saving at least part of the man's limb.

The two men nodded and went in search of something Bishop could use.

Several moments passed when Hoop appeared, carrying what looked to be a crowbar and a block of wood. "Found these behind the counter. Hell of a mess back there, though," he said, referring to the body of the gas station attendant that lay ruined on the floor behind the counter.

Bishop nodded and took the implements from his cohort. He carefully raised Jackson's arm and placed the block of wood underneath; Jackson moaned quietly as the drugs seemed to take effect. Bishop looked up at Hooper. "I'm gonna need you to hold his shoulders." Hoop grimaced but acquiesced. Bishop looked at his subordinate and sighed.

"Sorry about this, bud," he said as he raised the crowbar above his head and quickly came smashing down with crippling force. The crunch of bone reverberated throughout the small building with a sickening snap, and even with the influence of powerful painkillers running through his veins, Jackson screamed and instinctively tried to pull his injured arm away.

Hoop did his best to hold the flailing man down. The broken arm hung limply to the floor as Jackson tried in vain to pull it protectively into his chest.

Bishop grabbed Jackson's arm by the wrist and pinned it to the floor.

Jackson's eyes were wide open as he watched Bishop retrieve the scalpel from off the floor.

Quickly, Bishop began to cut into the communications officer's flesh, drawing the scalpel around the man's arm just below the tourniquet and well-above the bite wound, separating the infected flesh from the main portion of his body.

The lower portion of Jackson's arm came free, and blood merely oozed from the now-opened stump. Jackson's eyes rolled back in his head as consciousness left him.

Bishop grabbed a wad of gauze from within the medical kit and pressed it firmly to the remaining portion of Jackson's arm. He then began to wrap the stump tightly, thankful that the tourniquet had done its job—only a small amount of crimson leaked from the ragged stump. Bishop was glad that the poor man had finally managed to pass out, allowing him to at least momentarily escape the pain.

Bishop replaced the unused portion of medical supplies back in the first aid kit lest they should happen to need them again, which, in this type of situation, was more than likely going to be the case.

Bishop climbed to his feet, leaving the passed-out form of Jackson on the floor where he lay. Figuring with the amount of morphine he had given the soldier, he'd be out for a few hours, if he survived, that is. Bishop may not have known much about the K5 strain, but he knew the infection and mortality rate was off the charts like nothing they have ever seen before. From the reports that he'd read, once infected, the disease was always fatal, but the reports had never described anything even resembling what they were seeing now. It was almost as if the disease killed and then resurrected its victims. He knew that was impossible; however, he did have a fleeting suspicion that whoever had acquired the pathogen had made some kind of alterations to it. Bishop had seen many men and women take fatal gunshot wounds out there on the highway and just get up and keep coming as if nothing had happened. It wasn't until someone scored a headshot that the bastards went down. He couldn't quite wrap his mind around the whole thing. All he knew was that he and his men were going to have to keep a close eye on Officer Jackson.

Jackson lay still on the floor, his pallor taking on a grayish hue in the pale light that flooded in from the broken windows at the front of the store. His eyes remained closed as his orbs rapidly flittered back and forth under the thin membrane of his eyelids, as if he were dreaming.

Bishop could only assume that whatever the man was experiencing in his unconscious state had to be flat-out nightmarish, judging by the expression etched across the black man's face. A mixture of fear and pain flashed over the man's hardened features.

Bishop turned as the sound of someone entering the front door quietly resounded throughout the room. An old man in a black uniform stumbled in through the entryway, cursing as Jones followed closely behind. His slightly balding head was coated with sweat, and thin wisps of white hair clung to his forehead and temples as he limped across the front of the store and over to the island that resided in the shop's center. He paused as he came to stand by the countertop, leaning against its cool surface.

Marvin glanced over the top of the counter and down at the shop keeper who, only a short time ago, he had been forced to dispatch. The old Marine stared at the ruined corpse, with a continence of cold detachment. As if someone else, somewhere far away had committed the act.

Bishop eyed the man closely, studying the old man's reaction, and knew instinctively that this man had seen combat, which meant he was a soldier, a soldier like himself. This he may be able to work with.

A noise from the rear of the store caught their attention as Officer Scotty came bashing through the metal door that led in from the garage.

Winters' smirked as he saw the robust form of a man carrying in the damaged case that had resided on the workbench where he had left it.

Scotty carried the large case over to his commander and flipped open the lid. "Empty," he said dryly to his captain.

Bishop nodded, studying the interior of the case briefly. He looked over at Marvin, still leaning up against the counter, pretending to be interested in some scratch-off lotto tickets in a small clear plastic case atop the counter.

"Where is it?" Bishop asked with a slight edge to his voice.

Marvin ignored him and continued to study the scratch-off tickets seeming to take interest in one in particular. "Money Pit— five dollars for a chance to win big, match any three like symbols, win the amount listed below, chance of winning up to one hundred thousand dollars," he said, ignoring Bishop.

Bishop stepped closer. He wanted very much to start hounding the old man, to pry the information he wanted out of him; but judging from what he had seen thus far, he didn't believe scare tactics were going to get him very far with this one. No, he was figuring him for a soldier, probably Vietnam, Korea possibly judging by his age. No, he was going to have to try to appeal to the old man's sense of duty, to his sense of patriotism.

"Jones, take your weapon off of this man," Bishop barked.

Jones flinched at his commander's order, eyeing him dubiously. "Sir?" Jones questioned, furrowing his brow.

Bishop shot the man an annoyed glance.

Jones nodded, retreating away from his captive, and walked past the counter over to the front window and came to stand next to Vindetti.

Vindetti looked over and gave Jones a cursory glance, cocking what looked like a sly grin on his gnarled pockmarked features. Jones glanced at Sal out of the corner of his eyes. "What?" he said annoyingly.

Sal smirked, ignoring him, and turned his gaze back out into the parking lot.

Jones stared at the man for a moment, and then followed suit, hefting his weapon and aiming out through the shattered front window into the parking lot. Sun glinted off the shards of broken glass and created a serious of shifting shadows in the gas station's interior as clouds slowly shifted in the sky. "Asshole," Jones muttered.

Vindetti stifled a laugh just as he thought he saw movement to his right. His neck jerked right in the direction of the lambent shift and he studied the surrounding area. *Nothing*, he thought, as he searched the area around an abandoned fuel truck.

"What is it?" Jones asked, taking notice of Vindetti's actions.

"Just thought I saw something. Guess it's just nerves," Vindetti replied, still gazing in the direction of the fuel tanker. Jones nodded in agreement.

"Been a lot of that going around today," he said, scanning the area as well.

Bishop approached Marvin Winters and leaned up against the countertop next to the old man. "Sorry about that, sir," he said, gazing over at the old timer.

Marvin remained quiet using his fingernail to scratch the surface of a lottery ticket. Marvin blew off the latex dust, smiled, and held the ticket out for the captain to see. "Would you look at that. I just won twenty bucks," he said with a slight giggle and stuffed the ticket into his lapel pocket.

Bishop let out a breathy sigh. "The contents of that case, sir? Where are they?" Bishop said, trying his best to keep the irritation out of his voice.

Scotty held up the open case, showing it to the old man.

Marvin pretended to inspect it, adjusting his glasses he peered inside. "That's a fancy case, bub. Sorry, but I have no idea." Marvin gave a dismissive wave of his hand and turned to select another lotto ticket.

Bishop grabbed the old man's liver-spotted hand. Marvin halted his movement as Bishop tightened his grip.

Bishop leaned in close. "I don't have time for games, sir. If you hadn't noticed, there is a shit-storm going on outside, and the contents of that case may be the only chance we have of stopping it," the commander hissed.

Marvin looked over at the captain. "You mind taking your hand off of me, bub?" Marvin said flatly.

The captain released his grip and held up his hands. "Look, I can tell you're a reasonable person, so let's cut to the chase. You have information that we need. Give us that, and you're free to go," Bishop tried to fake a smile, but it looked out of place on his hard features.

Marvin eyed him suspiciously. "Let me go, just like that?" Marvin made an example by walking his index and middle fingers across the countertop. He considered for a moment and shrugged. "Nope, still don't know what the hell you're talking about, chief." He smiled.

Bishop's smile faded, and he took a step back nodding.

Scotty stormed forward and slammed the empty case down hard on the countertop and grabbed Marvin by his shirt collar. He thumped him hard against the counter's surface. "Listen, you old fucker. You're gonna give us what we want, or I'm gonna tear you a new asshole!" the burly red-haired Scottish officer said, sending flecks of warm spittle into Marvin's face.

Marvin blinked away the offending liquid and gave a sheepish grin. "You're gonna have to do better than that, bub." Marvin brought his implanted joint and artificial leg up, slamming it hard into the large man's groin.

Scotty's eyes went wide with shock as the metal implant struck his tender testicles and sent a wave of pain clear up the big man's chest, causing him to release his grip and double over in pain. Scotty gasped and reached to cover his nuts before the old man could deliver another blow.

Bishop reared on Winters, slamming a gloved fist into the side of his chin, knocking Marvin off center.

Marvin's false teeth nearly flew out of the side of his mouth with the impact. He involuntarily bit his cheek in the process of trying to keep his false teeth in place.

Bishop, using his feet, planted them in between Marvin's legs and shoved him sideways, grabbing his arm in the process. He wrenched the old man's arm free from the countertop and spun him around like a ballerina dancer.

Marvin went down hard, tripping over Bishop's feet, his face thumping hard against the flat surface. Blood pooled out from his lips as the captain wrapped the old man's hands behind his back, effectively restraining him.

"I didn't want it to go this way, sir," Bishop spat in Marvin's ear as he used his free hand to fish around Marv's pockets. After a moment, Bishop located Marvin's wallet. He tossed it aside and continued to frisk the man harshly.

Marvin started to chuckle as Bishop searched him. "Stop! Ha-ha! That tickles," he said doing his best to enervate the man.

"Scotty, pick up this asshole's wallet and see who the fuck he is," Bishop ordered.

Scotty mumbled and cursed as he shuffled his way over to the billfold and retrieved it off the floor. He flipped the old tattered brown leather wallet open and thumbed through its contents and retrieved what looked to be a driver's license and work ID. He held the ID up for his boss to inspect.

"Says here his name is Winters, Marvin Winters," Scotty said with his slight Southern drawl. "Says also that his partner is a Kyle Walker." Scotty tossed the IDs onto the shop counter in front of the two men. Bishop studied the small credit card-sized objects closely for a moment.

"So, Marv, if you don't know about the information we're looking for, perhaps your partner does. Where is he?" Bishop sneered.

"Shit if I know, probably a God damn pile of ashes by now after what you people did." Marvin's voice began to tremble ever so slightly at the thought of his longtime friend being burnt to a crisp. He just hoped that it had been quick. Or even better, that he had managed somehow to escape the blast. He doubted that outcome; however, the bomb they had dropped on that portion of 95 had no doubt vaporized anything within half a mile of the blast zone. He could remember his days in Vietnam, where the use of napalm was widespread and the subsequent devastation that followed the cleansing fire. What they used here was a hundred times more powerful than that.

"Hey, Cap, check this old biddy out. Maybe we should ask her." Scotty held out an old tattered photograph of a sweet-looking elderly woman.

Marvin shot his gaze over toward the burly man and the photograph. "You leave her alone, you sons of bitches!" Marvin struggled against Bishop's forceful grip. The captain pressed Marvin's face harder into the countertop, causing him to wince in pain.

Jones and Vindetti looked away from the window, watching the scene play out just as an explosion ripped through the, air sending metal debris into the store front. The gas station shuddered as a plume of flames shot upward toward the sky.

Jones was knocked to the floor under the weight of a wayward magazine rack that was picked up off the floor and hurled toward him. Shards of glass bit deep into his bicep, and he squealed in shock and pain.

Vindetti ducked and rolled to one side, narrowly missing an oncoming shard of scrap metal.

Startled by the explosion, Bishop momentarily released his grip on Marvin.

Marvin, feeling the captain's lapse in concentration, used the opportunity to break free of his grasp. Bishop reached for his sidearm. Marvin spun around and planted his foot directly in

Bishop's abdomen, causing him to double over. Scotty reached for Winters just as he felt something brush across the back of his neck.

Startled, Scotty whirled around only to see blank eyes staring into his. "Jackson?" Scotty breathed, startled to see the man standing on his feet. Jackson snarled and lunged. Scotty tried to sidestep the attack but slipped on broken glass shards that lay strewn across the floor. Jackson fell on him, tearing into his windpipe, clamping down hard with snarling teeth. Blood shot out as Jackson wrenched his head back, tearing the tender flesh from Scotty's trachea. Scotty tried in vain to scream as blood bubbled out of the opened wound, his vocal cords no longer able to create sound.

Scotty floundered on the ground as Marvin began to run toward the door.

Officer Hooper, late to the party, came bursting through the doorway of the garage and into the store. "Hey, what the hell is—" Hoop stopped as he took in the scene. "Holy fuck!" he screamed as he saw the form of Jackson tearing strips of flesh away from his former partner's face.

Shouldering his submachine gun, Hooper opened fire, striking Jackson in the back. Flecks of deep red and orange blood spilled out from the small wound pattern that exploded on his backside.

Jackson paused in his feast and slowly stood. He turned and faced Hooper and growled in a low feral pitch.

Hoop gasped as he saw the eyes of the man he once knew. The look was both intense and empty all at once. Like pools of nothingness reflecting his very soul. Dark rims lined his eyes, and blood spilled freely from his gaping mouth and dribbled over his chin, staining his shirt. The look of the man was horrific. Hoop stepped back slowly, keeping his weapon trained on the man. Hooper, in his mind, knew his friend was no longer with them. That the man he once knew was long gone and was replaced by this, this thing. He knew he should put him down. Yet he hesitated.

"Jackson, man, what are you doing?" Hoop stammered as he continued to back away.

The front door burst open as Marvin made a hasty exit.

Hoop glanced his way momentarily, distracted by the noise. Jackson lunged, throwing himself bodily into Hoop's distracted frame. Hoop, realizing his mistake, threw his hands up, blocking the man who snapped his jaws and lunged for his exposed neck. The two men struggled, Hooper doing his best to keep Jackson at bay as Jones managed to push the magazine rack off his legs.

Vindetti crawled to his feet and headed over to Jones' position, thrusting out a hand to help the big man to his feet. The two paused, watching as Marvin darted out into the parking lot seemingly lost in smoke and flames.

Hoop struggled with the snarling form of Jackson. His bloodied maw lunged and caught the collar of his uniform and tore off a strip of black fabric. Hooper screamed as a smallish wound exploded outward on the forehead of the attacking Jackson. His head slunk down and landed on Hooper's chest; Jackson's raging body went slack, all of his weight crushing the wind out of him.

Jones and Vindetti grabbed the dead man by the back of his shirt and hauled him off Hooper. Hoop gasped as air returned to his lungs. He coughed violently and turned to his side, vomiting. After a moment of shaking involuntarily, he steeled himself and sat up.

Bishop stood over him, pistol still clutched in his hand. Alex held a hand out to Officer Hooper. "You okay, soldier? He didn't bite you, did he?" Bishop said.

"No, sir, I don't think so," Hooper replied, still shaking. He looked himself over, checking for any obvious wounds. Spotting none, he took Bishop's hand. Bishop helped the man to his feet. "Damn, he got Scotty," Hoop said.

Bishop, as if remembering this fact, quickly turned. Taking aim with his pistol, he fired a single shot straight into the dead man's forehead. His subordinate's head jerked sideways as the round punched through his skull. Blood pooled beneath the wound and ran onto the glass-covered floor.

"What the fuck, boss?" Hooper backed up in shock. His eyes transfixed on the man that had just had his throat tore out. "He was dead, Cap. Why would you do that?" Hoop nearly shouted the last part.

"Because I intended on keeping him that way. I don't know if you've been paying attention, kid, but there's been some crazy shit going on around here." Bishop pointed a finger toward the parking lot. "How many of these things have you seen walking around out there with that same exact injury?" Bishop motioned toward the dead man on the floor. "Or worse, for that matter. Somehow this shit is bringing them back," Bishop said, pausing to allow that implication to sink in.

"Whoa, whoa, whoa, Cap, what the hell are you talking about?" Jones said, stepping into the conversation. "What are you not telling us?" He approached Bishop.

Bishop stood there in stoic silence as if considering his reply.

Vindetti stepped over to the group of men. "Uh, guys . . . In case you've forgotten, our prisoner just took off." Vindetti jerked a thumb toward the door.

Bishop shot a look toward the parking lot.

"Fuck!" Bishop shouted. "Come on, he couldn't have gone far," Bishop commanded, holstered his pistol, and retrieved his MP5 from off the littered floor. Slinging the weapon over his shoulder, he headed for the door. He paused and half turned toward his remaining men. "That's an order, gentlemen," and with that, he stepped out of the front door and into the blazing parking lot.

CHAPTER 21

Marvin scrambled through the shattered door frame and into the parking lot, using the distraction the explosion had provided to his advantage. Marvin risked a glance over his shoulder to see if his escape had been noticed. Luckily, for him, the men that he had left inside of the gas station seemed to be occupied with the snarling form of a one-armed assailant. Marvin observed the scene for a brief moment taking notice that the one attacking them happened to be the young injured man that had been lying on the floor when they had brought him in. *Damn*, Marvin thought, realizing the poor bastard must have turned after they removed his appendage. The man writhed and lunged at his captors with vicious ferocity. Marvin smiled to himself briefly. "Serves you assholes right," he muttered to himself. As he moved forward, waves of intense heat hit him as the tanker truck on the opposite side of the parking lot set ablaze.

The roar of flames was deafening in his ears as he made his way away from the building. Marvin froze as the sound of a gunshot resounded behind him. Putting his hands up, he slowly turned back toward the gas station. The doorway was still empty, the men inside obscured by heat distortion and smoke.

Marvin shook his head, feeling foolish. The gunshot had not been meant for him. At least not this time, but that could change at any second. Marv turned back around and looked for an avenue of escape. To his right was a wall of flame. After his years of working with explosives and pyrotechnic devices, it was blatantly obvious to Marvin that the explosion had been deliberate, but caused by whom? To his left, well, that had been the original pathway he'd come from and he didn't much like the idea of backtracking. *Not much choice, however*, he mused.

Marvin began to limp in that direction when movement to his right caught his attention. A lone figure materialized seemingly out of nowhere and stepped out from within the recesses of the flames. A charred, smoldering form shambled toward Marvin. Its clothing was completely seared away, save for shreds of a plastic-like material that bubbled along its feet. Strips of brightly colored rivulets stretched out, clinging to the asphalt beneath as it moved closer.

Marvin shuddered as the smell of cooked flesh assaulted his nostrils. The scent of burnt hair and fat wafted up and struck him full in the face like a hammer. The figure's exposed teeth gaped open as it tried to moan. Nothing escaped but a small hiss of air as the flesh surrounding his neck and trachea had all but been burned away. The figure stumbled toward Marvin, on charred legs, with outstretched hands. Marvin saw the cracks in the skin that ran along his fingertips and exposed bone and muscle beneath. Instinctively, Marvin reached for his sidearm. Realizing the moment he laid his hand on the empty holster that it was gone, his weapon having been stripped from him during his initial liberation from the cell tower.

Another figure shambled around from behind the burning vehicle. This one still wore clothing that was set ablaze. Flames danced off its shoulders and fanned upward as it moved.

"Ah, shit," Marvin cursed, backing up, nearly tripping over a discarded piece of scrap metal that must have blown away from the tanker truck when it had exploded. He glanced over his shoulder and, to his surprise, saw a familiar face staring back at him just within the tree line.

"Kyle?" Marvin shook his head in disbelief. "It can't be," Marvin breathed.

Kyle waved frantically to him from within the trees, motioning for the old man to run.

Marv cast one last glance at the approaching creatures and then over toward the gas station door, expecting his captors to burst through the opening at any moment.

Kyle waved again this time with more urgency.

Marvin relented. Gritting his teeth, Marv took off in his own semblance of a run. It was more like a fast paced wobble than anything remotely resembling an all-out sprint.

Marvin reached the tree line and ducked inside, nearly out of breath, and huffing like he'd just run a five-K triathlon. The pain in his knees was so intense he nearly fell to the forest floor as Kyle and another man caught him. The other man, the cop from the highway, Marvin realized, stood there holding him by the elbows. Marvin looked at the two men dumbfounded, resting his eyes on Kyle.

"Where in the hell have you been?" Marvin asked, cocking and eyebrow, giving his partner a once-over.

"Sightseeing," Kyle replied without missing a beat. A sly grin spread across Kyle's worn face; he stepped forward and embraced the old man in a bear hug that nearly tore the wind out of him.

****

"Hey, hey, hey, now ease up. You gonna break my hip." Marvin gave me a sly wink. I released him. Marvin coughed and rubbed his aching knee. He stood erect and clapped me on the shoulder. "Seriously, I thought you were dead." He let out a sharp sigh. "Glad to see you made it, kid." Marvin allowed a broad smile.

"Likewise, Marv. We thought you'd been roasted like a chicken in that tin can." I shook my head with the memory of the attack on the highway. "How did you manage to escape?" I asked casting a glance at Marvin's leg.

Marvin shrugged. "Well"—Marvin scratched his head—"Getting hit with that frigging missile was a good indicator that it was time to slip away," Marv said with an edge of sarcasm and thrust a thumb over his shoulder. "So I managed to sneak out before the goon squad showed." Marvin cast a glance back at the gas station. "Lot of good that did me." He frowned.

Richard quietly tapped me on the shoulder. I paused and looked in his direction. A look of concern was etched across his dark features, and he held a finger up to his lips, motioning for us to be silent. He then pointed out toward the parking lot. The infected that had chased my partner out of the lot were seemingly locked onto our position and headed this direction.

One figure was charred and blackened from flame, his skin flaking off in hot dark-gray cinders as he moved. Steam rose from his body and sent fine wisps of smoke streaming into the air. Its mouth stood agape, opened wide in what looked like a silent scream. The second figure walked several feet behind the first, this one seemingly in better shape, although half of his right arm and midsection were currently being consumed by flames. Dried blood coated his mouth and neck and stippled the front of his dirty T-shirt. This one snarled and quickened its pace as it spotted us in the tree line.

"Shit! I think we should get—" My suggestion was cut off as the front door of the gas station burst open. A large black man and aging white guy ran through the portal, followed by two other men shortly after. The four of them fanned out into the parking lot, taking care to steer away from the burning tanker truck. The infected that were headed our direction paused, taking interest in this new prey, and advanced on them.

The gnarled older agent was the first to react to the threat. He raised his weapon barely taking time to aim and fired. A round punched through the head of the closest fiend, the one that still held some resemblance of a human. It fell to the asphalt sprawling, the flames that consumed his side still licking upward and spreading onto its back.

The second limped toward the four men, pausing as if to choose between them. The muscle-bound black man took the initiative and closed the distance between them in a flash. Without hesitation, he swung the butt of his rifle up at the creature's skull. The rifle connected with its temple with a sickening crack. The charred thing's head seemed to implode with the amount of force that was behind the blow. The scorched bones shattered and flew apart as the large man followed through with a swing that would have made Babe Ruth jealous.

I actually envisioned the man pointing out into the distance as if to say where the creature's head was going to land. Sometimes I don't even know what the hell is going on up there in my lofty brain.

I refocused back on the situation at hand and gasped. A white-haired man, tall, slender, a sense of command about him, stared directly at me. He cocked a half almost-wicked smile and motioned to his men. His men polarized on our position and slowly began to head in our direction.

"Fuck!" I said in a harsh whisper. I gazed from Marvin to Richard. "What the hell are we going to do?" I rasped, feeling acid burn at the back of my throat. I felt the fringes of panic begin to build within me. *What the fuck were these guys after?* I thought.

Richard looked over at me and drew his sidearm.

I frowned, thinking that this was it. I was going to die here, in the woods, possibly in a ditch (Mom always said I would end up in a ditch someday). All I wanted to do was go home. Kiss my wife, run my fingers through her silky hair, and then collect our children and run for the hills. I didn't want to be here. None of this was right; none of this could possibly be happening. A voice bellowed out over the distance and snapped me back to reality.

"To you fellas hiding out back there in the woods, you can come out now. We're not gonna hurt ya. We just want to talk. We believe you have something that belongs to us," the white-haired man said, lowering his weapon to face the ground. I noticed his compatriots didn't follow suit.

"What could we possibly have that these ass-hats want?" I asked in a low voice, speaking to my friends. Marvin cast somewhat of a guilty glance over at me. "What?" I asked, catching his demeanor.

"There's a file," Marvin stated, "in that case that we were carrying to Brantley and Reese this morning. You know, the one with all the fancy doodads on it." Marvin made a blinking motion with his hands.

"Yeah, I remember it, I had a hunch it may have had something to do with that. What kind of file?" I asked, wondering what kind of information could cause this much of a ruckus. It was bad enough to be facing some potential plague that turned people into flesh-eating freaks, but to add being hunted by the government's golden boys was a bit much. Especially since, at least I would think, this disease would more or less take precedence over anything we would be transporting. You know, zombie-like creatures attacking people and making more zombie-like creatures trumps confidential documents sort of precedence. I paused considering the implications. "What was in the file?" I asked with a bad feeling creeping up inside me.

"Medical research, I think. I couldn't really make heads or tails of it but . . ." Marvin sighed and shrugged. "Part of me thinks we should just hand it over, but then again, the part of me that has been through war and seen this type of situation before thinks there is no way in hell they're going to take it and let us walk out of here." Marv gave me a dead-serious stare.

I didn't know what to think. What kind of medical research could make these guys want to kill us for seeing it? I mean, I know this stuff going on was bad, completely fucked actually, but why would they want to take us out for it? I scratched my head considering, *unless, unless they already knew about it . . . and this was their attempt at a cover-up.* I blew out a long breath and stood. I carefully walked over to the tree line, placing myself behind a rather sturdy-looking oak tree, figuring if these bastards started shooting, at least it would provide me with some type of cover. Marvin cast me a wild glance.

"Kyle, what on Earth do you think you're doing? Get down!" the old man hissed.

I waved him off. I peered around the base of the oak tree, hugging up against its rough-textured surface. A line of ants busied themselves up the side of the large trunk and I did my best to avoid crushing the little creatures. I peered out from behind the tree and observed the four expectant men, considering what I was going to say. I couldn't think of squat at the moment. *Ah, well, fuck it,* I thought.

"What exactly is it we're supposed to have, sir?" I said loud enough so that my voice would carry the two hundred or so feet away, just to be certain that the gathering of agents could hear me. The white-haired fellow looked dubiously over to his subordinates.

"Sir, we know for a fact that your man has what we're looking for," he said, giving me a hard stare.

I glanced back at Marv and he waved a middle finger in the air. I rolled my eyes and turned to face the agents. "And what exactly is it you're looking for, sir? Swear to God, if you say free samples, I'm going to start shooting," I said, casting Marv and Richard a sly grin. Marvin rolled his eyes knowingly; Richard slapped his forehead. In my line of work, people tended to ask that very same question about five hundred times a day. Everyone thought they were just the most clever and original sons-of-bitches on the planet. My automatic reply to said question was "Nope, but I think I just saw the ghost of Ed McMahon run over that hill with a giant check," referring to the old Publishers Clearing House commercials. Of course in this case, I could always say the infected corpse of Ed McMahon. A skinny grizzled-looking gentleman stepped forward impatiently and shouldered his rifle.

"Let me just shoot him, Cap, so we can get this shit over with," the man said with a gruff gnarled voice, sounding as if he'd spent the better part of the last thirty or so years smoking five packs of cigarettes a day and shouting at the top of his lungs.

The white-haired man, their commanding officer apparently, held up a hand. "Vindetti, ease up. Let me handle this," the commander said, and the skinny man cursed under his breath and backed off a step. "Kyle, isn't it? Kyle Walker?" the man said, looking in my direction. I cast a look of mixed confusion and betrayal at my partner.

Marvin grimaced and returned my gaze. "They got a hold of my ID card. Sorry, kid," Marvin said with a slight sense of guilt and shame washing over his features.

I shook my head as if to say *It's no big deal*. Marvin nodded in understanding. I looked back down on the men in the parking lot.

"So you know who I am, sir. May I ask then who exactly the hell you are?" It was a bold statement, but I figured if we had something they wanted, then maybe I could use that to my advantage. The white-haired man stepped forward slightly.

"I'm Alex Bishop, captain of the Homeland Security's strategic threat assessment task force. This"—he motioned to the others in turn while he spoke—"is my second agent, Jones. These two are Officers Vindetti and Hooper."

The three other men stared at me with blank expressions. The one he had called Vindetti looked as if he would rather twist my head off like a soda cap. I smirked slightly. From the looks of him, he could probably do just that; it gave me some type of grim satisfaction, however, knowing that I could have that effect on some people.

"Once again, sir, the file, we know you have it. We traced the case that housed it to this location. It's imperative that we take it back to our people. You have no right to it, and we've already lost men in its pursuit. So, just hand it over so we can all go home." The captain let the statement hang in the air.

I glanced over at Marvin, and he grimly shook his head. The words he spoke only moments ago hung in my mind like a wraith. They're not going to let us walk away after seeing this. I hadn't even seen the documents in question, but I believed the old man. Hell, I'd trusted him with my life every day for the past ten years, so why stop now?

"Actually, friend, you should check your facts. If we do indeed have this . . . file or whatever you're looking for, we were given sole dominion when it was signed over to us this morning," I said, trying to gauge their reaction from my position. "Just because you give me a fancy title doesn't mean *jack* in my book. You could claim to be the President of the United Freaking States, and I still wouldn't give it to you." I paused. "No, I think we'll take it to its assigned destination, then if they want you to have it, you can get it from them. Other than that, you can go fuck yourselves." I looked pensively over at my compatriots and shrugged. Hoping my words made some bit of sense. The agent in charge, Bishop I believe, looked over at his crew and nodded.

"Fine, we'll do this the hard way," he stated, and his men suddenly took off in all directions. They disappeared into the surrounding landscape in a flash. *Shit*, I thought, crouching behind the tree, and pulling my revolver. I looked over at my comrades.

Richard, who still held his Glock at the ready, sought cover on my right flank, taking up position behind another sturdy-looking tree. He crouched low and aimed his weapon into the distance.

Marvin, who was still unarmed, grabbed for a solid-looking branch that lay on the forest floor. He hefted the long piece of wood and took up position to my left, concealing himself behind some leafy branches.

Agent Bishop didn't say another word. He turned slowly and walked away. He disappeared into the white SUV that set in the gas station parking lot. I watched as the SUV's engine started. The captain sped off down the road, presumably to a preordained position to regroup with his men. *After they had killed us*, I thought. Great, all this crap going on, and we're fighting one another. I shook my head in disbelief.

The sharp crack of gunfire resounded from out of nowhere, and the trunk of the tree next to my head exploded and rained debris and splinters over my face. I shrunk back and shielded my eyes from the offending shower. *Holy shit*, I thought and nearly screamed with surprise. I brought my weapon up and scanned the area from where I believed the shots had been fired from. Seeing nothing but tree limbs blowing softly in the breeze, I cursed.

"That was a warning, bitch. The next one goes through your forehead," a voice bellowed seemingly from all directions.

I pinpointed where I thought it was coming from and fired a shot by way of reply. I heard a voice curse and noticed movement off in the distance. I adjusted my position, trying my best to present as small a target as possible.

Richard followed the movement in the trees and peppered the area with a hail of bullets from his 9 mm handgun.

The movement in the woods seemed to pick up pace, and another volley of shots struck out in our direction. The figure in the woods fired as he ran; the movement ceased as I assume he found a suitable area to hide.

"This is a frigging Mexican standoff!" I said aloud to my comrades. At the moment, aside from Marvin only being equipped with a tree branch, we were pretty well even matched. Three highly trained Homeland Security agents against two highly trained armored enforcement officers as well as the MDTA policeman, whose agency was known for their level of training with all they had to deal with on Maryland's highways and byways. *This was going to be interesting*, I thought, and for some reason the song "Dueling Banjos" popped in my head. Rolling my eyes at myself, I forced myself to focus; I noticed something strange off to my left.

Pale faces began to appear in the forest all around us. People, or at least what used to be people, began shambling into our area.

I watched in horror as one of them came frighteningly close to Marvin. Fevered hands brushed up against his side and caused him to pitch backward out of his hiding place before I could even call out a warning. Marvin swung his wooden bludgeon and barely nicked the monster's forehead. A thin ragged line appeared on the monster's brow. Marvin took a step back and swung again, this time connecting with the beast square in the noggin. His branch snapped with the impact; however, it also managed to end the infected's existence as it pitched forward and landed in the dirt beneath Marvin's feet. Blood pooled out of its eyes and mouth mixing in with the dirt and rotted leaves. A barrage of shots arched out of the woods and nearly struck the old man. If it hadn't been for him tripping over a root buried in the ground behind him, he may have very well been killed.

Marvin immediately rolled over to his knees, wincing in pain as his throbbing knees responded to the movement.

Several more figures began to shamble within view of the trio; Richard shot the first one to enter his kill zone and took him down quickly.

Another, a woman in a torn baby doll dress, stumbled directly in front of me, seeming to materialize out of nowhere. She managed to grab hold of my arm and pull it toward her gaping mouth. I grunted in surprise and smacked the lady in the side of the face with the barrel of my revolver.

She stumbled backward and lunged again. This time I kicked out and struck her in the side, and she pitched forward, landing hard on the ground. I drove the heel of my boot down on the back of her neck, resulting in a resounding crack of her spine. The woman's head writhed on the ground, unable to move anything aside from her mouth and eyes. Her face stared up at me almost pleadingly. I shuddered, wondering what she must be feeling, if she was able to feel anything at all that is.

More shots caught my attention. This time the rounds were not apparently meant for us. Shouts came out of the distance, and I realized this was perhaps our first opportunity at escape. More faces were appearing in the forest surrounding us; deep guttural moans began sounding throughout the area. I looked frantically from Marvin, and then to Richard.

"We need to find a way out of here now!" I shouted to be heard over the sounds of gunfire and the moans of the infected that were beginning to stumble into view all around us. I could only assume they had been from the area surrounding the gas station. Homes and small businesses littered the expanse in this subdivision of Baltimore County. I wondered briefly just how far this infection had spread, not to mention how it had spread so fast, and why we weren't affected as well? Questions for another time, I mused and scanned the area, judging our options, looking for an avenue of escape.

The gas station behind us was completely engulfed in flames by this point. The gas in the underground tanks having now ignited and spewing fire forth like the burning oil rigs in Saudi Arabia during Desert Storm. Fire shot straight upward in a steady stream. *Strange*, I thought, figuring it would have been a massive explosion; but knowing the properties of gasoline, that was not the case. It would burn but would not explode unless it had been vaporized. So at the moment, it was like a giant Tiki torch extending into the afternoon air.

Several homes nearby began to ignite under the intense heat; clothes that hung on lines outside drying out and catching in the superheated air spread the encroaching inferno.

That left the way back out of the question. I had already almost been roasted today and I had no desire to revisit that situation. That limited our options; we would have to escape into the surrounding woodland. Problem was, aside from the fact that I had no idea where exactly that would lead us, the location of our attackers was still unknown to us at this time. The sound of a gunshot and or the occasional scream was the only indication that the agents were still in the area. Then there were the infected. Men and women, young and old seemed to pile into the forest. The figures scrambling into the trees looked like something out of horror movies. Most of the approaching figures sporting ragged neck wounds or bits of flesh and muscle torn from exposed appendages. Their skin took on an almost waxy yellowish pallor. Blue veins lightly spanned out across their skin, creating a nightmarish visage. It was their eyes, however, that were the most disturbing.

The ones closest to me, an older-looking woman dressed in what could only be described as a *Muumuu* patterned with light blue flowers now ripped to shreds covered in blood and dirt snarled in my direction. Her eyes were dotted with deep red veins and burned with infection. Her gaze, however, despite the enraged look on her face, showed absolutely no emotion whatsoever. It was as if her mind was completely lost, dead.

Another, a middle-aged man in a gray tattered business suit, stumbled in close from the other side. Richard raised his 9mm and shot this one in the forehead before I even had a chance to react. He stumbled forward a few steps and collapsed on the ground in front of the old woman, causing her to trip and sprawl onto the forest floor. I gazed over at my friends.

"We have to move forward. It's the only way," I exasperated, knowing that we were in for the fight of our lives. In front of us was not only certain death at the hands of Homeland Security's goons, but also from what I could make out through the breaks in the foliage, were about a hundred or so infected, perhaps drawn to the noise of our exchange—like moths to a flame. Either way it really didn't matter; the decision was the only one we could make.

Richard racked his slide after inserting a new magazine and nodded at the ready.

I reached down to the forest floor and retrieved a lightweight yet solid-looking branch and handed it to Marv, who took it reluctantly, most likely wondering what good it would do. Something was better than nothing I thought, and looked the two over.

"Okay, guys, let's go." I raised my pistol, Richard and Marvin taking up position on my flanks, and we began heading forward deeper into the forest.

INTERLUDE 5

Director Hammond disembarked the UH-72A Lakota helicopter that had evacuated him from the office building that housed the Department of Homeland Security's operations center. He stepped out onto a small landing pad located in an obscure military base somewhere in western Maryland, followed by his escorting officer, which he learned midflight was Special Agent Roberts.

Roberts was a huge man. He had removed his balaclava during their flight to wipe the sweat away from his face. The man had a total lack of hair. A bald head reflected the sun's rays, and his face was a set of deep piggish-like features and small yet fierce eyes and virtually no neck to speak of. Upon closer examination, Hammond had come to realize that the officer was actually shorter than he'd originally thought; the heat of battle, adrenaline, and fear caused his perception to skew away from reality.

A U.S. Army jeep pulled up to their position, its hull decorated in the usual style of drab tan, camouflaged for a desert campaign that it had not made it into. Roberts instructed Director Hammond to step inside. Hammond said nothing, but Roberts forced himself to hide a smile as he saw the look of contempt cross Hammond's features. Apparently, Hammond did not like being told what to do. Oh well, Roberts thought, this was his show at the moment and the director was just going to have to deal.

The two men boarded the vehicle; a small scrawny corporal greeted them, saluting as they entered. Agent Roberts returned the gesture to the noncom even though the U.S. Army and the department of Homeland had a completely different ranking system.

Hammond simply nodded and took the seat next to the driver.

Roberts climbed in the back, taking notice of Hammond's choice. *Arrogant bastard*, Roberts thought.

The rotors on the helicopter they had just flown in on still spun as a fuel truck pulled alongside, taking care not to get too close. A crew of two men dressed in overalls jumped out and began busying themselves with the process of refueling the aircraft.

"Where are they going?" Hammond asked in astonishment, wondering why their ride was disembarking so soon.

"They're under orders to retrieve other personnel, sir," Roberts replied. "You didn't think you were the only one, did you?" The agent allowed himself a slight smirk.

"No, I just . . ." Hammond didn't finish his sentence as the jeep lurched forward and headed off down the airfield. "Where exactly are you taking me?" Hammond asked.

"There is a bunker here, sir. We would have routed you out to Washington, but that location had already met its maximum capacity. This location was the next logical choice." Roberts looked out over through the fences. Men ran alongside the fence line, taking up positions at hundred yard intervals. It was then Roberts took notice of the encroaching hordes of infected walking in their direction. People from the adjoining town he assumed, a town that now burned and smoldered in the distance, the smoke visible above the tree line. "You are to have full operational capabilities in the bunker, along with the protection and assistance of the soldiers stationed at this location." He paused. "The President and the joint chiefs are awaiting your arrival."

"What? They're here?" Hammond gulped hard, notably shaken by the information.

"No, sir, they're awaiting via satcomm. They've requested an update at your earliest convenience."

"Shit," Hammond cursed under his breath. It was more than likely just as he feared. The President was on a witch hunt. Probably already pointing fingers in his direction.

Hammond regarded the current situation as he knew. There were six incriminating cases scattered around Maryland, Delaware, and Virginia. All of which had been shipped separately to be compiled in one location at a later time. A preventative measure lest some wayward terrorist group learned the true nature of their existence. Theoretically, they could get their hands on one or two packages and still not know exactly what they had. They chose private couriers and even outsourced to a government contractor to compile and study the data, all in an attempt to keep it off the official books. This type of practice was almost standard in black budget operations, illegal by the public standpoint, but a necessary evil to ensure America's sovereignty.

He would have to get in touch with his field agents before he could make any kind of report to his superiors. Currently, his teams were in pursuit of one of the said cases, and he was hoping that they had located their objective. That would be at least one off his mind. It then came down to the remaining five cases, all of which in one way or another could possibly be linked in some way back to his department, back to him at least by someone who happened to be in the know.

The jeep pulled to a stop in front of a small white concrete dome that was housed at the edge of the military base. Hammond frowned a bit at the sight. This was where he was expected to work?

Unbeknown to the director was the fact that underneath the smallish dome was a massive underground complex comprised of four separate levels. The first and second levels were primarily used for operational departments consisting of offices, control rooms, and security stations. The two remaining floors were designed for storage and housing, with a barracks large enough to house an entire platoon of soldiers as well as enough food and water to last for well over a year, more if properly managed. The area of housing also held some of the creature comforts of living. A movie theater, a gym, and a fully stocked bar were also integrated into the structure, primarily to aid in the dissention of cabin fever that a group housed in the facility for long periods of time would most likely suffer.

The driver cut the engine and stepped out into the tepid air. Hammond and Roberts followed suit. The corporal extended an arm and pointed to a set of stairs that descended down into the earth. They stepped over to them and peered downward. The stairs led to a rather large fortified doorway that sat at the base of the concrete structure. A large wheel attached where a doorknob would normally reside. A keypad set above and blinked red in the pale light below.

The driver of the jeep gingerly walked down the stairs and motioned for the two men to follow. "This way, sir," he said, producing a key card. He swiped the card through a slot located at the bottom of the keypad and punched in his security ID. The sound of locks turning clanked and shuddered as wheel began to turn on its own. Slowly, the armored door began to swing open on hydraulic-powered motors.

The driver motioned to Hammond and Roberts to step inside. They did as they were asked and the driver stepped inside with them.

The door, as if on cue, closed and sealed shut with a rush of downward air. The air burst down as if under pressure, blowing any potential contaminates off their clothing. In front of them was yet another steel door, similar to the one they had just entered. The room they stood in was small, entirely composed of white brick and looked to act more or less like an air lock. A light on a camera blipped on and began to track back and forth observing the three men. The second door clanked and popped and swung open as well.

The three men entered into the facility proper and gazed down a long tunnel. The tunnel itself ran for what seemed like at least a mile downward into the Earth.

Hammond frowned at the fact that they were going to have to walk this pipe until the driver of the jeep stepped off to one side and depressed a button. A hidden door off to the right slid upward and produced a small black painted golf cart.

The driver climbed behind the wheel and beckoned the men to join him.

Hammond smiled. "I may just learn to like this place," he said as he climbed into the seat next to the driver.

Roberts sat on the rear-facing seat and grunted. The golf cart hummed as they drove downward into the darkness.

CHAPTER 22

Alex Bishop positioned his cruiser about a mile from the gas station where he had left his men. The steady snore in the back of his SUV assured him that agent Simmons was still indeed alive, having passed out from injuries sustained in the school. Bishop had pumped the man with enough morphine to allow him to sleep for several hours, so he had decided to leave him in the cruiser while he and his men had searched the gas station. Bishop eyed the man's leg that had been wrapped tight with bandages to help staunch the bleeding from his foolish self-inflicted wound. The bleeding had seemed to slow and merely soaked a small portion of the wrappings. Shaking his head in remembrance, Bishop turned his thoughts to his remaining squad members who were under orders to take out the armored car crew and retrieve the missing files.

He was fed up with this cat-and-mouse game. This mission should have been a piece of cake, not the holy cluster fuck that it had become. It was time to end it, he thought. Bishop saw that opportunity and took it. His men were well-trained, and aside from losing half of them to the infected bastards, he knew they could get the job done.

Infected people roamed around his SUV as if they could see him through the 100 percent tint of the cars exterior windows. Thankfully, the vehicle itself was completely soundproof to any that passed by. Bishop watched the wandering specters, intrigued at how they seemed to just know where prey was. Could they smell him? No, that didn't make much sense. The human capacity for smell was one of the least impressive traits in the animal kingdom. It could be sight, but that still didn't explain how they seemed to sense his presence here. Perhaps he was just reading into it too much, and they merely heard the sound of the engine as he cruised to this location. Yes, that had to be it. After all, that was the only sensible explanation.

Bishop turned his attention away from the infected meandering outside and regarded the instruments that inlayed the car's interior fascia. To most, the panel would look mostly like any other normal dash, gray-textured polyvinyl material. That, however, was where the similarities ended. Upon the push of a button, a small panel hidden atop the dash flipped up, exposing what appeared to be a standard GPS unit; it was anything but. Reaching underneath the center console, Bishop produced a full-sized keyboard that swiveled out to bring it within hand's reach. He tapped the keys and brought up the systems display.

The display illuminated a dull green at first and then faded into brilliant color; he tapped the keys, bringing up detailed topographical data. His squad showed up as bright green blips on the screen, courtesy of the personal GPS location devices each one of them wore attached to their tactical vests. Located in red was the last known whereabouts of his targets. Using the system's built in mapping software, Bishop could then position his men accordingly to effectively box them in. Alex smiled; at this point, they had nowhere to go. They had them. Then the radio squelched. It was Hooper, Bishop realized.

"Sir, we're under attack!" the man said frantically, the sharp sounds of gunfire carrying over the radio. Something snarled in the background and Bishop cursed under his breath. "It's not the targets, sir. It's . . . them." Hooper didn't need to explain who *them* were; Bishop already new.

Quickly, Alex punched the keypad, switching the topographical display to include real-time thermal data, a gift from the department of defense, and gasped as he noticed the scores upon scores of hot radiating bodies swarming toward his team's location. He had to warn them; he had to get them out of there. *Fuck, where had they all come from?* Bishop wondered. He retrieved the vehicle's microphone, and just as he was going to depress the talk switch, the radio squelched once more, this time the voice was that of someone he didn't expect.

"Alpha team, this is Director Hammond. I need a sitrep, over."

Bishop cursed as he looked at the screen, red and orange blips beginning to swarm into view.

"Not a good time, Don," Alex hissed into the microphone.

"Bishop, I don't give a fuck if it's a good time or not. You need to listen up!" the director barked over the car's loudspeaker.

Bishop wanted to pull his hair out in frustration. "My men are about to become human chow, sir. So if you don't mind, fuck off!" Bishop shouted the last part and called up his squad leader.

"Jones, Jones, can you read me? You and the men need to fall back." Bishop waited with no response. The loudspeaker chirped again.

"You should watch your tone with me, Captain," the director said menacingly, and then softened. "I can see the pickle you all have gotten yourselves into from here, Alex. That's why I'm sounding a general retreat for you and your men." The director let that statement hang in the air.

Bishop stared at the radio in disbelief. A retreat ordered by Hammond. He couldn't believe it.

Pushing the talk button, he responded, "Why, sir? Have things gotten that bad?" he asked, beginning to worry about his own family. He had no immediate family to speak of, not anymore, not here at least, but he had a brother three states over. If they were calling their forces in, did that mean it had spread there too?

"Alex, I've been going over the transcripts of your engagement, and the tech heads have pulled up some interesting info on your subjects. Particularly on one, Kyle Walker." The radio squelched as Hammond released the button.

Bishop noticed his question about the state of things had been completely overlooked or flat-out ignored; Bishop wasn't surprised that Hammond was made aware of their situation. Every field agent that worked for the DHS was equipped with state-of-the-art communications gear. This equipment not only allowed the men and women in the field to communicate with one another, but it also allowed the powers that be to stay informed of the goings-on of their officers. Bishop assumed that while communications had been down, the cached information was sent automatically upon the connection being reestablished.

"What about him, Hammond?" Bishop asked, annoyance creeping into his voice, although he tried his best to contain it.

"No time for that now, Bishop," Hammond growled. "Right now I need you to rally the remainder of your squad and head to these coordinates. Your new mission orders will be uploaded while you're en route." Hammond let the subject drop. A resounding click followed as the line went silent.

Bishop grimaced, staring at the gray and black dashboard-mounted radio, cursing under his breath. This conversation had already cost him critical time that he could have been directing his men out of harm's way. Not only was their mission a failure and he had lost half of his men, but they were now being pressed into service for yet another mission. This time without even the slightest notion of what it was. Bishop depressed the button on his walkie.

"Hoop, Vindetti, Jones, fall back and regroup to rally point one, over." Bishop listened to the static that hung in the air. He watched his men onscreen and knew that at least for the moment, they were still alive. At least they were still moving, that is. He wasn't quite sure as to what state they were in, however. The thought then occurred to him that if they had been bitten and infected . . . He let the thought drop. That wasn't an option. He was already going to have to explain to the wives of his fallen comrades why their husbands weren't coming home. Finally, after what seemed like an eternity, the radio hissed and popped and then two clicks.

Bishop knew instinctively that the two clicks was a signal from his men. Two clicks meant *message received* during times when the ability to speak was ill-advised. Paying close attention to the SUV's computer screen, he noticed the slow deliberate movements of his men. They were doing their best to stay ahead of the horde, all the while keeping silent as they moved. *Smart*, Bishop thought. At least he'd trained them well.

CHAPTER 23

One by one, shambling figures stumbled out of the din. Their sheer numbers were mind boggling. Where had they all come from? How had this shit spread so fast? Marvin and Richard walked nervously beside me. I could see their eyes darting from left to right, watching the infected advance through the trees. Gunshots sounded in the distance. Well, truth be told, it could be right next to us for all we knew. It was hard to tell with the sounds the infected made as leaves and branches crunched underfoot and they plowed through the trees. They sounded like a heard of bulls running through the woods.

I gripped my weapon with white knuckles, finger on the trigger, safety off. The infected seemed to take interest in the noise in the distance and began to shamble in that direction. Unfortunately, not all of them followed suit. A good majority of them were still fixated on us. I felt frozen in place, my feet rooted to the ground where I stood. As the horde approached, a vile scent reached my nostrils. The smell was that of fevered body odor and sickness. There was something else that clung there as well. Something I hadn't smelled in years. Not since my days of working in the private sector. It was the smell of death, decay. Cadaverine and putrescine gasses seemed to escape off some of the more badly injured victims. How could that be? Were these people dead? No, that couldn't be possible, could it? The thought made my already-goose-pimpled flesh seem to raise even more; my skin felt hypersensitive to the point that it was almost painful.

Our opportunity of escape was closing rapidly as the infected encroached on our position. I eyed my partner, and then Richard, a panicked look crossing over my pale features. The freaks were no more than twenty or thirty paces away.

Marvin held his tree branch up like a pro baseball player ready to strike.

Richard readied his service weapon.

"Go!" I said in a harsh whisper. We began to nervously tread forward.

A figure off to my left lunged at Marv, who, in return, swung out with the tree branch. His swing was instant, like releasing a taut rubber band. The branch slapped the encroaching figure in the sternum and knocked it back a few paces. It stumbled and fell to the ground in a heap. Marvin left it where it lay and quickened his pace.

We didn't have time to kill them all. There was just too many. All we could hope to accomplish was to possibly put some distance between us and them.

I heard a rustling of leaves off to my right as a young girl, who couldn't have been older than the age of sixteen, shot out.

Richard instinctively and without hesitation fired, the shot passed through the small girl's head, entering just around the bridge of her nose. A look of surprise or maybe even relief seemed to settle in her features as she pitched forward and fell to the forest floor.

The gunshot seemed extremely loud. Its effect was immediate. Although it had managed to save Richard from having a chunk removed from his body, it had also seemed to galvanize the advancing figures, even the ones that had seemed confused and wary, distracted by the sounds in the distance, seemed to instantly focus on us. All hell broke loose. They started running toward us.

"Oh shit!" I screamed. "Run, run now!" I bellowed.

We shot off into the trees, heedless of the obstacles. Still-damp tree branches whipped me in the face and stung my eyes as we moved. The infected seemed to be closing in all around us. We continued forward. One advantage we had—hell, the only advantage we had—was that we still possessed the cognitive ability to navigate the landscape. The infected seemed to have lost that particular trait, unable to determine a loose rock or a low-hanging tree branch. Several of the figures tripped and fell to the forest floor. I noticed one get caught in between a fork in a tree branch. If I hadn't been running for my life, it may have been almost comical. Its head wriggled back and forth, neck snagged in between two outcropped branches. It just stood there, too stupid to even back itself out. Its mouth snapped and snarled as drool ran down its face and clung to the tree branch.

I risked a glance behind me, Marvin having fallen behind slightly, his prosthetic leg obviously giving him trouble on the uneven terrain. I went wide eyed as a man of about 6'5" dressed in a torn sweat suit reached out to grab Marvin from behind. I raised my pistol and fired. Flame shot out of the barrel of my .357. The round passed over Marvin's shoulder and slammed into the approaching figure's neck.

Marvin, surprised, stared at me for a moment then glanced over his shoulder. His expression changed from determined weariness to sheer terror as the tall man behind him bled from the ragged wound in his throat, mouth hanging agape.

"Duck!" I shouted to the old man. Marvin, using his tree branch as a crutch, ducked low and quickly hobbled out of the way. I fired another round, this time finding the mark just between sweat suit man's eyes. His body struck the ground hard, his heavy mass landing on the forest floor with a thud. Marvin limped toward me, his eyes full of fear. Come to think of it, as much as we'd seen and been through together over the years, this was the first time I think I'd ever seen the man scared.

"You could have warned me," he said, nearly out of breath.

"I said *duck*," was my reply.

He nodded his head, too worn out to quip back.

"You ready? We need to keep moving," I asked, and Marvin exhaled sharply and gave me a *thumbs-up* approval.

I heard Richard curse ahead of us and another gunshot. I turned my attention in his direction as he stood over the body of yet another of the infected. Marvin pushed at my shoulder as if to say *go*. I nodded to the old man, then turned and took off in a run toward the action.

As I neared, I noticed blood coated the side of Richard's uniform. He must have seen the concern on my face and looked down. He looked back at me and began to speak just as I spotted another two infected approaching him. I quickened my pace and pointed past him, raising my pistol. The closest figure, the one off to Richard's right, took him by surprise. It grabbed onto him as he tried to backpedal. Richard tripped, and the two of them went down. I took off in a sprint, trying my best to reach my friend. I fired as I ran, striking the second assailant in the shoulder and chest. I cursed as I moved, knowing that a head shot was damn near impossible while moving and at this distance. Richard wrestled with the infected on the ground, struggling to keep its snarling mouth away from his flesh.

"Shoot it!" Richard shouted in near panic as he pushed the thing's head upward and into view.

It was disgusting. White, waxy, pallid skin stretched out across what I believed to be a female's face. Thin, blue spider veins added to the horrific visage. I felt my stomach roil upon the sight. I wanted to vomit. *My wife could be one of those things*, I thought dejectedly. No, there wasn't time for those kinds of thoughts. I took aim and fired as I moved. The bullet went wide and struck a tree, showering Richard and his attacker with bits of bark. I cursed, knowing that I only had one more shot left in my gun. I had to make it count. I took aim, trying my best to steady myself as I moved. I got the once woman's rage-filled eyes in my sight and . . . Something shot out from behind a tree off to my left. A blur of movement that caught me off guard as something hard slammed into my chest with a force that lifted me off my feet. Next thing I knew I was falling. I slammed into the forest floor hard, knocking the wind out of me. It was a wonder my gun didn't go off.

Dazed and startled, something large stepped out from behind the tree. I heard Marvin shout something from my rear, but in my stupor, I wasn't sure what he was saying. Standing above me was a man, a very, very big man. I blinked my eyes, rapidly trying to force the blurry image into focus. It was one of Homeland's goons. Jones, I believe, was what their commander had said his name was. He stood above me grinning, blood trickling down his mouth, a deep gash on his forehead. I began to raise my pistol, and he kicked out with a booted foot and knocked it away from my grasp. The Smith & Wesson bounced uselessly into the leaves out of my reach. Jones pointed a menacing-looking MP5 at my face. He glanced at Marvin and then to the still-struggling Richard and grinned even wider.

"You're mine now, bitches," he spat out viciously.

Flecks of warm blood and spittle hit me in the face as he spoke. Part of me just wanted to close my eyes and let this be over and done with. I laid my head back on the forest floor and gazed at the upside-down image of my partner hobbling forward.

"You let him go, you ass-hat," Marvin shouted as he hefted the tree branch in both hands.

"Or what, old man? You gonna hit me with a twig?" Jones seemed to laugh at the notion.

Anger flashed across Marvin's face, and he took a chance and swung the makeshift bat.

Jones stepped into the blow and caught the branch one handed, still clutching his MP5 in the other. He wrenched the stick away from Marvin and flung it into the woods. In a flash of movement, he backhanded the old man, sending him sprawling to the forest floor. Marvin lay there still and unmoving.

I tried to kick out, aiming for Jones' knee.

Anticipating the maneuver, Jones sidestepped and brought his leg down on mine, pinning it to the ground. "Where's the file?" he said vehemently.

I shook my head. Jones pushed his boot harder into my leg, grinding my ankle down into the dirt. Pain shot like lightning as he applied steady presser, the earlier wound to my leg causing me intense pain.

"I don't know!" I cried, feeling tears begin to well up in my eyes. Jones glanced over to Marvin's still form, and then to the backpack Marvin wore. Jones released my ankle and motioned over to my partner.

"Get the backpack," Jones stated flatly.

I glanced over at Marvin. I nodded and started to get to my feet.

Jones thrust the gun in my face. "Slowly," he said.

I acquiesced. Cautiously, I turned over and onto my knees. Instead of standing, I crawled over to where Marvin lay. His old Army-green backpack strapped atop his backside. I reached out for it and grasped hold of its rough canvas-like fabric. I wanted to shake Marvin to rouse him awake. I was relieved to see the steady rise and fall of his chest; at least Jones hadn't killed the old man, which was a small consolation as I took notice of the dozen or so shambling figures still advancing on our position.

I reached for the zipper and began to fumble with it. I took the clasp hold in my shaking fingertips and began to work it open. As I reached inside, two gunshots resounded behind me. I turned sharply to see Richard pushing the infected off the top of him. He flipped over into a prone position and fired on Jones. The big man cursed and spun out of the way and dove behind a large oak. Richard fired a few more rounds, providing me the chance to get to cover. I grabbed Marvin's backpack by the strap and began to drag him along with me, struggling to keep my grip.

Jones returned fire, sending a three-round burst downrange toward Richard. Rich grabbed the body of the fallen infected and rolled with it so that it acted as a human shield. The rounds struck the thing in the back and sent pelts of blood flying across the forest floor.

The sweat and dirt on my hands made it hard to keep my grip on Marvin's backpack as I pulled him along behind me. Another shot fired from Richard's position and startled me as I entered a copse of trees. I ducked down low and pulled Marvin in and leaned him up against a massive black walnut tree. I peered out from my hiding spot to see Richard still taking refuge underneath the dead thing he had just brought down. The body of the second infected lay merely inches from his feet. Jones fired another burst from his hiding spot and I cursed. Richard was pinned down, and at the moment I was unarmed, not to mention we were still drawing unwanted company.

Time seemed to slow down as I watched the horde of people wandering toward us. It was almost ethereal as the smoke from the gas station fire rolled into the woods, the infected coming closer and closer, seeming to materialize out of the haze. *How many were there?* I wondered, swallowing hard.

I scanned the leaf-encrusted ground for my sidearm. Finally, after what seemed like an eternity, I managed to spot its dull steel frame half buried under freshly fallen leaves. I poked my head out from cover, checking to see if the coast was clear. Jones huddled behind the oak tree so I took a chance. I darted out from behind the walnut tree and dove for my sidearm. I grasped hold of it just as a series of rounds stitched the ground where my hand had just been. Richard, noticing my dilemma opened fire once more, providing me with cover. I reached my hiding spot and crouched to the ground. Taking a shooter's stance, I aimed at the oak, waiting for Jones to stick his foul head out.

Something rustled in the leaves at my rear. I turned to see the snarling form of what looked to be an infected senior citizen. Christ, she still clutched on to her walker. A crazy thought passed through my mind, and I had to wonder for a brief moment if the tennis balls attached to the bottom of the granny walker came preinstalled or if they were aftermarket. Instinctively, I opened fire.

My last remaining round caught her in the shoulder and blew out the joint that connected her arm to her upper body. She kept coming, dragging the granny walker behind her; it caught leaves and sticks underneath the dirty yellow-green tennis balls. Her arm hung uselessly by a tendon and flopped back and forth as she scrambled forward.

Gore seeped from the horrific wound and caused my already-nervous stomach to lurch. I caught it in my chest and held my breath. Her stench hit me next. Never had I smelled something as grotesque as this thing that hovered in front of me. The scent reminded me of the Krokodil addicts I had seen in Russia almost a decade ago. Bits of their limbs decayed with gangrene from injecting codeine cut with gasoline or lighter fluid. At the time, that was the only reference to walking death I had ever seen, let alone imagine.

As she got closer, I could make out the decay that encrusted her upper body. Her dress was torn just below her sagging breasts, the flesh was shriveled and red, raw and inflamed all at the same time, and it ran along the length of her chest and up to the bottom of her chin.

"Jesus Christ!" I gasped as she lunged for me, dropping the walker behind her. For as old and decrepit that she was, she could sure move fast. Her one good arm reached for me, and by force of habit, I pulled the trigger on my .357, which seemed to laugh at me with an audible click. Remembering in that instant that the weapon was empty, I fell backward to the ground.

With my back against the soil, I reached forward and grasped her outstretched arm. I planted my foot against her chest and shoved upward, throttling her up and into the air. Her thin frame launched over me and landed directly in the middle of the pathway, right next to Jones' hiding spot. Somehow remarkably, she seemed to sense the big man standing there. I watched as she managed to scramble to her feet and charge around the tree. I heard the big man curse and open fire. Quickly, I hit the switch to release the cylinder of my sidearm and swung it out. I ejected the spent cartridges and grabbed a fresh speed loader off my duty rig. In an instant, I popped the new one in and gave it a twist, dropping the new rounds into the weapon. I snapped the cylinder shut and discarded the speed loader, dropping it to the ground out of habit.

People often asked me while on the gun range why I would toss my magazines to the side when reloading. I would then go into a long spiel about the necessity of this practice. If by chance you were unlucky enough to find yourself in a firefight, the last thing you wanted to do was waste precious seconds by worrying about your damn magazines.

"*Let it fall. Your life is worth more than the few dollars you spent on it,*" I would always tell the rookies I was expected to train. A bellowing voice brought me back to reality.

"Nice try, asshole!" I heard as the sound of sporadic gunfire peppered my location.

"Damn, you mean the ol' rabid granny ploy didn't take you out?" I said tauntingly. "Look, uh, Jonesy, we're kind of at an impasse here, and I don't know if you've noticed, but were starting to draw a crowd. Why don't we just call it a draw and discuss this some other time?" I said, hoping we could side with reason and try to make it to some semblance of safety.

"Sure, I'll tell you what. Let's make a deal. You give me the file, and then I kill you. How's that sound?" I heard Jones eject his magazine and load in a fresh one.

Crap, I thought and followed with a sigh. I gazed down at Marvin and noticed he was starting to fade back into the conscious world.

"Just make a run for it, Kyle. I'll hold this prick!" Richard shouted from down the pathway.

I heard Jones laugh in response. I crouched behind the tree and took aim. I was at an odd angle to my enemy, but a thought occurred to me. If he so much as poked his weapon out to take another pop shot at Richard, maybe, just maybe, I could shut him down.

"Not a chance, Rich! We're walking out of here together, man!" I shouted back in reply.

"Aw, ain't that sweet," Jones' deep voice muttered from across the expanse.

I cast a worried glance around as the moans of the infected were getting steadily closer to us.

"Go screw yourself," Richard answered.

Just as expected, Jones took aim in Richard's direction. The black barrel of his MP5 protruded from beyond the massive oak tree. I took aim and blew out all the oxygen in my lungs. If he fired before I could line up my sites, this was not going to end well. As it was, Richard's cover had all but been shredded, the back of the infected being all but disintegrated by the constant assault. I squeezed the trigger. The weapon in my hands kicked back, the bullet finding its mark.

Jones shrieked from behind his cover, a sound I thought was uncharacteristic of the big man. I heard him utter a curse as he dropped the weapon to the ground, the MP5 now useless as my round punched into it skewing the barrel. I knew, however, from seeing them previously, he had a backup weapon strapped to a leg holster situated on his thigh. I jumped up and dashed out from cover, firing in his general direction as I headed toward Richard's position, not wanting to give the man a chance at drawing down on me. To my surprise, the large figure retreated, disappearing into the surrounding landscape in a flash. I was shocked that a man of that size could move so damn quickly.

I ran over to Richard, hurdling over the body of the fallen infected at his feet. I reached down and carefully grasped hold of the dead thing that lay on top of him. Richard pushed the figure off him as I pulled, and I held my hand out to help him to his feet.

"You wounded?" I asked, giving the man a once-over.

"I don't think so, took a few rounds in the vest, but I don't think anything is broken." He sighed with relief. It was short lived. The infected in the area were once again getting dangerously close.

"What the hell is going on?" Marvin grumbled from behind the tree I had sought refuge in only moments ago.

Richard took a moment to top off his magazine as I dashed over to aid Marv. I reached the old man and smiled. Marvin sat where I had left him, rubbing the top of his bald head.

He squinted up at me and scowled. "I thought I was dead, but if you're here, then I'm definitely not in heaven," he snorted.

I shrugged off his gibe and helped him to his feet. "Well, you're too much of an asshole to die anyway," I quipped. "C'mon, we need to get going before we end up a happy meal." I motioned toward the infected moving toward our location.

We turned quickly, heading off to regroup with Richard. No words needed to be said. Marvin picked up yet another branch, and we took off into the forest.

CHAPTER 24

Marvin, Richard, and I shot out of the forest into the roadway running full tilt. I slammed into a small hybrid car and dented its exterior with my thigh. I cursed and jumped over the hood just as the infected came spilling out of the trees. There had to be at least fifty of them, all of them ranging in different levels of grotesqueness. Several of the shambling figures were missing limbs or displayed torn arteries or throats; all of them were focused on us.

"Go, go, go!" Richard shouted and pointed down the road. Apparently, he seemed to recognize this stretch of road.

Marvin and I followed the police officer, positioning ourselves in between the rows of cars in the street, trying to use them as a sort of barrier between us and the infected. Growling moaning figures plowed into the sides of the derelict cars, reaching out, trying anything it seemed to get at our warm flesh.

"This way." Richard pointed and shot off down a side street that led to the fuel depot area of the airport.

Gigantic white cylindrical tanks protruded from the earth, three in all labeled Jet Fuel. Signs like Keep Out and Danger were posted all throughout the area. As we rounded one of the tanks, a smallish building came into view. Lo and behold, it was the police station. *Keep the jet fuel by the police station*, I thought. *Makes sense to me.*

Richard ran directly toward the front doors of the building and stopped abruptly.

Marvin and I made it over to his position, the infected not far behind. "What is it?" I said, looking from Richard to the door, and then to the infected that were steadily closing in. Richard tapped the card reader imbedded in the brick next to the door. I examined it closely and took notice that the small LED light was dark. I cocked and eyebrow as I realized what the problem was. There was no power. No power meant the card reader wouldn't work no matter how many times you swiped it; hence, the door was locked.

"Don't they have a backup battery or something?" I asked, giving the bottom of the door a small kick in frustration. To my surprise, the door bounced open. "What the?" I said in shock, staring at the handle as if I had just imagined it.

Richard grinned at me. He reached down, clutched the door handle and pulled. The door swung open with ease, and we rushed inside just as the infected reached the building. Richard hastily slammed the door shut.

"Quick, find something we can use to brace this." Richard ordered.

I wanted to ask him why the hell the door wasn't locked, but I decided now was probably not the time. We stood inside of a small vestibule that led into a larger lobby area. I peered through a tiny window situated at the top of the door and gazed into the lobby proper. The lobby itself was dark as ink. I tried to listen for any sounds of movement, but the barrage of hands beating on the front door obliterated any chance of that bearing any fruit. I swallowed hard and brought my sidearm up to the ready. Marvin stood behind me, still clutching onto his broken stick.

"Marv, stay here. I've got this," I told the shaken man and he nodded. Looking at him for a long moment, I could tell that he was in intense pain. Prosthetic legs and knee implants were good for your everyday stroll, but when it came down to it, they just weren't designed for the type of rigorous abuse they'd been put through today. I gave him a quick nod as he wiped beads of sweat away from his brow. "You keep watch. Open this door quick if I come running. Got it?" I said.

Marvin eyed me with a small look of annoyance. "When have I ever let you down when it came to opening a damn door? Hell, been doing it for ten freaking years, kid." He chuckled slightly; it was an inside joke of ours.

In our profession, there were two components: the guys like me and the guys like Marvin. The guys like me were the ones who made the actual deliveries to your various banks and stores and so forth and so on. We were up and down all day long, back and forth, counting on our drivers to keep an eye on the scene, and hopefully warn us of any potential danger.

The guys like Marvin sat on their respective rear ends all day and opened the door as we would either leave or return to the trucks. So I would always joke around with the old man, telling him that he was pretty much a professional door opener. That would usually end up in a snide remark from the man.

Slowly, I pulled the door open and gingerly stepped inside. The room for the most part was pitch black, save for a small area illuminated by the bit of sunlight filtering through the porthole in the door. I reached down to my duty rig, hoping that somehow my mini-mag managed to stay attached. My hand brushed against its cool metal surface and I let out a thankful sigh. Pulling it out of my belt, I turned it on with a twist, and focused the beam to go wide.

I scanned the area with the flashlight. Rows of chairs set alongside plain white brick walls, a few end tables situated at the ends of each. It reminded me almost like a tiny doctor's office waiting room, with the exception that there was a small window where a desk sergeant would reside rather than a receptionist. The room itself seemed to be clear of any threats. I could still hear the muffled pounding on the other side of the door as I searched for something I could use to barricade us in. I walked over to one of the chairs and tried to pick it up. As I expected, the chairs themselves were bolted to the floor. Upon closer examination, I discovered the end tables were as well. Guess they didn't want anyone in here to have anything that could be used as a potential weapon.

I scratched my head in thought. There was another door that led deeper into the structure, but there was no way in hell that I was going to go roaming around a police station in the middle of all of this shit without some kind of backup—then it hit me.

"Of course. God, I'm stupid sometimes." I smacked myself in the forehead. Quickly, I hurried my way back toward the entryway.

Marvin opened the door in a flash, a look of concern crossing over his aging features. He peered over my shoulder, then looked at me as I entered.

I gave him a wink to indicate that everything was fine. I stormed over to Richard, who was doing his best to hold the door shut.

He stood there holding the handle with both hands, trying to keep the infected outside at bay, clutching the door to prevent them from knocking it open as I had.

"Rich, keep doing what you're doing. This is in no way weird," I stated as I reached down and ran my hands along his duty rig.

Richard gave me a confused and somewhat worried glance. "What the hell are you looking for?" he said as I located the item.

Unsnapping the compartment on his belt, I retrieved his handcuffs and held them up in the air, letting them dangle in front of his face.

A smile crossed Richards's hard features. "Well, go ahead and do it then," he said.

I attached one end of the handcuffs to the door handle and snapped them closed. The second more tricky part would be finding something to secure it to. The only thing there that would possibly even work in that capacity was a small mail slot that resided next to the door. It would be awkward, but I was pretty sure I could manage the task. Biggest problem was Richard. Rich's large frame happened to be positioned right in front of the damn thing. If he let go and repositioned himself, it would most likely leave an opening for the infected to get in.

I sighed to myself and said in my best John Wayne voice, "Man's gotta do what a man's gotta do." I closed my arms around Richard in a bear hug-like posture. To look at us was, well, downright shameful. Here Richard stood, half bent over a door, and I myself was pressed into his back side, arms around him, fishing around for a set of handcuffs. I had seen porno movies start out on less.

Marvin, sensing my discomfort, had to throw his two cents in. "Damn, son, you gonna buy him dinner first?" he snorted in the background.

Richard shot the old man a glare, and I simply shook my head and chose to ignore him. After fishing around blindly, I located the dangling handcuff. Grasping it in one hand, I felt around the edge of the door with the other. After searching for a moment I located, the cool metal slot set off merely inches from the door frame. Pulling the open handcuff over, I raised the mail slot open, and shoved the loose end inside and let the flap fall. Not the most secure of locks, but I hoped it would be enough, as it was judging by the way these things moved and acted, I highly doubted any of them would have the reasoning power to figure it out.

I let go of Richard and backed away from the door. I looked over at Marv, who was still standing by the opposite end, and motioned for him to go into the other room.

"You guys need some alone time?" he glowered and shot a thumb toward the lobby.

"Get in the other room, Marv," I said irritably. "If this doesn't hold, we're probably toast. At least you may stand a chance."

"Doubtful," Richard muttered.

I drew my sidearm and motioned to Rich to let go of the door. He nodded, stepping back quickly, drawing his piece as well.

Marvin quickly dashed through the other door; I suppose probably figuring it to be a good idea. He held the door open in anticipation, waiting to see if the infected would push through.

The handcuffs rattled like ghostly chains in the night as the infected pounded on the door's surface. Although the door bounced and jolted every few seconds, it seemed to be holding. I breathed a sigh of relief.

"Okay, guys, let's get moving," I said, never taking my eyes off the entryway. I couldn't help but focus on the coating of blood and mucus on the door's windows. It slid down the exterior slowly and smeared every time a hand or eager face pressed up against it. In some strange way, it reminded me of my dog pawing at the sliding glass door in anticipation, waiting for me to let him out.

Quickly, we backed our way out of the vestibule, entering the darkened lobby. All three of us reached down and removed our flashlights from our duty rigs. It seemed to be an instinct that we shared as we took the action without so much as a word spoken.

Lights turned on; the beams played across the small confines of the lobby, illuminating the rows of chairs and end tables. Light reflected off the glossy covers of magazines that occupied the small tables, throwing ghastly shadows over the room, playing on our already-frayed nerves. Although I had already cleared the area, my senses were so hyper-intensified; every sound, every movement registered in my mind in a fraction of a second. I had to try to slow myself down lest my adrenaline-soaked veins drive me into a state of sheer panic. *Slow down, take things one at a time*, I told myself over and over.

Richard shined the narrow beam of his SureFire flashlight directly at the booth that would have normally housed the station's desk sergeant. Frowning, Rich stormed over to the protective window that enclosed the booth. He pressed his face to the glass, cupped the sides of his eyes, and shined his torch into the room's interior. Seeing nothing, he groaned.

"Where in the hell is everybody?" Richard said with some confusion. "There should be someone here, there's always someone here," he exasperated. Frantically, Rich adjusted the direction of his beam and gasped.

"What is it?" I said, taking a step forward.

Rich gave me a look of desperation and squinted as my flashlight caught him in the eyes. I lowered the beam from his face and his eyes relaxed.

"Blood, a lot of it, on the floor behind the desk," Richard stated, the look of panic seeming to betray his normally stoic features.

I shook my head. *Was nowhere safe?* I thought. Even here, in the hub of law enforcement, I stepped over beside him and peered into the window and beyond the desk, looking at the pool of dark liquid on the ground. I followed a smeared pathway throughout the smallish room that led to an open doorway.

"Great," I muttered. Blood coated the office chair behind the desk and ran down to the floor. Upon further examination, it looked as if arterial spray had splattered the walls of the room. By all accounts, there should have been a body; alas, there were none. That gave me cause for concern. The room looked as if it had been painted in gore. Whatever this disease, or whatever it was that was spreading around, must have struck extremely fast—fast enough that it took these poor souls completely by surprise.

"Come on," Richard breathed as he headed for a door marked Restricted Access. I pulled my pistol, held it up against my flashlight, and nodded to Rich to open the door.

Marvin came to stand behind me, raising his bludgeon up in his arms, ready to swoop in and attack if the need arose.

Richard yanked the door open. The door swung open with ease.

I wondered once again as to why these security doors would all be, well, non-secure, and then it hit me—magnetic locks. Looking around the area, there was obviously no power; the locks themselves would have held iron tight so long as there was electricity. I had to wonder why the power had been shut off; perhaps it was some kind of control measure in the case of a terrorist attack. I wasn't completely sure, and that was probably a better thought for another time.

I stepped forward with my gun at the ready and shined my light inside of the smallish room. Gingerly, I walked around the pools of blood on the tiled floor, taking care not to rub up against the walls as I moved inside. Marv came in behind me and then Richard. Slowly I moved to the other door that led farther into the police station. I cast my light trough the partially opened door and peered inside. From this vantage, I could see rows of desks crowding the room. An area used for booking and paperwork, I assumed. Seeing nothing of interest at first glance, I pushed the door the rest of the way open. I walked inside, Marvin coming in next to me.

Something shot out to Marvin's side and caught the old man by surprise and he let out a shriek.

Richard was there in an instant, shining his flashlight down to see the figure of a once blonde-haired woman whose long locks were coated with gore and matted down to her head with dried blood. Her hands wrapped around Marv's leg as she sank her teeth in.

Marvin let out a gasp as he swung his wooden club down at the female officer, catching her in the side of her face. Her head rocked to the side, pulling on his leg with each blow, but she wasn't letting go.

Richard stood there staring at the woman, mouth hanging open in shock.

"Shoot the damn thing already!" Marvin cried as he struck her in the head once more.

She stared up at him with blood-soaked eyes and let out a snarling growl, teeth still latched on to his leg.

Richard looked down at Marv's leg and to the figure that was attached. He raised his gun and fired. The bullet passed directly through the top of her forehead, exploding the back side out, showering a grouping of file cabinets along the wall with gore. Her teeth lost their grip, and she slumped to the side.

Marvin pulled his leg free and stepped away from the corpse. To his surprise, Richard held his gun in Marvin's face.

"Hey, hey, hey now, buddy. What the hell do you think you're doing?" Marvin asked, cocking an eyebrow, scowling.

"You've been infected," Richard said, looking down to the old man's leg. Marvin shook his head. I stepped forward to intervene.

"Rich, we're not even certain how this thing spreads," I said, eyeing the man. The police officer didn't budge, gun still leveled at my partner.

"The hell we aren't. Have any of you been paying any attention?" he nearly shouted, pointing down at the fallen woman on the floor. "Tell me what you see? Look at her neck. As a matter of fact, I can beg to wager that ninety percent of those we've seen have had some sort of chunk taken out of them," he spat, anger seeming to well up in his voice. He wasn't wrong; the female officer who lay dead at their feet had a ragged and grotesque wound along the length of her shoulder and neck.

Marvin took a step back. "Enough of this horseshit. Look, moron," he said annoyingly as he hiked up his pant leg and tapped on the titanium alloy of his prosthetic leg. The artificial leg glinted with a dull glow as Richard fixed his torch beam on it. "I'm fine, so chill out, would ya?" Marvin allowed his torn pant leg to drop once again, obscuring his peg leg.

Richard seemed to relax, and then broke out into laughter. It was infectious as I soon began to laugh as well. Tears welled up in our eyes as we chuckled. Marvin stood there somewhat stupefied at the scene and muttered something about us being "bat shit crazy." As my laughter calmed, I fixated once again on the dead woman on the floor, and a disturbing thought hit me. If she had been bitten, then chances are that there was more of the infected wandering around inside of the building. I cleared my throat and put my hand up, trying to stem the tide of nervous laughter.

"Guys, I think we should probably clear the area. If she had been bit in here . . ." I let the implication sink in.

My two compatriots began to cautiously peer around the room, understanding what I was getting at. Thankfully, a quick search of our surroundings came up empty, save for a few trails of blood and strewn paperwork. We regrouped around the center of the room, taking up position in front of Officer Richard's desk.

Marvin eyed the stick in his hands. "You people have an armory around here, right?" he said, setting the length of wood on the desk. "I'm beginning to feel a bit naked," Marv said as he tapped his empty holster.

Richard nodded.

"That would be a good idea. I could use to top off my ammo supply as well. I'm sorry, Kyle, but I don't think we stock anything for your .357, though," Rich said, leaning over his desk.

I nodded by way of reply. "So what now?" I asked, eyeing the two men.

"Well, we could try to fortify this place, but with the state of the doors, I'm not certain how long that we'd last in here," Richard answered.

I shook my head in agreement. "First things first, Marv. You have those files you mentioned earlier. I would love a chance to figure out what the hell we're being chased for," I said.

Marvin reached to his shoulder as if just remembering the backpack that he still wore. It was a wonder that he hadn't been stripped of it during his brief incarceration with Homeland's goons, an oversight on their part that he was thankful for. Marvin slung off the backpack and set the green canvas bag on the desktop's surface, managing to knock over a small tray of paper clips as he did so. The tiny pieces of color-coated metal skittered across the floor of the station.

"Sorry," Marvin shrugged as he untied the bag's clasp. Reaching inside, Marvin produced a plain manila folder and set it in the middle of desk in front of me.

Taking hold of my Maglite, I unscrewed the top and removed it. I then placed the lens holder onto the bottom of light, forming a sort of candle-like light source. It was a handy feature. It allowed me to set the light down and illuminate the area without having to hold onto it. I took the folder in hand, scrutinizing the generic security seal emblazoned on the front cover displaying the word "Classified" across it in bright red lettering.

I opened the folder and began to sift through the contents. I wasn't too savvy when it came to medical documentation, but it was apparently obvious that the information had something to do with some sort of disease. Then I came across the photo. Marvin seemed to recognize the image as I moved it into view. The image was of a man, or more to the point, what used to be a man. It was also apparent that the photo had been taken some time ago judging by the graininess of the image. It was a black-and-white image of a man strapped down to a table. His eye's fixated on the camera operator, his face twisted in a grimace of rage. The label at the top of the page read "Kuru Variant 5."

"I guess that explains some things," I said as I continued to thumb through various charts and graphs.

"Explains what?" Richard asked, not quite putting two and two together.

"Why we've been getting chased all around God's creation. From what I can tell by looking at this crap, is Homeland knew something about this disease. Could you imagine what would happen if the public got wind of that? Think about it. Nine eleven—the FBI, and the NSA had information prior to that attack and did nothing to stop it. We ended up with our asses in our hand and going to war with two separate countries over that—one of which had absolutely nothing to do with it—all in an attempt to placate the populous, a war that is still going on, mind you. The same day they choose to ship this particular information, we get hit with it. They knew this was going to happen. Perhaps they weren't sure of when, but it's fairly obvious with this information that they knew of its existence. Judging by the looks of this photograph, they've known about it for some time," I said as Richard and Marvin exchanged understanding glances. "If the people found out that the government's new golden boys let something like this slip, well . . . it would be complete chaos." I finished my rant.

Richard furrowed his brow in thought. "That explains why they took out your rig and firebombed the interstate. Someone out there wants to cover this up," Richard said matter-of-factly.

"I agree. I think in the beginning they may have been trying to contain the spread of this shit, but . . . we've seen how that panned out. Now I think it's mostly a game of covering their asses," I said as I closed the folder and handed it back to my partner.

Marvin shoved the incriminating document into his backpack and returned it back to its former place. "So what should we do?" Marvin asked, letting out a deep breath. "Hey, what about that friend of yours you're always talking about, that doctor guy? You think he might be able to make heads or tails of this stuff?" He looked hopeful.

"I'm not sure. It might be worth a shot. I haven't talked to Shaun in some time, though," I answered Marvin.

Shaun was a old childhood friend of mine. After high school, we'd gone our separate ways, me taking the job with Air Force intelligence and him, well, he moved on to become one of the country's leading microbiologists working for Johns Hopkins. We'd kept in contact over the years, and well, life and family had gotten in the way.

"There's really one big hitch in that plan, however," I said, eyeing the men. "John's Hopkins is in the middle of downtown Baltimore, and if this stuff has spread there like it has here, then I'm not sure just how we're gonna get this info to him unless we can find a working fax machine," I said dubiously. "Honestly, I think Homeland is the one that cut the power out here. It's the only thing that makes sense. No power, no media, cell phones, or anything else." My two compatriots seemed to consider my argument. "I think the first thing we should do is arm up and see about getting out to our families."

Richard turned his attention over to the still form of the blonde officer that lay on the floor over by the entryway. "This was my family," Richard whispered.

Marvin reached up and put hand on the man's shoulder. "You okay, chief?" Marvin asked.

Richard shrugged off his arm. "No, I'm not okay. Nothing about any of this is okay." Richard lowered his head, shaking it back and forth, trying his best to stave off tears. Richard turned, facing the dead woman on the floor. "Laurie over there, she was a pro, and they still got her. I want to know how in the hell they even got in here. How did this disease get in here? Is this shit airborne? Do we all have it?" Richard seemed to be cracking under the stress of it all. "If Homeland is responsible for this, I want to see them pay," he spit out vehemently.

I could see him beginning to shake with rage in the darkness of the room. "We will, Rich," I said softly. "Can you get us into the armory?" I asked, trying my best to help the man focus on the situation at hand. I always found that during times of conflict, it was always best to keep men busy, give them a task to try and keep the demons in their minds at bay.

Richard nodded. "Yeah, come on. It's this way." He pointed toward a hallway that led off to the left.

CHAPTER 25

The three of us walked down the darkened hallways of the police station with as much stealth as we could manage. Richard took the lead and Marvin and I followed. We passed by empty offices and interrogation rooms as we moved, weapons poised at the ready. We knew that somewhere in the station was at least one more of the monsters. Officer Laurie was evidence enough of that, so we had to keep on our toes lest we end up in the same boat. Every so often as we moved, I would spot a trickle of blood on the floor, or a partial hand print on a wall; but so far, no threats had presented themselves.

"This way," Richard whispered and broke right down a T-junction in the corridor.

We followed closely behind. Every so often, I would turn my gaze behind us to make certain we weren't being followed. With every step we took, I could imagine the feeling of hundreds of infected eyes bearing down on me. The thought was terrifying. Shadows shifted and moved like ghosts as we passed through the halls. Every movement caused my finger to twitch on my trigger guard; it was a wonder that none of us had made the mistake of striking out against a potted plant.

After what seemed like an agonizingly long trek through the police station, we made it to a heavy door marked—you guessed it—Armory. Richard slowly pulled the door open as I stepped around and shined my flashlight inside, barrel of my sidearm following the beam. The coast was clear as I stepped inside.

The room itself was fairly large but typical of your average armory with the exception this one happened to be a complete wreck. A grayish-blue wireframe security door hung open. Boxes of ammunition were strewn across the floor from one end of the room to the other. Several rows of weapons shelves were completely empty, save for a few shotguns and what looked to be disassembled handgun parts, tear gas grenades, and tasers. I wondered for a moment just how one of the infected would react to being hit with a taser. I honestly doubted it would have much effect.

"Holy shit balls," Marvin managed to say as he stepped into the room. "Looks like they've pretty much picked this place clean." He frowned looking at the stick in his hand.

"Don't worry, Marv, I think I still see a few things we can use." I flipped the cylinder of my .357 open and eyed my three remaining rounds. "At least I hope this stuff is usable."

Richard stepped in behind us. "Shit," Richard muttered. "At least it looks as if my guys got a chance to get in here and get stocked up. Who knows, maybe most of them are still alive," he said hopefully.

I nodded in agreement. "Come on, let's see what we can salvage here," I said taking care to step over any loose rounds of ammunition that were spread across the floor. Several different calibers littered the slate flooring; .45, .40, and 9mm seemed to be the most abundant. I motioned to Marvin to begin trying to round some of them up. He scowled and set off about the task, muttering something about "Sure, make the old man bend over and pick up the shit." I chose to ignore him and stepped over and began sifting through weapon parts. From the looks of things, each weapon part that I had found seemed to belong to the police's standard-issue sidearm. a forty-caliber automatic pistol. I just hoped I could find enough pieces to build a complete and working weapon.

Richard went to work, inspecting several shotguns that he had managed to procure.

I laid out weapon parts in front of me. Granted, it had been a while since I had used any kind of automatic, but I had remembered from previous training what the various parts were. So far I had found several quick detach barrels, two duel recoil springs, three gas pistons, and two slides as well as various pistol grips and magazines. I went to work as fast as I could, doing my best to assemble the weapons.

Outside of the room, I heard a loud crash. Richard and Marvin both froze in place, cocking their heads to the side, listening.

Something went skittering across the floor. It sounded like a tin pie plate being kicked down the hallway.

Richard fumbled with the shotgun he currently held. "Marv, hand me some of those shells over there." Richard pointed to a box of ammunition that lay in the corner of the room, with his flashlight.

Marvin did as he was asked without so much as a remark and fetched the twelve-gauge slugs off the floor and carefully tossed them over to Richard.

Richard managed to deftly catch the box in one hand and quickly thumbed it opened. He held the box under his arm as he retrieved several rounds and began sliding them into the ammo feed. "Here," he said and passed the weapon over to Marv, who accepted it graciously.

Richard went to work on another shotgun following the same ritual as before. The sounds in the hallway seemed to intensify as whatever it was making the noise got closer.

Marvin took up position on one side of the door, standing several feet back, waiting to see if anything managed to stick its ugly head through. More sounds reverberated through the hallway, these apparently farther away.

"Goddamn it," Marvin muttered when the realization hit him that whatever was coming had managed to multiply. "You almost done screwing around over there, son?" Marv said in a harsh whisper.

"Just a few more seconds," I said as I finished assembling the second sidearm. "Just need ammo." I began to scan around the immediate area of the floor.

"Here," Marvin said as he fished around one of his pockets. He handed me about ten loose rounds, which I took from him and immediately started loading a magazine. I finished and slapped the magazine home and racked the slide, feeding a round into the chamber.

"I hope there's more ammo where that came from," I told the old man. He nodded by way of reply. "Here," I said as I produced another forty-caliber handgun and handed it to him.

Marvin grinned—glad to feel the warm metal grip in his hand. He slid the empty weapon into his barren holster and seemed to relax a bit.

"Thanks, been feeling kinda naked all afternoon." He grinned.

"Yeah," I replied. "Just don't forget to load it," I said and stepped over to join them.

Richard walked over to my position and nudged me with another one of the shotguns. I took the weapon and looked at it, deciding which would be better in this situation. The shotgun seemed to be the obvious choice, even though in these confined spaces they were going to be loud as all hell. I tucked the handgun into a leg holster that was designed to house my PDA and secured it with a Velcro strap that dangled beside it. It was an awkward fit, and the weight of the weapon felt strange on my thigh, but that was the least of my worries at the moment.

The noises in the hallway seemed to be getting closer. The only problem we had at this point was the fact that this particular hallway only had one exit. That happened to be straight down until we hit the T-junction we had entered through. According to Richard, if we followed the hallway straight down, we would pass by several holding cells and continue down to find the entrance into the motor pool, which is where we had decided to head next. Now it was just a matter of getting through what was beyond the doors.

"Ideas?" I asked, looking back and forth between Rich and Marvin. Both men shrugged and I let out a long sigh. "Well, we can't wait here. We don't know exactly how many are out there, but from the sounds of it, there's at least a few. I'm afraid if we wait too long, the assholes at the front door will figure out how to get in here and then we're up shit-creek," I finished and the men nodded in agreement. "Question is, after we hit the motor pool, then what? Where are we headed? I know where I want to go, but how's about the two of you?" I asked, pretty much already figuring the answer.

Marvin was the first one to pipe up. "I need to get home to my wife, bub," he said with a hint of desperation.

I gritted my teeth, knowing that the old man would probably never make it, not on his own anyway.

Marvin's household laid smack dab on the edge of the city. He and his wife resided in a small row home in what was considered to be Baltimore County but was more or less part of the city itself. I knew this to be the case, as many times the man remarked on the fact that some asshole always seemed to manage to park in his parking spot anytime we made it home late. Marvin would then call the police, whom would show up and have the car towed and the owner fined due to the fact that he had only one leg and the spot was reserved for handicap vehicles only. Marvin never liked the fact that he needed such a spot, but truth be told, at the end of a long day, walking three or four blocks to his home on aching knees and a prosthetic leg was not his idea of a good time. If the disease had spread out into the city where the population was much, much denser, then the old guy was in for some trouble. Personally, I'd prefer to stay as far away from the city of Baltimore as possible. I cocked the shotgun, preparing for the worst, and looked to Richard.

"Rich, you?" I asked and he shook his head somberly.

"I have no one to go home to. I guess wherever you go, I go," he said.

I was actually pleased to hear it, although I felt slightly guilty for the emotion. "My goal is to get home as well. My wife is a smart woman, but I'm not sure how she's gonna deal with all this," I said and pointed out toward the noises in the hall. "Anyway, enough of the chitchat. I think we should probably concentrate on getting to the vehicles before we nail down exactly what we're going to do." I moved to head off into the hallway, wanting to just get in there and do what needed to be done, when Richard stopped me.

"Hang on a second." Rich ran around to the opposite side of the room. He fumbled in the dark for a moment and let out a "Yes" and then ran back over to me and Marvin and began handing out what looked like old police radios. "Here, take these," he said and passed one of the ancient-looking devices over to me, and then handed one to my partner. "In case we get separated, we can communicate with these. They run on the old analog frequencies and shouldn't be affected by whatever it is Homeland is doing. I haven't heard a thing on my new radio in hours. I'm guessing something is interfering with the digital gear, probably some kind of jamming or something. Their range leaves a little to be desired, but they should work nonetheless," he finished.

I gratefully accepted the new gear and set about equipping myself with it. We gave the gear a quick radio check and everything seemed to be in order.

Richard stepped around in front of me and Marv and looked out into the darkness beyond the door. "I'm going to head in first. I've got scattershot rounds whereas you two are loaded with slugs. If we're facing a bunch of these things, I can slow them down with this, and you two take out the stragglers. Sound like a plan?" Richard exchanged glances with Marvin and me.

"Sounds good," we said in unison and tried our best to mentally prepare for what was about to go down.

CHAPTER 26

We burst through the armory door in a diamond formation with Richard taking the lead. Marvin and I took up flanking positions to the right and left slightly to the rear, providing us each a set of clear firing lanes. Last thing we wanted was to shoot Rich in the back as we got trigger happy. What we thought was the sound of only one or two infected turned out to be about a half dozen or so wandering down the hallway. The noises that we had heard were overturned trash cans and potted plants that lined the hallway's edge.

The closest of the infected, a black man dressed in a Redskin's jersey and a do-rag ran toward us, his hands still cuffed behind his back. He growled as he ran and Richard took aim. He didn't have time for a head shot, so he fired low. The sound of the weapon reverberated explosively loud in the narrow confines of the hallway, leaving us all partially deaf in the ears, the ringing blocking out most of growls and howls coming from farther down the hall.

Richard's shot devastated the running prisoner's legs and sent him pinwheeling to the floor. His ankles all but separated from his legs and exploded outward, showering the walls with a gory mist. He hit the ground hard with his chin and I gasped as his teeth protruded upward through his upper lip. Around his hands where the cuffs were still attached, you could see bits of broken skin and bone where the monster had struggled with the bonds, trying to break itself free.

I took aim with my weapon and fired a slug directly into the top of its head, ending its pitiful existence.

A second figure came hurling its way into view followed by a third, both of them wearing what appeared to be the tattered remains of gray transportation authority police uniforms. Richard hesitated a moment and then fired a burst that sent scattershot into the advancing figures at about chest height.

I watched in horror as the steel pellets did their job and decimated the creature's flesh. Rib cages blew open, and organs spilled forth from the wounds. Amazingly, they did not stop. One of the infected officers tripped on his own intestine as it slid out of his stomach and fell to the floor in a heap, then just as quickly, regained his footing and was on us once more. I raised my shotgun and fired past Richard. My slug caught one of the advancing officers in his upturned chin, snapping his head backward, nearly decapitating him. The figure flew back and hit the floor with a thud.

Marvin, almost in unison, fired as well. His shot, however, went wide, striking the advancing ghoul in the shoulder, sheering his arm away from its moorings.

The arm slapped to the floor and it took as much as I had to keep from retching at the sight.

Richard took aim and fired once more; his shot struck the figure in the head at close range, bursting it apart like a watermelon. Gore rained down the hallway as the body fell to the floor.

We advanced down the line, taking care not to trip on the fallen bodies as we passed. To fall now would more than likely spell disaster for any of us. We were down to the last three enemies, these standing farthest away from us down the hallway. The figures were slightly obscured by the darkness and gun smoke that hung in the air and reflected off our flashlights. We tensed, readying for another assault; it was then I heard a loud crash in the direction of the lobby.

"Oh Christ!" I breathed with the realization of what had just happened. "I think they breached the lobby."

That did it. We had to move, and we had to move quickly. All caution went out the window at that point. We broke into a run and rapidly came upon the figures at the end of the expanse. We fired shots as we ran, not taking the time to observe the damage. At the close range, the figures were spun around and knocked to the floor. We continued on. As we passed the T-junction, the door at the end of the hallway off to our left exploded open. What looked like hundreds of creatures spilled forth through the now-open portal.

White pallid faces snarled and growled as our torch beams found them. Deadened eyes stared at us and formed grimaces of rage and pain.

"Go, run, run, run!" I shouted.

We sprinted to the opposite end of the long, narrow hallway. We slammed into the opposing door and threw it open. It was then I noticed Marvin lagging behind. "Shit," I said as I seen the first of the infected round the corner of the T-junction.

Marvin shot a glance over his shoulder and tried desperately to quicken his step. Christ, they were close.

I ran back down the hallway to Marvin's position and grabbed him by the arm. The fevered stench of the infected hit me like a sack of bricks and caused my stomach to do flip flops in the din; the scent of vomit, body odor, and decay wafted down toward us and only seemed to spur me on as I damn near dragged Marvin along behind me.

We reached the door and hurled ourselves through as Richard slammed it closed behind us. Frantically, we searched for something to bar the door with. Thankfully, we had entered what appeared to be a garage of some sort. Off to my left was a wooden broom and dustpan. I grabbed the broom and quickly shoved it into the door handle like an old-fashioned crossbeam. I didn't think it would hold for long, but at least it would slow them down.

To our luck, the garage itself was empty of any threats. Sunlight shown underneath a set of rolling doors off to my left and illuminated the room with a dull ambient glow. A police cruiser raised atop a hydraulic lift set in the center of the room, a series of oil and fluid catches positioned underneath. Routine maintenance I gathered from the scene.

Richard waved us over to another door, this one leading us back outside. He paused next to a large aluminum lock box hanging on the wall next to the door and opened it. Inside of the box were rows and rows of spare keys, each labeled with a letter and number combination. Grabbing a handful of them, Richard stepped over to open the door.

Once again, Marvin and I stood off to the side and readied ourselves for what lay beyond.

Rich opened the door. I went through and flanked right, and Marvin went left, Richard then came in through the middle. Although we had never worked together as a team in the past, we must have looked like a seasoned unit of professionals to any onlooking observer.

The light in the yard was blinding at first, our eyes having adjusted to the darkness within the building. We swept over the parking lot, thankful for the series of heavy chain-link fence that had managed to keep the infected out. Now what came next was the task of finding ourselves a ride. Richard waved me and Marvin over and began passing out keys.

"I'm not sure which cars are still here. From the looks of it, the guys managed to get a few of them out this morning, so we'll need to look for the cars that match the numbers imprinted on the keys." Richard flipped the key fobs over and showed us the letter-number combinations embossed on their surface. "The numbers are all located on the trunk hoods of all the cars, shouldn't be too difficult," he said and went off in search of a vehicle.

After several minutes of searching, we managed to locate a few viable options, Richard settling on a large canary-yellow Ford explorer. Figuring it would be large enough to house not only ourselves but also any we managed to pick up along the way. I had my doubts about that, however. If it were just my wife and Marvin's, that would be one thing; however, when this infection struck early this morning, my wife's daycare business was in full swing, which meant she could have upward of eight children residing with her. The thought made my insides turn to acid. I hoped against hope that she had managed to protect herself and the children and get to someplace safe. I was under no illusions that she'd remain in our homestead. The double-wide trailer we lived in wasn't designed to stand up to much in the way of catastrophe; if she had managed to stay there, any and all hope of survival was lost. She was smart, however; this I knew, in fact, it was one of the main reasons I fell in love with her. She would have recognized the severity of the situation and followed the plans that we'd laid out and went over time and again, which meant she could be in one of two places.

There was a local drugstore at the end of our development; it was a short distance and a good sturdy location that we had picked in the event of a hurricane or a tornado, which, although rare in our area, could still happen at a moment's notice. It was a logical choice in the way of supplies; there was food, medicine, and other necessities. The problem was the front of the building was completely exposed; that made the second option seem more plausible. That option was my folk's place. It was comprised of solid brick and mortar on the lower level, the upper floors being made of wood, but not accessible from ground level. There was also a basement with a secondary exit and plenty of room for which to house the children. Figuring that to be her best course of action, I decided that's where I was going to be heading.

The streets outside of the police station at the moment remained void of activity, and if I had to wager a guess, I imagined most of the infected in the immediate area had managed to find their way into the police station. Richard opened the doors to the Explorer and waved me over to join him. I paused and gave him and Marvin a cursory glance.

"I'm going to make a suggestion, you may not like it," I said as the two men turned in my direction and looked at me with furrowed brows. Marvin cocked an eyebrow expectantly. "I think perhaps we should split up," I finished and Marvin about choked as he spoke.

"Bullshit," he said.

Richard narrowed his eyes in my direction.

"Listen, guys. Marv, I know you want to get to your wife. I understand that. I want to get to mine as well. Chances are if we waste any more time, the likelihood of that happening is about nil." I paused for a moment, gauging Marvin's expression. "You practically live downtown. My family is in the opposite direction. If we split, we can make it to them faster, and then we can see about rendezvousing later. I know it sucks, but it's the best chance they have. Besides, do you honestly think we can pile everyone into one vehicle?"

Marvin and Richard seemed to consider my words for a moment.

Richard had a look on his face that suggested he didn't quite understand the dynamics of it, so I elaborated, "Rich, my wife runs a daycare center, so chances are she's not alone. I'm gonna need an empty ride to fit everyone in, and it's going to be cramped quarters even if it's just me going." That last comment got Richard's attention.

"What do you mean, *just you*? I already told you wherever you go, I go," he said expectantly.

"And I appreciate that, Rich. Truth be told, Marv could probably use your help more than I could. No offense, man," I said, giving Marvin a sideways glance.

"None taken, bub." Marvin shook his head. "What you say makes sense. You're right, though. I don't like it, and what about Homeland's thugs? What do we do if they show up?" Marvin crossed his arms over his chest.

"I'm not sure, to be honest. Perhaps to be on the safe side, we should probably stash those documents here somewhere." I looked around the lot, and an idea formed in my head. "Why don't we stash the file in one of these trunks? We can swing by later and pick it up if we decide to take it to Hopkins."

Marvin nodded considering the idea. "That sounds good but . . ." He reached into his breast pocket and removed a small flash drive and held it between his thumb and forefinger. "Here, I found this in the case as well. I have no idea what's on it, but I would guess it's most likely the same information that's in the hard file."

Marvin tossed the small plastic device over to me. I caught it in midair and studied it for a moment, then stuffed it in my vest pocket.

"Okay, let's hope this thing isn't just full of downloaded porn, and there's something still up and running to read it. We'll slip the hard copy into one of these cars as a backup. At least I might be able to conceal this a little easier if the need arises." I tapped the breast pocket of my vest.

"You know them Homeland boys are known for their cavity searches, right?" Marvin quipped and cocked a sideways grin.

I smiled and sighed. "We should probably get moving. I'm not sure what time it is, but I don't want to be stuck out here on the road after dark." Something about that thought sent a cold chill down my spine, probably due to the fact we had just came out into the light after fighting for our lives in a dark police station.

I held three fingers up in the air in front of my face, using them to measure the distance between the sun overhead and the horizon below, an old survival technique that I had been taught some years ago. Judging from the distance, we had about four, maybe five hours of daylight left. Although it would normally only take me roughly forty-five or so minutes to get home, I had to figure with all that had transpired, the roadways were probably going to be choked with cars, or worse.

Richard climbed up into the cab of the Ford Explorer and started the engine.

"What car are you taking?" Richard craned his neck around the lot, observing the leftover vehicles.

"I was thinking I would take that." I pointed down the lot to a dull-gray Mustang that sat on the far edge. "I want speed and maneuverability. I figured that ought to do," I said, dangling the keys in my hand.

"One of the HEAT units. Good choice."

"Heat?" I said.

"HEAT stands for *High Enforcement Arrest Team.* The cars were designed for high-speed pursuit and equipped with special antiroll suspension systems and a protective roll cage—like on a formula race car. However, not the best choice for seating room. How are you planning on getting your wife and kids out?" Richard asked, a puzzled look creasing his chiseled features.

"In all honesty, man, I hope it doesn't come down to that. If she's gone where I think she has, then I may just be able to fortify and hold out there with them. If not . . ." I let the sentence trail off, considering my words. "If not, my wife has a pretty good-sized van. It will seat eight comfortably, but if I toss the seats out, we could probably cram about ten or even twelve in." I paused for a moment. "Do me a favor, guys. When you get to Marvin's place, give me a call on the radio, so long as I get to where I'm going. I'll be certain to answer. I think the best bet for all of us would be to hook up there."

"Marvin"—I looked to my old friend—"I think she may have taken the kids to my mother's. You remember the place?" It had been some time, but right after my divorce from my first wife, I was forced to bunk up there in the aftermath. There had been a few occasions when Marvin would have to swing by in the morning and fetch my hungover ass, me being too sick and woozy to drive out to the job. With everything I had suffered at that woman's hand, it had been Marvin who pretty much pulled me out of the gutter, not to mention kept me from being fired.

"Sure thing, bub. I remember."

He gave me a furtive glance, and I looked down at my feet somewhat ashamed. Marvin gave me a wink as if to say, *No worries, your secret is safe with me.* I walked over and gave the old man a hug and quickly released him as he gave me a disapproving look.

"Keep safe, my friend," I said, clasping him on the shoulder. I turned and looked over to Richard. "You too, man, and keep him out of trouble."

Richard nodded, and Marvin grunted as I poked a thumb in his direction.

"We won't be long. Get home to that family, kiddo," Marvin said, then dug the file out of his backpack and handed it to me.

I took it and decided to stuff it into the back of a dilapidated police cruiser that set on blocks at the other end of the lot, doubting that it would be going anywhere anytime soon.

Marvin gave me a nod and began to head to the passenger door of the Ford. He opened the door and stepped inside.

Richard closed his door and leaned out of the window. "Hey, one last thing." Rich paused and I looked at him expectantly. "Get the gate, would ya?" He pointed to the sliding chain-link exit directly ahead of the Explorer.

I nodded and jogged off to do as I was asked. I reached the gate and studied the simple mechanism. The gate opened via a standard garage door opener that had been placed sideways; the gate would hold shut even if the power was off. I pulled on it, and as expected, the gate did not move. I looked down at the machine and found what I was looking for. Dangling beneath it was an emergency pull cord that would allow the motor to be disengaged in the event something or someone had been caught in it. I pulled the cord and released the motor's hold. The gate slid open easily on well-oiled tracks.

Richard slowly moved the Explorer forward and gave me a wave as he drove past. When the SUV had made it clear of the gate, I slid it shut and set about hiding the file that was still in my hand.

CHAPTER 27

Richard navigated the large canary-yellow Ford Explorer with practiced ease through the streets of Baltimore County. An hour had passed since they left Kyle at the police station. The streets leading away from the station were, as predicted, insane. Normally, at least according to Marvin, the drive to his home in Dundalk would have only taken about twenty minutes from their previous location, but the way the roadways were clogged with cars, there was no way that was even possible. At times, Richard would have to pull the vehicle off to the side of the road or drive up onto the median to get beyond clusters of abandoned cars. Unfortunately, not all of the vehicles themselves were empty. Bodies could be seen slumped up against bloodied windows or hanging out of opened doors. Occasionally, they would pass by a car whose inhabitants still moved, the figures inside going insane and pounding on the windows, howling with silent rage behind glass as they passed by.

Marvin and Richard watched from behind the Explorer's windows. Smoke was everywhere as they entered the town. Fires burned unchecked in homes and apartment buildings as far as the eye could see. Every so often, screams could be heard from within the smoke, followed by a glimpse of movement as a survivor fled for his or her lives from small groups of the human monsters. It seemed to usually end up the same way—they would disappear from view, and either the screams would become too distant to be heard or . . . well, neither one of them wanted to think of the alternative.

Marvin gripped the shotgun in his hand, clenching and unclenching his grip around the stock as he wished he could do something to help these people. The people in this town were his friends, his neighbors, and all he could do was watch. Reason took hold of him every time he was about to protest their movement.

Marvin knew if they stopped the vehicle to help, they themselves would most likely become casualties as well. Marvin stiffened in his seat and pointed as they approached his street.

"Over there." He motioned and Richard headed in that direction, turning the big SUV into the direction that Marvin had indicated. As they approached Marvin's home, Richard cursed.

"Damn it," Rich said, looking into the rearview mirror. "We've got company." He shot a thumb behind him.

Marvin turned around to get a glimpse at what he was talking about. Directly behind them wandering down the street were about two dozen or so infected, apparently drawn to the noise of the engine. The sound acting as a dinner bell to any who had occupied the surrounding area.

"Great," Marvin muttered. "Drive around the block. Maybe we can lead them away and double back on foot," Marvin suggested.

Richard nodded in agreement.

Marvin gazed at his building as they drove past, thankful for the fact that his front door remained closed. His parking spot, however, had been occupied. "Damn punks," he grumbled and Rich looked over at him expectantly. "It's nothing," he said and motioned for him to pull over in an alleyway as they neared the opposite side of the block.

Richard did as he was asked and pulled over, taking care to angle the Explorer in a way that it obscured the alley, not allowing any approaching vehicle to make it through. He also hoped that the infected would have a hard time navigating around the obstruction as well. He cut the engine and pocketed the keys.

He and Marvin grabbed up their weapons and gear, keeping a close eye on the curious infected trailing behind them at several hundred yards. The duo stepped out of the SUV and readied their weapons, hoping they would be able to evade infected for fear of drawing more of them in with the noise of a gun blast.

"Come on, this way!" Marvin whispered loudly and began to limp hurriedly down the alleyway toward the front of his building. Reaching the end of the expanse, Marvin stopped and pressed himself up against the wall, and began fishing around his pant pockets until he found a set of keys. The infected in the alley had taken notice of them and picked up speed, several of them already reaching the Ford Explorer. As expected, they began to pound on the vehicle in frustration, unable to figure a way around it. "Dumbasses," Marvin muttered to Richard and grinned.

"Yeah, thankfully," Richard replied, taking a moment to gaze over his shoulder. "You ready or what?" Richard asked. "These things are starting to make a hell of a lot of noise, and I don't think we want to be standing here when more start to show up." As if on cue, the growls and moans began behind them.

Marvin nodded his head up and down in agreement.

"Let's go," he breathed and headed out into the smoke-filled street. Carefully and quietly, they moved past several doors that occupied the same length of row homes on Marvin's street.

Each home was your basic cookie-cutter brick buildings with generic-colored pale-green siding atop the second-floor level. Small brick stairways led up to tin-covered porches, most of which were decorated in artificial plants or goofy Welcome Home signs. At the end of the row was Marvin's particular dwelling, which, in only knowing the man for several hours, Richard was able to pick out. A large red U.S. Marine Corps flag hung from the tin roof and fluttered slightly in the breeze. Several potted plants hung over wrought iron railings that surrounded his porch, something his wife had obviously put there to add a woman's touch to the home.

Marvin and Richard approached and ascended the small stairway. Richard covered to the rear as Marvin fumbled around with the set of house keys. After what seemed like an agonizingly long second, Marv located the key he was searching for and slid it silently into the lock. To his surprise, as he began to turn the key, the door swung open. It had been unlocked.

CHAPTER 28

After I stashed the documents into the damaged police cruiser, taking care to hide them in the vehicle's tire well in the trunk, I made my way over to the Mustang and fired up the engine. I pulled the car over to the gate and went back through the ritual of opening the chain-link portal. I toyed with the idea of just leaving it open as I left, but if the need arose for me to retrieve said file, I didn't want to have to battle my way back through the parking lot to do it, so I took a moment to resecure the gate back into place.

I was anxious to get on the move and get to my wife, but with my current inventory of weaponry, I didn't think I would make it very far if it came down to a fight, so I wanted to make a quick pit stop at my home along the way. At present, I had the shotgun loaded with about an additional ten spare rounds and the forty-caliber pistol. The pistol had one full magazine with about fifteen rounds and a partial stored in one of my pant pockets. Good under normal circumstances, but in this situation, if I was caught in a firefight or hit by a horde of these things, I was pretty much screwed. I tapped the Smith & Wesson in the holster on my side. For that weapon I had a whopping three rounds left, so I made the decision that my trusty .357 would be my absolute last resort.

My home in Harford County was along the way to my parents' house, and in my closet was a virtual armory hidden away. I hoped like hell, however, that my wife managed to grab a few supplies for herself before she bugged out, if she bugged out . . . I shook my head, letting the thought drop. *Of course she bugged out*, I told myself. We had been through too much for her not to have done so. No, she was a strong woman, and I had faith that she would have made the right decision even though I knew she abhorred fire arms. At any rate, I needed to stop there if for no other reason than to make certain she wasn't there. The weapons and ammo were actually secondary to that objective. I had to be sure.

CHAPTER 29

Marvin entered his home first. He held his shotgun at port arms as not to startle his wife of the last forty-six years. The scent of candle wax permeated the air as they entered. A homey scent of apples and cinnamon wafted up and lingered in their nostrils. The lights were off and candles illuminated the living room area, casting the cozily decorated room in flickering shadows of orange and yellow.

Richard took notice of old photographs that hung above a fireplace off to his left. Candles set atop the mantle, casting light on the black-and-white images. One picture stood out among the rest; it was an image of a young Marvin Winters in full formal military dress holding on to what he had to assume was his lifelong love and companion. The woman in the photograph stood wrapped in his arms, her slender face pressed against his metal-adorned chest. Her hair had been styled up into a bun consistent with the style back in the 1960s. She wore a plain white or cream colored dress. In black and white, and in this lighting, it was impossible to tell.

Another photograph set below and to the right, this one a bit more modern. It was your standard 5" x 7" digital photo that people were accustomed to seeing these days and portrayed a fortieth anniversary party shot. Once again, the photo was of Marvin and his wife. This one showed the couple as they were now. Age had been kind to his wife. She still had slender delicate features, although her hair had gone white, and fine wrinkles creased her face. She had a sweet mom-looking quality about her that made Richard smile inwardly.

Breaking his attention away from the display, Richard cast a glance outside of the doorway once more to see if they had been followed. It was difficult to see out into the smoke, but from what he could make out, the coast was still clear. He stepped off to the side and closed the door softly, hoping not to alert any of the nearby infected to their location.

Marvin stepped farther into the living room. Everything seemed to look fairly normal to the old man. The room was as clean as it was when he had left this morning, and save for the dozen or so candles that burned around the room, nothing was out of place.

"Baby," Marvin called out expectantly. His nerves beginning to frazzle as his call went unreciprocated. Marvin breathed in deeply and peered around the couch in the middle of the living room. The couch was empty, a ruffled quilt lying across its patchwork surface. An ancient-looking tube television stared blankly back at them. Marvin smiled when he gazed upon the open pages of a romance novel lying on an end table.

"She's always loved her smut books," Marvin quipped to Richard, who took notice of the book as they passed.

Marvin stepped through the living room and entered the kitchen. The room itself once again was empty. Ambient light diffused through a sliding glass door covered with flower-patterned vertical blinds and spilled forth into the smallish kitchen area. Immediately, Marvin took notice of the syringe and an empty bottle of insulin sitting in the middle of their small, round dining room table. What struck Marvin as odd was the absence of his wife's blood glucose test kit that was usually sitting in the middle of the dining room table. If she'd injected insulin recently, there would have been at least one test strip lying about in the room. A quick glance at the nearby waste basket confirmed that none were present. He shook his head in confusion, and thought, *Perhaps she'd taken a dose at lunch and simply forgot to throw out the vial.* The testing equipment was odd, though. In the past fifteen years after she'd been diagnosed with the disease, the kit practically never left its resting spot in the center of the table.

Richard stepped lightly into the kitchen as Marvin moved over to the sliding glass door. Using his fingertips, he nudged the vertical blinds open slightly and peered outside. His tiny yard was empty, save for overgrown grass and the usual rusted lawn equipment. Marvin normally had some neighborhood kids tend to his lawn, but it had been several weeks since they'd been around.

He could see several figures lumbering out in the haze of smoke beyond his open fence.

"Goddamn it," Marvin grunted, noticing the gate hanging ajar. He must have forgotten to latch it the last time he'd been out there, which, truth be told, he couldn't even remember when that was.

Richard gave Marvin a worried glance.

"It's nothing. Gates open, so we just need to be extra careful we don't draw any attention to ourselves, yeah?" Marvin said, allowing the blinds to fall back into place.

Richard nodded in agreement.

Marvin led Rich over to a small door that set directly next to the refrigerator, partially obscured by the large appliance. He pulled the old door open and peered up the stairs. The staircase, just like the living room, was cast into darkness.

"Honey, you up there?" Marvin asked and listened intently. When no reply came forth, Marvin began to carefully ascend the staircase. The old wooden steps creaked and groaned under the weight of the two men as they made their way up to the top landing. "Honey," he repeated and still was only greeted with silence. A deep sense of worry boiled in the old man's stomach and ebbed out into his skin, causing every wayward hair on his body to stand on end. Marvin peered down the short hallway leading to his bedroom. He hoped like hell his wife was just taking a nap and perhaps didn't even have any idea of what was even going on outside.

Richard removed the flashlight from his belt and flipped it on. The light cast and ominous glow through the hallway, throwing Marvin's shadow against the door to his bedroom. The two men approached the door.

Marvin held his breath as he turned the knob. The door swung open with a creak, something Marvin had been meaning to fix for some time. Marvin stepped in the room and froze.

Richard entered behind him and shined the light around the room.

Marvin stood there stuck still as the light came to rest on the figure lying in the center of the bed. Marvin gasped and dropped his shotgun to the floor as he stared at the unmoving form of his wife.

His wife lay in the bed wrapped in a powder-blue night gown adorned with small white and yellow flowers. The first thing he noticed was the stream of frothy-looking blood that ran from her mouth and pooled on the bedspread. Her skin was pale, and blue veins stood out in stark contrast to her alabaster skin. They wove a spidery-looking tapestry along her arms, face, and bare legs. Marvin's eyes flicked to the nightstand. Another three vials of insulin stood empty atop its surface. Recognition hit him like a ton of bricks. She had overdosed. Something caused her to inject every bit of insulin she had. From the looks of her, the way her face was contorted and twisted in pain, and the fact that blood and drool ran from her open mouth, she must have had some sort of seizure, ultimately, a seizure that proved to be fatal.

Marvin ran forward and fell to his knees at the edge of the bed, the pain from shock to his aching knee not even registering in his mind as he broke into uncontrollable tears. He gathered his wife's hand in his own, held it to his lips, and began to whisper frantically to her, "Why, baby? Why? Why would you do this?" he asked to God or the Devil or anyone that would listen to his pleas. "No, sweetie, no. This can't be how it ends, not like this," Marvin cried, laying his head down beside her.

Richard moved forward and came to rest his hand on Marvin's shoulders. "Marvin, I . . . I'm so sorry . . ."

Richard didn't get a chance to finish the sentence as Marvin shot up from his crouching position with a speed and agility that Richard had not expected to see from the old man. He shot a fist out and caught Richard in the chin, knocking the police officer back a few steps.

"Fuck you!" he shouted, tears streaming from his eyes. "Fuck all of you . . ." he trailed off and went back down to his knees sobbing.

Richard stood there stunned for a moment. He rubbed his chin and shook off the blow when something to Marvin's side caught his attention. It was subtle, but it was definitely something. Sitting next to Marvin on the floor was what looked to be a very large boot print. Mud caked on the carpet in a distinctive tread pattern. At closer observation, Richard could see the prints led in and also back out of the room. Judging from the size of the print, whoever had left it, had to be at least 6' 5" or more.

"Marvin," Richard spoke quietly, and Marvin ignored him. "Marv," he tried again. "Look down to your right," Richard said softly, trying his best to keep the edge out of his voice. Marvin glanced down at the floor and saw the muddy imprint on the carpet.

"So what?" Marvin cried, gazing at the boot print through tear-stained eyes. "It's just a fucking footprint," he sobbed, not making the connection.

"Marv, look closer, that's not one of your prints. Unless you happened to be taller this morning," Richard said, trying somewhat to bring this man back to reality. This was a horrible situation, but if the old man continued down this path for much longer, both of them were going to die.

Marvin looked back down once more, then back up to his wife. The realization set in as he remembered the syringe sitting downstairs on the kitchen table, if she had injected herself downstairs and then again up here, the syringe would have still been with her. Marvin looked around the room to see if another needle lay in the vicinity. None had, which meant someone had injected her and then left her here, but why? Why leave the evidence lying around . . . unless, unless they wanted him to know it wasn't an accident. The thought tore through Marvin's mind like a thunderbolt, and he stood erect. "Homeland did this. I'm sure of it," Marvin vehemently spat out.

Richard stood there in silence.

Marvin gazed down at his wife's dead form. "Why would they do this, though? She's never done anything to anybody," he sobbed again.

Richard caught movement out of the corner of his eye. The police officer stared intently at the elderly woman lying on the bed. For a moment, he could have sworn he had seen her hand twitch.

Marvin walked over to the upstairs window and stared out into the din. He touched his fingers to his chin, his mind racing with a thousand and one thoughts about what had transpired. Why would they kill his wife? What the hell was the point? They had to be sending some sort of message, but he had no clue as to what it would be. The only thing Marvin could surmise in his brain's distraught state was that these people wanted that case more than any of them could have imagined, and if they knew where he lived, then Kyle was also in danger. They had to warn him.

Marvin turned to face Richard when his wife's body shot straight up in her bed. She stared at them with hollow eyes and lunged at Richard.

"No, baby, no!" Marvin cried as the creature that was once his wife slammed into Richard, knocking him to the floor. She climbed on top of him, snarling and snapping.

Richard grabbed her by her spindly arms and thrust her forward off him. She landed hard against the other side of the room and quickly scrambled back to her feet. Richard rolled over and deftly moved back into a standing position.

Marvin stood there, staring in stunned silence, rooted to the floor, his mouth quivering at the sight of his beloved's face covered in blood and drool. Her once lovely features twisted in rage. Richard brought up his pistol and prepared to fire as Marvin screamed out.

"No!" he shouted and moved to intercept as Richard squeezed the trigger. The shot caught the woman in the forehead and she fell to the carpeted floor in a mound of brittle bones and paper-thin flesh.

Marvin fell to his knees beside her once more, screaming out in pain and anguish. He gathered her up in his arms and held her close, rocking her back and forth as she stared lifelessly up at him once again.

This sucks, Richard thought. It was bad enough to lose a loved one once, but twice in the same night? At that point, the police officer was glad that he was unmarried and any family he had lived several states away.

A loud crash from downstairs caused Richard to wrench his eyes away from the grieving man on the floor. Richard lifted the shotgun that hung from a strap on his side and raised it up to his shoulder, and then moved over into the hallway.

He sprinted over to the top of the stairs and peered down to see the shadows of shambling forms entering in through the sliding glass window. The sounds of Marvin's screams and the gunshot from his sidearm must have alerted the infected to their position. Quickly, Richard ran back down the hallway, and peered into the bedroom.

"Marv, we gotta go!" he shouted to be heard over the increasing volume of the infected's wails below. Marvin didn't respond. He simply sat there, still rocking his wife's body back and forth in his lap. "Goddamn it," Richard spat out and crossed the room in an instant. The large police man reached down and grabbed Marvin by the arm and bodily hauled him to his feet. Marvin stood there in silence, too weak to fight and in shock, Richard realized. "Marv, you need to snap out of it, or we're both dead," Richard said, grabbing the old man by the shoulders, and giving him a shake.

The old vet simply closed his eyes. "Just leave me. I don't want to be without her. I just want to stay," Marvin whimpered.

Richard felt panic welling up in his stomach as he heard the infected begin to clomp onto the bottom of the stairs. Hastily, Richard grabbed Marvin's discarded shotgun and thrust it into his hands. Marvin reluctantly took the weapon and let it hang at his side. Rich dragged him forward and out into the hallway. He pointed down the stairs at the oncoming horde and shouted in the old man's face. "I don't know about you, but I don't plan on ending up like one of them! Do you think that's what she would have wanted for you?"

Richard's words stung in Marvin's ears, and that seemed to snap the man out of it.

Looking at Richard with tear-stained eyes, Marvin seemed to steel himself, allowing the aspects of their situation to sink in. The old vet nodded and wiped the offending liquid away from his face. He looked around the hallway and pointed upward.

"There," he said, pointing to a hidden drawstring in the ceiling. An attic, Richard presumed. Although Marvin would have needed a step ladder to reach the cord, Richard's 6' 2" stature allowed him to jump up and snatch it in the air. Quickly, he pulled down the trap door with a loud springy creak. He grabbed the folding stairs and pulled them down. "All right, you first," Richard ordered, pushing the elderly man toward the steps.

Marvin didn't resist; he simply grabbed onto the ladder-like stairs and made his way up into the darkness.

The infected stumbled atop one another, trying to get up the staircase and to the fresh meat that sat above them.

Hurriedly, Richard climbed up after Marvin; the metal coils creaked and sprang under his weight, the sounds almost deafening in the confines of the hallway. Richard made it to the landing above. Reaching down, he grabbed the closest wooden step and pulled upward with all his strength. The infected clawed at the bottom rungs as he hefted the heavy spring-loaded staircase up and into the ceiling.

CHAPTER 30

After driving through just about every country back road from the airport district to Harford County, I had finally managed to make it to my homestead. The roads I had chosen had been eerily devoid of anything moving, the normal sounds of birds and squirrels rustling through the trees were absent as I made my way home. Smoke from distant fires hovered on the horizon as I passed in and out of wooded areas. It wasn't until I made it to the main strip of Route 40 that I even noticed any of the widespread devastation that seemed to be all around me. Cars set empty along the middle of the expressway and forced me up and onto the shoulder. There were several points I was worried that the lowered formula Mustang would get hung up on a curb as the bottom of the car scraped along, showering the sidewalk in sparks. There were several tense moments where the lanes became so choked with cars that I feared there would be no way of getting around the obstructions short of ramming them.

I peered into many of the empty transports as I slowly made my way past them, looking for any signs of life still trapped inside. None were particularly forthcoming; many of the doors and windows hung open, cab lights and door alarms still binging away in the interiors of many still-running vehicles.

Finally, after what felt like hours, I made it into my neighborhood. I was shocked when I pulled in to see many of my fellow residents trailer's had been reduced to flames and ash, many of them still smoldering in the afternoon heat, adding to the oppressiveness of the day. Several bodies lay in the street, crowding gutters and sidewalks in the area, spread along the roadsides like rubbish. My heart leapt slightly when I turned onto my street and noticed that my wife's van was absent from the scene.

"Thank God," I breathed as I pulled alongside my driveway. A quick check of my surroundings led me to believe that for the moment, the coast was clear. I grabbed my shotgun from off the passenger seat and checked to make certain that a round was in the chamber. Satisfied that the gun was conflict ready, I exited the vehicle. I entered my home like a DEA agent on a drug raid and swept the shotgun left and then right. The first thing I had noticed upon entering was how the door hung open on wiry hinges. I cursed the manufacturer of the mobile home and continued on. One by one, I cleared the home—starting with my children's rooms.

At the moment, I was extremely thankful that my children were on vacation somewhere else. Hopefully safe, staying with my grandparents in the mountains of West Virginia. With any luck, this blight hadn't even reached there yet. Shifting that thought to the side, I made my way into my bedroom. The room itself was in complete disarray; bedding and clothing lay strewn across the room in unorganized heaps. My wife's knickknacks littered the floor, broken and crushed under footsteps that had obviously trampled them into the wooden floors. The bathroom door hung ajar and had been busted inward; the doorway leading to my closet was completely torn off its hinges. A body lying in between the bathroom proper and my closet told me that something had definitely went down, *as if I needed any more convincing*.

I gingerly stepped over the fallen corpse, taking notice that its head had nearly been removed from its shoulders, and set about gathering my supplies. Grabbing one of the many duffle bags from off the top shelf, I started loading it up. I dumped several boxes of various types of ammunition—including rounds for my beloved .357 Smith & Wesson. MREs were the next item to be added in to the pot; I loaded enough of those to last several people for about a week or more if rationed right.

A noise outside of the closet forced me to stop what I was doing and listen. I waited for several minutes to see if it would come again. Nothing but silence greeted my expectant ears.

Thankful, I resumed my task. I bent over and unlocked a heavy wooden chest and grabbed out the crowning jewel of my firearms collection. The AR-15 felt comforting in my hands; it was like an old friend came home for a visit in my arms. The custom stock provided an easy grip and helped reduce recoil when set to full auto. I had it mounted with a night-vision scope that would allow me to practically shoot the flea off a dog's ass at a hundred yards or more, even in lowlight conditions. I hefted it in my arms and gauged the weight; ultimately, I swapped the shotgun out in favor of the weapon and loaded it in the bag with the other supplies. I also stacked several .22 hunting rifles inside, mainly because the ammunition for those was not only lightweight, but plentiful.

After I finished loading the bag to what I presumed was its tear-weight capacity, I hefted it up and slung it over my shoulder. The heavy nylon strap dug down into the flesh of my neck as it settled into place. Hurriedly, I carried the burden out of the house, nearly tripping down the rickety wood stairs attached to my front deck, and crossed the yard. I threw the heavy bag into the backseat of the Mustang and gave my home of the last few years one final look. I settled myself into the driver's seat and restarted the engine.

CHAPTER 31

It took roughly forty or so minutes to make it over toward my parents' place. The ride for the most part was fairly uneventful aside from a few shambling forms that I had spotted in the distance. The ones I had seen for the most part either grouped around buildings or walked along pathways of congested cars. For some reason, activity seemed to increase the farther down the road I traveled.

My first thought was to simply drive into their cul-de-sac and park directly in front of the house, thus allowing me to transfer the heavy bag of supplies directly into my wife's van. Common sense, however, got the better of me. With the loud engine of the Mustang, the last thing I wanted to do was to draw a horde of the infected directly to my parents' front door; so siding on an air of caution, I decided to park the car along the side of the road about a half mile or so from the property. I chose an area that had an entrance leading into the woods.

My parents' home was surrounded on all sides by trees, and as a kid I ran and romped through the forest like it was my own personal playground. I could remember years ago crawling with my friends through the woods, carrying toy rifles, and hunting one another down like enemy combatants. We dug pits, built traps and forts, and had the time of our lives doing it. The thought had never crossed my mind that I would be back here someday, only this time doing it for real.

I let out a long sigh. I gathered what equipment I could carry on my back, deciding to leave the rest in the rear of the Mustang. If my wife was indeed at my parents' place, this road wasn't too far off that we couldn't just simply swing around over to it and grab the remaining supplies. Choosing my .357 and the AR-15, I reloaded each and grabbed several spare magazines and speed loaders, and then tucked them into my duty rig. I exited the vehicle, locking it securely, and headed for the trail leading deeper into the forest.

The trailhead lay just on the other side of the sidewalk and behind an old-fashioned wooden fence that someone had erected some time ago to keep the neighborhood children out. I shook my head at the thought of that notion. This is why most of our children now are overweight, lazy, and would rather be stuck in front of a video game than out here experiencing actual life.

I straddled the fence and hopped over. The old trail through the forest was barely visible through the heavy overgrowth that had taken place over the years, and I hoped that I could still remember which way to go given all the changes that had taken place.

I looked into the sky and decided the sun was going to be dipping below the horizon very, very soon, meaning more time had passed than I had realized. I needed to get a move on. If the sun was dropping rapidly out here, that meant it was going to be getting dark inside of the woods that much faster. I slipped into the thick underbrush stealthily, years of training taking over as I did so. I moved slowly at first, most of the overgrowth having taken place on the outskirts of the woods where the sun had more of a chance to penetrate down to the forest floor below. After breaking through the shrubs and brambles, I exited on the other side into the forest proper. I moved swiftly at that point, memories of my young exploits through the wilderness flooding back to me as I traveled. I passed by the remnants of an old dilapidated treehouse my friend Matt and I had built as children. It stood atop several large branches in an old oak tree and hung there in broken and rotted pieces. Following these old signs, I managed to pick up the trail leading to my folk's house with relative ease.

The area around me began to darken as I emerged from the woods out onto the top of a hill overlooking the cul-de-sac where my parent's home resided. I could make out candlelight inside of the home, which gave me a sense of relief that they had managed to buckle down and pull through. My view of the street below was obscured by another home that set at the bottom of the hill directly in front of me so I adjusted positions. My heart soared as I noticed the navy-blue Honda Odyssey parked in front of the house. There were shapes lying around the lawn that I had a hard time making out in the encroaching darkness of twilight.

I lifted my rifle up and flipped on the NVGs. Peering through the optics, I realized the shapes I had been looking at were indeed the remains of human corpses. I focused in on the bodies, making certain none of them were my own family members. Some of them seemed to look somewhat familiar being neighbors and such I supposed, people I had seen merely in passing as I dropped my children off on occasion to spend the day with their grandparents. I had seen so much craziness today that the offending bodies didn't seem to even make a dent in my psyche. I swept the rifle up and down the street, scanning for threats, when something odd caught my eyes. On the end of the road was a white SUV. The same kind of white SUV I had seen the Department of Homeland Security driving earlier that day.

"Shit," I cursed inwardly as I searched the area. From this angle, I couldn't tell if the SUV bore the seal of the department or not. It could have just as well belonged to one of the neighbors. I looked at the vehicle for a long moment and continued my scan. I was about to cease my reconnaissance and make my way down to the house as something shifted in the darkness behind me.

I turned to face the movement when my world exploded in flashes of light and pain. I heard the muffled sound of laughter as I dropped to the forest floor, and in my scrambled thoughts, I heard something else as well.

"I told you, you were mine, bitch," a deep voice rumbled.

My eyes blurred and rolled into the back of my head, and I fell into unconsciousness.

****

When I awoke, I could see through my swollen eyes that I was sitting in my parents' dining room area. Pain throbbed in my head, and I winced as I tried to raise my hands up to my face. This became a problem when I realized that my arms had been bound behind the back of the chair that I was sitting in. I looked down— my feet had been secured as well. From the looks of it, heavy layers of duct tape had been wrapped around each ankle several times, creating an unmoving bond to the chair legs. I raised my head in an effort to observe my surroundings. My neck ached and popped as I lifted it upward.

A darkened figure sat across the room from me, staring at me intently with cold blue-gray eyes. He leaned forward in my mother's rocking chair and rested his arms on his lap. He tapped his fingertips to his chin and spoke, "Welcome back, Mr. Walker," came a vaguely familiar voice. "I was wondering for a little bit if my friend over there had hit you too hard." The figure clapped his hands together. "Ha, you must have really pissed him off back there."

The man in front of me chuckled as I noticed a massive black man step out from behind me, holding an MP5 leveled at my chest.

"It's all good, Cap. We're even now." The large man smiled and gazed down at me with narrowed eyes.

"What the hell do you people want from me?" I asked in confusion, glancing around the room. It was then I noticed the pair of legs sticking out from behind an island that separated the dining room from the kitchen. I could clearly see the short stubby legs of my father protruding from behind the bar. A small amount of blood stained his pants and soaked into the floor. I jerked upright in my chair, trying to free myself to no avail. "What the hell have you done to him, and where are my mother and my wife?" I screamed in the direction of the two men.

The man in front of me stared back at me with a hardened look and grinned. "No worries, Mr. Walker, they're alive. Your father over there is alive . . . for the moment anyway. Consider it an incentive for your cooperation to our proposal." He paused, choosing his words. "I've been reading your service record, Mr. Walker. It was actually funny when I mentioned it to your wife. You should have seen her face when I told her you were a soldier." He shook his head. "It must have been hard keeping it from her for all of these years." He stood and began to pace the length of the dining room.

"You still haven't told me what the hell it is you want. Is it this stupid file? Don't tell me you did all this for a fucking piece of paper," I spat vehemently at the man.

The captain paused in front of me. "Originally, yes, the files that you were transporting were our primary objective. We were under orders to retrieve the information and deliver them directly to the CDC in order to combat this disease," he said in a flat tone.

"More like cover your own asses," I said incredulously.

Alex Bishop smiled. "You're a smart man, Mr. Walker. Your file was correct. Yes, we needed to naturally put some distance between ourselves and any connection to this outbreak. Unfortunately, the American people at large are a bunch of morons. When this gets cleared up, and it will get cleared up, the first thing the public is going to do is demand blood from whoever is responsible. Granted, we didn't cause this outbreak; our enemies saw to that. It was just dumb luck that as soon as we started our investigations, they struck, and therein lays the problem. If the public were to figure out that we had any prior information to this attack, whether or not if it was a day or ten years, they're going to demand a reason as to why we hadn't acted sooner. Unfortunately, this particular administration would most likely agree with them. My department would be finished, and in all honesty for all of our flaws, we do a hell of a lot more good than bad," he said pacing once more.

"That's a great story, sir, but it still doesn't explain what the hell you want with me." I shot daggers at him with my eyes.

Bishop nodded and turned to stare out of the back window. "The President has declared a state of national emergency. Apparently, this particular attack struck us at every major transportation hub across the country. Airports, train stations—hell—even bus depots, so this contagion has spread much, much further than any of us could have even imagined. Naturally, martial law has been put into effect across the entire nation. Problem with that is now my division's movements are limited. You, however, are not." Alex paused. "Homeland has been ordered to investigate the cause of this outbreak and backup the National Guard units being deployed across the country. So, needless to say, we're going to be pretty fucking busy. You, however, are not, plus you have a unique skill set and position that we find to be extremely useful to us in this situation."

I shook my head and shrugged.

Bishop ignored the expression and continued. "There are six cases in total, Mr. Walker, one of them you know of. We didn't find it on you, so we assume you stashed it somewhere. The others are spread out across the East Coast, each one being carried by a similar armored security group such as yours. Unfortunately, after things began to spread, we lost track of most of those cases, and well, being you yourself are familiar with that industry gives you an edge we do not have."

Bishop watched me as things began to form in my mind.

"And in light of our circumstances, you can understand why we need this done off the books. Something from what I have read of your past seems to be your specialty." Bishop smiled, half turning in my direction.

"So . . . what? You think I'm just going to mosey on out and be your errand boy?" I said sarcastically.

Bishop snickered. "We're not giving you a choice, Kyle. Your wife and mother, along with the children we found them with, have all been transported to an underground facility not far from here. They're safe for the moment, but mark my words, if you don't play ball, I will personally feed each one of them to these crazy bastards walking around out here. Then I'll drag them back inside and let our eggheads go to town dissecting them." Bishop stared at me intently. "Consider yourself reactivated, Mr. Walker."

I gritted my teeth in disgust. I wanted nothing more but to jump out of this seat and tear the man's head off with my bare hands, but the asshole had me, and there wasn't a goddamn thing I could do about it.

Bishop walked over toward me and set something down on the dining room table.

I peered at it with suspicion.

He smiled. "This is a satellite phone. Make certain you don't lose it. If we manage to find any information that will help you locate the remaining cases, we'll communicate with you via this. You will also, in turn, give us regular status reports with it as well. We'll also keep you posted about your family's well-being, and hell, if you're a good boy, we may even let you talk to your wife from time to time." Next, Bishop set my knife on the table as well, having removed it from my duty rig while I was unconscious.

"We've locked your weapons down in the basement as well. I have a feeling you're going to need them." Bishop turned and began to walk out of the room, apparently finished with this conversation.

I swiveled my head in his direction. "Bishop!" I called out as he began to disappear around the corner into the hallway.

The man paused and looked over his shoulder at me.

"I'm going to kill you for this," I said solemnly.

Bishop cocked a half grin. "Not today, son," and with that, he and his partner headed for the front door. "Don't worry, kid. We'll lock up on our way out."

As I sat there strapped down to the chair, I heard the door slam as they left the house. I cursed and struggled frantically with my bonds, flexing and relaxing my muscles, trying to break free, the chair hopping around, knocking on the hardwood floors as I moved. I screamed in frustration as I heard an engine start up and pull away outside. I let my arms sag in place, the fight draining out of me, and leaving me with a sense of helplessness. I broke down and began to sob, and then went into full-out wailing. I cursed and swore and finally relented. I sat there bound to the chair in silence. The only sound I heard was an antique coo-coo clock that resided in the living room; its constant ticking reminding me now that time was something we had very little of.

The End

CHECK OUT OTHER GREAT ZOMBIE NOVELS

Z BURBIA
by **Jake Bible**

Whispering Pines is a classic, quiet, private American subdivision on the edge of Asheville, NC, set in the pristine Blue Ridge Mountains. Which is good since the zombie apocalypse has come to Western North Carolina and really put suburban living to the test!

Surrounded by a sea of the undead, the residents of Whispering Pines have adapted their bucolic life of block parties to scavenging parties, common area groundskeeping to immediate area warfare, neighborhood beautification to neighborhood fortification.

But, even in the best of times, suburban living has its ups and downs what with nosy neighbors, a strict Home Owners' Association, and a property management company that believes the words "strict interpretation" are holy words when applied to the HOA covenants. Now with the zombie apocalypse upon them even those innocuous, daily irritations quickly become dramatic struggles for personal identity, family security, and straight up survival.

ZOMBIE RULES
by **David Achord**

Zach Gunderson's life sucked and then the zombie apocalypse began.

Rick, an aging Vietnam veteran, alcoholic, and prepper, convinces Zach that the apocalypse is on the horizon. The two of them take refuge at a remote farm. As the zombie plague rages, they face a terrifying fight for survival.

They soon learn however that the walking dead are not the only monsters.

 SEVEREDPRESS

facebook.com/severedpress

twitter.com/severedpress

CHECK OUT OTHER GREAT ZOMBIE NOVELS

900 MILES
by S. Johnathan Davis

John is a killer, but that wasn't his day job before the Apocalypse.

In a harrowing 900 mile race against time to get to his wife just as the dead begin to rise, John, a business man trapped in New York, soon learns that the zombies are the least of his worries, as he sees first-hand the horror of what man is capable of with no rules, no consequences and death at every turn.

Teaming up with an ex-army pilot named Kyle, they escape New York only to stumble across a man who says that he has the key to a rumored underground stronghold called Avalon..... Will they find safety? Will they make it to Johns wife before it's too late?

Get ready to follow John and Kyle in this fast paced thriller that mixes zombie horror with gladiator style arena action!

WHITE FLAG OF THE DEAD
by Joseph Talluto

Millions died when the Enillo Virus swept the earth. Millions more were lost when the victims of the plague refused to stay dead, instead rising to slaughter and feed on those left alive. For survivors like John Talon and his son Jake, they are faced with a choice: Do they submit to the dead, raising the white flag of surrender? Or do they find the will to fight, to try and hang on to the last shreds or humanity?

CHECK OUT OTHER GREAT ZOMBIE NOVELS

VACCINATION
by Phillip Tomasso

What if the H7N9 vaccination wasn't just a preventative measure against swine flu?

It seemed like the flu came out of nowhere and yet, in no time at all the government manufactured a vaccination. Were lab workers diligent, or could the virus itself have been man-made? Chase McKinney works as a dispatcher at 9-1-1. Taking emergency calls, it becomes immediately obvious that the entire city is infected with the walking dead. His first goal is to reach and save his two children.

Could the walls built by the U.S.A. to keep out illegal aliens, and the fact the Mexican government could not afford to vaccinate their citizens against the flu, make the southern border the only plausible destination for safety?

ZOMBIE, INC
by Chris Dougherty

"WELCOME! To Zombie, Inc. The United Five State Republic's leading manufacturer of zombie defense systems! In business since 2027, Zombie, Inc. puts YOU first. YOUR safety is our MAIN GOAL! Our many home defense options - from Ze Fence® to Ze Popper® to Ze Shed® - fit every need and every budget. Use Scan Code "TELL ME MORE!" for your FREE, in-home*, no obligation consultation! *Schedule your appointment with the confidence that you will NEVER HAVE TO LEAVE YOUR HOME! It isn't safe out there and we know it better than most! Our sales staff is FULLY TRAINED to handle any and all adversarial encounters with the living and the undead". Twenty-five years after the deadly plague, the United Five State Republic's most successful company, Zombie, Inc., is in trouble. Will a simple case of dwindling supply and lessening demand be the end of them or will Zombie, Inc. find a way, however unpalatable, to survive?

www.ingramcontent.com/pod-product-compliance
Lightning Source LLC
Chambersburg PA
CBHW020305200626
46814CB00006BA/2101